Also by Terry Spear

MATED
for Christmas

TERRY
SPEAR

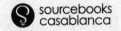

sourcebooks
casablanca

Published by Sourcebooks Casablanca, an imprint of Sourcebooks
P.O. Box 4410, Naperville, Illinois 60567-4410
(630) 961-3900
sourcebooks.com

Printed and bound in the United States of America.
BVG 10 9 8 7 6 5 4 3 2 1

Chapter 1

TWO WEEKS BEFORE CHRISTMAS, PRIVATE INVESTIGATOR Sheri Whitmore was at her office at the White Wolf Investigative Services in Ely, Minnesota, hoping she'd find a missing pilot and that he was alive and well—the best Christmas gift she could give to his wife, Sheri's client.

Sheri opened the blinds on her office window to view the reception area so she could see the sparkling lights on the Christmas tree. She'd even had fun decorating the aquarium for Christmas with Santa wearing scuba gear while in his sleigh pulled by seahorses.

She was about to make a call on her missing-person's case—another possible lead that she needed to check on before she went on a dinner date with Slade White, an Arctic wolf like her—when Betty Connolly got in touch with her first.

"Hello, Betty. I haven't been able to locate your husband yet, but I have a clue as to where to look for him next and was going to check on it—" Sheri said, but was quickly interrupted.

"He's home. Don't worry about it. I'll drop by your office and pay you what I owe you for your services."

"He's home?" Sheri was so surprised that she was totally

taken aback. This was the first big case she was working solo on and she hadn't expected it to be resolved on its own.

"Yes. So we don't need your services any longer." Betty Connolly spoke to her so abruptly that Sheri figured she had no intention of telling her where her husband, Gerard, a local pilot, had been for the last two weeks.

Sheri loved to have some closure in a case, but if she were in Betty's shoes, she might feel the same way if her husband had been off with another woman like Betty had thought. Betty sounded afraid that Sheri would look into the case further and learn the truth about his disappearance. Maybe she was embarrassed.

"I'm on my way over there now. In fact, I am nearly there," Betty said.

Boy, Betty really did want to end Sheri's investigation into the matter immediately. "Okay, sure, that's great. I'm certain you're thrilled Gerard turned up safe and sound."

"Yes. I'm pulling into your parking lot. I'll be inside in a minute." Betty didn't sound thrilled in the least—more angry with a mixture of anxiety.

The case had been a priority for Sheri and now that it was done, she wouldn't have to worry about locating Gerard. Tonight's dinner with Slade and the office Christmas party tomorrow would be her next priorities.

Slade was showing up in a few minutes and she couldn't wait to see him. Since he was a pilot like Gerard, Sheri had even asked him if he could think of anywhere else that she could look to find Gerard. Slade had given her a few tips and she was so glad he could be her expert advisor in the matter.

She truly was grateful Gerard was home and now she could tell Slade that. Even though he wasn't a PI, he had the same interest in her solving her cases, which pleased her.

"Case done," she told her fellow private investigators, Cameron MacPherson, Owen Nottingham, and David Davis, who were in their offices, their doors open to the reception area.

They were running a little short on PIs because Sheri's best friend, Elizabeth, and her mate, David, were both PIs, mated, and expecting twin boys in March. Elizabeth had begun to do some of the employment agency background checks and other investigations from home so she could rest more but still help out. Slade's twin sister, Amelia, and her mate, Gavin, had a set of twins who were only two weeks old, so Gavin, another PI, was taking some time off to help with the babies.

"Was it a good outcome?" Cameron asked Sheri, looking concerned. She knew he didn't want to give her cases that might have bad resolutions for her first missions.

"Yes! For Christmas, it couldn't be better news. Gerard is home."

"That's terrific."

A Jaguar pulled up into the office parking lot—a brand-new bright-red one—and Betty hurried out of it, looking a bit frazzled. As soon as she walked into the office lobby, she hurried to join Sheri. "Here's your payment. That's all there is to it, right?"

"Yes, of course."

Betty could have just paid for the transaction online and

wouldn't have had to come in at all. Though Betty knew that, for whatever reason, she had wanted to pay in cash. That didn't happen very often. The sixty-year-old blond woman had beautiful features and she looked half her age—cosmetic surgery, Sheri assumed. Her curly hair was shoulder length and she usually looked like she'd just walked out of a beauty salon the few times Sheri had talked to her in person. But tonight, her hair was in disarray, uncombed and tangled. She had smudges of mascara under her eyes. Her eyes appeared a little red, like she'd been crying. She didn't look like a woman who had just welcomed her long-lost husband home. On the other hand, maybe she had wept for his return and her makeup had smudged.

"Thank you. If we can ever be of any other service to you, feel free to call us," Sheri said cheerfully, trying to make the moment more upbeat.

"Thanks." Then Betty hurried out of the building, got into her Jaguar, and peeled out of the parking lot.

Owen raised his brows. Yeah, he'd seen Betty before, but looking like a beauty queen, not like this. "I would venture to guess she has something to hide," Owen said, having finished a call on his own case about a grocery store missing expensive bottles of wine every time a particular couple of employees worked at the store.

"I think so too." She was dying to know what had really happened.

She heard Slade park his SUV and smiled at him as he came inside, but he looked as frazzled as Betty. His dark-brown hair was always windswept and in disorder, which appealed to her, making her think of him as wild and untamable. He was wearing his favorite dark-brown genuine lamb's leather bomber jacket with a fur collar, just like the one Tom Cruise wore in *Top Gun*, but without all the patches, and it just suited him. To her, he looked like a war hero. His blue eyes were beautifully inquisitive, and when he saw her, he smiled broadly. "Wow, who was that in the Jaguar?"

"The woman who hired me to look into her husband's disappearance. She said he just showed up at their home."

"Gerard Connolly? Nice wheels."

"Yeah, that's the case I asked you about because her husband is a pilot too."

"Man, I need some of *his* business," Slade said, and gave Sheri a brief kiss because she knew he didn't want to be too amorous in the office.

But they didn't have any clients in the office right now, so she kissed him back a lot more passionately and he seemed to be thrilled by it, smiling back and kissing her with just as much enthusiasm. She loved doing that to him, kissing him more deeply when he wasn't expecting it and then him going right along with the move. Her PI partners wouldn't mind. The other mated couples hoped they would mate each other because they always seemed to be so into each other.

"So are we ready to go to dinner?" she asked.

"Uh, there's a change of plans. I'm sorry."

Sheri tried not to show her disappointment. She had really been looking forward to dinner with him all week. "Okay, no problem."

"I just got a Pilots N Paws mission, but you can come

with me, and we'll fly Cupcake, Mischief, and Brutus to their owners now."

"Oh, yeah, sure." It didn't matter about the dinner plans as much as that Slade still wanted to spend the time with her. She loved that he volunteered to fly shelter dogs needing a home to new families when he could.

"Okay, I know it's not the restaurant I planned to take you to, but we could grab something to eat after we drop the dogs off."

"Yeah, that would be fun." She was easy. She loved flying with him, and taking pets to meet their families made precious memories for her. Slade was so good with the dogs, and she loved them too.

Slade glanced at Owen, David, and Cameron, who had left their offices to grab some water from the water dispenser. "Hey, guys. See you at the office party tomorrow."

"Sure thing," they said.

She swore they had been ready to come to her aid if she had been really upset about the missed dinner date and invite her to dine with them instead. But she was getting used to Slade's emergency plane trips and they were always really important, so she certainly wasn't dismayed about it. There were times when she had job issues where she also had to cancel on dates with him and he was just as accommodating.

"Are you ready?" he asked.

"Yeah, let's go." Sheri grabbed the winter-white wool dress coat she wore on the job and pulled it on, then wrapped her favorite red-and-green-plaid cashmere scarf around her neck. She slipped her red angora hat on her head, seized her purse, and was ready to go.

After they said their goodbyes to Owen and Cameron, Sheri and Slade went outside to Slade's SUV and climbed inside. Then he drove her to the airport where his mother, Lolita, had readied the three dogs for the trip. They were already in a large crate with a nice soft pad covering the bottom of it, enough room for the dogs to stay together. Lolita had also packed bottled water, in case they got thirsty. She gave Sheri a warm hug.

"I'm so sorry your dinner date was put on hold. Amelia would have gone in his place, but with the young babies, she can't," Lolita said. She wouldn't be able to come either, since the family-run piloting business needed her to schedule flights and take care of other duties.

"We'll make it up for sure," Slade promised.

"I know we will." Sheri checked on the dogs. "Oh my, they're adorable. Aww, two are puppies. You'll have to tell me the reason we're taking the dogs to new homes."

"Absolutely," Slade said.

Then they took off in the plane and were on their way to Moorhead, Minnesota. "Okay, so Cupcake and her pups are cockapoos and were at an animal shelter. They needed to find a home pronto."

"How come they had ended up at a shelter?"

"Their family was moving overseas, and they didn't want to deal with the trouble with putting them in quarantine, the vaccinations, and other restrictions, so we found a family who are thrilled not only to have the young mother, but also her two sons. They normally have a couple of rescue cocka-poos living with them at one time. But their last one passed away and the whole family was heartbroken, until they learned of the three cockapoos needing a home."

"Then you're doing an early Santa gig."

Slade laughed.

"Have you gotten your Santa suit for the kids' toy giveaway already?" She thought it was so neat that his parents decided to have a Santa Seaplane Toy Drop, where businesses around Ely would donate gifts for children who wouldn't have much of a Christmas this year. Slade would pilot the plane and land in a field to give the presents out to the children—a beautiful cause for this time of year, the gifts delivered in a unique way.

"I sure do, and I also have the fake white beard."

"The belly?" She looked at his beautiful physique.

"I had just gone on a low-cookie diet and have been working out since last year, so I might not have the belly by the time of the presents delivery."

She loved his sense of humor. "Do you think you'll do it again next year?"

"Yeah, Dad and Mom have had such a wonderful response from businesses donating toys and our pack members gathering them from all the sources and wrapping them. Businesses are providing candy canes, marshmallows, and cocoa too, and are eager to do it again. That means we're all in to do this annually."

"That's wonderful. The kids will be glad to get something nice for Christmas. I think it's great that you do so much that is above and beyond your regular job."

"I love placing animals needing homes with families and the Santa job is just another way to give back to the community."

"For sure. So, my brother is getting excited about staying at the cabin with you in the Boundary Waters Canoe Area in a couple of days," she said.

"Oh, yeah. As soon as you all moved here, Hans and I talked about going to a cabin this winter and made the reservation right then and there. They book up really fast."

"Well, you guys will have a great time."

"We will."

When they finally landed at the airport in Moorhead, the family was there to pick up their dogs. They were wearing Christmas sweaters, blue jeans, and Santa hats to greet their new furry extended family, all of them beaming broadly.

Cupcake and her pups were overjoyed to meet the family, the pups jumping all over the kids. The dad picked up Cupcake and held her while she licked his face in happiness. The kids sat down to let the pups climb all over their laps.

Sheri took a picture of the happy family and asked for their email so she could send it to them.

"We thank you with all our hearts." The wife gave Sheri, then Slade a hug.

The husband wasn't letting go of Cupcake, and her pups were weaned, so she wasn't worried about them playing with the kids. He shook Slade's hand, and then Sheri's and thanked them also.

"Merry Christmas," Sheri said.

"It truly is," the dad said. Then he and the kids, holding a puppy each, and the mom headed to the parking garage, while the dad continued to carry Cupcake. It looked like the cockapoo family had their forever home and would get lots of loving, and they wouldn't end up in a shelter again.

"Okay, well, they actually have a lot of nice restaurants in Moorhead," Slade said to Sheri.

"This is really fun. We could have eaten in Ely any old time, but flying to Moorhead for dinner? Now that's a real date. What appeals to you?"

"It's your choice." He pulled up some recommended restaurants in the area, and she chose the Irish pub restaurant that looked good. He made arrangements to have an Uber pick them up and they were on their way.

This was going to be even fancier than the restaurant they were planning to go to in Ely. She couldn't have been more thrilled. A fun flight, a chance to give the dogs a good home, but also for the family to have an even better Christmas, and then dinner with the wolf Sheri was totally hooked on? Yeah, this was wonderful.

The car dropped them off at the Irish pub and Slade took her hand as they walked inside. It was nice and dark, perfect ambience for a date at a pub. The place was decorated with Santas in kilts and Irish wolfhounds wearing plaid bows, and the Christmas tree was covered in plaid bows and ornaments and colorful lights, adding to the joyful atmosphere.

Once they found a table to sit at, he helped remove her coat and pulled off his jacket while she took off her scarf and hat and they ordered their meals. Slade got fish and chips and she ordered corned beef and creamed cabbage. Both had sweetened raspberry tea.

She couldn't believe how well things had turned out for their date. This was just delightful.

———

"I'm sorry for the change of plans," Slade said, but he was glad he was dating such an agreeable wolf. As usual, her pretty blond hair was tucked up in a chignon. She was wearing a winter-white outfit: slacks, sweater, and even her long dressy coat were white. She made him think of a sugary sweet treat, pure, and delicious, her pretty blue eyes smiling as she sat next to him.

She was always so flexible when plans changed. He'd dated other wolves who had hated when he messed up their plans. They had shared with their friends how they were going out with him, and he thought that was the reason they were so miffed when he had to cancel things.

"Oh no, this is even better. I love it. I think you really planned it all along to make it extra special for us." She leaned over and kissed him.

He kissed her back. "Yeah, I was hoping you would see it that way."

A piper wearing an Irish kilt played music on his bagpipes as he serenaded patrons throughout the pub and then their meals were delivered to their table.

Sheri ate a bite of her corned beef. "Well, this is great food."

"The company is the best too."

"I'll second that. About the dogs' adoption—it looked like the family that took in Cupcake and her pups would give them a good home," she said.

"I agree. One year, I had flown a puppy to a couple who were so upset afterward because it peed on the floor all the time. They had no clue how to housebreak him and so they wanted him returned because he was unteachable."

"No. How long had they had him?"

"Two days."

She shook her head.

"So now we always ask a number of questions about a potential homeowner's past history of taking care of dogs, if they've ever had any experience housebreaking them, et cetera."

"What happened to the dog?" Sheri asked.

"Thankfully, I was able to coordinate with another family who lived in the same area who had an aging dog, and they were excited to take a puppy in. Their older dog would teach the pup right away where he was supposed to go. But puppies need constant watching so that you can take them out when they have to go. They don't know any better."

"Yeah, my parents had two Alaskan malamute puppies when I was ten and I was responsible for housebreaking them. I would put them on a chair while I attached their leashes. They wouldn't do anything until I could take them outside. We didn't have a fenced-in yard, so I had to walk them out on leash. I took them out after feeding them, after they got up from a nap, before bedtime, and after they drank any water."

"Exactly. It takes time and persistence and keeping an eye

on them. That's all. I figured if the couple didn't have the patience with a puppy, it was good that he found another home where the family didn't find any issue with him. He needed a good family that loved him and was willing to work with him."

"And? Did you ever get any updates?"

"Yeah, he's five years old now and serves as a therapy dog. His owners take him into nursing homes all the time. After growing up with them, he has never had an accident," Slade said, then ate another of his fries.

"Then he found the best home ever for him, but that must have been frustrating to take the dog on a flight like that, thinking that was his forever home, and it lasted only two days."

"Yeah, but it changed our way of making sure the family would be suitable for the pet. At least in my experience, I haven't had any issue with another dog being rejected like that. Everyone's so happy to bring a new fur baby into the home."

"That's good."

They finished their dinner, and they bundled up and got an Uber back to the airport to fly home. Once they were in Slade's plane, they finally had approval to take off and they were on their way. "When I get back from the trip with your brother, I'll take you out to dinner."

"I'm always up for another."

"Good. Are you ready for the Christmas party tomorrow?" This would be the first year Slade would see Sheri at the Christmas party, so he was looking forward to it.

"Yeah. Are you?"

"I am. Cameron's kids wanted me to play Santa for them."

Sheri laughed. "Are you going to?"

"No, I want to just enjoy the party."

"Good. That's what you need to do."

They just flew for a while in silence after that. He finally glanced over at her to see if she was watching out the windows, hoping she wasn't bored but was enjoying the trip. She'd fallen fast asleep, looking peaceful, comfortable, angelic.

He smiled. He had decided that he wanted to mate her more than anything else in the world, and if he hadn't already invited Hans to the cabin, he would have taken Sheri there instead to propose to her. They'd been dating since she had moved to Minnesota, and they really enjoyed being with each other. More than that—he knew they were made for each other.

Seven months was a long time for wolves to date, and he was beyond ready to mate her. Before the new year, before Christmas even. He wanted to wake up with her on Christmas Day, enjoying the holiday as a newly mated couple. But her father, Fred, had been adamant that Slade shouldn't try to convince her of a mating because her former boyfriend, Bentley, had controlled her so much. She never had a say in their relationship, which was why she kept telling Bentley she wasn't interested in mating him. Her parents had felt bad that they had encouraged their mating and didn't want to do that again with her where any other male wolf was concerned. Otherwise, her parents were excited to welcome Slade into the family.

But Slade just didn't want to wait any longer!

Chapter 2

SHERI STIRRED AWAKE, REALIZED SHE WAS FLYING BACK to Ely with Slade, and couldn't believe she'd fallen asleep on the flight home. Poor Slade. She'd meant to visit with him on the return trip, hoping she'd keep him entertained. Ugh, she was a boring companion. "Hey, sorry about that."

"No need to be." He smiled at her. "I know you've been putting in long hours at the investigative agency. More than I've been putting in at my job lately. You deserve it."

"Well, I normally can't sleep on planes. But your ride was so smooth, I must have zoned right out. Did I snore?"

He chuckled. "No."

"I meant to keep you company."

"You did. The trip there, dinner with you, and the trip back was enjoyable. It would have been boring for me if you hadn't come with me. So did you learn what had actually happened to Gerard Connolly when he had gone missing?"

"Oh, no, Betty sure didn't tell me a thing. She was in a rush to leave after she paid her bill."

"You had checked everywhere for him before he showed up at home, right?"

"Yeah, he hadn't been in a hospital, hadn't been treated at any medical clinic, hadn't been at any morgue, or in any jail.

He hadn't been in contact with his wife or any of his relatives or friends. His flight plan had been on file, but he hadn't followed it. The police were still searching for him, but they hadn't found any sign of him either. So where was he for the last two weeks?"

"That's the mystery. Seeing a girlfriend? A different clandestine meeting? Gambling?"

"Exactly. At least he's okay. I'm glad he's home and that I could do this with you. I'll see what else I need to do in the morning at the office, but later in the afternoon, I'll be helping everyone to set up our PI office Christmas party."

"I look forward to it."

She did too. It was the first Christmas that she and her parents and brother would spend as part of the white wolf pack of Ely, and they were excited about being with this group that was so positive and uplifting. Everyone in the pack seemed like family. It was such a change from their old one in Yellowknife, Northwest Territories, Canada.

"I talked to your parents and mine about us all having Christmas Eve dinner together. They are excited about it."

"Oh, that will be really nice." She was surprised that he had. Even though he liked her parents and brother too, she thought there was more of a reason for Slade asking their parents to have the special dinner together. She'd been hinting about mating, but Slade hadn't been biting. She figured he still liked being a bachelor wolf. Or maybe he was afraid she wasn't over her ex-boyfriend in Yellowknife, but she had gotten over him a long time ago. Her problem had been in getting Bentley to recognize that she was finished with him.

It hadn't helped that her parents had thought they were a good match and had believed she should have mated him.

At least now her parents and Hans seemed to be glad it was truly over between her and Bentley. Which was a good thing because she wasn't changing her mind about the wolf. He'd been way too controlling. She hadn't even realized it at times because she'd been so used to it, but her mom and dad weren't like that, so she knew that it hadn't been a healthy relationship. With Slade? Totally different and she loved him for it.

She figured Slade had wanted to take her out on a special date tonight because tomorrow night was the PIs' Christmas office party and the day after that, Slade was going with Sheri's brother to stay at a cabin in the Boundary Waters Canoe Area for a week. She and Slade wouldn't have a chance to see each other alone for all that time. The cabin was remote and there wouldn't be any internet or cell phone service.

They finally arrived at the airport at home, and Slade drove her to the office where her car was still parked. Everyone had gone home, and Slade kissed her goodbye. "I'll see you tomorrow for the party. Thanks again for coming with me. I appreciated your company."

"Oh, I had a ball. Dinner was delicious and seeing the dogs go to a new family was really rewarding."

"I agree. They have a super family to take care of them now."

"Absolutely." She wrapped her arms around his neck and kissed him soundly. She wanted to tell him she would miss him while he was gone with her brother, but she didn't want to sound clingy. "Okay, see you tomorrow at the party."

"See you tomorrow."

Then they had one last, long parting kiss, and both drove off in their respective vehicles. It had been a feel-good night. When Slade got back from his vacation with her brother, she was going to tell him that he was hers. No more holding off, no more waiting for him to ask. She was going to let him know he was the only one for her. She just hoped he was feeling the same about mating her as she was about mating him!

He called her on the way home and she laughed. "Miss me already?"

He chuckled. "I just want to remind you that we have a dinner date when I return from camping with your brother."

"Yes. It's on my calendar." But she was certain he wouldn't expect her to propose to him then. Maybe he planned to propose to *her*! Finally.

"Okay, night, Sheri."

"Night, Slade." She arrived at home and unlocked her apartment door. Then she wondered what they would do about their living arrangements. Move into one apartment or the other? Or build a home? Her dad built houses and that's what she wanted. She and Slade had to really start talking about these things too. Kids, finances, all that stuff. At least with their families, they all lived here, and they got along famously.

───────

The next day, Sheri was at the office, working on a couple of store burglary cases where the insurance companies wanted to make sure they hadn't been staged by the owners. One claimed that a whole shipment of computer equipment had never shown up, though someone had marked it as delivered. Since both thefts involved electronics, she suspected someone was stealing them.

After reviewing security footage for both stores, she suspected the jobs had been accomplished by employees. The day the merchandise went missing, the security cameras hadn't been working in either store. She didn't believe one person would work at both stores, though she did verify employee lists. She also checked to see if anyone had been fired around that time. No to that too. Then she ran background checks on the employees to make sure none of them had police records. None of them had, except for a younger man who had run up a couple traffic violations.

"Any luck on your insurance case?" Cameron asked, sporting a Grinch Christmas tie. She wondered if Faith had given it to him.

"Uh, no. I've been checking all the things I should."

"Okay, good." Cameron had given her the job this morning, increasing her responsibilities a case at a time because she was a new private investigator. She was glad the guys were so good with helping her and Elizabeth through the process of working cases, showing them the steps they went through to resolve them, though every case was different. Sheri and Elizabeth loved their jobs and working with their PI partners.

Next, she learned the trucking company that carried the merchandise actually had the shipments for both stores on the same manifest. Okay, so now that sounded like way too much of a coincidence. "What about the delivery truck driver?" Sheri asked the dispatcher.

"No one drove that truck," the dispatcher said.

"What? The truck just left the warehouse on its own?"

"Let me back up a bit. The truck wasn't driven by one of *our* guys. Someone dressed in one of our delivery uniforms showed up and had the truck filled up, then took off. No one even realized he wasn't one of our guys, and it took a couple of days to figure out the driver had stolen the truck."

"Oh, wow, okay. So you've reported it to the police?"

"Yeah, right away, but no one has found any sign of the truck or the merchandise."

"Can you identify the fake driver on your security video?"

"He was wearing a parka over his uniform, which makes sense because of how cold it was. Gloves too, and a hood so we couldn't see his face. It was as if he knew just where the security cameras were and how to avoid them. And he knew just which merchandise to take," the dispatcher said.

"Can I see the video?"

"Yeah, if you can help us or the police identify the guy and get our truck and merchandise back, we would be grateful."

"I'll be right over." Sheri told Cameron and Owen she was checking with the delivery company about the insurance case, and they both waved at her as they were taking calls about their own cases. They all told each other where they were going on their cases in the event anyone got into trouble. She loved how they all worked together on the investigations and watched out for one another's well-being.

When she arrived at the warehouse, she went in to speak with the dispatcher in her office. "Hi, I'm Sheri Whitmore and I talked to you on the phone about the missing delivery truck?"

"Yeah, the private eye. Come in and have some hot chocolate." The woman was gray-haired and wearing reindeer antlers with jingle bells on them. A spindly Grinch tree covered in little Christmas present ornaments and lights sat on the corner of her desk. "I sure hope you can help us find that truck. We really need it for deliveries, with the high volume we have for Christmas."

"The police have had no luck in the case?" Sheri asked.

"No. They've been overwhelmed with other thefts."

"Okay, I'll certainly look into it." Sheri then watched the warehouse's security video with the dispatcher while she wasn't busy. In the security-store feeds, there hadn't been anyone who looked overly interested in the electronics, other than customers, and most had walked out of the store carrying their purchases. The guy who stole the truck had covered himself up enough that she couldn't see his face the whole time he was getting the truck loaded and then climbing into the cab and driving off.

She couldn't tell if one of the store employees had helped to steal merchandise from the two stores.

"Do you have security video of the area beyond the building?" Sheri asked on a hunch.

"Yes, on the fences overlooking the entrance just in case someone came in after hours and tried to steal from us." Then the dispatcher pulled up the security video.

Sheri watched that and said, "There! He came in from outside the facility on foot. So he probably parked up the street from there."

"There are a couple of gas stations and a beauty salon in that direction. You could see if they have security videos that might have recorded where he went to and where he'd come from."

Sheri thanked her. "I'll let you know if I have any news."

"Thanks. I'm so glad to meet you and hope you learn what had happened to everything."

"Merry Christmas," Sheri said to the dispatcher.

"Merry Christmas," the woman said.

Then Sheri left to see if she could ask the businesses along the route that the delivery truck took if they had security videos that she could see. At the first service station, the manager allowed her to watch the outside security video for the day in question. A blond man was wearing the parka and delivery uniform the dispatcher and Sheri had seen in the video at the warehouse. He'd gotten out of a green Jeep Grand Wagoneer, but she couldn't see the license plate number. However, at least she knew he was blond and he drove a Jeep.

She continued to fast-forward through the video until four hours later on the security tape when a red pickup pulled into the service station. The blond guy got out of the red Ford pickup and walked straight to the Jeep, got in, and the two vehicles took off. Again, she couldn't see license plates, and she couldn't see what the other driver looked like in the red pickup, but it confirmed there was more than one person involved in the theft.

"I don't recognize either of the drivers."

"Okay, thanks. I'll let you know if I discover anything further." Then Sheri drove down the road until she reached the last business on the street in the direction the two vehicles had driven, but at the crossroad, she wondered which way they'd gone. So, she stopped at the beauty salon to watch their security footage. The video showed they'd continued straight. But she would have to go to several businesses to see just where the vehicles continued to go, and she didn't think she'd ever locate them that way unless she got a license plate number. For now, she needed to return home and get ready for the Christmas party.

She sure wished she could have gotten somewhere with the case she was working on, but it could take weeks, even months, to solve the mystery.

As soon as she arrived back at her apartment, she began changing into her Christmas sweater featuring an Arctic wolf in a Santa hat nuzzling another, a red skirt, and dress boots.

Then she put on her parka and hat, grabbed all her ingredients to make homemade wassail, and drove over to the office. When she reached the office building, she went inside, hung up her parka and hat, and said to Owen, who was in the middle of getting some papers printed off, "If you guys don't need me for anything, I'm heading downstairs to make the wassail."

"Go ahead. Everyone will join you shortly," Owen said. "See you downstairs." Then he got on the phone to call someone.

Sheri headed down the stairs where Christmas songs were playing in the background. She began to prep all the ingredients for the wassail. Once she had the wassail on the stovetop, she pulled out the cheese, beef, and chicken slider ingredients so the guys could make them. But the wassail began to boil over, sizzling on the hot stove. "Oh no, oh no!"

Just then, Slade came down the stairs, carrying a couple of loaves of french bread, and smiled broadly at Sheri. His blue eyes sparkled with good humor, dimples appearing in his cheeks, showing just how much he was amused. She loved his dimples.

She really hadn't wanted him to see her making such a mess of it. She thought of herself as organized and efficient, not prone to disasters.

"Do you need some help?" Slade asked. "It appears you have a lot going on." He kissed her cheek, then took over cleaning up the spilled wassail while she moved the pot to the back burner.

"Thanks." She totally appreciated a man who could help out during a minor kitchen crisis.

The whole basement of the PI office building was decorated for Christmas, just like their lobby and offices upstairs were. A large Christmas tree had been decorated by everyone in the pack, from Cameron and Faith's kids' papier-mâché snowmen, to strings of popcorn, bows, and Arctic wolf ornaments. Underneath the tree were all the white-elephant gifts for the exchange and prizes for the games they would be playing. A warm fire crackled in the hearth, the mantel covered in greenery, Christmas lights, and snowmen.

The basement was set up as guest quarters with a bathroom and a kitchen and a large living area that they used for parties during inclement weather. Since the original pack members were not born as wolves but had been turned by Sheri's former Arctic wolf pack, they had issues shifting into wolf form during the full moon and couldn't shift during the new moon. If they had any trouble while at work, they would just slip down to the guest quarters until they could get their shifting under control. Sheri and her parents and brother, Hans, were royal wolves, meaning they were born as *lupus garous* from a long line of shifters, so they didn't have any issues with the phases of the moon. The same was true of Elizabeth, Slade, and his sister and their parents—all royals, which meant they tried to hold down the fort when the other wolves had shifting issues.

"Where is everybody? I thought there would be more of us down here helping to set up the food for the Christmas party already," Slade said.

"Who needs them when we're here?"

"True."

"I'm sure everyone will be here soon." She was happy to be spending Christmas with her family and the white wolf pack led by Cameron and Faith. They'd moved here in June and every holiday spent with the wolf pack was new and special. Even Thanksgiving had been a whole-pack affair. She loved it. Being here was so different from being in Kintail's pack back home in Yellowknife where they didn't have fun gatherings as a pack like this.

But Christmas here was a family affair, and then the whole pack would get a wolf run in to enjoy Christmas night. Faith had already brought fruit and cheese and set the platters on the grazing tables, then returned to the house to get the kids ready to join the party. Sheri's best friend, Elizabeth Davis, had left her own special Swedish meatballs earlier for Sheri to warm up when the wassail—filled with apple cider, apples, cinnamon, cloves, lemon, ginger, nutmeg, and oranges—began to boil over.

Then Elizabeth came down the stairs with her mate, David. "Something smells like hot apple cider—delightful," Elizabeth said.

"It's the wassail. Help yourself to some. We just need to drain the whole cloves and apples and it will be ready to serve up," Sheri said.

Elizabeth had grown up with Sheri in Yellowknife. Sheri couldn't believe that Elizabeth and David had a set of twins coming in June. Well, she could believe it as far as how much the two of them loved each other. She was just so surprised that they had gotten pregnant so fast once Elizabeth had moved here to join David. Sheri's mother, Georgia, was a midwife and she would deliver Elizabeth's and David's twins, but she had also delivered Gavin's and Candice's two weeks ago.

Amelia joined them, bringing one of her twins in his carrier. "Hmm, something smells great."

"It's the wassail," Elizabeth said. "Sheri makes the best homemade variety."

Sheri glanced in the carrier at the sleeping baby boy.

"I just nursed them. Luckily, they're used to people talking and making noise and will sleep right through it," Elizabeth said.

"That's good." Sheri hoped when she had some of her own, they would be just as easy to take care of.

Then Faith and Cameron came downstairs with their six-year-old triplets. "I'm going to get the cookies started so everyone who wants to decorate them can do so after we eat dinner," Faith said.

"Gavin's finishing up a call upstairs and joining me so he and I can make the sliders," Cameron said.

Owen Nottingham joined them with his mate, Candice, the author of the bunch, bringing pecan-coated cheese balls with them. Gavin Summerfield arrived with bottled water and sodas.

"Is the office closed now?" Sheri asked.

"It sure is," Cameron said. "Of course, if anyone has an emergency, we'll deal with it, but it's time to party."

Shortly after that, Slade and Amelia's parents, Henry and Lolita, arrived and they were followed by Sheri's brother, Hans, and their parents, Georgia and Fred.

Henry had brought fruit mince tarts, Lolita, mini-Christmas cakes, and Fred was bearing bottles of pink champagne for later. Hans carried a container of his favorite eggnog. Georgia was carrying Amelia and Gavin's younger twin in his carrier. Faith brought the cookies out of the oven for everyone to decorate later after they cooled down and they'd eaten their meal.

"Let's eat," Cameron said. "The sliders are ready."

Then everyone grabbed plates and began filling them with food. They sat on chairs and couches, some at the dining room table that they also used for PI staff meetings.

"So what are some of the exciting cases that you're working on?" Candice asked.

Sheri had figured no one who wasn't one of the PIs would be interested in their ongoing cases, but she swore Candice was using them to write snippets of conflict in her fiction books. Everyone else was just as intrigued to learn about the cases too.

"I just wrapped up a case of jewelry stolen from a house—a supposed break-in and robbery. It turns out the owner had insured the jewelry only two weeks earlier and the insurance company was suspicious. They hired me to investigate, and I learned from one of the houseowner's teenage sons that his dad had hidden the jewelry in a wall safe," Cameron said.

"Why would his son tell on him?" Candice asked, sounding surprised.

"His dad had caught him smoking weed with some other teens and read him the riot act about doing something that was illegal. So it was a way to get back at his dad for getting after him. I don't believe the dad was very happy with him, but if he's going to try to teach his son right from wrong, he can't be caught defrauding the insurance company. Anyway, the dad has been charged with insurance fraud."

"Good deal," Lolita said. "It's people like that who make *all* of our insurance rates go up."

"Exactly," Georgia said.

"Tell them about the case of the missing guy, Sheri," Elizabeth said.

"Oh, you mean Gerard Connolly?" Sheri sure hoped

she didn't get as sick as Elizabeth if she got pregnant. "It resolved itself on its own. Gerard's wife, Betty, called saying her husband had gone missing." She filled them in on all the details. "He had filed a flight plan, was in the air for a while, and then radar lost him. He never called in a distress signal. It was as if he ended up in the Bermuda Triangle and just vanished.

"Then Betty called and said he had returned home. I wanted to ask where he had been all this time, but I didn't want to pry. She didn't volunteer where he'd been for the last two weeks, paid our services, and ran off. So that was my first really big case, and it was easily resolved."

"I want to know what had happened to him," Elizabeth said.

"All of us do," Gavin said. "But when a case is closed, that's it."

"Yeah, me too. She didn't seem like she was happy that her husband had come home safe and sound, which makes me all the more curious," Sheri said.

"Maybe she learned he was having an affair and didn't want to share her dirty laundry once she'd learned what had happened to him," Faith said.

"Truthfully, I was thinking the same thing," Sheri said.

After they all finished eating, they began the cookie decorating contest at the dining room table.

To Sheri's surprise, Slade was eager to spruce up his own cookie. He squirted green icing all over the cookie *and* the table and some got on Sheri's arm. Luckily, she had pushed up the sleeves of her sweater before she started to work on her cookie. She laughed as he washed it off her, and then she started decorating her cookie with a butterfly. The kids were right next to them, working on theirs.

"Who's judging the contest?" Cameron asked.

"You can," Faith said.

"Then mine wins," Cameron said before he'd even begun to decorate his.

Corey, his oldest triplet, said, "Daddy, you can't make yourself the winner."

Everyone chuckled.

Slade was making a mess of the icing on his cookie. "Okay, I have to admit I've never decorated a Christmas cookie before, and the frosting is coming out way faster from the tube than I thought it would. I'm naming mine the green blob."

"With red eyes," Corey said.

"Yeah, for the Christmas-colors effect… You know, red and green." Slade glanced at Sheri's cookie. "Now that's great."

"Thanks. I have decorated cookies with Elizabeth every Christmas. I love to make Christmas butterflies."

There were snowmen, a snowflake, a candy cane, and several Christmas ornament–decorated cookies. Elizabeth had made a Christmas tree on hers. Sheri's dad had decorated his cookie with a wreath. He glanced at Slade and said, "I've never decorated a Christmas cookie before either."

Slade laughed. "Well, you have me beat." Sheri swore Slade had more green icing on the table than he had on his cookie.

The triplets won the contest for a Yoda, a dragon, and an airplane. Slade asked the triplet who created the airplane, "Are you going to be a pilot like my sister and me, Corey?"

"Yeah!" Corey said.

Candice thought Angie's dragon cookie was the cutest. "I need to add a dragon to one of the stories I'm writing."

Everyone loved Nick's green Yoda wearing a Santa hat. "Star Wars fan, eh?" Sheri asked.

Nick nodded vigorously.

"Is everyone ready for our white-elephant gift exchange?" Faith was in charge of all the activities because she loved to organize parties. She did a great job as a pack leader and her kids were old enough now that they could be a real help too—when they weren't distracted or bored with assisting.

The kids shouted, "Yes!"

Chapter 3

NEXT ON THE AGENDA AT THE WOLF PACK CHRISTMAS party, all the adults got numbers so they could take turns picking out presents. The kids' gifts were decorated in cute reindeer gift wrap so they wouldn't be mixed up with the adults' gifts.

Because there were only three kids, two boys and one girl, each was given a gift that were just for them and their own name tag on it. Nick got a science kit with tons of experiments. Corey loved his walkie-talkies. Angie got a rock-painting kit because she loved to paint, but all the kids wanted to share their gifts with their siblings, which Slade thought was admirable.

Sheri ended up with the number one and picked out her present from all the rest. She chose a large box, though she knew great gifts could come in small packages. But the trouble with getting the first number was someone could take it away from her and every subsequent package she picked out!

Inside the box was an aqua mini waffle maker. "I can use that. As a single she-wolf, I only need to make a waffle for myself." Slade smiled at her and she was thinking she might just want a bigger one if they tied the knot like she hoped they would soon.

Then Elizabeth eyed Sheri's waffle maker. Elizabeth was number two in line. Sheri playfully narrowed her eyes at her. "Don't even think of it."

"It's a good thing we're best friends. You know how much I love aqua kitchen items." But Elizabeth picked out another gift and got a new set of knives. "Oh, these are just great."

When Slade got his present, he opened it and found a rechargeable hand warmer. "Perfect for our camping trip on Saturday, Hans." He was really glad about it.

"Yeah, I sure could use it." Hans smiled at him. He had been giving Sheri a hard time about going with Slade on the cabin retreat instead of with her. But Slade had asked Hans to go with him before he'd even begun dating Sheri, so he felt he was obligated to follow through.

Sheri poked her finger at her brother's shoulder in a light-hearted way. "Don't be mean. Let Slade keep it."

"Yeah, but I'm going to be hiking with him in the snowy cold too." Hans eyed the gift with interest. "Okay, sorry, buddy, but I'm going to take that one."

Slade gave Hans the hand warmer and warned, "Watch out for karma, friend." Then he picked out another gift. When he opened the next gift, it was a GPS drone. "Hot, um, cool. This is great."

Hans immediately said, "Aww, if I hadn't taken your glove warmer, I would have gotten that one."

Slade laughed. Thankfully, by the end of the gift

exchange, he'd managed to keep his drone, though the other guys good-naturedly hassled him enough about wanting it. Sheri also got to keep her waffle maker and she seemed glad.

Then Faith said, "Okay, it's time for the Christmas movie trivia game. Everyone had the assignment to watch the Christmas movies we'll refer to in the game. So if you guess the most answers correctly first for that particular movie, you will win the prize under the tree. Then we'll do the same thing for the other Christmas movies. We'll be paired up for the game and begin. The triplets can play too."

Everyone already had mates except for Hans, Slade, and Sheri, and one of the triplets needed a partner. Sheri was going to pair up with Angie, but Slade said, "Sheri's with me." He thought it was important to show he wanted ties with her and not to just date her forever.

Sheri smiled at him.

Hans said, "Angie's with me." Then he frowned at her. "Did you do your movie assignment?"

"I know them by heart," Angie said, putting her hands over her heart.

"Good, then we'll win," Hans said.

Then Faith began asking the trivia questions. "In *A Christmas Story*, what does Ralphie want for Christmas?" Faith asked.

"A Red Ryder BB gun!" Sheri shouted. Slade laughed. "Sorry. That one I always remember."

"What item does Ralphie's father win in a contest?" Faith asked.

"A leg lamp! And his mother broke it to get rid of it," Sheri said.

"Man, am I glad I picked you for my partner," Slade said.

"It's my favorite Christmas movie and I watch it every year."

"Lucky for me," Slade said.

"What happened to the Parkers' turkey on Christmas Day?" Faith asked.

"The Bumpuses' hounds ran inside and ate it," Sheri said.

"Who gifts Ralphie a pink bunny onesie for Christmas?" Faith asked, looking at Sheri.

"Aunt Clara." Sheri smiled.

"What does Santa say to Ralphie when he says he wants a BB gun for Christmas?"

Nick waved his hand. "You'll shoot your eye out."

"How does Ralphie's mom get Randy to eat dinner?" Faith asked.

"She asks him to show her how pigs eat." Corey demonstrated by pretending to be a pig eating food.

Slade wondered why Angie didn't guess at any of the questions when she had said she knew the answers by heart. But then he saw her painting one of the rocks she got for Christmas and realized Hans had lost his partner in the game. Hans smiled and shrugged. Slade suspected he hadn't watched the Christmas movies for the game beforehand.

"When Ralphie's dad read the words on the box with his prize inside, he told his family it said, 'Fra-gee-lay.' What nationality did he believe that was?" Faith asked.

"Italian!" Sheri said.

"Sheri and Slade won that round," Faith said. "Go ahead and pick a gift."

Sheri and Slade picked out a present, though he let her choose which one she wanted. They both unwrapped it and found it was a rechargeable hand warmer. "You can take that on your cabin trip with Hans, so you both will have hand warmers," Sheri said to him.

She looked like she didn't expect Slade to give her a hug, but he appreciated that she'd been on his side when he'd gotten some for a Christmas present and her brother took them. "Thanks. Anytime you need them, they're yours."

Then Faith started the game again but this time for *Home Alone* and Sheri didn't guess at any of the answers. Slade suspected Sheri loved *A Christmas Story* and she wanted to let others win prizes.

Elizabeth and David ended up winning that one. They opened their gift, and they got a rechargeable hand warmer to share too. Everyone laughed.

"Cameron and I found a sale for hand warmers on Black Friday. Because of how cold it is here, we got a bunch of them for prizes for the Christmas party." Then Faith continued the movie game with questions about the next Christmas movie, *Miracle on 34th Street,* and the winners were Owen and Candice. *It's a Wonderful Life* was next, and Amelia and Gavin won that contest.

Everyone was thrilled with their hand warmers. In winter in Ely, Minnesota, it was worth having them.

"Merry Christmas, everyone," Faith said.

"And to you too," Elizabeth said. "I've had a great time, but I'm feeling bushed."

Poor Elizabeth seemed so tired all the time. Slade hoped she'd get more energy soon.

"We've got to run. The babies are beginning to stir, and we need to feed them and change their diapers." Gavin said, getting his and Amelia's babies ready to leave.

"Yeah, we need to get these kids home too," Cameron said about his triplets.

"We'll help you pack, and the rest of us will take care of cleaning everything up," Candice said.

"Are you sure?" Faith said. "I can stay and help do it. Cameron can take the kids home."

"Nah, go home and enjoy your family time," Sheri said. "We've got this."

Then Faith, Cameron, and the kids grabbed some of the leftovers, their Christmas cookies, and their presents. Amelia's parents got some leftovers together and picked up Amelia's and Gavin's gifts and left with them.

Candice, Hans, Owen, Slade, and Sheri were left to pack up the rest of the food and their own gifts. It was wonderful that everyone was so eager to help each other out. Of course, Slade had learned that when Faith and Cameron became a mated couple and had triplets, Gavin, David, and Owen had been the only other wolves in the pack and they had been a great help to the new parents, just like real wolves would be with the pack leaders' pups.

"Why don't we leave some of the food here for everyone working at the office?" Candice asked. "Owen and I couldn't eat all this, but you and the others could enjoy the leftovers while you're at work."

"Okay, but Slade needs to take some of this with him so he and Hans can have it on their camping trip," Sheri said.

"Yeah, that sounds good," Slade said.

Then they finished cleaning everything up and Owen and Candice said good night. Slade said to Sheri, "I'll walk you to your car."

They dressed warmly and when they reached her car, he kissed her with the pent-up desire he always felt when he was with her. In a way, Slade saw this trip as his bachelor's retreat with another bachelor wolf, and after that, he would be mated to Sheri, if she was agreeable. He sure hoped she would be.

Chapter 4

THE NEXT DAY, SHERI AND ELIZABETH WERE DOING SOME background checks on individuals applying for jobs with some local businesses when Hans texted. She wondered what the matter was. He was supposed to be on his way to the cabin with Slade.

Hans texted: I'm sick and I can't go with Slade on his cabin stay. I hate disappointing him.

She immediately thought of how Slade and his sister, Amelia, had piloted the plane to come to Sheri's best friend Elizabeth's rescue, and Sheri had managed to finagle a spot onboard the private plane to make her getaway from Yellowknife too. Since Sheri and Slade had both been single, they'd started dating each other.

She texted her brother: You're really sick?

He'd been so looking forward to this that she figured he wouldn't have canceled on the trip unless he had a really good reason.

Slade was taking some time off now because this was their offseason for flying. He and his sister and their father would take paddlers to the Boundary Waters Canoe Area (BWCA) and also take visitors on sightseeing tours during the spring, summer, and fall. But now everything was snowed in and the water iced over. Though for emergencies, they would fly in to help. And he did have some sightseeing trips scheduled to see the beauty of the BWCA in winter.

This was the perfect time for skiing, snowshoeing, and ice fishing, no paddling *and* for taking time off to enjoy this trip.

Her brother didn't respond.

She texted him again: You'd better tell Slade. He's going to have to make other arrangements then. He shouldn't go out there on his own.

Her brother didn't answer back. Ugh. She didn't want to be the one to tell Slade. Shoot, she should have asked Hans what was wrong with him. She tried calling her brother, but he didn't answer his phone.

She glanced outside the window. It was thirty degrees today with a light snow falling, but she and her family and her best friend, Elizabeth, were from Canada, so the cold didn't bother her. She would love to go with Slade if she could get away from work.

Sheri called Slade right away. "Hey, my brother texted me that he's sick."

"What has he got?"

"I don't know. I texted him back and called him, but I didn't get any response. I'm running by his apartment now and I'll let you know what I learn. Can you ask one of my PI partners to go with you instead?" They all loved camping with the guys, so surely someone would be willing to take Hans's place.

"No, we already asked the guys when Hans and I first

planned this. The cabin has enough room for eight, but everyone's mated and busy for the holidays before Christmas. Someone might be joining us at the end of the trip, but not this early on," Slade said.

"Let me check on Hans then. I'll talk to you in a little bit." Sheri ended the call and told Elizabeth, "Hans is sick. I'm going to run by his place and see what he has got."

"He's supposed to be going with Slade on a glamping trip today, isn't he?" Elizabeth asked.

"Glamping?" Sheri laughed. "Yeah, he might not be able to go."

"Okay, well, give him our love," Elizabeth said. Elizabeth, Hans, and Sheri had grown up together, so she was just like Hans's sister too.

"Thanks. I'm sure he'll appreciate it. Be back shortly."

"See you soon."

Then Sheri put on her parka and left the office building to check on her brother. When she arrived at his place, she knocked on the door, but her brother didn't answer. "I'm coming in," she called out. She had a key to his apartment and their parents' home, like all of them had a key to each other's residences in case of an emergency.

She unlocked the door and called out for her brother, but then she heard him throwing up in the bathroom. So that's why he hadn't responded to her text or phone call. She got him a glass of water from the kitchen and peeked into the bathroom, where Hans was crouching at the toilet bowl. He looked pale, his dark-brown eyes soggy. "Hey, it's just me," she said.

"I feel awful."

"Is it the stomach flu? Or something you ate that didn't agree with you?"

"Stomach flu. I have a fever and all the lower GI issues. I ate with Mom and Dad for breakfast this morning and we had all the same food. Both of them are fine, so it can't be something I ate."

"I told Slade you were sick. I'll call him back and let him know you have the flu."

"Thanks. Can he go with one of your PI partners on the camping trip now that I can't?" Hans sipped some of the water.

"He said no. You know they're all married, and with it being so close to Christmas, they're busy with their families and their PI workload at least for the beginning of the stay. Not to mention Amelia and Gavin have two-week-old twins."

"You could go."

She laughed.

"No, really. You're an experienced winter backpacker, hiking in the parks in Yellowknife, ice fishing, camping. You and Elizabeth loved to go to the Tuktut Nogait National Park and Wood Buffalo National Park. You have the gear for it, the stamina, and you're used to the cold weather. And Slade really cares for you."

"I know, but I think Slade was looking forward to going with a bachelor male wolf, not a single she-wolf." Though Sheri thought it would be a great way to get to know each other.

"He needs someone to go with him. You said you had finished your last major investigative case and you're just waiting for another one to come along."

"I've got to make some calls." Sheri walked into her brother's living room, which was all decorated for Christmas—his mantel covered with greenery and poinsettia flowers and his six-foot tree with sparkling lights and Christmas ornaments. Everyone in the family had decorated their places for Christmas, helping each other, though they would spend Christmas with their parents.

As far as the camping trip went, she didn't want to impose on Slade or make him feel obligated to take her instead of one of the guys, all of whom he was really close to, as if they were brothers. What if Slade thought she was trying to make more of the situation between them than there was for now? That she hoped he wanted a mating? Which of course she did. But what if he really *wasn't* ready for it?

She sighed and called Slade. "Hey, Hans has the flu. Fever, throwing up, all the rest. I'm going to call Mom and see if she can take care of him. In the meantime, if it wouldn't be a problem, or a dumb idea—and I want you to be honest with me—I could take my brother's place. His gear is all packed. I just need to run home and get my personal items and clothes, but the rest can go as is."

Silence.

Well, she knew proposing such a notion wasn't a good idea.

Then Slade chuckled. What was so funny?

"Okay, well, I need to call Mom and Dad to let them know Hans is sick," she said.

"I'll pick you up as soon as you're ready to leave and we can drop by your brother's place to get his gear," Slade said.

Her jaw dropped. "Really? Are you sure? I know you wanted to go with one of the guys."

"Yeah, I'm sure. We'll have a great time. I want to do this more than anything in the world."

She was thrilled that he felt that way. "Okay, great. I'll call Mom and the office and tell them I'm abandoning them for a camping and fishing trip with you."

"Good. See you in a little while."

He sounded cheerful about it, and she was glad he didn't seem to feel obligated to do it. She called her mom and put the call on the speakerphone while she hurried to pack. "Hey, Mom, Hans is sick with the flu. I would have made him some homemade chicken soup, but you know he was supposed to go with Slade on the camping trip today. So I'm going to go with Slade instead."

"Oh no, okay. I'll make the chicken soup for him and take it over. Dad's going over to his place now."

"I'll see you in a short while. Slade will pick me up at my apartment and we'll arrive at Hans's apartment after that. We need to grab Hans's gear."

"See you soon then."

They ended the call and Sheri had to check on work. That was the great thing about working with the wolf pack. Everyone helped everyone out when anything came up that needed to be done. "Hi, Cameron? My brother's sick and I'm taking his place on the camping trip with Slade, if that's all right with you."

Cameron laughed.

Why did everyone think the situation was so funny?

"You don't have any cases right now, and we'll take care of the background checks that you were working on. We can handle the missing delivery truck case and everything else that comes up," Cameron said.

"Are you sure my being gone isn't going to be a problem?" She knew they were a little shorthanded.

"Yeah. We're good. We don't have a full-moon issue for a few weeks. And we have the work covered for now. Have a great time," Cameron said.

"Thanks. I'm sure we will." She just hoped she didn't forget to bring something important, since she hadn't planned to do this months ahead of time like her brother and Slade had. Or that Slade ended up regretting that he had agreed to take her with him. On the other hand, this would be the perfect opportunity to see if they could really get along in close quarters for a whole week.

She went to her place and began packing up her stuff. She took some Christmas napkins too because she knew her brother and probably Slade would just use paper towels otherwise. She grabbed a small tabletop decorated Christmas tree because she was sure the cabin wouldn't be decorated for Christmas. She wanted to take a little Christmas spirit with her.

———

Well, this was sure a wild turn of events. Slade hadn't expected to be taking the vacation with Hans's sister instead of Hans. He'd had to laugh about it because Hans had joked about him taking Sheri with him instead because he would have more fun that way.

Of course, because Slade and Sheri had been dating, everyone in the wolf pack believed a mating was in the works, though when Sheri's dad had cautioned Slade about pushing Sheri into something she wasn't ready for, he'd taken her father's advice to heart.

He was glad she was okay about going with him when she hadn't been his first choice.

When he arrived at Sheri's apartment, he gave her a hug. "I'm glad you're able to come with me." He was wearing a warm parka this time, not his leather pilot jacket.

"It's not safe to go alone. Staying at the cabin would be fine, but doing all your activities would not be, though I know people do it all the time. And sometimes they get themselves into real trouble for it."

"Yeah, I agree. And the cabin stay wouldn't be half as much fun. I just didn't know if you could do it or not, what with work, and I wasn't sure you would want to. Elizabeth said you and she and some others had gone winter camping and ice fishing in Yellowknife, so I know you had done it several times before and you enjoyed it when you were back home."

"Absolutely. If I'd been in the middle of an important case, I might have been reluctant."

"One of the guys would have picked it up from you." He grabbed her bags.

"I'm sure you're right." Sheri pulled on her parka, hat,

scarf, and gloves and then locked her door as Slade placed her bags with his in the trunk. They climbed into Slade's black SUV that she swore looked like an FBI vehicle. She settled against the seat and sighed. "I never thought I would be doing this for the week."

"I'm so glad you are." Then Slade reached Hans's place and saw Sheri's parents' cars there.

"Mom and Dad to the rescue. I'm so glad that when I decided to settle here with Elizabeth and all of you, my parents and Hans agreed to come and stay. Family means everything."

"It sure does. My dad will probably continue to fly planes for a while longer and Mom loves managing flight schedules. We've all stuck together—my parents, Amelia, and me—from the time we were in Seattle to Alaska, and now here."

"Exactly." They went inside to get Hans's gear. "Hey, Mom, how is Hans?" Sheri asked.

"He's in the bathroom again. I brought the ingredients to make homemade chicken soup, since it would have taken too long to make it at home and bring it when I wanted to be here for Hans right away if he needed me. But it might be a while before he can keep anything down," Georgia said. "You and Slade are bound to get tongues wagging in the pack again, you know."

Sheri laughed. "Yeah, like that hasn't been going on all along."

Slade just smiled at her mom.

Georgia hugged Sheri. "You be safe. You have a satellite phone, right, Slade?"

"Yes, I do. We'll have our cell phones, but once we get to the cabin at Clearwater Lake, there's no cell reception," Slade said.

"I've got Hans's satellite phone too," Sheri said. "And his hand warmers that he took from Slade at the white-elephant gift exchange."

"I told you karma could come back to bite you, Hans," Slade called out.

Hans groaned from the bathroom.

Fred came in and shook Slade's hand. "I hadn't planned to be here to give Hans a send-off when you and he were going camping, but now that I am, I want to tell you to keep Sheri safe."

"Oh, Dad, how many times have I camped out in the snow country in the wilderness?" Sheri asked.

"Dozens of times in Yellowknife, but not here. Just be safe."

"I will be." She gave her dad a hug, then walked over to the bathroom door and said, "Hey, Brother, feel better. I'll try to keep Slade out of trouble."

"You do that. Oh, and grab the food in the freezer— steaks, chicken, hamburger meat. The canned goods are already packed."

"Okay, thanks, but we should be able to catch some fish too," Sheri said.

Then they said goodbye and Slade and Sheri drove off to the cabin where they would stay for the week. She sure hoped that she and Slade would further their interest in each other and it wouldn't be a disaster instead.

Chapter 5

"You're sure you're not disappointed that I'm taking Hans's place?" Sheri asked Slade on the drive to the cabin.

"Not at all. I'm glad to be able to spend the time with you." Slade understood Sheri's concern that she had been his second choice, but he really didn't feel that way about it. Hans had been the one who had asked him to join him on the camping trip, and then the two of them had planned it for the last seven months. "Hans and I had asked if anyone wanted to join us at the cabin for the last couple of days that we're there, but at the time they couldn't commit. It can easily accommodate eight adults, so we could have six come and join us and go fishing, hiking..."

"And then running as wolves?"

Slade smiled. "Yeah, run as wolves at night when anyone else who is camping out in the woods is hunkered down for the evening. Or early in the morning before sunrise."

"Yeah, sure, that would be fun."

"We meant to ask the others again before this, but we both forgot." He got on his phone and called Cameron at the PI agency. "Hey, can you ask everyone again if anyone wants to stay with us at the cabin for the last couple of days to ice fish, cross-country ski, hike, and/or run as wolves? We have enough beds for six more adults, but we can accommodate your three little kids too. It has one queen-size bed, one full-size bed, and two futons."

"Let me check with everyone and we'll get back with you. Hans asked if any of us would like to do it several months ago, but we didn't know what our caseload would look like at the time. Now that we know, we can see who would like to do it. I suspect our new parents won't be able to make it."

"Okay. There's no rush on making a decision. The cabin is available if anyone wants to come."

"You'll have takers, I'm sure."

"Good. Talk to you later."

Two hours later, Slade and Sheri arrived at the cabin and used the access code that Slade had received when he had rented it. They started to unpack their gear from the SUV and carry it inside.

Sheri set up a tabletop Christmas tree on the coffee table. "Oh, did you bring the drone? That would be fun to use."

He smiled at the Christmas tree, thinking Hans and he would never have thought of doing anything to make the experience more Christmassy while they were here. "No, we'll have to test it out over our lake. The Boundary Waters Canoe Area restricts the use of drones. Plus, I have to get a remote pilot certificate to operate it and register it with the FAA. I planned to do it after Christmas."

"Aww, okay."

The cabin's interior was all light wood paneling, making it look rustic and perfect for a getaway. The living room and spacious entryway had wooden flooring and large, blue area rugs. The kitchen had a tile floor, and all the cabinets were honey-stained pine, the walls white, and large windows overlooked the lake and forests.

A woodburning stove sat in the middle of the living room. Two sofas, two coffee tables, and several chairs filled the large room that opened to the kitchen. That made it nice if some of the people staying here were cooking and others could still talk to them from the living area. Everything was decorated in blues and browns, very cozy for a cabin in the wilderness. Black bears were featured on the shower curtains in the bathrooms, birch tree wallpaper on the walls. Pictures of black bears, wolves, and moose dominated the walls. A bookcase housed books, DVDs, and board games.

Slade was really glad he'd made a reservation for this particular cabin. They even had their own private dock, if they'd come here to paddle when the weather was warmer. He had also picked up some mistletoe before he had dropped by Sheri's place that he wanted to hang up in the cabin without her catching him doing it.

"Upstairs is the queen-size bed and a full-size one in the one room and there's a bathroom. Downstairs are the futons and another bathroom, the living area, and the kitchen," Slade told Sheri. It was totally up to her how she wanted to work this. When it had been just Hans and him, they were going to sleep in the upstairs room in separate beds. But if they had guests for the last couple of days, they would figure it out then. If she wanted the room upstairs to herself, Slade was fine with that, though he truly hoped that wouldn't be the case.

"Okay, so we sleep upstairs." She hauled a couple of her bags up the stairs.

He smiled. Good. He had hoped she would say that. He continued to haul the items in from his SUV and set them in the living room. They could sort everything out later. For now, he wanted to put the groceries away and fix lunch.

She returned to the SUV to bring in more of the groceries. "What do you want to eat?"

"The steaks?"

"Yeah, that sounds good. Green beans and potatoes to go with it? Then before it gets too late, we can go on a snowshoe hike?"

"I would love to do a hike." He realized how different it would be staying here with Sheri instead of her brother. With her brother, he didn't feel the need to impress him about anything. They were more laid-back. But with Sheri, he felt the need to show her how he could cook a great meal, keep the cabin picked up, and plan some fun-filled excursions.

"It's so cute and rustic, yet modern and warm to return to after a day spent out in the cold. It even has a firepit, and you know what that means," she said, hauling in more groceries.

"Making s'mores?"

"Yep. At least we know the bears are all hibernating so we don't have to worry about them coming to see what we're roasting over the fire. We'll have to return here in the summer when we can go paddling. I've done some of it around Yellowknife, and of course on the lake where the wolf pack's homes are located, but I would really love to do it here too." Sheri hung up her parka, scarf, and hat next to his on the coat-tree and then she put the perishable foods in the fridge.

"I would love to do that too." Summer was his family's seaplane busy season taking paddlers out to the BWCA, but he could carve out some time to come here again with her for sure.

Slade had been afraid that Sheri might be feeling some rebound effects after she'd called it quits with her former boyfriend, Bentley, in Yellowknife. But she had seemed perfectly fine with moving forward to date Slade exclusively.

She cut up the green beans and started cooking them while he began peeling the potatoes and boiling them.

"I wasn't sure if you would stay here permanently with the rest of us… I mean in Ely," he said, though he was really glad she had.

"I only told Kintail I would return with him because I didn't want any of you hurt. The pack leader of Yellowknife is hardheaded and was angry that Elizabeth and I left the pack. As long as Elizabeth had a home here, I would deal with him. But you all stood up for me. There was such an outpouring of love for us that I hadn't expected at all. Kintail had to go home with Bentley and the other guys empty-handed, and that's the way it was meant to be." She flipped the steaks and then dished up the green beans.

Slade drained the potatoes and began mashing them, adding some butter and milk. "Well, I know for me, I wouldn't have wanted it any other way. I was ready to take Bentley and Kintail on myself. Kintail had already conceded defeat where Elizabeth was concerned. But with you? It had to be your choice, not Kintail's. Or Bentley's."

"You're absolutely right. I'm just so glad Faith and Cameron are democratic in their leadership. Kintail was a tyrant. As far as Bentley goes, he was just as controlling. I just didn't know Elizabeth had planned her escape like that with you and Amelia piloting her out of Yellowknife. Talk about the adventure of a lifetime."

Slade served up the steaks while she got some water for them. "Yeah, imagine our surprise when David and I saw you arrive with Amelia and Elizabeth and that you weren't just there to see her off but that you wanted to come with us."

"You were worried that my parents and brother would be upset about me leaving, more than that Kintail would be." She set the plates and silverware on the table.

"Cabernet sauvignon to have with our steaks?" Slade asked, showing her the bottle.

"Oh yes, that would be perfect."

He poured them each a glass of wine and then they sat down to eat. "Family means everything to us, and I know you're close to Elizabeth, but I knew you would also be missing your parents and your brother. Your brother sided with Kintail about Elizabeth to begin with, but now that he's here, he's with us all the way. That was some of the reason that we were going to go camping together. To get to know each other better." Slade cut up some of his perfectly tender steak.

"All I know is I love it here. Of course, when my parents and brother said they were going to move here too, there was no going back. Not that I had any intention of returning to the way things were back there. So I'm here to stay."

Slade smiled. "I can't tell you how glad I am to hear it."

"Good. I wouldn't have wished my poor brother's illness on him or anyone else, but I'm excited about being here."

After they finally finished eating their dinner, they washed up.

"That was sure delicious," she said.

"Yeah, Hans's steaks were great. I brought us fixings for chili and beef stew too."

"That sounds like it will be great. Are you ready for our hike?" Sheri asked.

"I sure am." Slade grabbed his waterproof, breathable pants and pulled them on. She did the same with hers. Then they put on their parkas, snow pants, snow boots, hats, and gloves and grabbed their backpacks filled with snacks, water, first aid kits, and their satellite phones. They both packed ice cleats too. They shouldn't be separated or lose each other, but it was always good to be proactive just in case something happened they hadn't planned on.

Wearing their snowshoes, they took the Daniels Lake Spur Trail to reach the Border Route Trail. He loved the quiet out here, the snow lightly falling, the fresh powder on the ground, white, pristine.

"It's so quiet out here," she said.

"Yeah, except for some geese honking off in the distance, it is. Only one other cabin is winterized, so the rest of the cabins and the main lodge are empty for the winter and that makes our resort even quieter."

"It's so pretty out here covered in white sparkling snow," Sheri said, her voice soft.

"It is. We're looking for a small wooden bridge that will take us to the rapids flowing down from a waterfall."

"Oh, wonderful," she said.

They kept a lookout for the bridge crossing over the frozen water, then finally found it. They crossed the bridge and followed the frozen rapids to the falls.

A canopy of snow-covered trees covered the whole area and was just beautiful. Then they finally reached the partially frozen falls and put on their cleats to cross the frozen rapids to get closer to the falls. Once they were close enough, they could see just how huge they were. Sheri and Slade were dwarfed in size compared to them. After they touched the ice and took all the pictures they wanted, they started to cross the rapids again and reached the bank.

"Do you want to fish tomorrow?" Sheri asked as they took off their cleats and put on their snowshoes.

"Yeah, and cross-country ski?" he asked. Now if his sister, Amelia, had been here with them, she would have had the whole trip perfectly organized from start to finish. While he was on vacation, he relaxed, though if Sheri wanted to organize things and have packed days, he was fine with that too.

"Sure. That would be perfect." Then Sheri asked, "Amelia told me about the harrowing flights she's had with Gavin—two of them, in fact—but have you ever had any that you piloted?"

"Oh, yeah, sure. The engine failed once, and I immediately

found a place to land and ended up in a cornfield. We were lucky and no one was hurt."

"Wow, now that would be scary."

"It was. We were just lucky the cornfield was nearby."

"Who was with you?"

"A girlfriend from when I lived back in Seattle. But she never flew with me again."

Sheri laughed. "I believe in getting back on the horse that bucked you off."

"Good for you. I'm the same way." Slade checked his GPS to make sure they were still on the trail. "What's the wildest time you've ever had?"

"When on the job? As a store clerk? Well, both Elizabeth and I were working at a dress store in Yellowknife, and three armed robbers ran into the shop, locked the door, and told us to get on the floor. We were afraid they would hurt us. Luckily, no one was shopping in the store at the time. But one of the men's arms was bleeding and we wondered if he'd been shot or stabbed."

Sheri and Slade paused to drink some of their water and began moving again.

"What did you do?" He wished he'd been there with her to help her out at the time. He wanted to know everything he could about Sheri on their vacation!

———

Sheri still had nightmares about the armed men taking her and Elizabeth hostage. "Elizabeth and I decided one of us would turn into a wolf. Our growly side wanted to take all three men down for threatening us with guns. With the distraction of me turning into my wolf, Elizabeth would go for the silent alarm button under the counter. The guys were busy watching out the window. We figured they had stolen something from someplace else and were on the run and the one guy had been shot in the process. At the time, we didn't know that they'd broken out of jail, had killed a guard, and were really dangerous. Anyway, I hurried to strip behind a rack of clothes as quietly as I could. And then I shifted into my wolf.

"One of the men turned and saw that Elizabeth wasn't where she'd been, and I was a wolf leaping toward him. All three men were so shook up that one of them lost his gun and tried to open the door to run. One fired a shot at me, but he was too scared to aim properly before I lunged and knocked him onto his back. At the time, I felt invincible. Afterward, Elizabeth gave me heck about it. In any event, the gunman I collided with hit his head hard on the floor and he was knocked right out. The other guy, the one who had been wounded prior to entering the store, tore off after his friend. Of course, I was growling and baring my teeth at them as they were scrambling to make it outside and run down the street. Then I heard the sirens. Elizabeth had set off the silent alarm and was on the phone to the police."

Snowflakes fluttered about them as Sheri and Slade saw a faded, wooden Border Route Trail sign pointing to both ways on the trail. She took a selfie of them next to the sign.

Then she said, "The other guy was still unconscious,

though I could hear his heart beating and I knew he wasn't dead. I raced back to redress. Elizabeth grabbed the guy's gun and we both took refuge behind the checkout counter until the police arrived. Elizabeth turned over the gun. We gave the police descriptions of the other two men, and they revived the one on the floor. He was raving about an Arctic wolf that had nearly killed him. They had EMTs check him over, and then they handcuffed him and took him out to a police car."

"Did you learn who the guys were?"

Sheri and Slade reached a fallen tree covered in snow and he helped her over it. This was a unique experience for her. When she hiked with Hans in the winter like this, he would figure she could get over it on her own. Once Sheri was on her feet on the other side of the downed tree, she and Slade began to hike again.

"One of the men had shot a store clerk when they tried to rob a drugstore before they reached our store. I guess they thought they could score some easy money from the drugstore, but the manager shot the one escaped prisoner after he wounded the clerk, and the three gunmen took off. The clerk didn't die, but they were wanted by the police for assault with a deadly weapon and attempted murder and murdering the prison guard earlier. It was one thing to threaten unarmed employees, quite another to deal with someone who was also armed."

"Still, the drugstore manager was outnumbered three to one."

"Yeah, I guess the convicts got spooked."

"Like you spooked them."

"Yeah, when they caught the other two men a week later, they told the same wild tale about a white wolf coming to eat them. The police had figured the one man had hit his head so hard, he'd had a hallucination, but the other men? They didn't know what to think, except they didn't believe them about that for sure. Yes, wolves are seen regularly in Yellowknife, but not Arctic wolves. Of course, Kintail was mad that I'd turned wolf, not in front of the gunmen, but to go after them. He hadn't wanted us to reveal our wolf halves. We had been afraid for our lives. *Kintail* hadn't been there to protect us. He might have been angry about it, but the townspeople were thrilled that we had caught one of the would-be murderers."

"What about the store security cameras? I would have worried that they would catch you stripping and shifting and proved what the men claimed had happened was true," Slade said.

"The owner had security cameras that were never on. He just had them for show."

"Good thing for you."

"We would have come up with another plan if that hadn't worked. We had asked him about the security cameras in case anyone had tried to rob us. It helped that we didn't have any customers at the time, and that the robbers had locked the door so no one new could come in. Oh, and they got away with a whole forty Canadian dollars from the drugstore. Not much to show for the extra prison time they all got."

"It's a good thing they were all incarcerated again."

"For sure. Whenever anyone entered the dress shop after that, Elizabeth and I worried armed robbers were coming in to take us hostage again."

"I don't blame you."

Then Sheri and Slade were quiet so they could listen to the sounds of any animals in the area. It was just the perfect solitude out here. Because of the remoteness of the trail and the minimal maintenance it had, Sheri had the paper map and compass to navigate by. They also had downloaded an offline GPS on their phones. Slade was using the online GPS so far. But because they were wolves, they could also navigate by their sense of smell.

The trail was littered with downed trees that they had to navigate because of a rare tornado that had hit unseasonably late in the year. Volunteers would remove them in the spring and summer, but not until next year now. The trail was difficult enough to traverse without the downed trees—narrow and rugged, lots of climbing up and down, icy or snow-covered rocks.

But then they saw a bull moose up ahead, about seven feet tall, his huge antlers spreading nearly six feet from end to end, his brown fur soft-looking. They both paused to watch him. He was so big, he could weigh around a thousand pounds or more. That was worth the whole trip! He caught sight of them, then started to eat some birch, acting as though he had nothing to worry about. In truth, they had more to worry about if he decided to charge them. He finally moved off, and when he was gone, they continued their journey.

Slade smiled back at her. "That was great."

"I'll say." She was glad she had gone with Slade to do this.

"Since we've been hiking for about three hours, I figure it's about time to head back."

Thankfully, with their wolves' vision, they could see in the dark since the sun would set before they reached the cabin.

"We'll see the sun setting. That will be nice."

"Yeah. Maybe even the aurora borealis later," he said.

This time, Sheri led the way, and they could just follow their own trail back. No one else was around at all, which was really nice. Then they heard wolves serenading them from off in the distance.

"We'll be doing that too," she said.

"Yeah, after dinner? A wolf run and s'mores after that?"

"That sounds like fun."

As soon as they came to another big, downed tree in their path, Slade hurried to squeeze by Sheri and helped her over it. Then she was in the lead again.

"What had you planned to do with Hans if he and you had been here? I don't want to mess up your plans," she said.

"We didn't have any plans. We were just going to wing it."

"Okay, super. I'm really good at winging things."

He chuckled. "Good. Me too."

They had walked for about an hour when they saw movement in the woods. They both paused and listened to the brush moving, then out came a pretty red fox. She looked around, then headed back the way they had come.

It was nearly four in the afternoon and the sun was

setting. The sun would rise at about a quarter of eight in the morning. They could even take a wolf run before that, if they wanted to.

The sky turned pink and blue, reflecting off the snow. So pretty. Sheri took a video of it before they moved on again.

"Oh, I've been meaning to tell you that all of us ladies, with the help of Cameron and Faith's kids, picked out the toys for about seventy-five kids between the ages of three and eight for your Santa Seaplane Toy Drop. I think it was wonderful that your parents wanted to make that happen for the first time here."

"That's great. The stores provided them, then?"

"They sure did. They were all in, free publicity, great charitable cause."

"That's wonderful! And the music?"

"A band will play Christmas music and a group from Ely will be dressed in Victorian clothing and sing Christmas carols with everyone there."

"I'm glad I'm playing Santa."

"Oh?"

He chuckled. "I don't sing. At least that anyone wants to hear."

Chapter 6

SHERI AND SLADE KEPT WALKING, THE SNOW POWDER soft, perfect for snowshoes, and they were getting a really good workout. She was looking forward to warming up, having dinner, and then running as wolves.

As soon as they arrived at the cabin, Sheri said, "Do you want chicken?"

"Yeah. I'll get the fire started."

Then they shed their winter gear and he helped her make dinner—lemon and pepper roasted chicken, mashed potatoes, and spinach. They made a great team when they cooked. They just jibed, each of them taking a job to get it done.

Then they sat down to eat. "Well, this is delicious," Slade said.

"Yeah, it sure is. We did a great job."

After dinner, they cleaned up and then Slade pulled her into his arms and kissed her. "Hmm, are you ready to run as wolves?"

"After the long hike we had today, a walk is more like it. A trot." Though as wolves, they could walk for miles without getting tired.

"Yeah, I agree."

They kissed again, then stripped out of their clothes. He opened the door while she shifted and ran out of it. That was the problem with staying at human-run places. No wolf door.

Naked, Slade stepped onto the snowy deck and closed the door. It locked automatically. It helped that they could use a code to get in and not have to worry about a key. Then he shifted and they ran off. Even though they were going to walk on the trail, they wanted to navigate a good distance from the cabin as wolves to make sure they didn't run into any humans. But the only prints in the snow were their own snowshoe prints from their hike earlier.

The northern lights were slipping across the sky now, bright green and pink and mirrored on the ice-covered lake. They were just amazing, like a moving art palette of colors, the various hues in the form of light. She howled for joy. He licked her face and howled too. Tomorrow night, she planned to capture the northern lights on her cell phone if they appeared again.

She and Slade were taking a nice leisurely walk, about five miles per hour for a wolf, smelling the scents in the area— another fox that had crossed the trail and the cool, crisp air surrounding them—as they listened to a squirrel up in a tree squeaking at them, fluttering its bushy tail, telling them to go away.

She was wondering what they should do about tonight. She wanted to join him in bed, but she wasn't sure he was ready for that. They'd made unconsummated love before— with no sexual intercourse, which between wolves would mean they were mated for life—but they'd never stayed together overnight. They would figure it out when they returned from their wolf trip.

They had been walking for about an hour when the winds began to pick up. The weather could be so unpredictable, especially in the last few years with conditions ranging from a rare late-season tornado, to pouring rain and then a flash freeze right away. The forecasters hadn't said anything about this. But even within the BWCA, the weather could be very different from one area to the next.

Trees began falling, crashing off in the distance, making Sheri and Slade's hearts race. They stopped in their tracks, looked up at the trees near them to make sure none were leaning over and ready to fall. Slade woofed at her. She knew it was dangerous to stay here or return through the woods to the cabin, but if they reached it safely, they would have shelter for the rest of the storm.

That's when they heard men's shouts off in the distance. That didn't sound good. But if anyone had been injured, Sheri and Slade couldn't rescue them as wolves. It could take hours for emergency help to arrive to aid anyone out here in the best of weather conditions. But at night during the height of a storm?

She shifted. *Brrr*, man, was it cold. "I should check on them and see if anyone needs help. You run back to the cabin and shift, dress, and come back with the first aid kit and satellite phone. I mean, I'll howl and let you know if anyone needs assistance first. There's no reason for you to come back for me if no one's in trouble."

He shifted. "If you howl and say they're okay, I'm still coming back for you."

"It won't take me long to reach the cabin, and there's no sense in us both being out in this."

"I'm returning for you. If you were to get injured, I wouldn't be there to take care of you."

"All right, that's true. Go. I'll be fine." She shifted and ran off in the direction where they'd heard the shouts. She hoped everyone was okay, but she appreciated that Slade would return for her so they could both go back to the cabin together unscathed, hopefully.

━━━━━━━

Slade would have done just what Sheri had suggested if Hans had been with him and it wouldn't have mattered who returned to the cabin.

As it was, he was running full out as a wolf, leaping over fallen trees, some of them newly fallen since the storm had begun. He wished he could fly back to the cabin and grab everything he needed in a flash. The longer they were both out here, the worse it could be. The best-case scenario would be if Sheri didn't find anyone needing medical attention and they would return to the cabin and enjoy the rest of the night with each other in relative safety.

His heart was pounding as he jumped on top of a downed tree and heard one crack to the left of him. He jumped back down off the fallen tree to avoid the crashing one and hunkered behind it. A small branch hit him on the top of the head, but not hard. That made him even more worried about Sheri being out in this too.

When they'd started their run, they had been walking through the snow as wolves, just sniffing around, enjoying themselves. So they hadn't really gone but about five miles from the cabin. But now he was running as fast as he could, about thirty-five miles per hour, but he couldn't run that fast for long periods.

They were the only ones who had been on this trail today, so their tracks were still there from their snowshoe hike and wolf prints. But with the blowing snow and new snow falling, the tracks were being obliterated fast. It took him twenty minutes to return to the cabin, loping the rest of the way.

Just as he reached the walkway to the deck of the cabin, he heard Sheri howl. It was a distress call. Someone needed help, which was just what he had feared.

Sheri had reached the campsite where the men had called out and it was a disaster. Two trees had fallen on top of their two tents. Two of the men were trying to move the tree off one of the tents using only their cell phone lights, but the trees were massive, and the men couldn't budge them.

She worried that someone was still in that tent trapped underneath the tree. A chain saw would be needed to cut the behemoth of a tree off the tent. Chain saws weren't allowed in the Boundary Waters so the campers wouldn't have one with them. Emergency crews could get an exception to save someone, but it would take too long to get hold of anyone to get approval and bring a chain saw to reach the trapped camper or campers, so she figured they were on their own for now.

When Sheri howled to Slade to let him know that the campers were in need of help, the two men stopped what they were doing and looked in her direction, but she was hidden in the woods, all white, blending in with the snow. Well, and it was dark out so they couldn't see at night like she could either. Still, when she howled, she was close to them, so they would know she was there even though they couldn't see her.

"Hell, that's all we need is wolves coming to dinner, Trenton," one of the bearded men said, shining his cell phone light at the woods in her direction, but the beam didn't carry that far.

"Hey, Morgan, Lionel, can you hear us?" Trenton called out, frantic to find his friends. She was glad at least two of the men had managed to get out of their tent safely.

"Yeah," a man groaned from inside the collapsed tent. "The tree pinned my leg. I can't move out from underneath it. Lionel, hey, buddy, are you okay?"

The other man finally groaned. He had to be Lionel, and the man with the pinned leg was Morgan. "Yeah, what the hell happened?"

The wind was blowing hard, sending the snow on the branches flying while it was snowing, the flakes being swept sideways in the stiff wind. Sheri hoped Slade would bring an ax. One of the men was trying to get something out of the other tent that had been crushed by a tree, both trees appearing to have been uprooted about the same time. It was still blowing hard, and she worried for their safety and for Slade's. She wished she could help the men.

Then she had an idea. She could pretend to be a helpful dog. But what if they worried about a dog coming out of nowhere and were afraid of her? Particularly if they really believed she was the wolf that had just howled nearby.

She came out of the woods and barked at them, wagging her tail. With her night vision, she could find things. And she could dig.

"What the hell?" One of the men finally grabbed a camp lantern from his tent, turned it on, and saw her.

"Shit, it looks like a wolf, Andy."

"An Arctic wolf? Nah, they don't have them out here. It's got to be a dog," Andy said. "But where's its owner?"

Thankful that Andy put the other men's minds at ease, she began to dig under the fallen tree where the men were trapped. The snow was deep underneath the tent, so if she could dig there, they might be able to pull the trapped men out.

"What...what is that?" the one guy pinned in the tent said.

"A big white dog and he's trying to dig you out, Morgan," Andy said.

She—she wanted to tell them. She wasn't a *he*.

"We don't know where he came from. Hopefully, his owner is okay and not injured somewhere in the Boundary Waters. We're helping him dig you out. We thought of chopping up the tree, but it would take way too long. The dog has the right idea, Morgan," Andy said.

"I–I just need to cut through the tent. I'm pinned down by the tent and my sleeping bag. If I could slice through them, I could get out," Lionel said.

"I'll see if I can find my knife." Andy returned to his and the other guy's tent and began trying to find it, using the camp lantern.

"Hurry it up, Andy. I can't see anything without the bigger light," Trenton said, using the light from his cell phone to see by.

"Okay, okay, the tree is on top of all our gear, Trenton. I can't find anything," Andy said.

"Well, bring back the light then," Trenton said.

Andy returned to Lionel and Morgan's tent and was beginning to dig when they heard Slade shout out, "Hey, is anyone hurt out here?"

Immediately, Sheri began to bark, to let him know she was down in the snow digging, no longer hiding in the woods, observing what was going on. She was so glad he was safe and here now to help.

"Yeah, tell us you're with a rescue crew," Andy said. "I hope this is your dog. We worried someone was injured out here or lost and the dog found us."

"She's mine. Sadie's a rescue dog and she got away from me on a hike when the trees started falling. When I heard her barking, I knew she'd found someone in trouble, and I got here as soon as I could. It took me a while to find her and you."

"So you're just a camper like us?" Andy sounded disappointed.

"We're staying in one of the cabins nearby. Have you called this in?" Slade had a flashlight, though he hadn't needed it because of his wolf vision, but he must have figured the men in trouble would.

"Yeah, we called the St. Louis County Sheriff's Office right away. They can't get to us for who knows how long. They told me several emergencies were called in over the blizzard and blowdown. If it had occurred in summer, a seaplane could have landed and they would have picked us up," Andy said.

Sheri was thinking that Slade might have flown his plane in to rescue people if he had been home and not vacationing out here. Then again, as violent as the winds were, flying a seaplane was probably a no-go. She sighed. In the worst way, she wanted to shift, dress, and help them out more, but she was doing all she could as a wolf.

"Do you have a knife on you?" Andy asked. "Lionel believes we can get him out if we can cut him from his sleeping bag and tent. He's stuck under the tree too."

"I've got it." Then Slade said to Lionel, "Talk to me." He began cutting away at the tent.

"I'm good. I hear you trying to reach me. It's much appreciated," Lionel said.

Sheri was thinking that they wouldn't be happy about losing their tent, though she knew they would be glad to get their friends out.

"Hey," Slade said, "I see your sleeping bag. Just hold still while I extract you from it."

"Yeah, holding still as a board."

While Sheri and the others were still digging, she heard Slade slicing through the sleeping bag. Then he was helping Lionel out of the bag.

"Are you okay?" Slade asked Lionel.

"I think so."

Slade helped him to his feet. Sheri was glad that he hadn't been injured...*if* he hadn't been. He might have some issues he didn't know about though. Heightened adrenaline could mask the pain from injuries at first.

Using Slade's flashlight, Andy went back to his tent to look for something else while Sheri, Slade, and Trenton worked by the camp light. Andy finally shouted, "Got them!" He trudged back through the blowing snow to the other tent carrying two folding shovels.

Great, that would really help.

Andy and Trenton began digging out their friend with the shovels and Slade began to dig with his gloved hands. Another tree fell nearby. They paused, and she swore they all had PTSD, anxious about the trees falling on top of them, which was totally understandable. When they realized they were all in the clear, they began digging as fast as they could again.

"I hope you're getting me out soon," Morgan said.

"What part of you is pinned?" Slade asked.

"My right leg, hip."

"Do you feel like you can move it at all?" Andy asked.

"Yeah, a little. But my leg hurts like a son of a bitch," Morgan said.

"Okay, can we ease him out now?" Andy asked.

"Yeah, let's do it." Slade took hold of Morgan's shoulder while Andy and Trenton took hold of Morgan's leg that hadn't been pinned and gently pulled.

Morgan groaned and they stopped. Sheri could smell his fear and pain.

"Are you okay?" Slade asked.

"I'm in a lot of pain."

Normally, they wouldn't move an accident victim until they could safely do so, but with the trees falling all around them and the subfreezing temperatures, they had to get out of this weather and move Morgan to safety. And truthfully, they were all at risk until they reached the cabin.

They finally eased Morgan clear of the tree. "Let's grab one of your sleds and gently lift Morgan onto it, secure him, and we'll go along the Border Route Trail to carry him to our cabin. We'll have to lift him over the fallen trees in our path. There were a lot down already, but more have fallen since my girlfriend and I traversed it earlier," Slade said, taking charge. "Everyone needs to bundle up in layers in the warmest clothes you can find."

"I guess your girlfriend didn't want to venture out in this weather, and I don't blame her," Andy said. "What made *you* do it?"

"I was taking my, um, dog for a walk before we went to bed, and she alerted me someone was in trouble. I'm a seaplane pilot and I've gone on several emergency rescue missions in the BCWA. I'm just not with an official rescue service."

"Hell, that's good news, that you're trained for rescues," Trenton said.

"Yeah, I agree. How far away is your cabin?" Lionel asked.

"About five miles at the point where your trail connects to the Border Route Trail. It's a half a mile hike on your trail. But it will be slow going." Slade helped them dig through their tents for extra clothes, another comforter, and blanket. "You'll need your snowshoes too."

At the same time, Sheri tugged a blanket out of Morgan's tent with her teeth and pulled it over him. She noticed Lionel wasn't helping anyone to do anything. Either he wasn't one to pull his weight, he was in shock, or he might have been too injured, and he wasn't letting on.

"You've got quite a dog there," Morgan said, then winced and groaned.

"Yeah, she's a great rescue dog. When she heard your cries after the trees fell on your tents, she alerted me right away. They have such great hearing," Slade said.

Sheri woofed at him, and he smiled at her. But she noticed Lionel was having to catch his breath when he finally began trying to gather warm clothes for their journey.

"Are you sure you're okay?" Slade asked him.

Chapter 7

Slade was proud of Sheri for finding the campers in distress. He just hoped they wouldn't have any more trouble on the way to the cabin. But at least emergency services would be able to get to them more quickly and easily there. In the meantime, they all needed to warm up before hyperthermia set in, and inside the cabin they would be able to see to Morgan's injuries and Lionel's too.

Andy finally said, "Hey, I got ahold of Trenton's and my snowshoes. But we also need Lionel's."

Slade helped Trenton to look for another pair of snowshoes in Morgan and Lionel's tent and finally found them. "Got them," he said.

Once everyone had water and warm clothes, they were going to head out, but Slade considered how pale Lionel looked and he smelled like he was in pain. "Hey, why don't we take another sled, sleeping bag, and blankets, in case someone else needs it."

Everyone else looked at Lionel. He shrugged. "Yeah, we might have another disaster befall us and someone else will need to be carried out." But he acted like that truly meant someone *else*. Not *him*.

They got the other sled packed up and Slade called the

rescue service. He told them who had called before, where they were now, and where they were headed.

"Is anyone injured?" the emergency operator asked.

"Yeah, one of the men might have a broken leg, and another man might have bruised or cracked ribs. We're carrying the one out on a sled. It will probably take us a couple of hours to get there."

The operator told them she was sending a rescue team to their cabin, and if they hadn't made it there by then, they would help them on the trail. They would check the men out and take them to emergency care if they needed it.

"Okay, let's go," Slade said. "We can take turns pulling Morgan."

"I've got you, Morgan," Andy said.

"I'll pull the other sled," Trenton said.

"I guess that leaves you, me, and the dog to lead the way," Lionel said to Slade.

"Yeah, let's do it." Slade was keeping an eye on Lionel for sure. He was afraid Lionel would need that other sled before long. Slade just hoped Lionel didn't suffer further injuries because he was being stubborn about admitting he was hurt. Slade worried about moving Morgan too and injuring him further. He realized he needed to pretend he was calling his girlfriend to let her know what was going on. "Hey, Sheri, honey."

She smiled up at him, panting, her breath frosty on the air.

"Yeah, listen, two men were injured and I've called emergency services. They'll meet us at the cabin. All right, honey. It's slow going but we'll get there as soon as we can."

They hadn't gotten very far before they heard another tree crashing too close to them for comfort. Everyone immediately crouched down low on the trail, but the tree didn't reach them. Once they were reassured they were as safe as they could be, they started on their way again. Sheri woofed at Slade, and he knew she wanted to run ahead and return to the cabin, shift, dress, and rejoin him. He shook his head at her. If she just went back and stayed there, he would feel better about it.

Then he said to her, "If you'll go to the cabin and stay."

She shook her head.

"Man, has she got a great personality," Lionel said. "I swear she is disagreeing with you and knows just what you mean."

She sure did and she was.

They came down to a large fallen tree and Sheri jumped on top of it and waited for them. Slade helped Andy lift the sled and carried Morgan up on top of the tree. Then Slade climbed over the tree and waited for Andy to join him. The two of them lifted the sled over and set it on the snowy trail. Slade was going to go back to help Trenton with the other sled, but Lionel said he would. No way. Slade was afraid he'd aggravate the injuries he was hiding.

"I've got it." Slade helped lift the second sled on top of the tree. He figured they would have to lift Lionel too.

Lionel tried to reach up to climb the fallen tree and groaned, holding his ribs.

"Okay, bring the sled back down. Let's put Lionel on it. You can't climb these tree trunks. You're hurting too much.

You might have bruised your ribs or, worse, broken a couple," Slade said.

"Mary would kill us if you died because you wouldn't let us take care of you," Andy said.

"Hell. All right, all right," Lionel finally conceded.

Slade and Trenton pulled the sled down and put it on the ground. Then they got Lionel settled and strapped him on it.

Lionel shook head. "This is so unnecessary."

"Right, but it will make us feel better about it," Slade said.

Then Slade and Trenton lifted the sled up on the trunk and Andy steadied it while Slade and Trenton climbed over the tree and down on the other side. This was going to take them forever to navigate all the downed trees on the path.

Once they had carried the sled to the ground, Trenton hauled it while Andy pulled Morgan.

"Do you need me to swap off with either of you guys?" Slade asked.

"Maybe you could do so for one of us in a little bit." Andy had been towing the heavy load carrying Morgan all along.

"Let me know when and we'll take a water break and I'll pull Morgan," Slade said.

"Man, is your ex-wife going to be pissed, Morgan," Andy said, sounding amused.

"Why?" Trenton asked.

"Morgan is supposed to have his three kids all week," Andy said. "His ex, Ginny, is going on a cruise with her sister to Jamaica."

"Maybe Ginny will take Morgan back when she learns he has been injured," Lionel said, sounding breathless.

The guys all looked at Morgan. Trenton and Andy both said, "Nah."

After two and a half hours of climbing over fallen trees on the trail in the wind-driven snow, Sheri barked at Slade, telling him she wanted to take a turn pulling the sled. If the sled had been lighter, not pulling around a one-hundred-and-sixty-five-pound man, then she might have.

He shook his head at her. Then she raced off ahead of them.

"I hope she's not chasing a rabbit or something," Andy said. "It would be awful if she lost her way in this weather."

"She's going back to the cabin." Slade didn't blame her for wanting to get there and shift before help arrived. She would get a fire started and be ready for them. He just hoped she wouldn't come back to help them once she had shifted and dressed.

―――――――

When Sheri reached the cabin, she thought she heard someone coming and hesitated to shift. But when she realized it could have been just the noise from the storm, she shifted, put in the code, and entered the cabin and shut the door. She raced upstairs to the bedroom. Even though it would take some time for Slade and the others to get here, she thought the emergency rescue team might be here first. She hurried to dress warmly, then went downstairs to start the fire in the woodburning stove. She sure hoped Morgan and Lionel would be all right. Well, and Slade and the others in this storm. But if they got themselves in trouble, she would head out for them. For now, she was staying here.

She went outside on the porch out of the wind and called her mom on the satellite phone to see how Hans was. She had to tell them what was going on with them because the newscasters might be reporting the storm and maybe even injuries in the BCWA, and she didn't want her family to worry about her and Slade. She needed to call Slade's parents too.

"Hey, Mom—"

"Oh, goodness, Sheri. Are you and Slade okay? We've been watching the news and they've rescued campers at Lady Boot Bay of Lac LaCroix already. How is it in your area?"

"It's bad. We were bringing a couple of men who were injured back to our cabin. We didn't expect the storm, or we wouldn't have gone for a wolf run tonight."

"Or found the men, right?" her mom said.

"Correct. I heard them shouting for help. Anyway, Emergency Rescue Services are coming here to pick them up."

"Are you going to cancel your trip?"

Sheri was watching the road for any sign of help arriving, listening for a vehicle's engine. "No, the winds seem to be dissipating now." Some, thankfully. It didn't mean more trees that were leaning over and ready to collapse wouldn't fall, even after the storm settled down. It was still snowing.

"You let us know if you need any help."

"We sure will. How's Hans?" Sheri asked.

"He's still sick, staying hydrated the best he can. I left

the chicken soup for him. Dad said he would stay with him. Hans was more worried about you and Slade though."

"Yeah, who would have figured it?"

"Exactly. Okay, well, I'll let you go. I'm headed home."

"All right, Mom. I'll keep in touch." Then she called Slade's mom. "Hi, it's—"

"Oh, Sheri, are you and Slade okay? We've been watching the reports on the storms, and we were worried about the two of you," Lolita said.

"Yeah, we're okay." Then Sheri told her what had happened and why Slade wasn't here calling his mother or father himself. He most likely was pulling a sled by now to relieve one of the guys of the burden. But he probably also didn't want to tell his parents that everyone was fine when he wouldn't know that until they reached the cabin. "We'll call you as soon as he arrives. We'll have to take care of the men until help can come for them."

"There's no rush. I'm just glad to know you and he aren't injured."

Sheri knew half the wolf pack would be coming for them if they had been. They ended the call, and she went back inside, but she was watching out the window for any signs of the men.

Then she heard them coming, Slade shouting, "We're nearly there!"

She went outside to greet them. Slade was pulling Morgan. "No emergency crews have arrived yet, but I called our families to let them know that we're safe. They're hearing about it all on the news."

"Can we use your satellite phone to call our families?"

Andy asked. "My satellite phone died after I called this in to begin with."

"Yeah, sure, you can use both our satellite phones," Sheri said.

"You must be the girlfriend," Morgan said, smiling at her. *And the dog.* "I'll start hot cocoa for everyone. I imagine you'll need to warm up a bit. The fire is going."

"Did Sadie get home all right?" Morgan sounded worried.

"Yeah, she let me know you were coming." Sheri opened the door for them, and Slade and Andy hauled Morgan inside. She hoped they didn't ask to see their dog.

Then Slade helped Trenton carry Lionel inside. Sheri wasn't surprised to see Lionel on one of the sleds. She went in last and shut the door. Andy pulled off his gloves, hat, and parka and began removing the blankets and sleeping bag from Morgan to check him out.

Sheri began making cocoa for them while Slade and Trenton were stripping out of their outerwear and then removing the coverings on Lionel to see what they could about his injuries. Both injured men were wearing pajamas and wool socks, though Lionel had put on his parka over his pajamas and boots. Trenton unzipped Lionel's parka, then unbuttoned his shirt.

Lionel groaned and Sheri knew he had really been hurt.

When Trenton opened Lionel's shirt, Slade said, "You're bruised. You could have broken or bruised ribs. Let's get some water in you, and then some hot cocoa. Your lips are a little blue." Then he covered Lionel back up.

Sheri brought the hot cocoa into the living room and

went back to grab warm bottles of water for the guys. She set a pillow under Lionel's head and helped him to drink some water. After that, she helped him manage the cocoa.

"Have you got your knife handy?" Andy asked Slade.

"Yeah, here you go."

Andy took the knife and cut Morgan's pajama pants leg while Slade looked on and Sheri called her parents and Slade's to let them know they were all here and safe.

"It looks like it could be a fracture," Slade said. "There's lots of bruising and swelling. At least if it is a fracture, it's not a compound one. But it could just be torn ligaments, which can be worse because they can take longer to heal."

"Maybe they can put you in a walking cast and you can still take care of your kids while your ex-wife's on vacation," Andy said to Morgan. He helped him to drink some water and hot cocoa after that.

Trenton was drinking his cocoa too, and then Slade finished his off.

"Thanks, Sheri." He pulled her into his arms and kissed her. "This is not exactly how I had expected us to finish off the night."

Sheri kissed him back. "I'm just glad you're all safe here now."

"Thanks for helping us out back there," Andy said.

"Yeah, we would have still been stuck out there with nowhere to go," Trenton agreed.

"And freezing too," Lionel said.

"We were glad to help. Does anyone want any more hot cocoa?" Sheri asked.

Everyone wanted more and Sheri was glad she was making them feel a little better until they got picked up.

"This is a nice cabin," Lionel said. "Maybe the next time we should rent one like this."

The guys all laughed.

Sheri didn't blame them about not wanting to be in the forest on another camping trip if they were going to get into a storm of this magnitude. They would still need to get all their gear once they had help clearing the trees off their tents.

She fixed them more cocoa and then everyone was enjoying their second cup. "Help is coming," she said, hearing it off in the distance because of her heightened wolf senses.

"I don't hear anything." Andy looked out the window. "I don't see anyone either. Are you sure?"

"Yeah, she's right," Slade said. "I hear someone coming."

It didn't take much longer before the other guys heard the vehicles coming. Slade got bundled up and went outside to wave to them and Sheri watched through the window, relieved beyond measure that help had arrived for the injured guys.

Then the emergency vehicles and a couple of police cars parked. Slade came inside with four guys with the Emergency Rescue Services and a couple of deputy sheriffs. The ERS techs began checking the injured men out first. They called in that one of the men had a possible fractured leg, and another man possibly had broken ribs, then packed the two men up to take them to the hospital.

The men from the sheriff's office gave Trenton and Andy

a ride to a hotel and they thanked Slade and Sheri and their dog again.

They waved goodbye to the campers and closed the door. It was really late by then, and they were all for hitting the shower and going to bed.

"We made a great team." Slade locked the cabin door, and they turned out the lights, made sure the fire was out, and headed up the stairs. "We'll have to make s'mores tomorrow night."

"Yeah, it's too late for it now. And way too dangerous."

When they reached the bedroom, Sheri started stripping off her clothes. "I know you wanted to be the one to stay with the guys initially as a wolf, but I needed you to get the first aid supplies. I figured you would make it over those tree trunks better because you have a longer jump and you run faster than me. I also know you didn't want me to be out in that storm, but we needed to do the rescue mission together but separately."

"I agree. It all worked out perfectly, and you coming to their aid as a dog and digging them out was the smart thing to do."

"I had to do something because I'd howled as a wolf first, and they'd worried I was one."

"I'd wondered about that."

"Plus I wanted to help them in the worst way—both to help rescue them and to be doing something."

"Yeah, we're both that way."

"Exactly. I'll hop in the shower. Pick whichever bed you want to sleep in." She grabbed a pair of her pajamas.

"All right," he said.

She took a fast shower and dried off, then pulled on her snowman pajamas and left the bathroom. He was sitting in his boxer briefs on the queen-size bed, waiting to take his shower. "Enjoy your shower," she said.

"After all that work, I'm ready for it," he said.

"I know. You had a job of it."

"You too."

She climbed under the covers on the queen-size bed. If he was going to sleep in it, she was going to join him. When he finished his shower and came out wearing a pair of pj bottoms decorated in Christmas candy canes, she pulled the covers aside for him.

"Are you sharing that bed with me?" he asked, smiling, all warm and sexy-like.

"Only if you're sharing your candy canes with me."

He chuckled and joined her under the covers.

"Will they let us know how they fared?" Sheri snuggled with Slade.

"Yeah, I gave them my number and they can call us when they learn about their injuries."

"Good. I like to have closure."

"Me too." Then he kissed her, brushing his fingers along her jawline with tenderness, turning her on, and she parted her lips for him, inviting him in.

"Are we going to—" Slade asked, kissing her cheeks, her eyes, her jaw, her throat.

"Yes," she said, and began to kiss his mouth while she worked her hands under his pajama bottoms to cup his butt and felt his smooth, muscular cheeks, and squeezed. "Hmm, nice. Super nice."

He slid his hands down her pajama bottoms. "Yours are too. Sexy and perfect." He slipped her shirt over her head, baring her breasts, and massaged them, making her feel heavenly. She moaned, loving the feel of his large hands on her skin, her nipples tightening and becoming more sensitive, tingling with need.

Then he was kissing her, leaving her breathless.

She wrapped her arms around his neck and pressed her lips against his, kissing softly at first, then pressuring, opening to him, and touching her tongue to his and stroking. She could already feel his burgeoning arousal pressing hotly against her body as he moved against her, rubbing her mons, and she was ready to just capitulate and ask him to mate her now. But she still thought it might be too soon for him.

She nipped at his ear, and he licked her lips, but then he moved his mouth down to her breast and sucked. She groaned out loud. God, his exquisite touches sent her to the moon. He smiled and stroked the other breast with his hand, taking pleasure in tweaking her peaked nipple. Then he captured her nipple in his mouth and took his time skimming his fingers against the other breast, molding his hand to it.

He finally slid his fingers down the front of her pajama bottoms and found the feminine slit between her legs and began to stroke her swollen nubbin so good. Oh, heavens, he was terrific at this. Yeah, they were definitely ready. Heartbeats were ramping up, blood was heating, pheromones were calling to each other, and she felt she was on cloud nine. She was so wet for him as she surrendered to his touch.

The pulsing heat rippled through her as the climax hit. Wave after wave of pleasure washed over her.

He kissed her mouth with genuine love, and she knew he was the one for her without a doubt. Then she slid her hand down to his arousal, felt how massive it was, silky, jumping to her touch, and she smiled and began to pump him, eager to make him come.

———

Slade listened to Sheri's thundering heart, loving the way she touched him and kissed him with alternating tenderness and passion. Her sweet jasmine scent and she-wolf musk swept around him in a silky, sensuous way. Her soft sighs and moans caressed his ears, and he loved hearing them. Her luscious lips pressed against his and opened to encourage his exploration. Tongues swept over each other while she stroked his arousal, and he was lost to her touch. She was so precious to him, and he didn't want to delay a mating much longer.

She was making the moves on him in the most perfect way. No matter how he tried to hold on to the erotic feelings consuming him, he came in an explosive way. They kissed each other again passionately until he broke free and said, "I guess we should have taken our shower *after* we made love."

She laughed. "Yeah, come on, hot stuff. Let's shower."

He got out of bed, lifted her off it, and carried her into the shower. She was laughing and he loved this new exploration of intimacy between them. And then it was a new adventure all over again. Wet, wild, sexy, and fun.

Chapter 8

SLADE WAS SO GLAD THAT HE AND SHERI HAD MADE unconsummated love last night. They'd made love like that lots of times after returning home from dates. They couldn't have stopped the urge if they'd tried. They'd seen movies, had dinners out, attended the carnival, sure, but really being together overnight, sleeping together, waking up to each other in the morning? This was damn nice. A game changer, Slade felt. They'd always just made love and then kissed goodbye because of their early-morning work commitments.

But now, they were still enjoying just cuddling in bed this morning and weren't ready to jump up and head out to do anything. He loved this with her. He was ready to do this with her back home too for now and forever. She was sexy and sweet, sympathetic and sensitive when it came to how others felt. She was determined to solve her case mysteries, and in general, just so much fun to hang out with. Fortunately, she got his sense of humor, and he loved hers too.

He leaned over and kissed her forehead. He loved relaxing with Sheri just like this.

"Hmm, this is so nice," she said, stroking his arm.

"Yeah, I feel the same way." If she kept stroking him like that, they weren't going to get out of bed.

"I don't know why we never stayed together overnight like this before," he said.

"Work. But I'm not going to use that as an excuse again," she said.

"Good, me neither."

"We're never going to have time to do anything if we don't get up. Though I have to admit, I love this," Sheri said, and then she finally pulled her covers aside and climbed off the mattress.

"Yeah, me too." Feeling relaxed, he slowly left the bed. Then he hugged and kissed her. "But that was damn nice." When she was asleep, he had slipped downstairs to hang the mistletoe up. He hoped she would get a kick out of it.

"It sure was." While they were dressing, she said, "It's time to make breakfast so we can go on a new adventure."

"I'm ready for it."

When they went downstairs, she saw the mistletoe hanging up with a bright-red bow and smiled. "Ohmigod, that is too cute. That wasn't there before, was it? I can't imagine I missed it."

"Nope. I finally managed to sneak down here and hang it up."

"That is so sweet and romantic. And it's fresh. You had to have just bought it."

"I did right before I picked you up. I wouldn't have if only Hans was coming with me."

She laughed, grabbed his hand, and pulled him under the mistletoe. Then she wrapped her arms around his waist, pulled him snug against her body, and kissed him. "You are a romantic."

"I try to be." He kissed her mouth softly at first, and then they deepened the kiss, his hands in her blond hair, loving the soft silkiness of it.

They finally broke free of the kiss, smiled, and headed into the kitchen. Sheri began scrambling eggs and peered out the window. "It's dark out, but there's a negligible wind and it doesn't look stormy this morning."

He started frying some bacon. "I hope it stays that way for the rest of the time we're here." Then he popped some bread into the toaster.

"Me too. Do you want to go on a wolf run first thing this morning?" She set the table, giving them each a Victorian-dressed Santa napkin.

He poured them both cups of coffee and added milk and sugar. "Yeah. A quick run and we'll set up to go ice fishing?"

"That would be great. We can have fish for lunch, if we can catch anything. What if we find anyone else in trouble after last night's storm when we go for our wolf run?" As soon as the food was done, she served up the bacon and eggs.

"Hopefully we won't find anyone needing help or we'll have to do the same routine as we did last night. One of us stays—" He brought over the toast, blackberry jam, strawberry jam, and butter.

"Me."

They both sat down to eat. He smiled at her and buttered his toast. "You, so you can watch them or help in any way you can, and I'll return to the cabin to get supplies." He slathered strawberry jam on his toast.

"Good idea." She crunched into a slice of bacon.

After they finished eating, they cleaned up, removed their clothes, each of them eyeing the other with interest, which couldn't be helped! Then she shifted. He opened the door and was confronted with a ton of snow piled up outside. She leaped through the snowdrift. He joined her, closed the door, and shifted. It was still dark out and perfect for a wolf run. Stars filled the sky and a sliver of a moon lit the way.

Then they ran as wolves before the sun rose. They loved running through the fresh snow. If they'd gotten up around four this morning, they might have seen the northern lights again, but they'd needed to sleep in a little because of the late night they'd had—especially because of their extracurricular activities afterward.

More trees were down, and they had to watch for deadfall—trees that were dead but hadn't fallen yet. But as wolves, it was easy for them to leap over or on top of the fallen trees.

When they arrived at the trail that they'd taken to find the men last night, they heard talking off in the distance. She woofed at Slade.

Yeah, it sounded like Trenton and Andy had returned for the gear they'd left behind before the sun even rose. They had to have been disappointed about having to leave early, not to mention being upset about their friends' injuries and the damage to their camping gear.

Sheri turned around and headed back to the cabin. He smiled. He knew she wanted to help them, and they both raced off. They finally reached the cabin, and he shifted and unlocked it and they went inside. She shifted and they began to dress. "Rescue mission?" she asked.

"For camping gear this time?" he asked.

"Yeah. Let's help them out. We need to shovel the snow off the porch too when we get back."

Slade felt the same way about helping the men. With their wolves' eyesight, they could see what the campers couldn't in the dark. They finished dressing in warm clothes and headed out with an ax, a shovel, and a first aid kit, water, and protein bars, in case the guys didn't have any.

Then they headed back out. When they finally reached the trail connecting to the Border Rogue Trail, Slade hollered, "We're coming to help you all."

Trenton shouted, "Is that you, Slade?"

"Yeah, and Sheri's with me."

"Hell, thanks," Trenton said.

"Yeah, thanks," Andy said.

Slade was glad they could help.

They finally made it to the campsite where they saw the two men digging with their shovels, trying to get to their gear buried under the snow, several lamps set up to light their way.

"We never expected you to assist us this morning," Andy said.

"We were taking a hike to see what was going on out here when we heard your voices," Slade said. "I'm surprised you're here so early."

"We worried someone might come across some of our gear and take it. Not only that, but we want to drop by

Morgan's home and bring him his things and take him a get-well gift and something for his kids for Christmas. We also want to give Lionel a get-well gift. He doesn't have any kids though. There was no sense in delaying getting this done."

"I don't blame you," Slade said.

Trenton shook Slade's hand. "Well, thanks so much for helping us again."

"You're welcome."

"How long are you going to be here on vacation?" Trenton asked.

"Through the end of the week," Slade said, digging through the snow.

"Good. Hopefully, you won't have any more issues for the rest of the time you're here," Andy said.

"That would be welcome," Slade said.

"How are Morgan and Lionel doing?" Sheri pulled out a sleeping bag and two blankets from Morgan and Lionel's collapsed tent.

"Morgan had a simple leg fracture. Lionel had bruised ribs. So he got away with fewer injuries than we were afraid he had. Though both will take some time to heal from their injuries," Andy said. "We were going to call you about it after we finished packing this up and leaving here."

Then they got to work on locating all the rest of their camping gear. With four of them digging and chopping away at the tree, they managed to get some of their camping equipment out. Their tents and Lionel's sleeping bag were unsalvageable. They still had to take them out of the BCWA with them and dispose of them properly.

Morgan and Lionel's sleds were still there, so Slade and Sheri helped the men pack up their gear on them. It took them a couple of hours to dig everything out, and once they were sure that there were no other items left behind, they finished securing their gear.

"We can't believe you're spending your vacation on rescue missions," Trenton said, getting a drink of water from his thermos.

"You've become our favorite guys to rescue," Slade said.

Everyone laughed.

"Well, we really appreciate all the help," Andy said.

"We're glad we could assist you," Sheri said. "Where are you going to now?"

"To where our vehicle is parked about two miles from here. But we had a good night's sleep at a hotel last night, so we're ready to go," Trenton said.

"That's good," Slade said.

"Where's your dog?" Andy asked.

"Oh, she's curled up by the fire. After taking her for a brief walk this morning to do her business, she wanted to stay by the woodburning stove," Slade said.

"I don't blame her," Trenton said. "Oh, we wanted to mention something to you also. If we hadn't had this unfortunate experience, we would have looked into something we came across and wanted to check out further. It was some kind of debris from something, but we didn't know what. If you're interested in trying to figure out the mystery, here are the coordinates." He gave Sheri and Slade the location.

Slade made a note of it. "Thanks. We'll check it out."

"Thanks again." Andy shook their hands.

Trenton did too, and then they headed out on the trail leading to the trailhead where they'd parked their vehicle.

Slade and Sheri took the trail back to the BRT and headed to the cabin to get ready to ice fish. "I'm glad we were able to help them again," Sheri said. "We can investigate whatever they thought they had found at the coordinates Andy gave us afterward."

"Yeah, I agree. I'm glad too that we saw them. It brings us some closure and they appreciated our help."

"I didn't expect them to ask about our 'dog.'"

"I know, right?" Slade gave her a hug. "I'm glad you didn't mind me calling you a dog."

"No, they had to believe that."

Once they reached the cabin, they both shoveled off the snow on the porch. Then they got their fishing equipment out and hoped they would catch enough for a meal.

But Slade couldn't help wondering about the debris Andy and his friends had seen.

Chapter 9

LOOKING FORWARD TO ICE FISHING, SHERI AND SLADE skied out on the snow-covered lake. Slade pulled the sled with their equipment and then they found a spot farther out where the water was deeper. They drilled two fishing holes in the ice and then set up the blue pop-up tent. After setting their chairs inside the tent next to the fishing holes, they sat down, baited their hooks, and dipped in their lines.

They were just waiting for the fish to bite when they heard a dog barking off in the distance. Keeping a pet under control was one of the enforced rules for people who brought dogs into the BCWA. They had to keep their dogs on leashes, in their campsite, not chasing wildlife, not barking continuously. Sheri was glad Andy and the others hadn't seemed to notice that Sadie the dog hadn't been on a leash when Sheri had gone to rescue them. Normally, Slade would have been required to keep her on a leash for a walk when she got away from him and found the men.

But Sheri suspected something more was wrong now because the dog was barking constantly.

"We need to check it out," Sheri said. Being a private investigator, she was always eager to solve a mystery, but she was worried that something was really the matter, especially after the storm had caused so much trouble for them last night. What if someone else had been injured but they hadn't been able to contact anyone for help? Maybe he was pinned in his tent like Morgan and Lionel had been. Or he didn't have a satellite phone to call for help. "What if the dog's owner is in trouble?"

"Or the dog is. The dog is barking about five to six miles away. Because of the density of the woods, I would say it's closer to five miles." Slade looked back at their fishing holes in the ice.

She knew he wanted to fish. So did she. "Should we take the sled?"

"Yeah, and the first aid kit, water, sleeping bag, blankets, satellite phones, in case we find someone in trouble. We'll ice fish again, once we learn what's going on," Slade said.

She was glad he wanted to check it out too.

With sled in tow, they quickly skied back to the cabin and packed it with emergency rescue items and their snowshoes. "We'll ski across the lake to reach the location closest to where we heard the dog barking and then move inland. That way we can avoid all the fallen trees on the Border Route Trail." Then they headed out, Slade hauling the sled.

The dog continued to bark, sounding like he was heading toward them but then returning in the direction he'd come from.

"He's frantic," Sheri said. "He's worried about his owner, I bet you anything."

"Yeah, I agree."

They were going as fast as they could ski on the

snow-covered, frozen lake while pulling the sled. The dog was still barking. They predicted it would take them an hour to reach the dog's location by skis if he was as far away as they suspected he was. He sounded like he was close to the edge of the lake now, though, which helped because they could ski much faster to him than by hiking along the BRT.

Slade called out, "Hello! Is someone out here who needs our help?"

They didn't think anyone would be this close to them if the dog was still barking from that far away, but maybe the dog would come to them. The dog hardly moved from where he was, like he was protecting his owner, afraid to get too far away from him.

"Maybe the dog is tied up," Sheri said, thinking maybe it wasn't that he was sticking by his owner. Maybe his owner had left him, and the dog was unhappy about it.

"Hell, that might be it. But it's still worrisome that the dog's owner isn't returning to his campsite to calm him down."

Finally, they reached the place where they heard the dog barking deeper in the woods about a quarter of a mile from the shore on the lake. Then a beautiful male husky came running out to them. He grabbed at Slade's parka sleeve with his teeth, tugged at him to come with him, and then ran back toward the direction he'd come.

"I bet his owner is hurt," Sheri said. "Do you want to run ahead with the first aid kit?"

"No, I'm not leaving you alone in case there's any danger to us."

She appreciated Slade for saying so, though she wished they could get there faster. They finally reached the campsite and the dog scratched at his owner's tent before going inside it.

She hoped the guy wasn't dead. She'd kept thinking he might need medical attention, not that he was dead.

Slade went into the tent and said, "He's alive."

"Oh, good." Sheri was so relieved. "What's wrong with him?" Then she had the fleeting idea that he had the stomach flu like her brother.

The dog kept going inside the tent and then leaving it, as if he thought Sheri should go and check on his owner too.

"Mr. Lincoln believes he had a minor heart attack. He says he took medicine for it, but he looks pale and says he doesn't feel well. We need to get him out of here and he needs to be taken to the hospital." Slade poked his head out of the tent. "I'm calling it in."

"Do we need to take him back to our cabin? What about the dog?"

"I'm giving the emergency team the coordinates. They'll get to him to the hospital quicker if they pick him up at our cabin. He's in stable condition right now, but we need to get him on the sled and take off. We'll take the dog with us and anything else that Mr. Lincoln needs." Then they situated him on the sled and packed everything he didn't want to leave behind.

"Who do you want us to contact for you," Sheri asked, "if you haven't already done so?"

"My wife." Mr. Lincoln patted his parka's pocket and Sheri

reached in and found his phone. He gave her the number to unlock it. "Nancy is my wife."

They couldn't get reception out there on the cell phone, so she called the number on her satellite phone.

"Your husband might have suffered from a heart attack, at least he thinks he could have. My boyfriend and I are taking him to our cabin so he can be picked up and taken to the hospital." She gave her the location of their cabin.

"All right," Nancy said. "Is our dog okay?"

Sheri was kind of taken aback that Nancy hadn't seemed more concerned about her husband, though she understood how Nancy could be worried about the dog too. "Yeah, he's coming with us."

"I'll get hold of someone to come for him," Nancy said. Then she hung up.

Sheri expected his wife to be more upset about the situation with her husband!

Once they were ready, Slade said, "We're hauling you to our cabin. It'll take a little over an hour to get there and your dog can stay with us until someone can come get him for you."

"Thanks."

Sheri found the dog's leash and hooked him up so he wouldn't run off, though she suspected he would stick close to his owner. But she didn't want to get into trouble should anyone see the dog with them off leash. Besides, what if the dog did run off?

Then they made their way along the trail until they reached the frozen lake and could put on their skis. Once they were all set, Sheri tied the leash to the sled rope so her hands would be free to use the ski poles. Then they began skiing as fast as they could, the dog running beside the sled, looking invigorated to have a nice run like this. She suspected Mr. Lincoln hadn't been in any shape to run with his dog in the time leading up to the heart attack.

"I'm so glad your dog was barking and alerted us that you were in trouble," Slade said.

"I figured that someone would get annoyed and come looking for me to make me shut my dog up. Jet is truly my hero for alerting you," Mr. Lincoln said.

"He is." She was glad Mr. Lincoln was talking to them, and that he wasn't passing out from pain.

"The storm was the culprit," Mr. Lincoln said. "I was so scared because of it. With the trees falling down all around me, I figured I was a goner for sure. Then I heard a tree snap close by and was waiting for it to crash into the tent. I was so stressed out, I'm sure that's what brought the heart attack on."

"Have you ever had a heart attack before?" Slade asked.

"Mild chest pains. But I figured it was just heartburn from eating too much spicy food."

"But not this time," Slade said.

"No. This time I was sure I was going to die."

The dog was panting, looking like he was really enjoying the run. After an hour, they reached their cabin and an ambulance and EMTs were already there to take care of Mr. Lincoln, to Sheri's relief.

"We're airlifting you to the hospital," one EMT said after checking his vital signs.

Mr. Lincoln looked a little gray and nodded.

Sheri was surprised. She had thought from the way he'd been talking to them all the way to the cabin, he wasn't too bad off. But his condition seemed to have worsened since they had started their journey to the cabin.

Sheri called Nancy and said, "Hi, this is Sheri again. Your husband is being air evacuated to the hospital."

"My husband's cousin, Fitz, knows the place where you're staying. He'll be there within the hour to pick up our dog."

"Okay, we'll be here." Sheri prayed that Nancy's husband was going to be okay.

Then they ended the call. Jet wanted to go with the ambulance, but Slade and Sheri kept him inside the cabin. This had been an emergency and they couldn't have left the dog outside in the cold, but Slade knew that dogs were allowed in the cabin as long as they didn't get on the beds and weren't left alone in the cabin while the renters were off on some of their adventures.

Slade gave Jet some water. "When Mr. Lincoln's cousin arrives, I'll go with him to show him where Mr. Lincoln's campsite is located so we can pack up his stuff and the cousin can take it with him. You could stay with the dog and keep him company. I'm afraid he would bark the whole time otherwise. And we can't take him with us as I'm afraid he'll run off looking for Mr. Lincoln, unless he really likes Fitz and will mind him."

"Okay, sure." But Sheri wanted to do something, even go fishing and catch them some dinner in the meantime. Except the dog might just bark his head off if he was left alone in the cabin and she wasn't supposed to leave him alone, even if he wasn't their dog. At least for now, he was just looking out the living room window where the ambulance had taken off.

After Sheri and Slade made grilled ham and cheese sandwiches for lunch, they ate and cleaned up, and then Mr. Lincoln's cousin finally arrived.

They greeted him, and he said his name was Fitz Connolly. Brown-haired and bearded, he had nearly black eyes that narrowed when he saw his cousin's dog. He was good-looking, but something was off about him. Sheri sensed a darkness, maybe because he was frowning, unsmiling, smelling annoyed, not anxious or upset about his cousin having a heart attack like she thought he should be.

Sheri wondered why his last name sounded familiar, then she recalled the situation with the pilot who had gone missing. It was a long shot, but she wondered if they were kin. "Are you related to Gerard Connolly?"

"Uh, yeah, he's my brother. Why?" Again, Fitz's reaction made her think he was irritated that she'd even bring it up.

"His wife reported him missing a while back. She said he'd returned home on his own. I was glad to learn of it," Sheri said. "I'm the private investigator who had been looking into his disappearance."

Fitz's eyes widened. "Yeah. Can you give me the coordinates to my cousin's campsite? I need to pack it up and take his stuff and the dog with me and deal with some other business pronto."

"Yeah. I'll go with you, and I can help you pack it up," Slade said.

"There's no need to," Fitz said, his answer abrupt, and

Sheri didn't believe he was just giving Slade an out but truly didn't want his help for some reason. If he was in a rush to get to some other business, Slade could actually make it go more quickly.

"If you're sure—" Slade said. She was glad Slade made another attempt to offer his help just in case she was wrong about Fitz's reason for declining the assistance. Maybe he just didn't want to ask for help from a stranger or put them out in any way.

"Yeah, thanks. Just point me in the direction and I'll be on my way." Again, Fitz was gruff, like he wanted to get this over with as quickly as possible. Which she didn't blame him for, really. He most likely wouldn't have planned an outing like this that could take quite a bit of time. Maybe he didn't even like the wilderness.

She thought Fitz would have acted a little more concerned about his cousin's health, though, unless they really weren't all that close. Fitz looked like he was about twenty years younger than Mr. Lincoln, about thirty, so they might not have really bonded that much growing up.

"We skied on the lake to the shoreline about five miles from where we were fishing. I'll show you where we were and you can see our tracks that go toward his campsite and follow them there," Slade said.

"Okay." Fitz called to the dog and then he and Jet went outside with Slade. They walked out to the lake where the fishing holes had been drilled into the ice. Sheri wanted to tell Fitz he needed to put the dog on a leash, but she figured he would do what he wanted to do, and it wasn't any of her business. If he got into trouble for it, he would have to pay the consequences.

Slade pointed to the direction they had taken while Sheri watched them out the window. She couldn't understand why Fitz wouldn't want Slade's help, but that would make it better for Sheri and Slade so they could go fishing again, hopefully uninterrupted this time, and maybe they would have some luck at catching some fish too. In the meantime, she removed the emergency equipment from the sled.

But she also thought Fitz acted oddly about his brother returning home safely from wherever he had disappeared to. He might not care that much about a cousin, but his own brother? It just made her suspicious. Maybe he didn't like anyone in his family. The PI office had enough paid PI cases that the investigators didn't need to take the time to solve mysteries that weren't jobs, but she still really wanted to know what had happened to Gerard and why his wife and brother were acting so strange about his return.

After sending Fitz on his way, Slade entered the cabin and smiled at her. "You're ready to go fishing."

"Yep. It's time to catch some fish."

Chapter 10

Slade and Sheri watched as Fitz was still trudging in snowshoes across the lake. Without skis, it would take him a lot longer to reach Mr. Lincoln's campsite than Slade and Sheri had.

A yellow shelter and a red shelter had been set up on the lake farther off in the distance, and four more fishermen were sitting on camp chairs in open air while fishing now. The sky was so blue and pretty that Slade thought about taking down the shelter to enjoy the great outdoors more, but he didn't want Sheri to get too cold. A chilling breeze was blowing across the lake and the tent protected them from it.

"What did you think of Fitz's reaction to you asking if he was related to Gerard?" Slade asked as they baited their hooks, then sat down in their tent and began fishing. He was glad Sheri wanted to try this again. Some fishermen swore by fishing early in the morning, but there were so many fishermen out here now, he figured this was as good a time as any.

"His reaction was odd. Just like I thought Betty's reaction had been strange about Gerard's return. I suspected Fitz didn't want your help taking down Mr. Lincoln's campsite because he didn't want us to ask him any further questions about where his brother had been."

"I think you're right. I'd kind of gotten that impression."

"But I figured it was fine that he didn't want your help because it would give us time to get back to fishing. Otherwise, you could have been gone for a couple of hours or so, making your way there, packing up the site, and then coming back." She watched her fishing line in the water, waiting for any movement on the hook.

Slade pulled his line up a little and tensed, thinking something was nibbling on it, then not, and he relaxed. "Fitz might be kind of a loner and maybe he felt put out to even be here."

"Oh, sure, you could be right. He might have been busy with something else and didn't like the interruption. Still, I thought it was odd that he didn't seem concerned about Mr. Lincoln's health."

"I thought that too. Does it make you want to investigate the situation further?"

Sheri nodded. "I sure do."

"What was the clue you had that you were going to check on before Gerard's wife told you he had returned home and was fine?" Slade got a tug on his line but lost the fish.

"Oh no," Sheri said, peering into Slade's fishing hole.

"He got my bait too. Sneaky guy." Slade put a minnow on his hook and started all over again.

"About your question about the clue concerning Gerard," Sheri said. "Someone had spotted a plane flying awfully low in this area. It fit the description of the plane Gerard was flying. I was going to confirm with the airport to see if he'd landed there, but then his wife called me before I could check and said he'd returned home. I figured that answered my question."

"But you weren't satisfied with that."

"No, because he had disappeared for two weeks. Where had he been? Then I wondered if he had been doing something illegal and that's why it was all suddenly hush-hush. That his wife hadn't known about his involvement, but someone else did and told her to call off the search."

"That could be. My first thought was that he was ferrying drugs someplace."

"That could very well be. My first thought was that he was having an affair. I called on Gerard's close friends to see if he had told any of them where he'd been off to, hoping someone knew that he was seeing a woman. But no one had believed he was seeing anyone else.

"Not that he and Betty hadn't had their share of fights during their twenty-year marriage, according to friends, but no one believed he was having an affair or had run out on her. No one knew where he had been going either. Betty had sounded ashamed that she didn't know, but she'd told me it was always like that when he flew off. It had all been very mysterious."

"I'll say."

They continued to fish for a couple of hours. They both lost their fish a couple of times. Sheri threw one back that was too small, attached fresh bait, and put her line back in. The rest of the time, Slade envisioned the fish swimming by, ignoring their bait.

"So are you going to check with the airport to see if

Gerard landed there in time to arrive home to see his wife before she called you?" If Slade had been the PI investigating the case, paid or not, he would.

Sheri smiled. "Yeah. I might not have done so before, but after witnessing the wife *and* Fitz's strange reactions, it confirms my sense of unease about what is truly going on. If we'd known before that Mr. Lincoln was related to Gerard, I would have asked him about his cousin. He might have been more forthcoming. Or he might have slipped up and told us something that would have clued us in as to what was going on. When I return to the office at the end of the week, I'll check into it. I mean, if I had been Fitz, I would have said, 'Oh, yes, my brother came home safe and sound. We were so relieved. Thanks for looking into it for us.'"

"Exactly. But Fitz and Gerard might not have been very close, and Fitz might not have cared if Gerard had shown up at all."

"That's true. Not all families are all that close to each other. Age-wise, they looked like they could be a couple of years difference is all, unlike their cousin, Mr. Lincoln." Then Sheri got a tug on her line. "Ooh, I have a live one. This is so much fun. I've been ice fishing in Yellowknife at some of the parks, but this is my first time in Minnesota."

"And even better—you're with me."

Sheri laughed. "Yes!" Then she pulled up a northern pike twenty-four inches long and put it in the ice chest.

"That's enough for about five meals," Slade said, hurrying to take a picture of Sheri's pike.

"It sure is. So I guess we ought to filet it and then leave a couple of filets out for lunch and freeze the rest. I'll have to let you do the fishing next time so I don't get to catch all the fish."

He laughed. "It's all good."

They packed up their fishing stuff and Slade pulled the sled back to the cabin, then got a call on the satellite phone, stopped, and pulled it out. "Slade speaking."

"Hey, it's Candice. Owen and I would love to come to the cabin on your last two days and nights there. I just turned in my deadline book and I'm so thrilled to be able to celebrate finishing it. Owen was worried he might be needed for investigations because of Gavin's new babies, but everyone said that Owen was due for a vacation, that business was slow because of the holidays, and to go for it," Candice said.

"All right. Well, we look forward to seeing you. We, uh, I mean, Sheri just caught a northern pike." Slade rubbed Sheri's back. She smiled at him.

"Wow, that's great. Save some for us."

"We'll have to catch some more for everyone."

Candice said goodbye and Slade put his phone away. Then he began pulling the sled again. "They'll enjoy being here. I'm sure the others didn't want to bring the babies here. Or Cameron and Faith and their six-year-olds. We would have fun, but—"

"With the babies crying at night?"

Slade chuckled. "Yeah. And with the triplets, it would just be different dynamics." He was glad it would be just all adults for this vacation.

"I agree." Sheri pulled out her satellite phone. "I'm going to call my brother and see how he's feeling. We have plenty of room at the cabin for him to come too. He doesn't have to wait until the last couple of days if he's feeling well enough to join us earlier."

"Yeah, I was thinking the same thing."

"Hey, Hans, how are you doing? Okay, totally understand. Well, we want you to know that you're welcome to join us at any time, okay?" Sheri said. "Candice and Owen will be here for the last two days, but seriously, come as soon as you're over this. All right. Feel better. Love you." Then she ended the call. "He's still sick, but he said he'll let us know how he's feeling, and he'll join us when he can."

"Okay, good. So here we are," Slade said as they reached the cabin. She unlocked it, and they went inside with their fishing gear.

They shed all their outdoor clothes, hats, gloves, parkas, boots, and snow pants and he started a fire in the wood-burning stove. After they processed the fish, they froze some of it, then made the rest for lunch with french fries and coleslaw.

"The wind is really beginning to pick up," she said, glancing out the window. "I thought we could snowshoe to the location of whatever Andy and his friends found out in the woods at the coordinates they gave us, but I think because of the winds and deadfall, we would be safer staying indoors for now."

"Yeah, I was thinking we might just stay inside and play some board games for the rest of the evening, then run as wolves tonight. What do you think?" He finished peeling the potatoes, then began slicing them into french fries.

"That sounds like fun. They have some books on the shelves to read too if you feel like just reading."

"We could do that." Even though Slade loved to read, he really wanted to play a game with Sheri and talk to her about some things that he felt they needed to discuss if they were going to mate. Reading books wasn't conducive to doing that. Plus, he hadn't played any board games with her before. "We could go snowshoeing tomorrow and try to find whatever Andy and the others had seen. As to our meal, would you like a glass of chardonnay with our fish?"

"Sure. That would be super, and I think it would be great fun to go on a treasure hunt tomorrow. There's no telling what we might find."

Chapter 11

"YOU KNOW, THE LAST FEW YEARS, WE HAD TO MOVE A few times until we settled down here and found the perfect pack to be with. But we always decided on things as a family. Amelia and I were fully grown, but as wolves, we wanted to stay close to each other." Slade wanted to make sure Sheri felt the same way since someday he hoped they would have more of a family with each other.

"Of course, that's totally understandable." Sheri took a sip of her wine and set her glass down. "You have always had a family-run seaplane business and you're there for each other."

"Until we came here and had even more support," Slade said.

"True. We also are a great support to the newly turned wolves of the pack who can use our help. It's hard for me to explain to anyone who wasn't part of that pack in Yellowknife how things really were. Kintail was a tyrant. His henchmen were as well. No one in their right mind went against what he dictated. My parents went along with it because what other choice did we have? They belonged to the only Arctic wolf pack up there. We felt safety in numbers. And unless anyone ousted Kintail, nothing was going to ever change. Elizabeth was like my sister. I saw my chance to escape, but then worried that I'd brought Kintail down on everyone's heads in this wolf pack. Once my parents knew I wasn't going back, they were all in with staying with us too. I think they realized it was their way out too.

"Hans was stubborn, but he knew family was more important and saw that not all wolf packs were ruled with an iron fist. So we might not have all made the decision to leave there and come here at the same time, but believe me, if I hadn't slipped away with Elizabeth on your plane, my parents and brother would never have chanced leaving Yellowknife." She lifted a french fry off her plate and waved it at Slade. "You know, I would have tried everything in my power to change my parents' and brother's minds about coming down here to stay if they hadn't already decided it for themselves. They knew that if I mated, I would most likely have kids and they wanted to have grandchildren to love on. Hans wants a nephew or niece or two to dote on."

That was all Slade needed to hear. "Speaking of kids, how many do you think you want?"

"Well, since our kind often have multiple births, we'll probably have more than one. But if I had only one, maybe take a chance and try again?"

He smiled. "Absolutely."

"Well? What about you?"

"That sounds right to me. Being a twin, I can't imagine not having another sibling to play and fight with."

"Boy do I agree with you there."

Then they finished eating and cleaned up.

"I'll see what kind of board games they have here." He

looked through several, then found the perfect one. He pulled it from the bookshelf in the living room and set it on the table. "How about this one? It's a Christmas Monopoly game."

"Oh, that looks like fun. Perfect for Christmas. I'll make us some hot cocoa if you would like while you're setting up the game."

"Sure, that sounds good." Slade opened the box and began to set things up. "Which player piece do you want to use? The candy cane, train, teddy bear, reindeer, Scrooge, or a lump of black coal?"

"Oh, the teddy bear."

"Okay, I'll be—"

"Not the Scrooge."

He smiled at her.

"Or the lump of black coal. You're too sweet for that."

"I can be a really growly wolf."

"But not for a board game."

"You never know—not when I want to win."

She laughed and once the cocoa was ready, she brought their mugs into the living room.

"I'll be the reindeer," he said.

"Aww, okay, I love it." She leaned down and kissed him, then sat opposite him to start playing the game.

They both drank from their mugs of cocoa as they began tossing the dice and moving their reindeer and teddy bear forward, buying properties and buying presents to purchase Christmas trees, until Sheri ended up blowing a fuse in the game. "Oh no!"

Slade laughed, until he got run over by a reindeer. "Hey, *I'm* a reindeer. They should be running with me, not running over me. Okay, so while we're buying properties on the board, what would you say about us having a house built? I mean, your dad's a builder. He could build a house for us on the lake near the other families' homes. Cameron and the others bought all that land around part of the lake so that more of the members of the pack, should it expand, could live there too."

Sheri had just tossed the dice and overthrew them, and they rolled off the table and landed on the floor. "What?" She sounded shocked to hear him make the suggestion after all this time.

"Yeah. I don't know about you, but I'm ready for us to make the commitment to join households." He retrieved her dice for her and handed them to her.

"Do you want to mate?" Her beautiful blue eyes were wide.

He smiled. "Yeah. But your dad said I had to wait until I was sure that you didn't feel like you were being forced to mate me."

Sheri's jaw dropped. "What?"

"Uh, yeah. Don't get mad at him. He and your mom felt guilty that they were trying to push you to mate with Bentley when you still lived in Yellowknife." Slade didn't want her to be annoyed with her father over it. He knew her father had just worried about her not having a say in her life if Slade had been too alpha with her.

"Yeah, my parents thought I just couldn't make up my mind about Bentley, but the thing is I hated how controlling he was. He wasn't the one for me."

"They just didn't want you to fall into the same situation again." Slade was trying to smooth things over with her in case she was really irritated with her dad over this.

She let out her breath. "I can't believe my dad would tell you to hold off on mating me."

"I think we need to get serious about some other matters though too."

"Oh?" Sheri was surprised Slade would bring up a mating over a Christmas Monopoly game, but she knew he wanted to discuss more business before they really agreed to do this, and she was glad.

"Yeah. I've been dating a she-wolf for seven months and you know our kind normally don't wait that long to mate."

"When I asked you if you minded if I went with you when my brother couldn't, you laughed." She'd wondered what was up with that!

Slade smiled. "Your brother kept telling me I needed to take you instead of him. When he became sick all of a sudden, I thought he was faking it. But not when we went to his apartment."

"Ahh, okay. Cameron laughed about it too when I called to say I was going with you if he didn't need me at work for the week."

"Yeah, you know, everyone is just waiting for me to ask you to mate me."

Sheri laughed. "But you were afraid I would say no?"

"In the back of my mind, I kept thinking you were still thinking about your ex-boyfriend or might want to return to your home of Yellowknife."

Ugh. She wished Slade had never known about Bentley. On the other hand, it was probably good that he had. "No way. Not with my family and my best friend being here now and, most of all, you."

"We have the best sexual chemistry," Slade said.

"Oh yeah." That was for sure.

"After sleeping with you overnight, I don't want it to be any other way. I want to kiss you, hug you, fit you into my life in every possible way."

She smiled. She felt the same way about him. "Oh?"

"Yeah, I want you every night and every day. I want to be there for you when you need me, and I know you'll always be there for me."

She wrapped her arms around him and kissed him. "All I need is you. You are the best thing that has ever happened to me. You are so strong but so good about giving me a say in what we're going to do."

"As it should be," he said. "I wouldn't have it any other way."

She truly loved him for that. "That's why you're the right wolf for me. I mean, ever since I met you on the getaway plane that both you and Amelia were taking turns flying, you've been there for me—trying to protect me against Bentley and my former pack leader. Family is so important, and I love that your family is as loving to me as you are. You knew flying Elizabeth and me could have caused you and your sister more trouble, but both of you didn't even give it a second thought."

"No, it would have been wolves abandoning those in need, and David wouldn't have let anything come between him and Elizabeth, and we certainly weren't going to leave Elizabeth's best friend behind to take the flak from their pack leader for her slipping out of his grasp."

"Well, I thank you."

"When I first saw you, I wanted to date you."

"I was certain it was because I was the only lone she-wolf in the area." Sheri had felt the attraction to him right away, though she couldn't imagine how someone who was so sexy and sweet hadn't settled down already unless it was because there were no she-wolves in the area who were eligible.

"No, I wanted to know if you were single right away and I wanted you to know I was very much available. I was just glad David wanted Elizabeth as his mate, that you were leaving an ex-boyfriend behind, and we hit it off so well. Yeah, I was totally interested in you from the moment I saw you and learned you wanted to stay with your best friend. You were loyal to the core to her from the very beginning. That means a lot."

"She has always been loyal to me. I have to say that seeing a hotshot pilot in a bomber's jacket was a total turn-on. I was so surprised when you said you were single."

He laughed. "Yeah, I wanted you to know that right away."

"Well, now, soon, you're not going to be." She sighed and kissed his mouth. "While living in Yellowknife, I didn't figure I would ever have someone I could fall in love with and mate. Boy, once I was here, you changed everything for me."

"I'm glad you came with Elizabeth to make your escape. Amelia told me my tongue was hanging out as soon as I saw you."

Sheri laughed. "She knows you well. About another important topic, what about finances?"

"I make good money, and you do too. I have enough saved up to build a house for us. I'm amenable to us putting our money together or having separate accounts, or a joint account *and* separate ones. Whatever you want," Slade said.

"Let's have our money all together to simplify things. My parents always had their accounts together."

"My parents also have all joint accounts," he said.

"I have money in savings to put into the house too," she said.

"That sounds good. Both of us have furnished apartments, so we'll have fun shopping for furniture for our new home after it's built."

"Oh, I would love that," Sheri said. "What about a honeymoon? A wedding?"

"A wedding held locally with all our pack members," Slade said. "We could have it at the lake."

"So we could have the wedding in September of next year? That should give us time to have the house finished. My dad really gets to work and sees them built right and in a timely fashion."

"Yeah, that sounds good. We just need to look at house plans, purchase the land from the wolf pack, and get the permits, have your dad look over everything, and get it done."

"What about the honeymoon? Where would you like to go?" Sheri asked.

"Hmm, tropical? A ski vacation?"

Sheri thought about it for a moment. "Let's go skiing.

We'll take a pre-honeymoon trip after the mating—well, after Christmas, instead of after the wedding. That way the ski resort will still have snow."

"We can take a tropical honeymoon too, after the wedding. For the first, Silver Town is wolf-run, and I've heard they have a great ski resort. I'll make reservations for us at the Wolff Timberline Lodge, if they have anything available."

"Okay, great. Hopefully they have a room."

"I'll make reservations right away. If they don't have anything, we can find someplace else to go." Slade immediately got on the satellite phone and called the lodge. "Hi, I would like to make reservations for a room." He gave Roxie Wolff the dates. "We're going there for our honeymoon, but we realize it might be too late to get a room." He smiled at Sheri. "That would be great. We're excited to enjoy all that Silver Town has to offer. Thanks, Roxie."

When he ended the call, he hugged Sheri. "Roxie Wolff is part owner of the lodge, and she said that a groom had gotten cold feet at his wedding and canceled his reservation for a honeymoon suite. We've got it!"

"Yes!" Sheri was so excited. "Then we'll just have to let everyone know we need time off for that and hopefully they can do without us. As long as we do it before the full moon when those who are not royal wolves will have difficulties with shifting. So I'll need to be there for them."

"Absolutely. Okay, well that's the plan. Now, we just have to do one more thing."

Sheri said, "That's the most fun thing we have to do."

"And then we tell our families? The pack?" Slade asked.

"Yeah. They'll be so happy for us."

"I hope your dad will be." Slade sounded a little worried.

"Oh, he will be because I'm so happy."

Chapter 12

SLADE PUT THE DICE ON THE TABLE AND PULLED SHERI into his arms, ready to ask her the question that if she agreed to it would change their lives forever. "I want to mate you. *Now.* I don't want to hold off any longer. If your dad hadn't insisted that I wait, I would have asked you a lot sooner. I've always had so much fun with you that I knew we had what it took to be mated wolves. But he had his heart in the right place."

"I thought you preferred being a bachelor male wolf for longer. But I had planned to ask you to mate me when you returned from this trip with Hans. I'd even wanted to mate you last night when we were making love."

Slade kissed her. "Hell, I was going to do the same with you for that dinner following this trip, and I felt the same about making love all the way last night. So I don't want to wait, do you?"

"No way."

"Do you want me to ask your dad for permission?" Slade would do anything to make it right between Sheri and her father.

"Absolutely not." She glanced down at her properties on the Monopoly board, and she smiled. "I won. Let's go to bed."

He laughed. "I think I won."

She glanced back at the board.

"By getting you for my mate." Slade lifted her into his arms. "You make me a winner."

She rested her head next to his chest. "We both won."

After climbing the stairs to the bedroom, he set her down and they began to kiss each other again. "I'm so glad we're doing this," Slade said, loving her like he had never loved a she-wolf before. "I love you. I love how you are so flexible about cancellations, and even though I know you've been disappointed a couple of times because you really wanted to spend the time with me, you've always been so supportive. Not all she-wolves would be. You always care about others' feelings. You enjoy playing with the kids and cuddling the newborns. I love watching you with them. No matter who needs help, you're there to offer it, even if you're busy with something else. You make everything more special, and all I can think of is when we'll be able to get together again the next time and the next, and the next. I have to say that when you said you would go with me on the camping trip because no one else could, I was thrilled. I was pumping my fist in the air, and unless you hadn't been ready for this, I really was hoping it would come to this on the trip."

She wrapped her arms around his body and crushed him in a hot embrace. "I love you, Slade. I love your generosity, your protectiveness, your helpfulness, your kindness. You're strong, but sensitive too. And man, most of all I love how sexy you are and fun to be with. When you make a decision, you do it. Though I was feeling the same way about you."

They were actually going to do this, and Slade was over the moon.

———

Slade cupped Sheri's face and began to kiss her slowly, luxuriously, hotly. He was so hot and sexy whether he was bundled up in wool socks and a sweater, cargo pants, and long johns, or naked, bearing all those beautiful hard-earned muscles. He knew just how to use them to make her feel like she was the only one for him.

Wanting to feel his silky skin against hers, she pulled his red sweater over his head, mussing up his dark hair that always looked like he'd been making love to her all day and night. She kissed his chin, but before she could start removing his cargo pants, he lifted her so that she could wrap her legs around his and pressed her against the bed, his body captured between her thighs, claiming each other in a seductive wolf shifter's way. She kept him snug against her body, making her hot with desire.

She kissed his sensual mouth, and he kissed her back with even more passion, pressing for an opening, licking the seam, taking charge. She loved it when he did and started to explore his mouth, probing, tasting, enjoying the moment, knowing that this time they made love, it would make them mated wolves forever. She felt heady with the idea, a partner in everything, yet an individual able to make her own decision. She was thrilled to be able to do both.

She stroked his tongue with hers, teasing and touching

and tantalizing him. Their hearts were pounding, their pheromones zipping around them, shouting to the world they were the ones for each other, and to go for it.

He nuzzled her cheek with his, stubble grazing against her soft skin. She loved feeling it like the brush of his wolf face when he nuzzled hers. Then he was gently rubbing her throat with his mouth, kissing here there. He began to pull up her sweater. Like him, she was wearing a thermal shirt underneath it, though hers was pine green and his was black. He slipped off her sweater and ran his hands up underneath her thermal shirt, then began peeling it off too. She started to work on his, and they alternately tugged them off each other.

Then he pulled down her red-and-white polka dot bra to release her breasts and pushed them together, molding his large hands over them and kissing each reverently. She ran her hands through his tousled hair, loving the silky feel of it.

He took her other nipple in his mouth and tugged gently on it with his teeth. Sheri moaned as the sensual feeling washed over her and she was lost to his touch. So intense, so perfect, so sexy. Then he was tonguing her other nipple, the sensitive tip begging for more.

He slipped his hands behind her back and struggled to unfasten her bra. She was going to do it herself, but he wasn't letting her. It was his task, his fun to strip her naked, just like she wanted to do with him.

Then she felt her bra release, felt the band loosen, felt relief, and he smiled, looking perfectly satisfied to have completed that part of his mission. He pulled the straps off her shoulders and tossed the bra aside. She had gotten it for herself for Christmas and was glad she had worn it for this special occasion. He moved off her and lifted her foot to remove one sock and then the other, caressing her feet with a gentle massage. Then she tugged his socks off, massaging his in kind.

He looked at her for a moment and smiled. He had such a wolfish predatory gaze—like he had caught his prey and she was all his now. She arched a brow and started tugging off his cargo pants, admiring his beautiful bare chest. She leaned down and kissed his chest. He pressed kisses on top of her head.

Then he finished removing her pants and kissed her breasts at the same time. She tilted her head up, licked one of his nipples, then the other, and they peaked to perfection. She loved how easily she could arouse him. Even now his erection was pressing for release in his boxer briefs, and she reached down and cupped him, rubbing her thumb over his arousal, making it jump eagerly to her touch.

They rubbed their bodies against each other, the friction escalating the desire to mate. His hands were on her shoulders, massaging; hers were on his back, caressing. She slid her hands down his boxer briefs in back and squeezed his buttocks. She loved how firm they were. He slipped his hands down her bikini panties that matched her bra and squeezed her cheeks.

"You feel so good," he said.

"Oh, I love how hard you are." She squeezed his butt again.

He smiled. "And you're perfect."

They nearly bumped heads pulling each other's

underwear off and then they were on the bed, him between her legs again, only they were totally naked now.

She kissed his mouth, their kisses lingering, soul-searching as they rubbed their bodies together, increasing the friction, the intimacy, making the connection. The physical affection between them was the most wondrous experience. Then he was stroking her between her thighs, and it was amazing. She didn't know why she hadn't told him months ago he was hers whether he was ready for it or not. He made her feel loved and so special.

But right now, he was caressing her sweet spot and sending her to the moon. She arched against his finger, begging for climax. And then she was coming in a big way and cried out his name with such fervor that he smiled.

"Are you ready?" he asked.

It was important for wolves to make sure that this final commitment between them was what they truly wanted because for them, it was a lifetime pledge.

"Oh yeah, I sure am. I have been for a long time."

"Good. I love you."

"I love you too."

He pushed his erection into her, and she felt like he was right where he belonged. Just like she was. He felt incredible. She felt incredible. He thrust into her deeper, and this was it. She loved him more than anything in the world. His thrusts were more frantic now as he tasted her full, soft mouth, and she tongued his. He skimmed hot kisses over her collarbone, slowing his pace, and then he began deepening his thrusts, racing for climax, and came in a guttural growl.

She howled for the moon. He followed suit, howling along with her. They were mated wolves and she couldn't have been happier.

They showered and ended up making love again there. They couldn't help themselves now that they were mated.

"We'll have to tell the others that we mated," Sheri said, kissing his wet chest as he turned off the shower.

"Yeah, absolutely. Though I suspect they'll guess what we've been up to while we've stayed here alone." He handed her a towel and then grabbed one for himself.

"You're probably right. I'm glad we didn't wait any longer," Sheri said.

"Me too. We make a great team in the kitchen, for one thing."

"Rescue missions?"

He dried her off and she dried him too. "We do a superb job."

He took their towels and hung them up, but before she could walk back into the bedroom, he grabbed her up and carried her in there and set her on the bed, then joined her.

"Relaxing and having fun?" She cuddled with him on the bed.

"Yeah. I look forward to enjoying doing things with you once we have our own home too. We can run when we want when we're off from work, unlike while we are living at our apartments and have to drive over to the lake to run with the others. Speaking of the apartments..." he said.

"Well, I'm not living alone any longer." Sheri squeezed his hand. "So I don't care where we're going to be, but I want us to be together."

"Yeah, same here. I'm thinking we'll give notice on one of them and move in together. It'll take about nine months to build our new home. I'm fine with staying at either place. It's your choice, but you have a few more pieces of your own furniture at your place—and the room for them. My place is smaller, so it would probably be better to stay at your apartment."

Sheri tucked a blond curl behind her ear. "That's what I was thinking, but I didn't want you to feel you had to give up your place."

"Nope, I'm happy with that. Your place is definitely homier until we can have our home built."

"Okay. That sounds good."

"As soon as we get home, I'll give notice."

"All right, and we can start moving your things over right away."

"Absolutely."

Sheri said, "Are you ready to tell our families we mated? Then the rest of our pack?"

"Yeah. I wouldn't have done anything differently, but I hope your dad isn't angry with me."

Sheri kissed Slade on his nose. "He won't be."

They called her parents first at Slade's insistence. He was so sweet. He really was afraid her father would give him a hard time about mating her without his approval.

"Hey, Dad, can you call Mom to the phone too?" Sheri asked.

"Yes, I'll get her. Georgia! Sheri's on the phone."

"What's wrong?" Georgia asked, sounding out of breath.

"You're not having any other problems with more storms, are you?"

"Nope. We have some solutions. We're combining households," Sheri said.

Slade smiled at her.

"So…you're moving in together?" her father asked, sounding astounded. "For a trial period?"

"It better not be. We need to talk to you about building a house for us."

"A…"

"We're mated, Dad, Mom," Sheri said.

"Oh, that's terrific. We wondered when you would get around to it, and we thought this cabin retreat might be the time for it," her mom said.

"You told Slade to hold off on a mating, Dad?" Sheri asked.

"Uh, yeah. After the business with Bentley—"

"Slade isn't anything like Bentley."

"Yeah, I realized that as the weeks went on. I shouldn't have told Slade that. It wasn't my place." Her dad sounded regretful.

"I appreciate that you talked to him from the heart, worried I might be pushed into a mating I wouldn't be ready for, but Slade is a dream, not anything like my former boyfriend. Anyway, we're so happy we mated, and we can't wait to celebrate it with the family and friends."

"Oh, honey, we're so glad that the two of you love each other. I didn't know Fred had said anything to Slade or I would have had a little talk with him," Georgia said.

"Man, am I in the doghouse, and for a wolf, that's pretty bad," Fred said.

They all laughed.

"We love you, Dad," Sheri said.

"Yeah, I'm glad you talked to me," Slade said, "but we know that this is the best place for us."

"Find the home design you want, get your land, and we'll get it built," her dad said.

"What about the wedding?" Georgia asked.

"Oh, we'll plan all of that. We want to go on our mating honeymoon at the ski resort in Silver Town once we've had Christmas with the family here," Sheri said. "But then we'll go on another one after the wedding."

"We could have the wedding there on the lake," Slade said.

They talked more about that, and Fred said he would talk to them more about the house plans as soon as they were done with this trip so he could get started on building once they had their permits and the land sorted out.

Sheri's parents congratulated them for mating, and they finally ended the call so Sheri and Slade could call his parents next.

"Hey, Mom, can you get Dad on the phone?" Slade asked.

"No more trouble in the woods, right?" Henry asked.

"No, it's all good. We got mated," Slade said.

Henry and Lolita whooped and hollered. "Have you told Amelia yet?" Henry asked.

"Not yet. We're telling our parents, then our brother and sister," Slade said.

"Well, we're so proud of both of you and are excited about having another daughter in the family," Lolita said.

"Well, I'm thrilled to be part of your family too," Sheri said.

"We figured when Slade wanted to have us all together at Sheri's house for Christmas Eve dinner, this was where this was headed. Well, even before that. Once Sheri took Hans's place to be with you, Slade, we couldn't imagine you being with her all that time and not ending up mating," Lolita said.

"Yeah, I felt the same way," Henry said. "We're so happy for you both."

"Her dad is going to build the house for us on the lake as soon as we buy the property," Slade said.

"Good. If there's anything you need us to do, just ask. We'll be there for you," Henry said.

Sheri was thrilled his parents were as happy they were together as her parents were. After that, they called up Amelia, who was with her mate, Gavin, and shared the good news. They were ecstatic and they were excited about helping plan the wedding and the house too.

Last, they called Sheri's brother and let him in on the news.

Hans just laughed. "I couldn't have gotten sick with the flu at a better time."

Slade and Sheri laughed. "Yeah, Bro, I wouldn't have wished it on you, but I'm glad it worked out for Sheri and me."

"I'm so glad you ended up with Slade, Sheri. Sorry I was pushing you to mate Bentley. I was wrong and I have no excuse for it," Hans said.

"It's okay. Living in Yellowknife with the old pack made us all a little dysfunctional."

"For sure. I'll help you with the house too. I'm so glad for the both of you and I'm glad you ignored me about mating Bentley, Sheri. About me staying with you at the end of the week—"

"We want you to come," Sheri said. "How are you feeling now?"

"I'm feeling much better. I really want to stay with you, but with you being newly mated, this is like a honeymoon for you," Hans said.

"No, you planned to be here all along, and we plan to take a ski trip for our mated honeymoon."

"Okay, I'll be there Friday. And congratulations again."

"Thanks," Sheri and Slade said.

Then they called Cameron and Faith so they could tell the rest of the pack that they were mated.

"What about your living arrangements?" Faith asked.

"We're moving my stuff to Sheri's apartment," Slade said.

"We'll help and have a pizza party afterward at the office?" Faith asked.

"Yeah, that would be fun," Sheri said.

"We want to buy the property next to your cabin, if that works for you," Slade said.

"Yes, that's why we bought all that land for more of our pack members to enjoy living on it. We'll go over the lot boundaries when you return home, and I imagine Sheri's dad will build your home for you?"

"Absolutely. He does beautiful work."

"Yeah, he does, and we love that we have a wolf in the pack who can build our wolves homes that are so nice. When you both return home, we'll go over it with you and get the deed to the property in your name."

"Thanks, Cameron and Faith. We can't wait to get started," Slade said.

After they finished the call, it wasn't long before Candice called. "I'm so glad you mated each other. Congrats! Are you sure you want Owen and me to join you at the cabin at the end of your stay?"

"Oh, absolutely," Sheri said, not wanting to renege on the arrangement. Besides it would be fun having them there because they were another couple, and Sheri and Slade were now too. Even though Hans would be the odd man out, she wanted him there to enjoy what he should have before she took his place.

"Okay, but if you change your mind, just let us know."

"We won't. We have plenty of room and we'll have a great time. Hans is joining us too. He says he's feeling much better now," Sheri said.

Once they ended the call, she said, "Are you ready to go on a mated wolf run?"

"You bet."

She shifted and raced down the stairs and he got the door. Then he went outside with her, closed the door, and shifted. Then they leaped into the snow and ran off. Once they were far enough from the cabin, they left the trail and played with each other, nipping and biting, frolicking in the snow in the woods. They startled a fox, and it skittered off in a hurry.

They howled at the same time as if their mating had made them one. As soon as they did, other wolves off in the distance howled. She loved hearing wolves howl whether they were their own kind or wild wolves.

Sheri licked Slade's face and he nipped her back. They were mated, taking their mated run. They couldn't have had more fun running as wolves than this!

She loved him as they pounced on each other, then ran off and chased one another, nipping at each other's tails. He showed her just how much he loved her back. Best of all, they were going to be sharing a home together and making lots more good memories as a mated couple.

They woofed and they chased each other back to the cabin, having a ball.

It was time to return and make s'mores. As soon as they arrived at the cabin, they dressed warmly and he brought out the ingredients while she gathered blankets. Then he started the fire in the firepit. They were soon sitting next to each other on a bench, bundled up in the cold, and roasting their marshmallows.

"We need to roast hot dogs too," Sheri said.

"Yeah, I saw Hans had bought hot dogs and buns. Besides having some of the fish while Hans, Candice, and Owen are here, we can roast hot dogs and s'mores."

"Yeah, that sounds like fun." Sheri's marshmallow got a little too close to the fire and started flaming. She hurried to blow out the fire.

He laughed, until the same thing happened to him. Then it was her turn to laugh.

Once they'd made their first s'mores treat, they ate it and smiled at the marshmallow and chocolate remaining on their mouths. They took care of that in a hurry, not with napkins, but licking each other's lips and cleaning them off. Then they were ready to make their next s'more. What made it even more special was that the northern lights began to sweep across the dark sky.

"Oh, this is beautiful. This couldn't have been more fun, having s'mores and a gorgeous colorful display across the sky as if we had a symphony of lights choreographed just for us," Sheri said.

"I agree. It's the perfect ending to a beautiful day."

"The rest of the night is still to come."

He smiled at her. "Absolutely."

Once they were done with their s'mores, he pulled her onto his lap, and they just enjoyed cuddling in front of the fire and continued to watch the light display. Finally, when they were both ready to go in and warm up, they put out the fire and went inside and locked up. Then they pulled off their gloves, hats, parkas, snow pants, and boots. He chased her up the stairs to the bedroom. By the time she reached the landing, he lifted her into his arms and took her to the bed.

"Time for the final activity tonight," he said, and sat her on the bed, then began removing her clothes.

She was so glad they were mated and going all the way from now on, no more holding back. She couldn't wait to make love to her wolf mate again.

"Merry Christmas, early, my beautiful wolf," he said.

"Merry Christmas, my sexy wolf," she said. "I couldn't be happier."

"Me either."

Chapter 13

THE NEXT MORNING FELT LIKE DÉJÀ VU AS SHERI AND Slade snuggled together. It was so nice waking up next to him and she didn't want to leave the bed—again. She was never like that. Once she was awake, she was ready to do something, anything. But man, with Slade in her life, she felt totally different. This was heavenly—listening to Slade's relaxed heartbeat, breathing in his male wolf scent, enjoying his warmth.

"Do you want to run as wolves first thing?" she asked, stroking his bare chest.

It was still dark out, but Slade didn't seem to want to leave the bed either—like the last time. He kissed her breast. "Yeah, sure."

"After we return, we could go look for whatever Andy and his friends had found out in the woods, just for curiosity's sake," she said, eager to check it out. She'd been thinking of it on and off and wondered what had piqued the campers' interest enough to share the find with them.

"Yeah, I was thinking of that too."

They dressed, went downstairs, and made Christmas cinnamon pancakes for breakfast, swirling the cinnamon in the batter before cooking it, then sat down to eat, and afterward cleaned up. They hugged and kissed before they left on their wolf run, each of them tasting the cinnamon on the other's lips and licking them clean, smiling and laughing.

She was thinking how nice it would be to have a wolf door at the cabin. All the wolves' homes had them. Since she, Slade, and her brother had apartments, they didn't have that luxury. But then they didn't run from their apartments as wolves. They would go to the lake where the white wolf pack's members had their homes.

They had been running for some time in the wintry woods when they heard voices off in the distance and then saw something that was about two feet tall by three feet wide, painted white but scratched to bare metal on places sticking out of the snow. She frowned.

Slade shifted. "It's part of a plane. The main cabin door, buried about a foot in the snow." Then he shifted back into his wolf.

Ohmigod, was it a new wreck? Were the people whose voices they heard looking for anyone who had been injured or was dead? But she and Slade would have been alerted if the plane had crashed while they were here, she figured. Unless it had happened the night of the storm when the trees were falling all around them. The blowing snow and thirty-five-mile-per-hour howling winds could have masked the sound of the crash.

Sheri and Slade kept moving closer to where the men were talking. What if they had been aboard the plane and had been injured? She and Slade needed to return to the cabin and call it into the police, but before that, they really needed to learn what they could about the situation. Maybe the police and aviation investigators were the ones who were already there.

Then she saw the illumination of flashlights poking into the woods. Two men were gathering items in the snow, but they were dressed in winter camouflage clothes and didn't look like police or aviation investigators. The plane wasn't old and rusted, so it hadn't been here for a long time either.

Sheri and Slade stayed hidden in the woods watching them. That's when she saw part of the plane ID and thought it might have been Gerard Connolly's plane. She needed to verify the numbers. But Sheri would have heard if his plane had gone down, and if it had been found or had been reported. It would have been all over the local news in the surrounding areas. What had happened to Gerard? Had he returned home and then taken another trip and this time crashed? Or had he crashed when he went missing? Unless the plane hadn't been his.

What if he hadn't made it home and his brother and his wife were covering up his disappearance? Then who were these men? Just hikers who had run across the broken-up plane, or had they known it was here and they were looking for whatever the plane had been carrying? She wondered if she and Slade had happened across the coordinates of the item that Andy and his friends had found.

If Gerard had been carrying drugs, like Slade and Sheri had considered, these men could be dangerous.

Then they saw Gerard's brother, Fitz, join the men, which surprised her. She had suspected he didn't have anything to do with his brother, given the way he had acted about Gerard's return after having been missing for two weeks. "Keep looking. Hurry it up. If my damn cousin hadn't had his untimely heart attack and I hadn't had to deal with his shit, we would have been finished with this by now."

"Yeah, and if Gerard's plane hadn't crashed, we wouldn't be here either."

Ohmigod. That's why Fitz had been in a rush to take care of other "business" and hadn't shown any concern about Mr. Lincoln's heart condition. He was involved in this.

"Do you think any of the merchandise survived the crash?" a blond, bearded man asked. He was poking around under pieces of plane wreckage.

"Maybe not, but we need to get rid of the evidence even if nothing is salvageable," Fitz said.

Evidence? Of what? Sheri wished they would say. She sniffed the air, but she couldn't smell any drugs. She hadn't liked Fitz as soon as she had met him at the cabin. She hadn't believed he'd cared about either his cousin's or his brother's welfare.

Slade was also smelling the air. She knew he was trying to determine what the cargo was, and probably the other men's scents too so they could identify them later. She wanted to report the plane wreckage to law enforcement so they could take over and learn what was going on. Maybe they could even catch these guys in the act of trying to salvage things from the plane. It made her wonder if Gerard had made it home, or if he had died in the crash and was buried in the snow. Or maybe they had already removed Gerard's body. If they had found him, why not just report that he'd died in the crash? Because they had to get rid of whatever the cargo had been first? Possibly because they were all implicated?

She wanted to remain glued to the spot in case they said something more incriminating. She was afraid if she and Slade left, they could miss seeing some evidence of a crime. Slade appeared to feel the same way, not moving an inch, just observing the men searching for stuff. Of course, she or Slade could return to the cabin to contact the police while the other remained there, watching the whole thing, a witness to whatever they might dig up. But she didn't want to leave Slade alone, and she was certain he wouldn't want to leave her here alone if she stayed to observe the men.

Now she figured that's why Fitz hadn't wanted to talk to them about his brother. She knew something hadn't been right about the whole affair.

Was the wife involved too? Or had she not known what her husband was up to, but Fitz had learned she'd gone to the police and then a private investigator and told her to say Gerard had returned home after all. Sheri suspected the wife hadn't known what her husband was doing.

Maybe Gerard had returned after the crash, and he was just fine or had suffered only minor injuries that hadn't required seeing medical personnel or any hospitalization. Now, more than ever, Sheri wanted to check out his story.

"Hell," Fitz said. "I can't find anything here."

"We might have to wait until the snow melts off," the blond guy said, kicking at a pile of snow. Sheri realized he looked familiar, but she couldn't place where she'd seen him before.

"Anybody could run across the wreckage by then," Fitz said. "We can't let that happen. You know that, Danbury."

Danbury nodded. "I still want to know how in the hell the plane managed to crash."

"Yeah, well, we all do." Fitz walked off into the woods, out of Sheri and Slade's sight.

Danbury went off in a different direction. A dark-haired man with a scrubby beard headed Sheri and Slade's way. Slade nuzzled Sheri and they moved away from the path the man was taking.

"Shit!" The man saw them, pulled out a gun, and aimed it in the wolves' direction, and they took off running, heading back to the cabin. He fired off a couple of shots, but they hit nearby trees. He wouldn't be able to shoot them, as fast as they moved.

The fact he was carrying a handgun was bad news. She had wondered if Slade wanted to turn and head back to the crash site, keeping out of the shooter's view, but he kept on the path they had made to reach the cabin. Slade was probably afraid the other men would be alerted by the gunfire and join the shooter. Then they could have three men shooting at them if they were all armed.

"What the hell were you shooting at?" Fitz yelled.

But then Slade stopped, and Sheri had to backtrack to stand next to him as he listened to the conversation. They were far enough away from the crash site to be safe, but close enough to hear the men's conversations with their enhanced wolf hearing.

"There were two wolves out here."

"Then just throw a damn branch or rock or hell, a piece of the plane to scare them off, Otis. They would have run off. Firing our guns could alert campers in the area that we're trouble, and they could notify the police," Fitz said. "Nobody's supposed to be shooting with a handgun, and we don't have a permit to hunt on top of that. Use your damn head."

"Well, you weren't looking eye to eye with two hungry damn wolves," Otis said.

"If you were so close to them, how did you miss hitting one?" Fitz asked.

"I wasn't that close to them," Otis admitted. "It was just damn scary. I didn't even know we had Arctic wolves out here."

"We don't, you clown. They were probably white German shepherds. Hell, shooting dogs isn't allowed either. And if they were wolves, the same thing. Get back to work. Look for whatever we can find. And whatever you do, don't do anymore damn shooting."

Slade began searching around the area farther out from the plane's crash site, sniffing at the snow, pawing at it. He was exploring for whatever had been on the plane. Sheri hurried to help him look.

Then he began really digging and she joined him, smelling the scent of cardboard, Styrofoam, and metal underneath the snow. That was the thing about being a wolf. They could smell things buried deep in the snow. She was certain this wasn't something abandoned from someone's earlier campsite, but something new that was from the plane's wreckage.

Chapter 14

SLADE HAD WANTED TO CONTINUE TO WATCH THE MEN, but not when one was shooting at them. At least they knew the three men's partial names and even more about Fitz. But then Slade smelled a new cardboard box of something metal encased in protective Styrofoam. As soon as he started digging at it, Sheri was digging right next to him. Plane crashes could scatter debris for great distances and these men might not ever find all of it. But others just hiking through the area could. Even years later, plane debris could be discovered by hikers.

That sure made him wonder what had gone on with Fitz's brother, whether he was truly dead or he had made it out alive since both Gerard's brother and wife had acted so strangely about Gerard's supposed return. The area had seen significant accumulations of snow since Gerard had disappeared, and the temperatures hadn't warmed up enough to melt the snow. In the forest, it was so shaded that only slips of sunlight were able to peek through and melt dabs of snow in tiny areas that refroze.

Then Slade's wolf's nails hit something solid, and he realized he had found what he had been looking for. A box—new, a little crushed on one corner—but hopefully the goods inside were undamaged. He continued to dig around it and so did Sheri. He was glad she had been with him on this cabin stay, though he did worry about her safety because at least one of the men was armed with a 9mm.

Slade and Sheri finally revealed enough of the merchandise that they could see the description on the box. A laptop, sealed in the box, unopened. Stolen property? That's what came to mind, particularly since the men were trying to find the "evidence" and remove it from the area before anyone else discovered them doing it.

But now they had a dilemma. He wanted to keep the laptop from the men, should any of them walk this far to look for the items. But he couldn't carry it as a wolf, and he couldn't shift to carry it as a naked human and walk back through the snow in the freezing weather either.

Sheri woofed softly at him and then tore off through the woods back to the cabin. He knew she was going to shift, dress, and return to carry the package back. He was left with guard duty, though if those men came to get the package, he wouldn't be able to do anything about it. Not when at least one of the men was armed with a gun. He was certain they would shoot him to get the package.

He didn't hear anyone coming this way, so he prayed Sheri would return soon. It seemed like forever before he heard someone coming and saw her. He smiled. She had a collapsible shovel, his clothes, and his snowshoes. Though he was filled with relief to see her, he was also concerned that she not put herself at further risk. He shifted and hurried to dress while she dug at the box until she could get ahold of it and pull it the rest of the way out of the snow.

Fully dressed, he lifted it off the ground and she filled the snow into the depression where the box had sat. Once she had smoothed out the snow on top, they hurried back to their cabin. If the men chanced to find the disturbed snow, they could know someone had found something and tried to cover that up. No matter how much Sheri had tried to make it look undisturbed, the difference between the freshly fallen snow and the snow smoothed out on top would be visible to someone observant.

Sheri and Slade didn't speak, just in case the searchers had moved any closer to where they were. He knew the searchers could follow their trail and see that it led straight to the Border Route Trail. No one had come that way but Sheri and Slade, so it would be easy to presume they had been at that spot and went back in the direction of their cabin. The searchers could have seen the wolf tracks too and thought Sheri and Slade had a couple of dogs with them. But Fitz might be confused about it because they hadn't had dogs of their own at the cabin when he had picked up Jet, his cousin's dog.

When they reached the Border Route Trail, Slade said, "We need to call this in."

"Right. I was in a rush to dress and rejoin you. Then I wanted to wait until we were farther away from the men before calling the police." She pulled out her satellite phone and called the police. "Hi, I'm Sheri Whitmore, and my boyfriend and I found the wreckage of a plane in the Boundary Waters Canoe Area." She told them about the three men searching the wreckage, the searchers' names, and how one of the men had shot at them, using a handgun.

Slade knew she said that to alert the police that at least one man was armed and dangerous and not to take any chances.

"Yes. We were on a hike when we came across them." She gave the plane ID number. "I'm a private investigator with White Wolf Investigations and I was hired to locate Gerard Connolly, whose wife reported him missing. The plane number might be from Gerard's 2022 Cessna 172S Skyhawk. I haven't had time to verify it. But Fitz did say the plane was Gerard's when he was talking to his cohorts. Gerard's wife said her husband had returned home, so the police should have this on file too.

"Uh, yes. We're headed back to our cabin with a laptop we found buried in the snow near the plane wreckage. We believe the men are looking for more of the same in the vicinity of the crash site." Sheri frowned, looking exasperated, and let her breath out in a huff that mixed with the cold air and misted. "We wanted to take this into custody to safeguard it for the police so they can learn what is going on. If the other men had found it and everything else that they were looking for, all the evidence could disappear and then the police might not learn what this was all about." She paused speaking to the operator while Slade helped her climb over a fallen tree.

"No, we're fine, but our trail could lead them to our cabin. If you can reach our cabin, we can show you the direction to the crash site. Okay, thanks." She squeezed Slade's arm and ended the call. "They're sending policemen right away."

"Good. When we get to the cabin, we can take pictures

of the box, who it's addressed to, and where it came from so that you can start working on your own undercover investigation into the matter," Slade said. "Once the police confiscate the laptop, you won't have a chance to look into it."

"Exactly. She said we should have left the evidence where it was until I mentioned that Fitz and his cohorts might have discovered it."

"Right. I'm sure the police will overlook that we moved a piece of evidence when they might not even have found it in the first place. Or that Fitz and his cronies could have found it instead and have ferreted it away."

Sheri shook her head. "When Fitz was searching for the 'merchandise,' I assumed that Gerard had been carrying drugs."

"Yeah, me too. Though it's still possible this wasn't anything to do with anything being criminal."

"How much do you want to bet that it is though?" she asked. "Since they mentioned they could be in trouble if anyone found this stuff, I would say it was stolen merchandise."

The two of them were moving as quickly as they could. He was relieved when they finally reached the cabin and unlocked the door with the key code, went inside, and locked the door. He had hoped the police would already be here.

"You know Fitz could discover that we were close to the site," Sheri said.

"Only if they notice our tracks and the disturbed snow. They may never notice that we were in the area of the plane wreck otherwise."

Sheri nodded. "True. That's what I'm hoping for. Since Gerard had been missing for a while, I assume it went down about the time he vanished. And the sighting of the plane flying low over the BWCA? That was about the time that Betty reported Gerard had gone missing."

"Yeah, I agree." Slade looked on his phone. "The coordinates that Andy gave us match the vicinity of the plane wreck."

"So Andy and his friends *did* find something important." Sheri shivered.

Slade rubbed her back reassuringly. "Right. We'll have to let them know what we discovered. It was a good thing they didn't run into these men if they'd had the chance to go back and see what they could find."

"Oh yeah, for sure. I hadn't thought of that." They were both watching out the windows for the police—and for Fitz and his friends if they ended up coming here. "What do we do if they come and the police aren't here yet?" Sheri asked.

Slade said, "We keep everything locked up and call the police again and let them know we're in trouble."

They heard voices just outside the cabin, but they hadn't heard a car so they knew it wasn't the police. Slade feared for Sheri's safety most of all. The windows rattled as if someone was trying to find an unlocked one.

"Fitz?" Sheri whispered, crouched close to Slade.

"Yeah, that's who I figure it is." He squeezed her hand. Damn, he hoped the police would get here soon.

"This is so not good."

"We don't answer the door. At least one of the men has a gun, so we can't risk it," Slade said.

"I agree." Sheri got on the phone to call the police again. "Hi, this is Sheri Whitmore, calling again about Fitz Connolly and his friends. They're here at the cabin now, trying to find a way to get in. At least one of the men is armed with a handgun. We're inside the cabin. We're not going to open the door, but what if they force their way in? Where are the police?" Sheri glanced at Slade. "All right. Well, they need to hurry." Then she ended the call.

"They're still on their way here?" Slade asked.

"Yeah. A lot of good that will do us if they don't hurry up and get here. She said they are five minutes out."

They heard the men moving around the outside of the cabin, checking other windows.

"They're not coming to the door," Slade said.

"They're looking for another way to get in," Sheri warned.

"All the windows should be locked." But Slade was checking the ones the men hadn't messed with yet, keeping low, making sure the men didn't see him inside and shoot at him. He was afraid they would try to break in even if the windows were locked. Then he started to remove his clothes. He might not have a gun, but a big Arctic wolf would have a fighting chance.

"You're going to turn wolf?" she asked, sounding surprised.

"If they get in, we need to stop them from hurting us. I think you should too." He shifted and was ready to deter anyone who tried to break into the house.

"All right." She hurried to undress and then shifted too.

Slade went to the back window of the cabin, and she followed him. But then he had an idea. If he acted like a guard dog, the men might not try to gain entry. They might be worried someone would hear the barking dogs, or that if they entered the house, they could be attacked. Slade started to growl and bark like crazy.

Sheri took the cue and began barking and growling too, but her voice was different. The men could definitely hear two "dogs" making a ruckus. Hopefully, that would deter them.

The men stopped moving outside the cabin. Sheri turned on a light in the living room with her paw, effectively making it appear that the dogs barking had woken her and Slade up, which was a good idea too.

Police sirens sounded off in the distance, probably too far for the men to hear them.

"We've got to make sure they didn't take something from the wreckage," Fitz said.

Then the police sirens were close enough for the humans to hear too.

"Ah, hell, it's the police," Otis said.

The men hurried off on the Border Route Trail as fast as they could go through the deep snow.

Sheri shifted and started to dress. So did Slade. By the time the police turned off their engine, Slade was wearing his parka and headed outside, holding his hands up high to show he wasn't armed or one of the bad guys. "I'm Slade White. Sheri, my girlfriend, called in the report. The three men were trying to find a way into the cabin until they heard you arrive. They headed back down the Border Route Trail."

"Let's see some ID," the one officer said to Slade, the other holding a gun on him.

Slade pulled out his driver's license. Once they verified that he was who he said he was, Sheri came outside and showed her driver's license.

"I called the police about all this," she said.

Then Slade said, "The computer is in the cabin still in its new box. The men went that way." He pointed to the Border Route Trail. "We had also gone that way and then you can see our tracks veer off to the right. That's where you'll find our tracks heading to the crash site."

A couple of the police officers examined the merchandise.

"We were wearing gloves when we handled the box. Maybe you can obtain some fingerprints off it," Slade said.

One of the police officers asked, "Can you go with us to confirm the direction of the wreckage?"

"Yes, I sure can." Slade glanced back at Sheri.

"I'll stay here and keep the doors locked," she said.

"Okay, I'll be back soon." Slade was going to go with the police officers when they heard another vehicle arrive. More police officers. Good. Maybe they would catch the men in the act and arrest them. Then two of the men left one of the cruisers and shook their heads at him.

Slade smiled, glad to see them. Tanner Papadopoulos and Conway King. They had worked on a number of cases where Slade had rescued paddlers in the BWCA. So they knew him on sight. If they'd arrived here first, he wouldn't have had to convince them who he was.

"We had to come out to see if we could help you when

we learned you were rescuing people in the BWCA again," Conway said.

Slade couldn't tell them he just had excellent hearing and sight and that's why he was much more aware of what was going on around him in the wilderness. "Well, I have to say this is the first time I've been to the BWCA in winter where I've seen this much trouble. I'm just glad my girlfriend and I were here to help out."

"That was quite a storm," Tanner said. "We've had to deal with a lot of injuries because of it. We just didn't expect you to find a plane too, and we had to check it out."

"We didn't expect to find parts of a plane either." Slade led the way on the trail back to the site while one of the officers told the others where they were going. One of them stayed with Sheri in case the men returned.

Slade sure hoped they would reach Fitz and his cohorts before they got away. The problem was that if the three men did evade the police, there wouldn't be any proof, other than Sheri and Slade's word, that they had been there. Unless Fitz and his buddies had uncovered more merchandise from the plane wreckage and the police caught them with it.

Slade hoped they would. Still, when he led them to the wreckage, even if they couldn't locate the men, the police would search for evidence of wrongdoing and investigate what Gerard had been up to.

When they finally reached the crash site, one of the officers got on his radio. "Mr. White showed us where the plane went down. We need to have some aircraft accident investigators here to learn what had happened there. Okay." The officer gave the coordinates to the plane wreckage.

Slade showed the police where he and Sheri had found the laptop. "We covered up the hole where we extracted the laptop so that no one would discover we had been here. But as you can see, the men dug in the hole to try and find the item and then they must have followed us to the cabin." He explained that Sheri was a private investigator and had been hired by the pilot's wife to find him because he'd been missing.

"Yeah, Gerard Connolly," Tanner said. "His wife said he turned up at home and we closed out the investigation."

"Did anyone check to see if he really came home? Mrs. Connolly also told Sheri the same thing—that Gerard had arrived home—so Sheri quit investigating the case. But now we find Gerard's plane and it made us wonder why he didn't report that his plane had crashed."

"We're checking into it now," Conway said. "We're going to stay here to secure the site, but Tanner will walk you back to your cabin."

"Thanks," Slade said, eager to get back to Sheri.

"Slade," Tanner said, walking back with him. "You've had a busy few days. I learned you and your girlfriend saved the campers who had been injured when the trees went down, and then also the heart attack victim."

"Yeah, Mr. Lincoln. He's a cousin to Fitz. He might not know about any of this business, but he might."

"We'll check into him too. I hope the rest of your vacation is without incident."

Slade was thinking the same thing!

Chapter 15

ONE OF THE OFFICERS WHO HAD COME TO JOIN THE others stayed with Sheri. She was glad that he had, just in case Fitz or his friends turned up. She watched the officer call in the information on the laptop from the plane wreckage.

"Yeah." The police officer read off the serial number and, after a couple of minutes, nodded. When he ended the call, he said to Sheri, "A delivery truck and its contents were stolen, and the truck was ditched on some farm road. When the police looked into it, the truck was empty. But this was one of the packages on that truck."

"What about the driver?" Stolen packages were one thing, but what if they had killed the driver?

"The delivery truck had been stolen."

"From which place? I was investigating a case of stolen merchandise from a warehouse and a missing delivery truck."

The officer confirmed the delivery truck was from the same place.

"Okay, so no one was hurt while they were stealing the merchandise. But any of the packages you recover will have to go into evidence and the people who were supposed to get them won't be getting them," she said.

"The customer can file a claim and get a replacement. We'll notify the buyer that we've found his laptop and it is evidence in a criminal case."

"Oh, good. These guys could have ruined Christmas for a lot of people," Sheri said.

"Yeah, I agree."

More police cars pulled up and parked, and an aviation investigating agent from the National Transportation Safety Board also arrived. About that time, Slade and the police officer escorting him returned to the cabin.

"It looks like this is out of our hands now," Slade said, pulling Sheri into his arms and kissing her.

"Now that is more like it." She wrapped her arms around his neck and kissed him back. "More after we're alone."

"Do you feel like you need protection?" the police officer asked. "We can check with our supervisor and see if one of us can stay here with you until these men are picked up for questioning."

"We're good." Sheri figured they could turn into their wolves and deal with it. Though they couldn't bite the men or chance turning them into one of their kind. There was no way they wanted to turn men who were a menace to society into *lupus garous*. But she really wanted to have this alone time with Slade, and they couldn't turn into their wolves if a police officer was staying at the cabin. It was too cold for an officer to stay outside.

Then the officer left with the laptop and put it inside one of the cruisers. The two other officers left to join the others at the crash site.

"I hope they find Fitz and the other men before long," Sheri said.

"Yeah, I do too. I doubt they'll return here, but we'll keep a watch out and make sure we don't smell their scents more recently in the area."

"That's what I was thinking."

"Do you believe Mr. Lincoln knew about Gerard's plane crash? About the stolen merchandise?" Slade asked.

"They're family, but he might not have known about the theft. And I suspect Gerard's wife didn't know about it either, or she wouldn't have called the police or hired me to look into it." She sighed. "I wish we had internet out here."

Slade smiled at her.

"Okay, I know. We're supposed to be enjoying the wilderness and not be distracted by other things."

"Like work."

"Right. But don't you want to know what's going on?" Sheri asked.

"I do. You could call Cameron and see if he could check into it."

"No way. He and Owen are already doing the bulk of the investigative cases. Besides, this isn't a paid case any longer," she said.

"True."

"I'll just have to think it over. For now, let's have some lunch. What appeals to you?" she asked.

"How about that chili I planned to make?" he asked.

"That would really be good for a cold day."

"Do you want to have a cocktail to go with that and then we can play some games?"

"Absolutely, what are you going to make us?"

"A winter snowflake cocktail made of Irish cream topped with whipped cream and scented with cinnamon."

"Hmm, now that sounds delicious."

"I wasn't going to bring the ingredients when Hans was coming with me, but I figured as much as you like sweet drinks that you would enjoy it."

"Oh, sure. You guys probably were going to just drink beer. I love Irish cream." Sheri opened the cans of tomato sauce and chili beans and chopped up onions for the chili. "I guess we'll know when these law enforcement officers finish with their work because their vehicles are all parked here."

"Right. We could ask them if they found any more items then." Slade started cooking the hamburger.

"Unless they think we were involved."

"How so?"

"It's just us saying we saw these men and that one shot at us. The police never saw any sign of them. And we found the wreckage."

"Aww, like someone finding a dead body." Slade added onions to the pot.

She set the table. "Like that. And then if we're questioning the police about the items they recovered—"

"They could believe we want to know what evidence they gathered because sometimes the person who perpetrates the crime comes back to see how the investigation is going."

"And they want to help the police find the 'real' bad guys."

"Like us saying that Fitz and his friends were involved."
Once the onions were cooked through, he added the tomato
sauce and chili beans. He seasoned the chili with chili
powder and continued cooking it. She threw away the empty
cans and wiped off the counter.

Slade made their cocktails and handed her a glass. He
clinked his glass with hers.

She took a sip of her drink. "Mmm, this is so good."

Slade drank some of his. "I agree. So we're not going to
ask them what they found?"

"Sure we are."

He laughed.

When the chili was done, Sheri dished it up and spooned
some sour cream on top. Then he sprinkled on some shred-
ded cheese and crowned the chili with corn chips. Slade set
the bowls on the table and they sat down to eat.

But then they heard a vehicle drive to the cabin and park.

Slade went to look out the window to see who it was.
Immediately, Sheri worried Fitz and his men had returned to
interrogate them about the plane wreck merchandise.

Then again, maybe it was just the police and she and
Slade could interrogate them.

Chapter 16

"ANDY, TRENTON, AND LIONEL," SLADE SAID, OPENING the cabin door before they could knock and he invited them in. He realized Andy, who had been standing behind Trenton and Lionel, was holding a large cellophane-wrapped gift basket of a variety of cheeses, meats, fruits, and nuts, and a bottle of champagne tied with a big red-and-green-plaid Christmas bow. Lionel was also carrying a little Christmas box.

"This doesn't even begin to express our thanks to you for coming to our aid during the storm that night. We wouldn't have made it without your help," Lionel said.

Slade hadn't expected them to bring them a gift and was really taken aback, but appreciative. He hoped that if Sheri and he hadn't assisted them, an emergency crew would have reached them in time, but he was glad they'd been the ones there to aid them.

"Thanks so much for the beautiful gift basket. Did you fish at all while you were out here?" Sheri asked them as they came in.

"No, we sure didn't," Lionel said. "We planned to do that the next day, but then the storm hit, and you know how it was after that."

"We're having chili, if you would like to join us for lunch. We have plenty for everyone, too much for just the two of us, in fact," Sheri said.

"Yeah, come in and join us since you made the trip all the way out here," Slade said.

"Are you sure?" Andy asked, though he looked like he would love to stay for lunch.

"Yep. Besides, we have news about the coordinates you gave us to check out," Slade said.

"We saw all the police cruisers parked by your cabin and wondered what was going on, but were afraid to mention it," Andy said.

"Not only that," Lionel said, "but we were afraid you both might have not been here, in trouble yourselves, and that's why all the police cars were here." The three men began taking off their outer winter clothes, appearing eager to learn what Sheri and Slade had found.

"What had you thought you had seen in the woods on your hike?" Sheri asked as she served up bowls of chili for the guys.

"We weren't sure," Andy said. "Something metal. Possibly a plane, but we didn't want to call it in case we were totally off base. As for lunch, what can we do to help?"

"If you would like, you could unwrap the gift basket and we could have some of the fruit and cheeses, salami, and pecans with our lunch," Slade said.

"Are you sure?" Lionel asked. "We got that for you to enjoy."

"We will. But it's even better enjoying it with friends," Sheri said.

The three men all got to work setting out some of the gift basket items while Slade asked, "Would you like an Irish cream cocktail?"

"Yeah, sure," Lionel said.

Slade made them cocktails. Sheri set out the Christmas napkins.

Andy said, "Now that's what I call real class."

"Yeah, she sure makes meals truly exceptional during the holidays," Slade said, kissing her forehead.

"I love the Christmas tree too," Lionel said.

"That's all Sheri's doing too," Slade said, proud of her. They'd never expected to have company for a meal, except when their friends and her brother arrived, and her Christmas touches made it even more special.

"The mistletoe?" Trenton asked.

"That was all Slade's doing," Sheri said. "We've found it very useful."

The guys all laughed.

"So, about the coordinates we gave you for that item we saw out in the woods... Did you find the piece of metal we saw?" Andy asked as he set out dishes for whatever else they wanted to eat from the fruit basket.

"Well, we don't know if it was the piece you actually saw, but we found some of the plane, including a door and an ID number. It definitely was a wreck, if that's what you thought you had seen. But more than that, it was carrying at least one piece of stolen merchandise," Sheri said.

"No," Trenton said, pouring everyone glasses of water.

"Yep. Which is why all the police vehicles are out here.

And worse, the men who had something to do with it were there searching through the wreckage for the merchandise," Slade said, "so we were glad you hadn't come upon them when they were there."

"But you did?" Trenton asked, taking some green and purple grapes and adding them to his plate as they sat down to eat.

"We saw them, and one of the men fired off shots at us. Then they followed us back to the cabin," Slade said. "So they're dangerous. We called the police and they had aircraft accident investigators come to investigate, so they have roped off the area and are looking for the men now. Just a warning, I wouldn't go hiking through that area, in the event you had the notion to."

"No." Lionel paused before he ate another bite, his spoonful of chili suspended midair. "Except for dropping off the gifts, we have no intention of hiking through the woods anytime soon."

"Yeah, I'm sure all of us are feeling that way," Andy said.

"Man, you two have had more trouble on your vacation," Lionel said. "I'm glad they didn't actually shoot you."

"Yeah, we were thinking about how it would have been if the four of you had returned to check out the wreckage. How are your ribs?" Sheri asked.

"Awful, but they'll heal. I'm just glad I didn't have any fractures." Lionel ate some more of his chili. "Man, is this good."

"Thanks. I'm glad you didn't have any broken ribs. What about Morgan?" Sheri asked.

"He sends his thanks," Andy said. "We should have said

that in the beginning. The Christmas box is filled with chocolate fudge topped with walnuts and crushed candy canes. That's from Morgan's mom. She was extremely grateful that you helped get him assistance as fast as you did. He wanted to come but couldn't navigate the snow and icy conditions with a broken leg, besides the fact he's at home with his three kids and his mom. He's doing well, considering. But he's just as grateful as the rest of us are for your help."

"I'm glad to hear he's on the mend. We were afraid that moving both of you might have been harder on your injuries," Slade said. "Thank Morgan's mom for the fudge for us. We both love it."

"We will. The doctor said Morgan's broken bone hadn't moved and he would have been more worried about us suffering from hypothermia if we had stayed put," Lionel said.

"And the potential of being struck down by a fallen tree was on our minds," Andy said. "We did the right thing in moving to the cabin until we could be picked up by emergency services."

"I agree it worked out for the best. This cheese is really good," Sheri said, sampling a piece of the provolone from the gift basket.

"Yeah, and I love the muenster cheese too," Slade said.

Even though the guys ate a little of the food from the gift basket, Slade thought they were trying not to eat too much of it because it was Sheri and Slade's thank-you gift.

"You asked if we got to go fishing. I felt awful that we didn't get to because of Morgan's and my injuries. We all had fishing licenses just for this trip too," Lionel said.

Slade glanced at Sheri. She smiled and nodded.

"Why don't we all go fishing, if you're up to it, Lionel, and you can all spare the time?" Slade asked.

The guys all looked at each other. Andy said, "We wouldn't want to impose."

"It'll be fun," Sheri said. "Come on. We have the gear, we can take turns fishing, and if you catch anything, you can take it home with you."

"Let's do it," Slade said.

And with that said, the three men looked thrilled they were going to go fishing after all. Sheri and Slade were glad to have them join them.

After they finished their meal, they cleaned up and put the leftover food away. Then they packed up the sled to go fishing and everyone dressed warmly for the trip across the lake.

Once they headed out to a good deep spot on the lake, they set up to fish in the tent—though it was a little crowded and the three guys sat on waterproof pads instead of camp chairs. They all took turns fishing.

"Man, you've got the right spot." Andy caught about a five-pound pike. "My girlfriend will be so thrilled when she sees I brought home fish for dinner when she thought I was just delivering a gift basket to the both of you."

"She was looking forward to having some, so you'll have made her day once she gets home from her nursing job tonight," Trenton said, then caught his own pike. "This is a good spot."

"The bait works good too," Lionel said, snagging his own fish. He caught another after that. "That one is for Morgan."

Andy laughed. "I'm glad you caught a fish for him, or I might have had to give up mine so he wouldn't have felt left out. If I had given up mine and my girlfriend had learned about it, I would be out on my ear for the night. Or she might have even threatened to return my Christmas gifts."

"He's serious," Lionel said.

Everyone laughed.

Sheri had thrown back a fish that was too small and Slade managed to catch one that was about the size of Sheri's that she'd caught earlier.

Then they finally packed it up as their friends had caught what they wanted for their dinners while Slade and Sheri had plenty of fish to eat. Besides, they wanted to fish with Hans, Candice, and Owen when they arrived on Friday.

Andy hauled the sled with the fishing equipment on it while they all trudged back to the cabin, and then the guys packed their fish in an ice chest they had cold beers in and thanked them again for everything.

"We enjoyed the company, thanks for the gifts, and Merry Christmas," Sheri said.

The guys wished them a Merry Christmas too, and then they got into their SUV and drove off.

"Well, that was fun," Slade said.

"It sure was. Oh, I forgot all about the fudge. We should have offered them some."

Slade smiled. "As much as I love homemade fudge, I'm all for keeping it to ourselves."

She laughed. "So you weren't all that willing to share."

"I thought about it."

Loving his honesty, she kissed him. "I think we made their trip out here a little better after all that had gone on. I'm glad Lionel was able to fish even with his bruised ribs. I was afraid he wouldn't be able to make it." Sheri grabbed a purple grape and ate it, then snagged Slade's hand. "It's time to enjoy some bedtime now."

"My thoughts exactly!"

Then they made exquisite love and she realized how much she valued making love to him all the way.

———————

That night, Tanner and the rest of the police officers dropped by the cabin and told them they were heading out, done for the night, but they would be back tomorrow.

Sheri and Slade made grilled cheese and ham sandwiches for dinner and then went out to make more s'mores at the firepit. But this time, Sheri put some green icing on the top of their s'mores to make them more Christmassy. "I forgot all about the icing I brought for the s'mores. I wasn't even sure if you would want to have them, but Hans loves them and had packed them with the rest of his stuff, so I figured you would enjoy them too."

"Yeah, with you, they're perfect. I love how you added the Christmassy touch this time—very creative."

"Absolutely. I make them like that every year. I wanted to make this a camping trip that still had some Christmas spirit."

"We'll have to try the fudge tomorrow." Slade slathered

the green icing on the top of his s'more and managed to drip the frosting on his knee.

She laughed. "Shades of you decorating your cookie at the office party."

"Yeah. I bet if I used a different color, I wouldn't have so many problems."

"You're cute, you know?"

He smiled and kissed her.

After they finished eating their s'mores, he cleaned his snow pants inside the cabin. Then they stripped and shifted and went for a wolf run. Both of them looked in the direction of the plane crash site, then at each other. They wanted to check out the site. They took off that way down a different trail. As they approached the site, they cautiously drew closer, making sure no one was there for now. They listened for sounds of anyone talking, digging around the area, moving, but they didn't hear anything.

Finding no one, they began to explore the wreckage. Yellow crime-scene tape roped off the area as they began to smell the scents of the police officers and Fitz and his companions— nothing recent. Then Sheri and Slade began smelling for any sign of more merchandise that might be buried in the snow. Lots of areas had been dug up and piles of snow moved to other spots as officers had searched for plane wreckage and packages. Sheri and Slade might not find anything around this location, so they headed way beyond the taped-off section and started to sniff around, looking for anything else they might find that the investigators and Fitz and his cohorts hadn't located.

About a quarter mile from the site, Sheri picked up the

scent of cardboard boxes, each having a slightly different smell—different people who had handled them, different packaging materials, different items in the packages. It appeared they had found a bunch of merchandise that had been buried under the snow and the area looked so undisturbed that no one would have found the packages until the snow began to melt off. Again, they had the dilemma of what to do. But it was easier this time. They couldn't dig out the stuff in their wolf coats, but would leave it like it was, buried deep so that if Fitz or the others came across the area, they wouldn't see it. She woofed at Slade and he nodded, then the two of them bolted for the cabin.

When they finally arrived back there, they hurried inside to shift and dress warmly. "I think we've found several boxes of merchandise," Slade said.

"Yeah, I agree. We don't want to disturb the area though. We need to call the police and get them out here. They can dig up the merchandise and confiscate it."

"There's only one problem with that. How will we be able to tell them we knew it was there? There's nothing at all there to indicate that anything is buried deep underneath the snow," Slade said.

"Hmm, you're right. Do you have any ideas?"

"None that would make it sound as though we just stumbled across the packages."

"A friend dropped by with his dog, we took it for a walk, and she smelled the packages?" she asked.

"Then the police might want the dog to help them find them. They might ask if the dog is trained for searches."

"I don't know what we could do then. I mean, we could say we were searching around the area beyond the taped-off crime scene and saw a corner of a box sticking up, but if we did that, we would have to dig up a box and that would tell a different story," Sheri said.

They had to report it, had to get the merchandise into the police officers' hands, but how to do it without making themselves look suspicious?

"Okay, so maybe we return to the area and search around some more. Maybe we can find parts of the plane and then direct the police to that," Sheri said. "Though if we don't find any other pieces around where we found the merchandise, it won't help our case."

"But they might expand the search to the other areas. Do you want to go as wolves or not?" Slade asked.

"If we go as humans, we can still smell the buried merchandise. But at least we'll have our satellite phones on us and can call it in if we find anything that is exposed," Sheri said. "Otherwise, if we're running as wolves, we'll have to return to the cabin and call them."

"All right, but just keep a lookout for Fitz or his men. We need to be sure we don't get shot at again. As humans, we won't be able to move as quickly to outrun their gunfire."

"But we still have the advantage of nightfall. They won't be able to see us that well, and we'll hear them moving around a lot sooner than they'll hear us. Oh, I have another idea."

"I'm all ears," Slade said.

"What if we dig up the buried merchandise and…"

Slade raised his brows and smiled a little. "I thought that

would lead the police to believe we had something to do with the merchandise being there."

"Right, but what if we say we saw Fitz and his men out in the woods looking for the merchandise at night, and they had uncovered a couple of boxes—maybe partially—when we spooked them, and they took off?"

"So we're going to make something up?" Slade smiled at her. "But if the police can verify that they weren't at the scene of the crime, then they'll wonder why we lied to them."

Sheri sighed. "Right. Come on. Let's look for any other signs of the plane so we can report that. Maybe something will come to us about the buried boxes."

"Okay, I'll buy that." Slade began to put on his outer gear and so did Sheri.

They headed out but went a more direct route to the location of their new find instead of in the direction of the taped-off plane crash site this time. They had flashlights and emergency gear in backpacks, plus their satellite phones, but they weren't using their lights, just using their wolf sight to navigate by. They were both listening intently to any sounds in the woods. They heard a fox nearby, then saw it peering at them from behind a tree. Then it took off.

When they finally reached the area where they had located the buried packages, they spread out a bit and continued to look for more plane parts or smell any other scents of buried packages. They kept each other in view, but stayed quiet to ensure if anyone else was in the area, they wouldn't be heard.

Then Sheri found part of a wing and wanted to jump up

and down and pump her fist in the air. Instead, she howled. Howling was preferable to trying to use their satellite phones or calling out to each other. Even in their human forms, they could sound like full-fledged wolves.

Slade didn't howl back but trudged in his snowshoes to where she was. He smiled. "Another find," he whispered.

Then they heard voices. *Great.*

"I can't believe we're doing this in the dark!"

Sheri couldn't believe it either and was certain the police or aviation investigators wouldn't be out here looking for evidence this late at night—unless it had been a rescue mission or a case of finding a murder victim—but would be back at it in the morning. She thought the man who spoke was the guy who had fired his gun at them, Otis.

"Tell the whole world, why don't you?"

Now that sounded like Fitz. He always sounded annoyed.

The men who were speaking drew closer to Slade and Sheri. They moved farther away from them. She knew Fitz and the others wouldn't find the packages, not as deeply as they were buried, but they might see snowshoe tracks in the snow and where they led to—the packages and now the location of the airplane wing. If the men followed them in the opposite direction, the tracks would lead them back to Sheri and Slade's cabin. She was certain if that happened, they would try to break into their cabin again.

Flashlights came from three different parts of the forest, but the men were still moving close together and seemed to be the same three men that Sheri and Slade had encountered before. At least they knew that Fitz and Otis were here.

She really hadn't believed they would come here at night looking for the merchandise. Then she actually saw them. Yep, the same three men dressed in parkas and snow pants, wearing snowshoes and trudging through the snow using flashlights and, oh great, metal detectors.

"I don't know why we didn't try the metal detectors before," Otis said.

"Because we didn't realize the merchandise would be buried in the snow," Danbury said.

"Can you keep it down?" Fitz said.

"Why? There's no one else out here. The police wouldn't stay out at night looking for stuff," Otis said.

Sheri was afraid the men just might find the merchandise after all. She wanted to report them to the police right this minute, before these thieves found what they were looking for and got away with it. She whispered to Slade, "They might find the merchandise. Let's call the police and alert them."

He nodded and they made a wide circle around where the men were. When they were far enough away from the men, Sheri got on her satellite phone. "I'm Sheri Whitmore and I need to report that the same three men, one of whom shot at us before, Fitz Connolly and two of his friends, are out near the plane's crash site at the BWCA and they're looking for the stolen merchandise that was on the plane. They've got metal detectors this time. We were just taking a night hike and ran across them." She gave the dispatcher the coordinates. "It's about a quarter of a mile due southwest of the crash site and we found part of the plane's wing. We're headed back to our cabin." She gave them the name of the lodge. "We can take the police out there if they come by the cabin and maybe they can catch these guys in the act this time."

"Sending a unit now," the dispatcher said.

"Hey, get the shovel out," Fitz said. "I've detected metal here. Hopefully it's some of the electronic equipment and not more of the damn aircraft."

Sheri and Slade continued to move back to their cabin. She figured that if the men found the equipment before the police arrived, she and Slade had done all they could to try to safeguard it. It was up to the police to handle it now.

When they arrived at the cabin, they were surprised to see two patrol cars pull up and park. This time the policemen who had worked with Slade before were first on the scene, plus two more officers.

"You really ought to join the police force," Conway said to Slade.

Slade smiled. "Are you ready to catch these guys this time?"

"Yeah, let's get to it. We were coming out to do a security check on the crash site when Sheri made the call, which was why we were so close by."

Then another police car drove up and parked and two more police officers got out. Good. They needed to catch the three guys. With six police officers, that bettered the odds a bit. But what shocked Sheri—and Slade—the most was that the female officer who arrived in the last car was a wolf. A gray wolf. And none of the members of the white wolf pack had known about her before this.

She looked just as shocked to smell their scents and

then she smiled. "Well, I'm Dulcie Wulff and I'm pleased to meet you." She offered her hand and shook Sheri's first, then Slade's.

Sheri smiled broadly at her. "We're sure glad to meet you too."

Slade agreed.

"Wulff's going to stay with Ms. Whitmore while we go track down Fitz and his friends," Tanner said.

"That sounds good to me," Dulcie said.

Sheri thought she might have wanted to go with the other officers to help take Fitz and the other men into custody, but then again, meeting fellow wolves and learning more about them? That had to have made Dulcie's night.

Chapter 17

"Ohmigod," Dulcie said, giving Sheri a hug, now that the other police officers were gone. "I'm so glad to meet you. When I moved to Ely, I never thought I would be so fortunate as to meet up with other wolves."

Sheri hugged her back. "Yes, this is wonderful. I'm originally from Yellowknife but came here with a friend and we're part of a whole Arctic wolf pack. Slade is my mate. We're so thrilled to meet you. And you have to see the others. Where did you come from?" She was thinking it would be wonderful to have a wolf in the pack who was on the police force. It just made it easier to explain to a fellow wolf how they knew things that humans normally wouldn't.

"I'm originally from Minneapolis, but I wanted the slower pace in a small town like this. I wasn't part of a pack. So you're a private investigator, Tanner was saying." Dulcie followed Sheri inside the cabin.

"Yes. I began working here as one with a group of Arctic wolves who are former police officers from Seattle. Slade is a seaplane pilot. Would you like some cocoa?" Sheri walked into the kitchen.

"Oh, sure. Yeah, Conway King said Slade had been involved in several rescue missions and he and Tanner had worked with him on them." Dulcie removed her hat, gloves, and snow boots at the door. Then she pulled off her parka and hung it on the coatrack. "Wow, I just can't believe you're both wolves. Oh, oh, so is that how you found the laptop in the snow?" Dulcie joined her in the kitchen.

"Yeah. We were actually running as wolves and smelled the cardboard, Styrofoam, and metal, and dug it out."

"So when you said one of the men shot at you two, you were wolves, not in your human forms," Dulcie said.

"Right." Sheri added whipped cream to her mug of cocoa and asked if Dulcie wanted some too.

"Yes, thanks. That makes perfect sense. Did they realize you were wolves?"

"That's what one of the men said, but Fitz told him Arctic wolves don't live out here."

Dulcie thought about that for a moment and then said, "You were running as wolves tonight."

Sheri smiled. "Yep. We smelled the packages—about three of them—but we were afraid of digging them up and having to give details on how we had found them this time." She explained about going back out as humans and finding part of the wing and hearing Fitz and his men again searching for the goods. "I thought you might have been upset to have to stay with me instead of going with the other officers to capture Fitz and the other men."

"Normally, I might have been, though my job was to protect you from harm and that's just as important. But when I realized you were wolves, I knew this was where I needed to be."

Sheri added a sprinkle of peppermint candy to top off their mugs of hot chocolate, and then they carried them into the living room and sat down to talk.

"Truthfully, the reason I moved to Ely was they had a position open they were trying to fill at the sheriff's office and I wanted to be at a place where I could really run as a wolf. I just never expected I would meet up with a couple of wolves or a whole wolf pack." Dulcie took a sip of her cocoa.

"You just missed our Christmas party, but we'll have a get-together soon. Actually, Slade and I just mated and he's moving out of his apartment and into mine until my father can build us our home. Several of the wolf pack members are coming to help us move him, though there's not that much to move. But afterward we're having a pizza party to celebrate at the White Wolf Investigation Services office building where several of us work."

"Oh, I've seen the office building, but never thought to put two and two together that wolves ran it."

"Well, I'm sure there are a lot of businesses with a wolf name that aren't wolf-run, but here, it is. So are you a royal?" Sheri asked. It was important that they added more royals to the pack to help those who weren't.

"Through and through. We were wolves from so long ago, we always thought we were from the very first wolves that were *lupus garous*. What about you?"

"Yes, we're royals. Some of the pack members are more newly turned, so we help them out when they need our assistance." Sheri drank some of her cocoa.

"Oh, sure. Um, are there any…" Dulcie looked embarrassed to ask. "Bachelor males in the pack?"

Sheri smiled. "My brother, Hans." She didn't want to try to matchmake and upset Dulcie or her brother in the event they didn't like each other. "He's an accountant. Dad builds homes. My mom is a midwife."

"Oh, both must come in handy."

"Yeah, Dad will be building a home for Slade and me. And we just had two new babies in the pack. My good friend from Yellowknife is due in March."

"That's wonderful. It's great having more of our kind here." Dulcie drank some of her cocoa. "Oh, this is so good. I love the peppermint sprinkles on top."

"Double the chocolate. It's the only way to go. And the sprinkles are perfect for the holidays."

"I'll have to try that the next time I make it. I'm so glad to meet you and Slade. I'm sure I'll be seeing more of him when he's doing rescue missions in the future. Arctic wolves." Dulcie shook her head.

"Yeah, the pack ended up getting a couple of large white dogs, a German shepherd and a white Alaskan malamute. They stay mostly at Cameron and Faith's home because their triplets love playing with them. But if anyone sees our kind running at the lake where several of our homes are located, we can show off the dogs and say it was just them. The homes are right by the Wolf Investigative Services office building so it's convenient for going home and such. So do you have any family?"

"No family," Dulcie said.

"Well, you'll have plenty with us if you don't mind that we're Arctic wolves."

"Not at all. You are gray wolves too."

"That's true," Sheri said. "More cocoa?"

"Oh, absolutely. I hope the others catch the thieves, but I'm glad I got to safeguard you."

Sheri laughed and they both went into the kitchen to make some cocoa. She was hoping Slade and the officers were all right though.

Since Slade was an unarmed citizen, two of the police officers took the lead, following Slade and Sheri's snowshoe tracks, keeping quiet, while two flanked Slade and another took the rear. Slade didn't like that they had to use flashlights, which could alert Fitz and his cohorts that they were coming. But at least the officers were keeping quiet.

Then they heard Fitz say, "There! Damn, we found a laptop."

All the officers turned off their flashlights and moved toward the area where the three men were digging into the snow, using a couple of lanterns, headlamps, and flashlights. Slade smiled. They finally had them now and the men had been caught in the act.

Slade stayed put as the police officers moved stealthily forward, guns drawn. As soon as they were in place among the trees, Tanner called out, "St. Louis County Sheriff's Office. Everyone put your hands in the air."

Fitz made a run for it in one direction, the other two men splitting off from each other. It was a good move, rather than everyone running in the same direction. They were all wearing snowshoes, but anyone could walk or run in them just as well as walking or running without them. They just had to use a slightly wider stance and lift their legs higher. Slade had done it at times so he knew how to do it, and as soon as the men took off running, he joined the officers. It was so instinctive for a wolf to chase its prey. As long as the man he was trying to take down—which was the leader of the gang, Fitz—didn't pull a gun on him, Slade could safely make a citizen's arrest.

Tanner was hot on Fitz's tail, but Slade had been closer when Fitz ran in his direction, a huge mistake on Fitz's part. The other officers had taken off after Otis Risotto and Daniel Danbury. Slade hoped they nailed them as he got closer to Fitz by the second. He trusted he wouldn't annoy Tanner if he took Fitz down first, but if he could land him, Fitz couldn't shoot and that was the main thing.

Slade could hear Fitz's racing heart, his hurried breath, the crunch of his snowshoes against the crusted snow, and smell his anxiety showing just how fearful he was. Which Slade was glad for. It was time for them to be under the gun, so to speak.

Slade was nearly touching the back of Fitz's snowshoes with the toes of his own when gunfire sounded about an eighth of a mile away. Four shots rang out. Damn!

Was it one of Fitz's cohorts shooting at the police, or the police shooting at one of them? He couldn't worry about it for now, but he was sure Tanner wanted to go to his fellow officers' aid. Still, he was close behind Slade, and he couldn't leave him with a suspect on his own. Slade gained on Fitz, actually stepping on the back of Fitz's snowshoes, tripping him up. Slade tackled him down into the snow, burying him enough that he couldn't reach for a gun if he tried.

Tanner was right there then, and Slade got off Fitz so the officer could yank Fitz's arms back behind him, cuff him, and give him his Miranda rights.

Slade helped Tanner get Fitz to his feet, his beard and eyebrows covered in snow, his dark eyes narrowed with hatred as he glowered at Slade. If he could have, Slade was certain Fitz would have shot him right then and there. Tanner relieved Fitz of two handguns, a .45 and a 9mm. "Serial numbers removed on both of them."

"Figures." But that meant they were illegal weapons, and the police could charge Fitz with more criminal offenses.

Slade and Tanner took hold of Fitz's arms and headed in the direction where the shots had been fired. Slade hoped none of the officers had been shot.

Tanner got on his radio and called the other men. Conway answered, "I've got the guy named Otis Risotto. Daniel Danbury is still running. Sanchez, Peterson, and Miller are chasing him down."

"Who fired the shots?" Tanner asked.

"Danbury, but none of our guys were hit."

"Good." Tanner called it in to the sheriff's office and warned that shots had been fired at the officers and two of the men were in custody, but they needed backup to take in the shooter.

More shots were fired, sounding like they were from the same gun as before—which meant that Danbury was shooting at the other officers again.

The officers returned gunfire and then there was silence. Slade wished he knew what was going on with the other officers and the suspect.

Hauling Fitz with them, Tanner and Slade finally reached Conway.

"Hold on to this guy," Tanner said to Conway, who was standing over a cuffed Otis, now sitting on the ground. Tanner looked torn about helping out the other officers who were getting shot at.

"I'll help Conway with these two," Slade hurried to say.

"I hereby deputize you then," Tanner said. "I'm going after them. Slade, you're authorized to stay here with Conway and keep the two men under arrest or assist him to move them back to the patrol cars parked at your cabin."

"I'm good with heading back to the cabin if Conway is." Slade didn't like that Danbury was still on the loose and wanted Tanner to help with the apprehension of the shooter. Besides, he preferred going back to the cabin, should Danbury head that way.

"Yeah. We'll go together," Conway said. "I need to take these guys back to the patrol car anyway and the two of us can manage it. It's better than standing idle here in the cold." Conway and Tanner always treated Slade as though he was on the force with them because he was so helpful, and they had deputized him before in situations where he was needed.

"Yeah, that works for me."

Conway could use his help hauling these two guys back there to the patrol car.

"Okay, good." Then Tanner took off running to catch up to the other men.

Slade wondered where Fitz and his men had come from. They had to have parked a vehicle as close as they could to the site and then hiked in. He was certain that Danbury was going to try to reach the vehicle and tear off from there.

Slade glanced at the area where shovels and metal detectors were lying in the snow and a hole had been dug surrounded by flashlights and lanterns. Next to the hole, Fitz and his cohorts had unearthed one of the laptops. "Do you want me to get it?" Slade asked. "There are others there too still buried in the snow." He wasn't going to say why he knew that, but hoped the officers would trust in Slade's instincts.

"Yeah, sure," Conway said, since he needed to keep a free hand to reach his gun if he needed to. "We'll come back for the others once these guys are locked up."

Slade grabbed the box and tucked it under one arm and then took hold of Fitz's arm and pulled at him to walk through the snow to the cabin. Conway had hold of Otis's arm and was tugging him along too. It was one thing to walk in deep snow on their own, but when forcing a reluctant prisoner to walk with them? This was going to take forever.

Conway called Dulcie and gave her an update so as not to startle her when they arrived at the cabin. "Hey, we're bringing two of the men in. Other officers are en route to reinforce us so they should be arriving at the cabin soon. Tanner and the other officers are in pursuit of the last suspect. They've exchanged gunfire. Yeah, hopefully, they'll take him down without any injuries or worse. Okay, see you soon."

When Conway ended the call, he said, "Dulcie said reinforcements have just arrived at the cabin. We'll turn these two over to them and I'll return to search for Danbury and, after that, look for more of the stolen goods."

"I can help you if you want," Slade said. "I'm sure Sheri and Dulcie would also want to." He figured the more wolves searching the area, the more they would find. He decided they could say they saw odd indentions in the snow. And the officers could use the metal detectors the suspects had left behind. Slade was afraid that the suspects would get bonded out and they could be right back here again. He wondered if they already had buyers for the merchandise and that's why they had risked coming back here to look for it. Or maybe they had the notion that if the police didn't find the other merchandise here, they wouldn't have enough evidence to get them on much of anything.

Slade and Conway were still fighting with Fitz and Otis, who were giving them grief the whole way back. Slade swore if he'd just knocked Fitz out and carried him to the cabin, it would be easier than fighting with him to take him to the cabin this way. Here he had thought taking the two injured men, Lionel and Morgan, to their cabin had been difficult. But at least they were agreeable, and when Slade, Trenton, and Andy hadn't been lifting the sleds over the downed trees, it had been smooth going.

Which made him think about how it was going to be to get these two over fallen trees when they would fight them every step of the way.

Chapter 18

SLADE, CONWAY, AND THEIR PRISONERS WERE FINALLY ON the Border Trail Route. They had yet to reach the first downed tree, but it was coming up. The difficulty was that the trail was narrow for two men trying to walk side by side. Conway wanted Slade and Fitz to go first so he could make sure he could see that Fitz didn't get loose or injure Slade.

Slade tugged an uncooperative Fitz along the trail. Fitz kept trying to step on Slade's snowshoes like Slade had done to Fitz to take him down. They slipped on an icy patch and Slade held his footing, but Fitz went down. At first, Slade was glad that Fitz had fallen and not himself, but damn, it was hard to get a reluctant man to his feet when he didn't have a good grip on the ice either. He was determined, though, and managed to yank Fitz to his feet. Both nearly fell because of the steeper, icy conditions.

Conway was patiently waiting for Slade to get his charge under control—as patient as he could be. He looked as growly as Slade felt. Slade hoped the other officers were on their way here to help out soon.

Once he began moving forward with Fitz again, he paused at a flatter area and watched Conway move Otis through the icy area. Both kept their footing and continued on their way.

But when they came to the first big tree that had fallen across the path, Slade knew they would have a renewed struggle and this time he and Conway might not be successful in navigating the hazard with their prisoners. Plus, Slade was carrying the laptop, which put him at an additional disadvantage.

"Maybe we should wait for the other officers to reach us," Slade said to Conway. He normally didn't give up that easily, but the men were handcuffed behind their backs and moving them over the trees was impossible like that. For Slade and Conway's safety, they couldn't remove the handcuffs. More men could help get their prisoners through the maze of fallen trees more easily.

Slade set the laptop on top of the tree trunk and then tried to help Fitz to climb over the tree, but Fitz struck at him with his body with every ounce of strength he had. Slade knew they couldn't make it this way. It was too hard to get through the trees and underbrush to the lake or he would just take them that way.

Conway called his fellow police officers on his radio. "Hey, it's King. We can't get our suspects to you over the fallen trees on the Border Route Trail. We'll need your assistance."

One of the officers responded over the radio to him that they were equipped with Tasers, no problem. Conway laughed. He was also carrying a Taser, but if he used the Tasers on the prisoners, he and Slade would need to carry the men all the way to the cabin afterward, so it was better to have additional help.

Slade hated waiting in the cold though. He wished they

could move these guys along and shorten the distance at least. The other officers would take about half an hour to reach them.

That's when Slade heard something moving behind them on the trail. He didn't have a good feeling about it. "Down on the ground now," he told Otis and Fitz. They looked at him like he had to be kidding! They weren't taking orders from a civilian, even if he was deputized.

Trusting Slade, Conway took his cue and grabbed the men and forced them down on the ground. "What's up?" he asked Slade.

"Someone's coming. It could be anyone, but if it is Danbury, he's armed and willing to use his gun." Then Slade motioned to the trees where they could wait to ambush Danbury if he came along the trail. No one could hear anyone coming like Slade could, but he'd earned Conway and Tanner's trust that he had excellent hearing.

Conway called Tanner to tell him what they were hearing.

Slade set the laptop down on the snow. Fitz called out as loud as he could, "What are you afraid of? Bears? They're hibernating this time of year."

Again, Slade wanted to knock the troublemaker out. Slade didn't hear anyone coming then. He suspected whoever it was had stopped to try to figure out a different way to reach them, and if it was Danbury, he would try to free his cohorts. Slade knew Fitz was trying to share their exact location with Danbury, if that's who was coming.

Conway glanced at Slade. Slade signaled that the man was silent. Conway nodded. He could be a bulldog when it came to catching his perp, but he was also the most easygoing person Slade knew and wouldn't hurt anyone in the process if he could help it.

Then he heard someone moving through the woods north of them. The person had to be Danbury because Slade doubted that he would have left the trail otherwise. Traveling in snowshoes through the dense underbrush would have been nearly impossible. If nothing else, he would give Danbury kudos for being loyal to his friends.

Slade indicated to Conway that the person was approaching north of him now.

Conway shook his head. He motioned for Slade to take his place. Fitz and Otis were still lying on the ground next to the fallen tree, but Conway and Slade couldn't be at the same location in the woods, or the two men could run the other way. But Conway was armed, so he wanted to be the one to confront Danbury, if that was who was coming.

Slade wanted to turn wolf in the worst way. If he could, he would run through the woods and tackle the guy, end of story. They each took the other's place. They both crouched down behind trees and waited.

"You might as well give us up," Fitz loudly said. "You want to enjoy Christmas with your families, don't you?"

Slade and Conway remained quiet.

Fitz sat up and Otis did the same as if they were planning to get out of there. With their hands cuffed behind their backs, they would have a harder time getting to their feet while wearing snowshoes in the deep snow. They would most likely need help to stand. Which was why Slade had told them to get down on the ground in the first place. Plus, if gunfire was exchanged between Conway and Danbury, the other men would have a better chance of not getting hit by a stray bullet.

Then someone fired at Conway, but it sounded like the slug hit a tree. Slade hated that he couldn't do anything to help the situation. He had to stay right where he was to make sure the other two guys didn't try to escape with the diversion. Conway returned fire. Danbury cried out in pain.

But it didn't mean Conway had hit anything vital, and Slade didn't trust that Danbury was being honest either. He could be faking being hit so Conway would think Danbury was incapacitated.

Conway called Tanner on his radio, "Hey, it's King. Danbury and I have exchanged gunfire. We're hunkered down at a fallen tree on the BRT."

"We're nearly there," Tanner said.

Slade was relieved to hear it. He hoped the officers would get here sooner than later. Everything was quiet for now. No groaning, no movement, but he didn't trust that Danbury was mortally wounded or dead.

Slade noted that Conway was staying put, keeping cover, remaining there to make sure the other prisoners didn't escape. Some officers would be in too much of a hurry to try to take down Danbury, but Conway was doing his job the right way.

Then Slade heard movement in the woods headed toward the trail but on the other side of the huge fallen tree. Slade whistled to get Conway's attention. He glanced back.

Slade pointed in the direction he heard Danbury going now. Conway changed his stance to confront Danbury should he suddenly appear. Slade suspected Danbury was trying to reach the tree and then come up and over it and shoot Conway.

Again, Slade wanted to do something. He was eager to climb the tree deeper in the woods and take Danbury down before he could reach the tree. But he reminded himself that he needed to stay put and make sure Fitz and Otis didn't try to get away.

Then Slade heard the crunching of snow on the trail from the direction they had been traveling and figured that was Tanner and the other officers. Slade whistled to get Conway's attention again and indicated someone else was approaching them on the trail.

Slade was aware of footfalls on the other side of the tree trunk and assumed Danbury was making a last-ditch effort to free his friends. He was taking an awful risk for them.

Slade motioned to Conway that Danbury was moving in behind the tree on the other side. Conway gave Slade a thumbs-up.

Fitz was watching them and shouted, "Don't do it! They're waiting for you. Get out of here!"

Everything was quiet then and Slade suspected Danbury was taking Fitz's words seriously. Footfalls moved back into the woods. Danbury was probably making a run for it.

Tanner and the other officers came into view and Slade said, "He went that way."

"We're on it," Tanner said. "Are the two of you okay?"

"We're good," Conway said. "I called in more reinforcements. They're on their way here now. They'll help us get these two to the cars. I might have hit Danbury, or he might have been pretending that he was injured."

"Okay. Got it." Then Tanner and the other men began tracking Danbury.

Slade wanted to go with them because he could hear and smell Danbury. "He's headed back north through the woods," he called out. He knew he was definitely making an enemy of Fitz and his cohorts.

Tanner and the other guys were crashing through the woods, while four new officers and Dulcie headed toward the fallen tree from the other side.

Dulcie called out to Slade, "Two officers are with Sheri. Tanner called me to help his team to track down Danbury."

"Good," Slade said. Since Dulcie was a wolf, she would better be able to aid Tanner and the others. And she was armed.

Once Dulcie took off after Tanner and the others, the new officers climbed over the fallen tree and Slade assisted them in getting the suspects over it. One of the officers grabbed the boxed laptop still sitting in the snow.

Then Slade told them, "I'm going ahead to the cabin."

"Are you sure, Slade?" Conway asked.

"Yeah. I'll catch you later." Slade could make some more headway if he was on his own, not trying to help the police move the two cuffed men to the patrol cars over all the downed trees. If he smelled or heard Danbury going in his direction, Slade would take him down. He wanted to call

Sheri, but if Danbury was headed back this way, he didn't want to alert him that he was walking this way on his own.

Slate had moved so fast without having to deal with the prisoners that he was soon out of sight of the police. That's when he saw a tiny trail of blood droplets on the snow off the trail. Aw, hell. He had to follow it and see if he could catch Danbury. What if the guy was bleeding out? Again, Slade didn't want to call anyone and alert Danbury he was closing in on him.

A human couldn't hear Slade coming from a distance as he slowly moved though the underbrush, watching for more drips of blood on dead leaves stubbornly clinging to twigs, snowshoe prints in a few places, snapped branches. When he drew closer to Danbury, Slade smelled his scent—frustrated, angry, injured, in pain.

Slade was barely moving now, smelling Danbury's odor more strongly. He saw some snowshoe prints in the tangled underbrush, then heard a muffled cough. He went in a wide circle, judging the direction of the cough so he could sneak up on Danbury from behind as carefully as he could, not wanting to get shot.

Then he saw Danbury sitting, leaning against a tree, clutching his chest, his other hand holding the gun. He looked like he was still ready for a fight. Slade found a stout branch he could swing at Danbury if he tried to shoot him. He just hoped he could get close enough to disable him if he needed to without either of them being hurt.

Slade brushed up against a branch, making it snap. *Hell.* Danbury turned sharply around, his gun trained to shoot.

Slade threw the stout branch at Danbury. The stick struck Danbury's gun arm, knocking it away. The gun fired a round upward, slicing through a tree branch.

As soon as it did, Dulcie came out of practically nowhere and seized Danbury's gun. She and Slade handcuffed Danbury in front of his chest. Then Slade pulled out his personal first aid kit and unzipped Danbury's parka. He couldn't believe how hardheaded this guy was in wanting to free his friends, considering the wound he had suffered.

He pulled up Danbury's sweater and shirt and started to bandage the gunshot wound to slow down the bleeding while Dulcie called Tanner on her radio.

"We got him," Dulcie said.

"Hot damn, good news," Tanner said.

She gave them their coordinates. "Slade got here first." She winked at Slade.

Tanner and the others soon joined them, then carried Danbury to the trail and began making their way to the cabin and the patrol cars. "Call it in, will you, Wulff?"

"Absolutely." Then Dulcie called for an ambulance.

Slade was glad they'd caught all three men and he hoped they would be incarcerated for a while at least. "Since all three men are in custody, I'm on my way back to the cabin."

"Thanks so much for all your help," Tanner said.

"Anytime." Slade hurried off and called Sheri, eager to return to her. "All the men have been caught. I'm on my way home."

"Oh, that's wonderful on both counts. Dulcie left me here with a couple of men so she could help track Danbury down."

"Yeah. She and I got him. He suffered a gunshot wound after shooting at the police."

"Oh, no. Are all the officers all right?"

"Yeah. I thought we might return to help them locate the merchandise, but Dulcie can do that as well as we can, and after all this, I'm ready to hit the sack with you."

"Absolutely. I'm so glad we met her. I invited her to our pizza party. She's eager to meet everyone."

"The others will be glad to learn we have one of our kind on the police force," he said.

"That's for sure."

When Slade arrived at the cabin, Sheri welcomed him home as if he was the most special person in the world. He really loved how affectionate she was with him. But the other two officers were there so he and Sheri couldn't do what they wanted to do immediately.

She frowned when she saw the blood all over Slade's parka and his gloves.

"Danbury's blood, not mine. I bandaged him the best I could to help stop the bleeding," Slade said.

The officers thanked Slade for his assistance with this case, took his statement about what had happened, and thanked him again.

"You're welcome. Anything to get these guys into custody." Slade began pulling off his gloves, hat, and boots. Then Sheri helped him out of his parka.

"I'll start cleaning the blood off your gloves and parka," she said.

"I'll help you."

They worked to get the blood out of Slade's clothes, then hung them up in the downstairs shower to dry. Then they heard an ambulance arrive, and as soon as the police brought Danbury to the cabin, a couple of EMTs saw to him. Fitz and Conway weren't fighting the officers any longer—too many police officers to deal with this time.

Fitz gave Slade the evil eye, appearing to promise him retribution. Because of having a whole wolf pack to back him up, Slade wasn't too worried about it.

Otis and Fitz were taken to a couple of squad cars, and once they were sitting inside them, the officers drove them off to jail. Danbury left in the ambulance with a police escort.

Tanner and Conway thanked Slade and Sheri for their help and Dulcie said she looked forward to seeing them again soon.

Once everyone left, Slade hugged and kissed Sheri.

"I'm so glad they caught them," Sheri said. "Now, it's time to go to bed."

"My thoughts exactly. But first, it's shower time." Slade wanted to make love to Sheri and cuddle with her the rest of the night through. Forget about stolen merchandise, Wild West shoot-outs, thieves on the run, crashed airplanes—it was time for them to be a mated couple and just enjoy being with each other.

They made short work of their clothes and then they were in the shower, soaping each other up, kissing, rubbing their bodies together, laughing, and loving each other with glee.

Chapter 19

THE NEXT MORNING WAS ANOTHER LATE START FOR SHERI and Slade. After such a late night, they were happily intertwined in each other's arms, legs likewise tangled together, kissing and nuzzling.

"I'm so glad we're moving in together," Sheri said, "but"—she licked Slade's aroused nipple—"we might be late to work lots of mornings."

Slade laughed. "We'll just have to go to bed right after we're done with work and have had a quick bite of dinner."

"Okay, that works for me." She was glad they were going to have another week where they were just strictly together having a great time, which she was totally looking forward to. Except this time, they wouldn't have to deal with thieves on the run. Hopefully. In a wolf-run town like Slade said Silver Town was, the local law enforcement could deal with any issues they encountered. She suspected they would have a totally fun vacation skiing, running as wolves among even more wolves, trying out the eateries there, and just enjoying everything Silver Town had to offer. But especially treasuring their time alone together.

She put her arms on his chest and rested her chin on her hands as she looked at him. "Are you ready for breakfast? It's a little late for running as wolves this morning. Besides, as many times as we've gone to run as wolves and had issues, I'm ready to just go cross-country skiing. How does that sound to you?"

"That sounds great. We'll ski all across the lake," Slade agreed, and kissed her, but then he was on top of her, and they were making love again—before breakfast.

Once they showered and dressed, they made soft and fluffy skillet cinnamon rolls with homemade cream cheese icing and cinnamon sugar for breakfast. The rolls were sweet, buttery, and exquisite, perfect. They had some ham and eggs over easy to go with them, and mugs of coffee. Afterward, they called Faith to let her know that they were going to have a new wolf pack member, only she was a gray wolf, and she was on the police force.

"Oh, that's terrific. Cameron's in the middle of a case right now, but I'll let everyone else know."

"She's eager to meet everyone and I asked her to join us for the pizza party after we move Slade's things to my place," Sheri said.

"Oh, that will be perfect. Too bad we didn't know about her sooner. She could have come to our Christmas party," Faith said.

"I agree. Her name is Dulcie Wulff and she's from Minneapolis, no other family, and she's a royal, so she'll be a big help to the rest of the pack members."

"Wonderful. She'll be part of the family for sure," Faith said.

"We meant to tell you last night, but we got in so late. We'll have to tell you all about that later. We're going skiing now."

"Oh, fun. Enjoy skiing."

"Thanks! We will."

Then they ended the call and got all bundled up to ski, grabbed their skis, and put them on at the lake. They raced each other across the ice, avoiding the fishermen catching fish, though they all called out greetings to one another.

They slowed their pace, taking it leisurely after that, just enjoying the late morning, the blue sky, a few wisps of clouds, the pristine snow-covered lake, and the exercise. A steady breeze was blowing, sweeping a dusting of snow with it and making it appear as though they were skiing through a low screen of powdery mist. She thoroughly enjoyed this.

They skied over a couple of ice fishing holes dug the previous day and saw a number of blue, yellow, and red tents set up while fishermen were sitting inside fishing. She and Slade even waved at a Boy Scout troop, the scoutmasters and kids setting up to fish. They saw a fisherman pull a northern pike out of his fishing hole and hold it up to show it off to them. They waved and congratulated him.

This was so much fun.

The lake was 907 acres long, so they skied to the end of it and returned, traversing the lake back and forth. They skied for about three hours and then finally headed back to the cabin to have lunch and warm up.

"How about grilling hamburgers for lunch?" Slade unlocked the door, and they carried their skis inside.

"Ooh, yeah and we could have cranberries and blue cheese sauce on top of the burgers for a Christmassy touch," Sheri said.

"Now that sounds really good. Do you want to take a drive to the trail that leads to Magnetic Rock in Minnesota's Superior National Forest after lunch? It's about a forty-minute drive to the trailhead and a one-and-a-half-hour hike."

"That sounds perfect."

"We need to take the compass so you can see why the rock is called Magnetic Rock."

"That sounds like fun."

After lunch, they took the trip out to the trailhead and parked. They got out and hiked along the two miles on Magnetic Rock Trail, seeing the rolling tree-covered hills and northern lakes covered by a white blanket of snow. Pristine, beautiful.

They finally reached the monolith of Magnetic Rock—a sixty-foot rock standing on end, towering over the trees in the forest surrounding it. It was interesting to see the remnant of the rock, as if it was a standing stone erected by early inhabitants of the area. Other stones lay scattered around it. She wondered what the area would have looked like before the glacial period and how one standing stone remained.

"This was originally from the glacial period," Slade said.

"It's amazing that only one glacial stone would remain standing all on its own." Sheri tested her magnetic compass with the rock composed of magnetite, and the arrow was spinning slightly around.

"If we had a magnet with us, we could actually stick it on there."

"This is so cool. It really would mess up where you're going, though, if you were trying to use your compass and

you were close enough to the rock. This is great fun though."
Sheri pulled out her phone and took pictures of her and
Slade smiling in front of the rock and then each of them hug-
ging it between them though it was so large, they were far
apart from each other.

"You can actually climb it to the top," Slade said.

"No, thank you."

He laughed and gave her a real hug. "Yeah, the rock could
be icy."

"You want to climb up there. I can see in your expression
that you want to."

He smiled. "That would be a sixty-foot drop if I fell. Yeah,
I would love to climb to the top, but not when it's icy."

"Okay, if we come back to the area to stay at the cabin
in the summer, we'll come here, and I can video record you
climbing it."

"You're not going to give it a go?"

"No way."

He laughed. "Okay, we've got a deal."

They made their way back on the snow-covered trail to
the trailhead where they had parked his SUV.

"You know, I keep thinking about the blond guy who was
with Fitz," Sheri said.

"Danbury, the shooter who got shot and ended up in the
hospital?" Slade said.

"Yes. You remember that earlier case I had with the stolen
delivery truck and merchandise?"

"Right. And the police officer told you that the one laptop
we had dug out was from that heist."

"Exactly. The guy who was driving a green Jeep Wagoneer had stolen the truck—"

"Hell, that was Danbury?"

"I think so. I just need to confirm that Danbury owns the Jeep. Of course, he could have been driving someone else's vehicle. But if Danbury does own the Jeep, it could be evidence that he actually stole the delivery truck and the merchandise from the warehouse."

"I would say that was a good bet."

"Okay, then I'll call it in to Conway." Sheri pulled out her satellite phone and called Conway and told him what she believed.

"Thanks, Sheri, I'm going to sure look into it. We'll investigate the security videos from the businesses in the area again too and use his phone records to see if they correspond with him being in the area at the time and maybe nail him for the stolen goods."

"You're welcome. I couldn't identify who the other person was that had driven the man to his vehicle, but he was driving a red Ford pickup."

"I'll check into that also. I'll see if either Fitz or Otis owns a red pickup," Conway said.

"Great. I hope you find that they do and that will help to prove that case."

"Believe me, we do too and want to wrap this up."

"If I think of anything else, I'll let you know," Sheri said.

"You have done a great job on all this. If you ever need help with a case, just call Tanner or me."

Or Dulcie, Sheri was thinking. Though she had called

Conway because he had been working on this case from the beginning. "Absolutely. Thanks so much."

"Enjoy the rest of your vacation."

"Oh, we are." Then they ended the call. "Conway's going to check out what vehicles Fitz and his cohorts have."

"Good. I sure hope they can get even more evidence on that to help really get these guys," Slade said.

"Me too." Sheri got a call then from her brother.

"Hey, Sis, Candice, Owen, and I will be arriving tomorrow about ten. Is there anything we need to bring?"

"If Candice and Owen have another fishing tent, or if you want to bring yours, that would be great. We just have Slade's tent, so we'll need another. Fishing equipment, of course. I have your fishing pole that you can use."

"Okay, done. We'll see you tomorrow then."

"See you then!" Sheri was excited to have them come at the end and enjoy spending some time with them.

"They're all coming tomorrow then," Slade said.

"Yep. We're going to have fun."

"Yeah, we will." They reached the SUV and Slade said, "Do you want to go to a pub near here for dinner? I was going to fix beef stew, but I thought it would be fun to go out to dinner since we're close to the pub now."

"Yeah, sure."

"It has great reviews for food. And chocolate malts you have to eat with a spoon."

"Oh, I'm totally sold on it. No cleanup afterward and we can go running as wolves when we return to the cabin."

"That will work."

They soon reached the restaurant, which was decorated with white Christmas lights and a small Christmas tree sparkling in one of the windows. They went inside and got a booth and ditched their coats. The menu had a little of everything, and Sheri ordered the Swedish meatballs. Slade got a hot brisket sandwich and fries. And both ordered chocolate malts.

"Wow, everything is so good," Sheri said. "I'm glad we took off the night to just order a meal."

"I agree. This has been nice."

"We'll have to really run off all this when we go out as wolves."

Slade laughed. "Yeah, we will. Though we could go back to the Magnetic Rock and climb it."

Sheri smiled and shook her head. "You said yourself it's too icy."

"Yeah, but climbing it would burn off a few calories."

"We'll keep our feet on the ground and run off our calories that way."

He sighed.

She chuckled.

After dinner, they headed out to his vehicle and drove back to the cabin. Then they were in a hurry to strip and run as wolves. They needed to straighten up the place before everyone arrived tomorrow too.

Late the next morning, Owen and Candice arrived, and then Hans showed up, caravanning together, all bearing treats and well-wishes. They'd brought Christmas cookies the triplets, Faith, and Cameron had made for them, bottles of champagne, and more food.

Slade and Sheri were thrilled to see them and spend some time having fun in the wilderness with them with hugs all around. They went outside to bring in their bags for the next couple of days.

"We have to warn you, when we go home, the whole pack is going to celebrate, so just expect it," Hans said, pulling off his parka.

Sheri and Slade laughed. "I love this pack," Sheri said and squeezed Slade's hand.

"Yeah, the pack celebrates everything," Slade said. "I'm not surprised they would do it for us for this special occasion. Before my parents and sister and I arrived here, we weren't part of a pack, just had our own small family unit. So being with the white wolf pack has been a real treat for us. Not to mention that because of David's mission to rescue Elizabeth from the Yellowknife Arctic wolf pack, I ended up with a mate and another whole family to love." He pulled Sheri into a hug and kissed her soundly.

"For sure. I know we're doing the pizza party after we move you to Sheri's place, but we still have to have a real celebration of your mating." Candice hung up her parka on the coatrack.

"Then we can help you move from Sheri's apartment to the big house when it's done." Owen removed his parka and hung it up.

Slade smiled. "That would be great. We'll have to have another celebration there."

"Everyone will be at your apartment to help you pack," Hans assured him.

"I don't have that much stuff at my apartment," Slade said.

"That won't deter everyone from showing up for pizza and solidarity," Hans said.

Slade was more concerned about having room for everyone to show up at his place.

Hans had brought more steaks and Candice carried a cream corn casserole into the kitchen. "I brought more s'mores ingredients and hot chocolate, whipped cream, and chocolate sprinkles in case you were getting a little low," Candice said.

"Oh, that's wonderful. We've been serving up a lot of hot cocoa, especially because of all the excitement we've had since we've been here," Sheri said. "What do you all want to do today after lunch?"

"Fish," Candice said.

"Yeah, I'm all for that," Hans said. Owen agreed.

Then they got busy making a lunch of steaks and the casserole Candice had brought and once they were ready, they sat down to eat.

"I love your Christmas touches," Candice said, waving her Santa napkin at the Christmas tree in the center of the table.

Hans laughed. "If I'd gone with you, Slade, I wouldn't have given it a thought."

"I know. Me neither," Slade said. "But Sheri knows how to do things right."

"Thanks, Slade. But Slade was the one to hang the mistletoe," Sheri said.

Candice smiled. "Perfect for a romantic retreat."

"We were going to share our fish with you, and still can, unless we catch more, and then we can have fresh fish tonight for dinner?" Sheri asked.

"Yeah, that sounds good," Hans said.

They all ate their lunch and afterward they cleaned up and dressed warmly to go fishing. Owen and Candice had brought more gear, including another fishing tent and another sled. They headed out across the lake and found a nice deep location to fish at. Owen and Hans began drilling holes in the ice, while Slade helped Candice and Sheri to set up the tents. Then they set up chairs in each of the tents and got the fishing poles ready to go fishing.

They had been sitting on the ice for some time, waiting for the fish to bite, when Sheri thought it would be enjoyable and festive to have some hot chocolate to warm everyone up and make the experience more fun. "I'm going to get some thermoses of hot cocoa for everyone." No one was catching anything right now anyway.

"Yeah, I'm all for it," Slade said. "Do you want me to help you?"

"No, you catch us some more fish. If Hans takes over your fishing pole while he's fishing with his own, he'll claim the fish is his," Sheri said.

Hans laughed. "You know me too well, Sis."

Sheri smiled at him, loving that he was always playing

along with her. Then she left their shelter and poked her head into Candice and Owen's tent. "Hey, are you both up for some hot cocoa?"

"Yeah, do you want me to help you get it?" Candice asked.

Owen didn't look like he was going to offer because he was too intent on catching a fish.

"No, I've got it. Be back in a little bit." Sheri wanted Candice to enjoy fishing too, though in retrospect, she wondered if Candice had wanted to get out of the cold for a bit.

She walked across the lake, back to the cabin. When she reached the door, she heard a vehicle pull up behind it in the parking area, not a car she recognized. Immediately, after all the trouble they'd already had, she worried that Fitz and his friends had been bailed out and that they'd come back to get revenge. But what she hadn't expected was to see Betty coming around the end of the cabin.

"I'm so sorry for coming here while you're on vacation, but I need your help," Betty said, looking totally frazzled again.

"Where is Gerard?" Sheri wanted to know the truth this time. Was he even alive?

"That's why I had to come and see you. I–I… Can we sit inside and talk?"

Sheri hesitated. Now what did Betty want? She couldn't believe she would come here to their cabin to seek her out. Had she called Cameron and he sent her here?

"Yeah, sure." Then they went inside, and Sheri said, "I'm making cocoa for my fishing companions. What did you need to talk to me about?"

"I need you to find Gerard for me."

Sheri had just begun to pour milk into a saucepan and turned to look at her. "You said he had returned, then we found his plane in bits out here in the BWCA with merchandise from a stolen delivery truck. Gerard's brother and two of his friends were involved in all of it. How did Gerard survive the crash? Did he survive the crash?" She began pulling thermoses out of the kitchen cabinet. "Why not go to the police?"

Betty wiped away tears. "I–I didn't know about any of it. But Gerard wasn't flying the plane. His plane." She didn't say anything about going to see the police.

"What?" Suspicious about what was going on, Sheri set the last thermos on the kitchen counter and turned to face her. "Who was flying it then?"

"I don't know. But after I learned Gerard's plane had crashed, I knew he hadn't been flying it."

"Because you said he had returned home." Sheri stirred cocoa into the milk in the saucepan.

"Right."

That meant Betty hadn't lied about Gerard returning home and Sheri was glad for it. "So where had he been the first time he disappeared if he hadn't flown the plane?"

"Seeing a woman. I had been sure of it. He finally came home and said he'd made a mistake."

"But now he's disappeared again?" Sheri asked, and poured cocoa into the thermoses, then topped them with whipped cream.

"Yes. Then I learned all about this business with the plane and I'm afraid he's on the run from his brother."

"Gerard is running from Fitz?"

"Yes."

Sheri secured the tops on the thermoses. "Okay, so why is he afraid of him?" Sheri turned and folded her arms, observing her.

"Fitz planned this whole thing. He was blackmailing Gerard to fly for him. Gerard refused to fly the plane that night. He actually had hidden from his brother, not ever believing Fitz would get someone else to fly *his* plane. Gerard hadn't wanted to get caught with the goods and play Fitz's game."

"What was Fitz blackmailing Gerard over?"

"Gerard wouldn't tell me."

"Okay, so did you go to the police about Gerard's disappearance again?" Sheri asked again, suspecting Gerard's wife was telling the truth. Her scent and posture said she wasn't hiding anything.

"Yes, but they treated me like I was the boy who cried wolf. Then they said they believed Gerard is the mastermind in all this and that he ran away to avoid facing the consequences of his actions. I want you to find him, and I want you to prove that he didn't have anything to do with the theft of the goods."

"So you're hiring me to locate him again."

"*And* to prove he is innocent of all the charges."

"What if he isn't innocent?" Sheri didn't trust that he wasn't involved in all this. What had he done that his brother could blackmail him over? He was seeing another woman too. Or was that the same issue that his brother had over him? Who was the pilot who had taken over the flight and what had become of him?

"Gerard is innocent, or I wouldn't hire you to find him. But I'm worried Fitz will find him first and kill him."

Sheri had to find Gerard first. She knew there was more to this whole case. "All right. Who was the pilot Gerard gave the job to and what happened to him? Did he die in the crash? Make it out alive? Where is he now?" Sheri was just voicing the questions she needed the answers for out loud.

"I don't know. Gerard didn't know who Fitz got to fly his plane."

She hadn't expected Betty to answer her, but she wished she had more information on all of this. "Why didn't you just call me? Why did you drive all the way out here?"

"I was afraid you wouldn't help me if I didn't speak to you face-to-face. I would do anything to help resolve this."

"Okay, okay. Yeah. I'll do it. I want Gerard to be safe. It'll be the usual retainer and fees."

"You've got it. Thanks." Then Betty left.

Sheri couldn't believe it. But then she realized she really didn't have that much time to locate him. Only a week until Christmas and she was going with Slade on the ski trip at Silver Town two days after that.

She put all the thermoses into a bag and carried them out to the lake. She finally reached Candice and Owen's tent first, peeked in, and handed them their thermoses. "Did you catch anything?"

"Not yet," Candice said. "You probably would have heard us scream out with joy if we had."

Sheri laughed. "Well, I got a job looking for Gerard Connolly again."

"Oh?" Owen asked. "His wife called you again? I thought she would go through Cameron."

"Betty Connolly just dropped by the cabin. Maybe she talked to Cameron first and he told her I was here. Or, no, she probably knew from Fitz and his friends getting caught out here, that Slade and I were staying here and helped the police out. I'll tell you all about it later. I have some more cocoa deliveries to make."

"Oh, wow, that's unbelievable. I'm glad she's got you to help her, but the others will help you with the case too." Candice sipped from her thermos. "Thanks. This is delicious. I was getting cold."

"You're so welcome." Sheri was glad her fellow investigators would help her with the case if she needed them to. Then she carried the rest of the thermoses to the other tent. "So who caught some fish?"

Slade and Hans laughed.

"We needed you to be here to be our lucky charm." Hans paused to take a drink of his cocoa. "Your double chocolate is always the greatest."

"Thanks. I think I need to show you how to fish right." Sheri reached out for Hans's fishing pole.

Hans smiled and handed it to her. He was good-natured about it.

Slade drank some of his cocoa. "I heard you tell Candice and Owen about Betty Connolly hiring you again to search for her husband."

"Yeah, that was a shock. I was worried when I heard the car arrive. I didn't recognize the vehicle's engine sound. She wasn't driving her Jaguar this time." Then Sheri felt a tug on Hans's fishing line. "Here, Hans, take your line. I need to take a drink of my cocoa."

She handed him the line and he said, "Hot damn, there's a fish on the hook."

She laughed and drank some of her cocoa. Slade leaned over and kissed her and whispered, "I love you."

Hans was too busy reeling in his fish to notice the lovebirds kissing.

Chapter 20

Slade got a tug on his line right after Hans did, then concentrated on pulling in his fish. He loved how Sheri showed her brother how to catch the fish in jest, and then handed the pole to him when she had a bite so her brother could reel it in. He loved to see the interaction between them—good-natured fun. Even though he loved being here alone with Sheri, he enjoyed being with the others too.

He wanted to ask Sheri about the Gerard case, but he figured she wanted to tell everyone about it at the same time over dinner. Hans pulled his pike, and Slade managed to catch one too.

"Yes!" Hans said. "We can have a fish fry tonight and then take the rest home for a fish fry with the pack if we have enough left."

"Or we could have hot dogs and save the fish for home," Slade said.

"Woo-hoo!" Candice said in the tent nearby.

He smiled. "It appears Candice got one."

Sheri was fishing but wasn't catching anything. Slade was afraid Owen wouldn't either.

It took another hour before Owen caught a fish, and the

others were cold, so they broke down their tents and packed everything up on the sleds and hauled them back across the snow-covered ice to the cabin.

"We've seen the prettiest northern lights at night. Maybe we can see them after our wolf run, while we're making s'mores. Do you want to save the fish and have hot dogs over the campfire?" Sheri asked.

"Oh, hot dogs sound good," Hans said.

"Yeah, we can save the fish for home," Candice said. "A fish fry with the whole pack for all those who couldn't make it to the cabin?"

"Yeah, that would be really nice," Sheri said.

After they unloaded their stuff and cleaned the fish, then put them in the freezer, they grabbed the hot dogs and headed out to start the firepit to cook them. Owen brought out the bottles of champagne to help celebrate their mating and filled glasses for everyone.

Then they sat all bundled up, roasting the hot dogs over the fire, talking about Sheri's case.

"If this case gets too dangerous, we're all on it," Owen warned Sheri.

"Yeah, sure. I'm all for the help if I need it. I'm not too proud to accept it." Sheri took a sip of her champagne.

Slade was glad about it. He loved being a pilot in his family's business, but he realized how much he wanted to help Sheri with her cases now that they were mated!

Sheri got a call and said, "Oh, no. All right. I'll tell everyone else. Thanks, Cameron." She set the satellite phone down on the table. "Okay, not so good news. Fitz and Otis both got bail. They had never been up on any other charges before, so the judge let them go with low bails."

"It's a financial crime, and no one has been murdered *yet*," Slade said.

"Unless Fitz gets ahold of Gerard, if Betty's worries are founded." Owen drank some more of his champagne.

"Yeah. Fitz wasn't too happy with me either for helping the police to bring him in," Slade said.

"They deputized you again, didn't they?" Owen asked.

"Ohmigod, they actually deputized you?" Sheri asked. "You didn't tell me that."

"Yeah, to help bring the perps in. The other deputies were trying to take down Danbury, the shooter. Conway only had me to help him take in the other two men." Slade swore Sheri looked impressed that he'd been deputized.

"Wow." Sheri put her hot dog on a bun and squirted on ketchup. Then she took a bite. "Hmm, good."

The others finished roasting their hot dogs and began adding condiments.

"Oh, these are good," Candice said. "I haven't had roasted hot dogs like this in a long time."

"Yeah, we thought they would be tasty over the fire," Sheri said. "The champagne goes well with them too."

They all ended up getting seconds on the hot dogs and after they ate those and finished another bottle of champagne, Sheri said, "Save room for s'mores after our wolf run!"

"About the wolf run," Owen said, "you're taking us to the crash site, right?"

Sheri smiled. "Sure. It's taped off, but we found other merchandise beyond that area."

"Which is probably taped off too now, but as wolves exploring the site? It won't matter," Slade said.

"True," Sheri agreed.

Candice said, "Everyone take mental notes about everything. I'll use it in one of my stories."

They all laughed, but they knew Candice was serious. If she didn't have a camera, a recorder, or a pad of paper with her, she asked everyone to help her remember details.

They stripped out of their clothes and shifted, all but Slade, who had to open the door and close it afterward, then he shifted.

Slade and Sheri led the way, the other wolves following them along the trail. Now, Slade thought, Candice could really envision the downed trees and the difficulty for humans to travel this way after the bad snowstorm for her story.

First, they took them to the crash site and the wolves went under the crime-scene tape and smelled around the whole area. They didn't smell any more merchandise though. Then Slade and Sheri headed for the next area where they'd found packages before, but this time they heard digging. Slade was afraid that Fitz and his friends had returned once again.

They moved silently in that direction, but if it was Fitz and the others, they were quiet this time, no one talking, just digging in the snow. And they only heard one person digging. It didn't make any sense. Unless someone had seen the news about the plane crash and stolen goods on board and was looking for a free laptop or other brand-new electronic devices to grab.

As soon as he reached a tree that was close enough, Slade saw Dulcie digging in the snow with lanterns around and a headlamp on. She'd already found a laser printer. She wouldn't have needed the lighting, unless she was taking pictures to document the finds. Sure, then she'd need them. He listened for any sign of any other officers in the area before he let her know they were there. In the meantime, the other wolves joined him and watched Dulcie.

Then Slade figured she was by herself and woofed at her.

Dulcie startled and turned to look in Slade's direction. He smiled at her and woofed again.

"Slade?"

He nodded.

Sheri came out of the woods and woofed at her and then trotted over to her and started helping Dulcie dig out the package.

"Sheri," Dulcie said, smelling her scent. She smiled. "Wow, imagine me seeing you guys out here." She saw the other wolves then and smiled again.

Slade joined Sheri and Dulcie and began digging. But Hans, Candice, and Owen were wandering around, sniffing for any other scents. And then Hans woofed and started to dig at the snow. So did Candice and Owen.

Before long Dulcie, Slade, and Sheri uncovered two more boxes, but they didn't know what they were. Dulcie lifted them out and set them with the printer.

Then Dulcie began smelling for any more scents. Slade

watched Hans and the others digging deeper in the snow. Then he and Sheri began looking for any more items out here. He was surprised Dulcie was out here on her own. Then again, in a way, it was easier for her to locate the items on her own without witnesses than try to explain how she had found them.

With all the wolves digging, Dulcie concentrated on pulling out the merchandise from the snow. She left markers everywhere that they had found the buried merchandise. Then they found the last of the packages in the area. They moved off to another area to do more searches and found a few more items. Once they were done, Dulcie called it in to the sheriff's office.

"Yes, I know. I couldn't sleep, okay? I kept seeing in my mind's eye where all the packages were buried. In any event, I used a metal detector in a few new areas and have recovered another fifteen packages. Anyway, I'm done for the night if anyone wants to come out here and pick these up to secure as evidence." Dulcie laughed. "Sorry about your show... Yeah, I really, really am. Okay, see you in an hour." She secured her satellite phone and said to Slade and the others, "Thanks so much to you for helping me. I couldn't have gotten half of this work done without you."

They woofed at her.

"Tanner and Conway are on their way. They'll be here within the hour. There's no need for you to stay here any longer."

But they didn't budge. Slade knew the others wanted to stay here with Dulcie too, to make sure Fitz and Otis didn't return and steal all this from Dulcie and hurt her. At least Danbury was still in the hospital from the gunshot wound, and since he was the one who had been shooting at everyone, maybe the others wouldn't resort to those kinds of tactics, but Slade and his pack members couldn't take that chance.

Besides, they were nice and warm in their fur coats. He imagined poor Dulcie was cold for however long she'd been out here before they had even arrived. They figured they would have quite a wait for the officers to show up, but half an hour later, they heard a siren in the distance and knew Tanner and Conway were parking at the cabin. Slade smiled. They had rushed to come to Dulcie's aid.

When they heard Tanner and Conway finally approaching on foot, the wolves moved off into the trees. They could have gone back to the cabin, but Slade wanted to make sure Dulcie didn't get into trouble for coming out here on her own to do this. Though he totally understood why she had.

"Hey," Tanner said. "We knew you were a workaholic, but really, this is beyond what I could have envisioned."

Conway shook his head. "She's just trying to show us up at the office because she's new at the job. She's doing a damn good job of it too."

They all seemed to have a good working relationship with each other, which Slade was glad to see.

"She is. But I'm glad she did it so we didn't have to be out here all this time. It must have taken hours to uncover all this stuff," Tanner said.

It would have if she hadn't had the wolves' help.

Tanner and Conway helped document all the finds and

locations of the merchandise, and then they packed the items up on two sleds and hauled them back.

The wolves followed them, giving them safe passage all the way to their vehicle at the cabin. He wondered where Dulcie had trekked in from.

When the officers drew close enough to the cabin, Slade and the other wolves dashed through the woods ahead of them. Once they arrived at the cabin, Slade shifted, unlocked the door and everyone went inside, and he locked the door. Then they all shifted and dressed.

"Wow," Candice said. "At least the bad guys didn't show up, but the rest was great for a story."

Owen laughed. "I'm glad we could help Dulcie uncover a bunch of the stolen merchandise."

"Is she single?" Hans asked.

"Yes," Sheri said, "and she asked if there were any bachelor males in the pack. I mentioned you, but I didn't want to push you two together if you weren't interested in each other. She'll be coming to the pizza party at the office after we move Slade's things to my apartment."

"Great. I can talk to her then. I guess she didn't know I was the bachelor male there helping her out."

"She'll smell your scent when you're at the party and know you were there," Sheri said.

Slade was amused, but he was glad he already had his mate. Sheri was just perfect for him.

"I was going to say we could go out and have some s'mores, but maybe we should wait for the officers to all leave in their cars first," Sheri said.

"No. I mean, we could invite them to join us. I mean, since the three officers had to give up part of their night to come out here and—" Hans said.

"You want to meet Dulcie," Sheri said.

Slade would have done the same thing if he were Hans.

"Let's do it," Candice said. She was already heading to the kitchen to grab the graham crackers, chocolate bars, and marshmallows and smiled at the container of green frosting. "I remember you adding red and blue frosting to the s'mores for the Fourth of July party. This will be so much fun." Then she took all of it outside while everyone grabbed some water bottles and blankets and headed out after her.

Hans got the fire started. Sheri passed around the roasting forks, and then everyone began to roast their marshmallows when they heard Tanner talking to the other officers as they moved in the direction of the cabin from the trail. "Yeah, at least my show is on a streaming service, and I can watch it anytime."

"That's good to know," Dulcie said. "I knew I could count on the two of you to come out and help me with this."

"You should have called us sooner," Conway said.

They saw Slade and the others roasting marshmallows and Slade called out to them, "Come join us! We didn't know you would be out doing some more digging for buried treasure tonight."

"We didn't either," Tanner said. "It was all Dulcie's idea."

"Yeah, we'll join you," Conway said. "I haven't had s'mores since I was a Boy Scout."

"I haven't had them since I was a little girl," Dulcie said.

"I have them every Fourth of July." Tanner frowned. "What's that on them?"

"A little Christmas color," Candice said.

"Well, that works for me." Dulcie motioned to the cars. "We'll just get these loaded in the cars and then be right back."

A few minutes later, the three officers joined them. Slade was glad Candice and Owen had brought more fixings for s'mores. Then introductions were made all around, though Tanner and Conway had met Owen before on a case he had been looking into.

Dulcie seemed interested in Hans, once she realized he was Sheri's brother and the bachelor male wolf in the group.

When Candice said she was the novelist, Dulcie smiled. "I read your novels. I'll have to have you autograph them."

"Oh sure, I would love to."

Then the officers were making up their s'mores, adding green icing to them, Tanner saying, "This is like Grinch s'mores." Everyone chuckled.

"So we heard that Otis and Fitz were bailed out of jail," Slade said.

"Yeah. We hoped they wouldn't be because they had been resisting arrest and carrying illegal weapons in the BCWA, but the judge thought otherwise. No past criminal charges, no threat of flight risk—so the judge believed. It won't be the same for Danbury though," Tanner said. "Not only because he'll be hospitalized for a few more days, but because he was shooting at our officers."

"Good. Do you believe these guys had never pulled off a job before?" Sheri asked.

"It's possible, but unlikely," Conway said. "I mean, there are cases where someone or a team of people pull off a heist and they had never done any crimes before that. But most of the time it's a case of they never got caught on any other crimes they've been involved in so there's no record of it."

"Okay, well, Betty Connolly came to me today at the cabin and asked if I would find her husband, Gerard, and clear him of being a suspect in the case," Sheri said.

"Yeah, she was in today to speak with me." Tanner made another s'more. "I swear she's like the boy who cried wolf. When she first said her husband had gone missing, we figured he was a grown man, he was having an affair, and that's all there was to it. Now, that's not to say we didn't look into it. We did. We checked all the usual places to make sure he hadn't died or been injured—accident reports, all of it. But there was no sign of him. Then she calls the office and says, 'He's home. He's all right.' Then you call in the airplane crash, we verify it was his plane, you tell us about the stolen merchandise, and this is now a whole different story."

"Did Gerard's wife tell you who was really flying the plane?" Sheri asked.

"Nope," Conway said. "She said Gerard didn't know who had and now he has gone missing again. We have no way of knowing who the pilot was or whether he survived the crash or was injured and whether he even knew what he was transporting. Of course, Gerard might very well have been flying the plane. We did have cadaver dogs out there searching the area to see if we could find a body. But we didn't find any sign of one."

Slade was thinking they would have smelled an injured or dead man while they were looking for the packages, and they hadn't. Which he was glad for. Maybe the pilot had made it out alive just fine.

"Well, while I'm conducting my new investigation into Gerard's disappearance, I'll let you know if I locate him or learn anything about the case. Did Betty tell you he was being blackmailed by his brother, Fitz?" Sheri asked.

"Yeah." Tanner wiped his hands on one of the Christmas napkins Sheri had set out for everyone to use. "She said it had been because he'd been unfaithful. With whom? I had asked. She didn't know. She sure doesn't know a lot. Supposedly, Gerard wouldn't tell her. But Mrs. Connolly did say she had all the money in the family—inherited wealth. And if Gerard had been unfaithful, she would divorce him and there would go his chance of getting any of that money. She had him sign a pre-nuptial agreement. He was, or still could be, a real ladies' man and Mrs. Connolly knew that when she had married him."

"So then the blackmail could have triggered a divorce and him losing the money he was accustomed to having." Slade thought that might make more sense. And the Jaguar Betty had been driving? It wasn't from Gerard's income as a pilot, but her own wealth.

"Exactly," Conway said.

Hans looked like he wanted to add something to the conversation, opening his mouth to speak, and then clamping it closed as if he thought better of it.

"We tried to call you, by the way, to let you know we were parking at the cabin since it's the closest location to the plane's crash site, but we didn't get any answer," Tanner said, sounding apologetic.

"Oh, we were taking a walk and none of us had a satellite phone on us," Hans said. "We were lucky we didn't run into any trouble."

Of course, in reality, they'd been running as wolves and didn't have their satellite phones with them. Dulcie smiled at Hans.

The officers finally finished their s'mores and thanked them for the treats. Then they left and Owen said to Sheri, "You know what this means, don't you?"

"What?"

"You're no longer in training as a PI. I don't think any of us has done as much work on a case when we were on vacation as you have," Owen said.

"Yeah, but that's because it all kind of fell into my lap. Though we might have to make Slade an honorary PI for all the help he has been to me on the case," Sheri said, giving Slade a hug.

"Believe me, I've been happy to do it."

Then they all went inside to have some more champagne to celebrate the happy union between Slade and Sheri.

Chapter 21

"So about the sleeping arrangements, Slade and I are amenable to doing anything you want to do. You all could stay upstairs, and we'll stay downstairs, or—" Sheri said to her brother and Candice and Owen.

"We already discussed it," Hans said. "We're staying downstairs. The two of you have been upstairs all this time, right? There are two couches that fold out into double beds. We'll be good."

"Yeah, we have. We figured we could take our sheets to a foldout couch, but if you are good with the way things are, then we won't have to," Sheri said.

Slade was glad they were having the bedroom to themselves, though from now on, the two of them would be sharing a bedroom of their own when they returned home. That had a great ring to it.

Then they all toasted to a long life and happy mating, drank their champagne, and got ready to take showers and settle down for the night. Sheri and Slade found extra sheets and blankets for the foldout couches while the others were setting up the beds.

Sheri and Slade were making their way upstairs to the bedroom while they heard Owen and Candice head to the downstairs shower. After Sheri and Slade showered together and retired to bed, they snuggled for a while.

"I'm glad my brother, Candice, and Owen are here, not only to fish with us and take a wolf run, but also to help Dulcie with finding all those goods. I'm glad she got the credit for being there for so long to do that, even though she hadn't been there *that* long because we'd helped her instead."

"Yeah, I agree, and you know she appreciated us. Plus, she was glad she was able to meet other wolves in the pack. She would have given us credit for helping her if she could have without outing us."

"Yes. It was better that we let on we hadn't been out there too. That might have looked a bit suspicious, don't you think?" Sheri asked.

"Possibly. It was best we played it low-key this time."

"No more searching for merchandise though. It's up to the police to take care of it. Should we go for a wolf run in the morning and then go for a snowshoe hike through the woods?" Sheri kissed Slade's bare chest.

"Yeah, that sounds good if everyone likes the idea."

Then they made love, and before they were fully awake the next morning, they heard their companions downstairs, laughing while making breakfast.

Slade hugged Sheri. "I thought everyone would sleep in a bit."

She smiled at him. "I guess they want to make the most of their time here. They probably want to run as wolves this morning before sunrise."

"That's probably true." They both got out of bed and dressed, then headed down the stairs.

"Good morning," Slade and Sheri said to everyone.

Candice and Owen smiled brightly at them. They were both morning people. Hans looked like he could have gotten a little more sleep, but he also loved to get going early when he was on a vacation somewhere.

"Are we going on a run as wolves after breakfast?" Candice asked, making them tea, coffee, eggs, sausage links, and hash browns.

"Yeah, but we're not heading in the direction of the crash site this time," Sheri said.

"It's time for just pure wolf fun," Candice agreed.

But Slade knew Candice never just had pure wolf fun. She was always gathering information for another story, no matter what she was doing. He'd even seen her writing dialogue down on napkins at a restaurant when she had heard some juicy conversation she wanted to incorporate in a story. Of course, everyone in the pack who was with her enabled her and offered their own unused napkins to help further her cause.

They all sat down to have their breakfast, then cleaned up and got ready to run. Even though they ran at their homes on their own lake, it was always fun to go to new locations, smell new scents, and enjoy the different scenery. It was still dark out, a billion stars lighting the sky, the moon growing fuller, which meant that Candice and Owen would have more trouble fighting the urge to shift when the full moon was here. At least Hans, Slade, and Sheri didn't have any issue with it.

They all went out to run in a different direction, biting at the snowflakes swept off nearby trees, hearing the howling of a wolf pack off in the distance. Slade howled and so did everyone in their pack. The wild wolves weren't the only ones to be out here claiming their territory.

Everything was covered in a fresh coating of white. It must have snowed last night after they all went to bed. The cold, crisp air felt great on their faces, their tails held high, their fur fluffed out. They nipped at each other, played chase, and just had fun. Every time Hans tried to take down his sister, Slade thwarted him. It was a natural instinct for Slade to react that way as her mate, though he would have done it before they were mated too. He knew Hans was just play fighting like they all were, but he had to protect Sheri. No one but Sheri went after Candice either, for the same reason. In that case, Owen let the women have their fun. If Hans or Slade had gone after Candice, Owen would have been there to stop them from reaching her. Again, in fun. But Hans was Sheri's brother, so the dynamics between them were a little different. Still, Hans didn't stand a chance when Slade was protecting Sheri.

Which seemed to please Hans immensely. He appeared to be much more interested in tackling Slade every time he thwarted him from trying to take down Sheri. Slade was getting a kick out of it. Owen didn't seem to mind that he was a little left out, though he did tackle Slade once and Hans another time for good measure to show he could. And he played with Candice when Slade, Sheri, and Hans were mixing it up.

Then they happily trotted back to the cabin but saw a vehicle parked there and a man knocking at the door. Now what?

When the man realized no one was home, he left a card on the door. A salesman? Surely not out here in the wilderness. For a moment, Slade was worried it might be the owner or manager of the lodge and cabins who was upset with them for all the police traffic they'd had at the cabin, wondering if they had caused trouble while they were there.

The man finally had stood out in the cold long enough, really not dressed to be out here for any length of time, so he got into his car and drove off. When he was way down the road, Slade hurried to the cabin, shifted, and unlocked the door, then went inside. The others raced across the snowy field from where they'd been hiding in the woods and entered the cabin. Slade had already pulled on his boxer briefs and pants. Once they were all inside, he shut the door and locked it and the others shifted.

"Who in the world was that?" Sheri asked.

"A reporter," Slade said as they all got dressed, while he read the business card the man left behind.

"Oh, that's just what we need. A reporter snooping around while we're running as wolves," Candice said.

They all knew the hazards of having reporters trying to learn what they could about the wolves and the wolves trying to keep what they were undercover.

"What does he want?" Hans asked, pulling on a thermal sweatshirt.

"Probably something to do with this case concerning the downed plane," Slade guessed.

"If that's all it is, we're okay," Sheri said. "What do you want to do until lunchtime? Go for a snowshoe hike—not in the direction of the crash site?"

Everyone laughed.

Slade figured they would want to continue to do outdoor activities since this was the only full day they had here. Tomorrow, checkout was by half past ten so they would need to do something early before they packed up and left.

"Tonight, we have to stay up late and watch the aurora borealis if it appears," Candice said.

"Absolutely. It's gorgeous out here. Like at home, but even better here because there are no lights on the lake so the northern lights are even more showy and vibrant," Sheri said.

They all got dressed warmly to go a different direction for the hike so that they were on a portage for two miles, then crossed the frozen lake and ended up on an island. It looked like the windstorm hadn't touched the island, but that was the way it was in the BWCA. One place would get hit with a storm while another was left untouched.

They snowshoed around the island and saw a fox take off from behind a tree. A bunny was hiding very still in the underbrush and Slade figured it had been trying to avoid being the fox's lunch, but now it worried about the humans wandering around on the island.

"We need to schedule a stay at the cabin when we can paddle on the lakes and waterways, though it's really fun to be able to access the islands and all by crossing the frozen water on skis or snowshoes." Candice peered down at the ice at the edge of the beach.

"What do you see?" Sheri asked.

"A dead body."

Sheri frowned and everyone drew closer. Owen laughed. "A story idea, betcha."

"Yes, can't you see it?" Candice asked. "I know it's not a very Christmassy thought for this time of year, but I'm thinking that with the winter freeze coming on, someone had drowned in the lake and then a camper sees the body floating face up."

Murder mysteries were Candice's specialty. Slade and all the other wolves loved how her mind worked.

"I was afraid that the person you were seeing in the lake, who obviously isn't there, was the pilot hired to fly Gerard's plane," Sheri said.

Candice laughed. "Sorry, I had forgotten about that." She looked up at the sky. "Up there, really high in the sky is an eagle soaring in the heavens. What a beautiful sight."

"For real?" Sheri looked in the direction Candice was talking about it.

"Yes." Candice smiled. "For real."

Slade caught sight of it too. It was nice taking a breather and just seeing the wildlife that lived all around them in the wilderness. There wasn't anyone out here. Not as many people liked to visit the BWCA in the wintertime. It was untouched, beautiful, a white wonderland, quiet and still.

They finally started to walk again, exploring the island, and then headed back to the cabin to have lunch. "Okay, how about we quickly climb to the top of the towering 400-foot cliffs where we can see beautiful views of Canada and beyond after lunch? We haven't gotten around to doing that yet," Slade said.

"Yeah, that's exactly something I would like to do," Hans said.

So that was the plan. When they returned to the cabin, they made ravioli for lunch that Candice had brought with her, and while she was baking it, Sheri started beef bourguignon in a slow cooker for dinner.

After they had lunch, they packed up to hike on the Border Route Trail, taking a spur and then finally reaching the top of the cliffs.

Man, this was spectacular.

They all took pictures of the view, of each other, of the group, and then finally began to make their way down the cliffs.

When they reached the base, Sheri got a call. She answered it, wondering who would be calling her now. It was Conway. "Hey, you were right. Danbury owns a green Jeep Wagoneer and Otis owns a red Ford pickup, the ones we saw in the video. You do good work."

"Yes!"

"So we know Otis and Danbury were involved in the actual theft of the merchandise. We just still need to prove Fitz was responsible. When we questioned the two men, they lawyered up."

"I'll see what I can learn and let you know."

"Thanks, that sounds good."

Then they ended the call and Sheri smiled at her companions. Slade gave her a hug. She told them what had happened, and everyone cheered her for the good news. Yeah, this was great. But she still needed to find evidence to prove Gerard was innocent and learn where he was now.

Chapter 22

When they were back at the cabin, Slade was so glad Sheri had started a slow cooker of beef bourguignon that afternoon. Everyone was cold, and after the physical workout, they were hungry. The aroma of the beef bourguignon had greeted them before they even reached the door, and Slade heard Owen's stomach grumbling.

Candice rubbed Owen's back and chuckled. "Am I glad you started a meal earlier," Candice said.

"That's one of my favorite dishes that Sheri makes," Hans said. "She makes the best beef bourguignon. I've never eaten better."

"That's because I always feed it to you when you are really hungry," Sheri said.

Everyone laughed.

Once they removed their outerwear, Slade and Candice began setting the table, getting water for everyone, while Hans made hot cocoa and Sheri cooked the noodles. Then she served up the dinner.

"Later, I'll make hot buttered rum to have on the deck and we can watch the northern lights if they appear," Slade said.

"That sounds good," Hans agreed as he got a fire going in the woodburning stove.

They were starting to get warmed up, so by the time they finished eating, they would be feeling warm enough to sit out in the cold again. But they would have a fire going in the firepit and blankets too.

"Oh boy, this is so good," Candice said. "I would ask for the recipe since I wasn't paying attention when you were working on it while I was making lunch, but I'm sure I wouldn't make it taste half as good as you do."

Sheri smiled. "That was like when a friend of mine would make a special chicken, broccoli, and cheese dinner that was so good, but when she gave me the recipe and I made it, it didn't taste half as good. When I told her that, she admitted she had made it for so many years, she just added things without really measuring all that well, so a little more cheese, a few more spices, a little more—I think more likely a lot more—sour cream and it was sooo good."

"Oh yeah, I know just what you mean," Candice said. "So that means you just have to fix it for us when we have celebrations or for a special treat from time to time."

Sheri laughed. "I can certainly do that."

That evening, they enjoyed hot buttered rum and s'mores and talked about Sheri and Slade's trip to Silver Town.

"We'll be back before the full moon is here," Sheri reassured them.

Owen clinked his glass with hers. "That's a good thing. When you and Elizabeth arrived, it was perfect once you had your PI licenses. Elizabeth said she's feeling much better now so we'll be able to help with more of the cases again."

"I'm just glad I have a job where I don't have to worry

about the timing of a shift," Candice said. "Though I have to admit there are times when I get some great scene ideas forming in my mind when I'm a wolf and can't write them down."

"She paces a lot when that happens," Owen said. "And once she's able to shift back, she's totally focused on writing down the scenes."

"Yeah, before I forget them!"

Sheri was just glad she didn't have any shifting issues and neither did Slade, especially for when they had kids of their own. Elizabeth would be fortunate for the same reason, though Gavin wouldn't be able to help her with the twins when he had to shift. But everyone else who hadn't shifted would help her with the babies if she needed their assistance.

The next morning, they ran as wolves first thing, wanting to enjoy the morning in the BWCA for the little bit of time they were there. They had just as much fun as they did the other times they ran as wolves together.

Then they had breakfast of eggs and potatoes casserole, filled with onions and bell peppers and topped with cheddar cheese. Slade made them mimosas to celebrate their last meal here in the BWCA and at the cabin.

They sat down to eat and made toasts.

"This has been delightful," Candice said. "Thanks for sharing your cabin space with us."

"Yeah, fishing, hiking, mountain climbing, digging out

buried treasure, running as wolves, visiting with you all... It's been grand," Owen said.

"I'm glad I finally was well enough to come here and stay with you too," Hans said.

"Yeah, we had a ball with all of you being here." Sheri raised her glass and took another sip.

Slade was glad everyone had come to visit with them for the last two and a half days. It had made the stay even more special.

Then they finished their breakfast. Since they had to leave by half past ten that morning, they all hurried to pack, cleaned up, and carried their bags and gear out to the vehicles. They had to sweep the snow off the vehicles too.

Hans took all his camping gear that they had used. "When do you want us to help you move?"

"Sheri and I are going to her place first when we get home to unpack all our equipment. Since it's Sunday, we could pack up all my stuff after that while everyone's off from work," Slade said.

"Yeah, that works for me," Sheri said.

"For us too," Candice said. "I'm starting on a new deadline book on Monday, so I'm all for getting this done when we get back. We'll just drop off our camping things at the house and then meet you at the apartment."

"Okay, I'll call Cameron and tell him what we're going to do." Slade still couldn't see all of them showing up to help. Especially Amelia and Gavin because of their young twins. "Hey, Cameron, we're going to be home by noon, and Hans, Candice, and Owen said everyone wanted to help me move to Sheri's house, but I don't expect that. We'll have a pizza party at the office afterward."

"We'll help set up the office retreat room for the pizza party. You know Faith. She loves to organize parties," Cameron said.

Slade laughed. "Yeah, and we love that she does. Okay, we'll see whoever wants to come by the apartment when we get there."

It was a three-hour drive home and they caravanned there together. But then Candice and Owen headed to their house to unload their things and Hans dropped by his apartment to leave his stuff off. Slade and Sheri likewise went to her apartment first to empty his vehicle of camping equipment, food, and their bags so they could pack his things up from his apartment.

When they arrived at Slade's apartment, they found a big surprise. Everyone was arriving there with packing boxes, including their parents. And Dulcie too! Slade and Sheri hugged everyone.

Amelia and Gavin transported their babies in their carriers and set them in the living room while everyone, including Cameron and Faith's kids, were packing boxes, taping them up, and loading them into various vehicles. Some of the duplicate frying and saucepans, silverware, dishes, and other items they didn't need were boxed up and would be donated to charities.

Faith had brought bottles of water to keep everyone hydrated, while Candice, Owen, and Hans shared fish tales. "But Sheri still caught the biggest fish. Maybe we can have our pack fish fry when we return from our ski trip to Silver Town," Slade said. Everyone loved the idea.

It took only an hour and a half with all the help they had to finish packing and hauling the boxes to Sheri's apartment. They unloaded them there and would organize it later. They all headed over to the office to have pizza after that. They turned on the Christmas lights and played Christmas music. The room had been decorated with balloons, and a banner of congratulations hung overhead.

Slade and Sheri laughed. "Thanks for doing this for us," she said.

"Yeah, thanks," Slade said.

"Naturally. It's our pleasure." Faith motioned to the boxes of freshly delivered pizzas. "Dig in."

After all the congratulations and hugs, they started getting pieces of pizza and setting them on Santa paper plates. The kids had ginger ales with a splash of cranberry juice for a Christmassy appeal. Slade made Christmas margaritas and Amelia and Elizabeth both had hot cocoas.

They settled down to eat their pizzas and drink.

Cameron said, "We'll have to let Elizabeth start working some of these harder cases since she's feeling much better. We sure lucked out when we helped train you two ladies to be PI partners."

"Yeah," Gavin said. "It's perfect for us being able to take off on trips when we need to and still cover our clients' needs. But also with the full moon coming, you both have been a godsend."

"Oh, will you be all right without me being here when we go to Silver Town?" Sheri asked.

Slade and Sheri wouldn't be gone when the moon was

at its fullest, so he figured the other royals would jump in to help in any way that they could if the nonroyals had issues.

"Yeah, we're good," Cameron said.

"That's for sure," both of Sheri's parents said.

Georgia started making another margarita for everyone who wanted one. "Whatever we need to do to help, we will. If Fred is busy with builders on the house he's working on now, I'll come and do anything you need me to. I don't have any baby deliveries to take care of anytime soon."

Elizabeth said, "I'm back at the office full time. I might need an afternoon nap, but I'm not having any morning sickness any longer."

"Well, I have police resources and I can take off a couple of days from work and serve in the capacity of a PI," Dulcie said.

Dulcie! Slade had forgotten that she was trained in investigations, though he wouldn't have considered she would actually take off work and come to their aid. She was going to fit in nicely as one of their pack members.

"We should have congratulated you for being our newest pack member," Faith said.

"I'm so glad to find a pack to belong to. Though I'm a gray wolf," Dulcie said.

"So are we, only the Arctic wolf variety of gray wolf," Hans said.

Then Fred began talking about house plans with Sheri and Slade, showing them a bunch of different plans for homes on his phone. "Oh, I like this one," Sheri said.

Slade would be happy with any house that Sheri picked

out. It would be nicer than their apartments: larger, more spacious, a bigger kitchen, more room for parties.

Cameron brought out a map and showed them the lot they would have to build their home on. Slade smiled. He couldn't believe Fred and Cameron had brought the map for the site of their home and blueprint plans to help them get started on this right away.

They were thrilled and even though Slade was leaving it to Sheri to decide on the home, she roped him in to make some suggestions too. They agreed on a one-story, with three bedrooms, three baths, an open kitchen and living room, and a den. It would fit the style of homes the other wolves had, blending in with the woods, and a lot of native trees would surround it in keeping with the wild state. They would be sitting on the lake too.

"No need to pay for the land. I inherited a bundle and Owen and I gifted the land to you," Candice said.

"Oh, wow, thanks so much," Sheri said.

"All you need to pay for are the permits and materials for the house. Georgia and I are absorbing the costs of building the home," Fred said.

Slade's dad said, "We're donating the costs of materials for the home."

So surprised, Slade and Sheri thanked them both.

"The rest of us are going to put in some money toward furniture for your wedding gift since you have a furnished apartment and will need some when you move in," Amelia said.

"Oh, absolutely," Sheri said.

Dulcie was listening with rapt interest, appearing

intrigued as to how the pack worked. Slade knew she'd fit right in. "Put me on the list for furniture buying."

"Mommy said we're making something special for your house," Nick said.

"Yeah," Corey said and opened his mouth to speak further, but his triplet sister stopped him.

"But it's a secret," Angie said. Faith and Cameron smiled.

"Wow, thanks to all of you for everything," Sheri said.

"Yeah, you all are amazing," Slade said.

"On another topic, is everyone all set for the Santa Seaplane Toy Drop?" Henry asked.

"Oh, absolutely," Sheri said, squeezing Slade's hand.

"I sure am ready," Slade said. "I've even been practicing my ho-ho-hos."

Everyone laughed.

Dulcie smiled. "I didn't realize that the wolf pack was involved in all that."

"Yeah, the Whites wanted to do it and all of us got involved," Faith said.

"I'll be there with a couple of officers for crowd control and to make sure only the kids that are supposed to receive the toys get them," Dulcie said.

"We're going to be elves, Momma says," Angie said.

It truly would be a whole pack affair.

———————

Slade and Sheri were glad that they could get started on the plans for the house right away. Then there was some discussion about the wedding for the summer, but they would go over more details for that later.

Everyone was just thrilled about them mating, though, and Cameron and Faith and the kids were excited they were going to build on the other side of them.

Both Slade and Sheri's parents were hoping they would have grandchildren soon—though Slade's parents were already enjoying Amelia and Gavin's twins. But for Sheri's parents, this would be their first.

"Are you sure you weren't faking being sick so that I would go with Slade instead on the camping trip?" Sheri teased Hans.

Hans laughed. "I knew the two of you needed the time to get together, but no, believe me, that was totally unplanned."

Faith and her kids had even made a large brownie cake with *Congratulations, Sheri and Slade* on it and after everyone was finished with their pizza, they all had brownies.

Slade wondered if Sheri wanted to run with the others as wolves, a closing celebration activity for the evening. She seemed to sense what he was thinking and took hold of his hand and squeezed. "Does anyone want to go for a wolf run?" she asked.

They were here where they could run in the woods as wolves without any issues. Once they were at their apartment, they couldn't run as wolves, so this was a nice way to do it with the pack.

After a beautiful night there in celebration, running with the pack afterward and returning to shift and dress, everyone said their goodbyes. Sheri and Slade returned to her apartment, saw all the boxes stacked up all over the place, sighed, and went off to the bathroom to shower.

"I can't believe we went to the cabin together and you ended up permanently living with me at my apartment upon our return," Sheri said as they washed each other in the shower.

"I can't believe it either since I'd intended to ask you once Hans and I returned home. It worked out better than I could ever have arranged it."

She laughed. "And here I had planned to ask you to mate me when you returned."

"At least we were on the same page, and I'm so glad."

They left the shower, dried off, and walked into the bedroom where more stacks of boxes towered around the room. They would sort things later when they could. It was late and they went to bed to make love because that was all that was important for now.

Chapter 23

THE NEXT DAY, SHERI BEGAN WORKING ON HER CASE AT the office while Slade was busy trying to organize his clothes and other items he'd brought to her apartment. He had already given written notice for his place.

Sheri started really digging into the business of Gerard having a girlfriend. She wanted to see Gerard's cousin, Mr. Lincoln, who lived in Minneapolis and whom they had rescued after he had his heart attack in the BWCA. Maybe he would know who Gerard was seeing. His brother might, but she figured Fitz wouldn't tell her. The problem was if Fitz did know and he was out to get his brother, he might think the same thing as she did—that Gerard was with a girlfriend.

Since Sheri still had Mr. Lincoln's wife's phone number, she called her. "Hi, this is Sheri and I spoke to you before in the BCWA when your husband had his heart attack. How is he doing?"

"He's home, grouchy because his doctor put him on restrictions. Thanks for calling about him."

"You're welcome. I'm just so glad we found him before he got worse. I'm also trying to locate his cousin Gerard Connolly for his wife, Betty. Would you or your husband have any idea where Gerard might be?"

"We don't know where he is." Nancy sounded harried.

"Do you know if he was seeing someone else—another woman?" Sheri asked, though she really wanted to ask Lincoln because he might know more about his cousin than his wife.

"No."

Sheri wondered why Nancy was so abrupt with her, like she had something to hide. "Can I speak to Lincoln?"

"Oh, I'm afraid not, dear. He's sleeping right now. That's the only time when he's not being a grouch."

"Okay, can you have him call me back when he wakes?"

"Sure."

"Thanks." But Sheri wasn't sure that Nancy had any intention of doing that.

Gerard and Lincoln might not associate with each other. Even if they did, Gerard could have been really secretive about having an affair so his cousin could be clueless about it.

She wished she could check to see who might have a pilot's license in the area, which would narrow down her options, but she still needed a name to investigate records.

She began looking into Gerard's social media postings again, though she hadn't found anything before to indicate where he was or if he had a girlfriend. But now that she knew he was supposed to have one, she might learn more about her. And then she discovered a clue that she could check into further—a girl of about twenty named Jessica Gardener had posted a happy birthday message to Gerard a week ago. She hadn't seen any other postings from Jessica, but when she checked out her profile, Sheri thought she bore a striking resemblance to Gerard—the same dark-brown eyes, round face, and smile.

She checked Jessica's pages. There were pictures of her and her friends, tons of them, but none of them showed Jessica being with Gerard. But then Sheri saw that Jessica had been excited to earn her pilot's license six months earlier. She checked the records, and sure enough, Jessica had a pilot's license. Had Gerard taught her how to fly?

Ohmigod, could Gerard have given her the job of flying his plane and carrying the stolen merchandise? Putting her life at risk? Her freedom?

What if...What if Jessica was his daughter from a union between Gerard and some other woman early in his marriage to Betty? And Fitz knew it and was blackmailing Gerard over it? Gerard could be afraid of losing his wife if she learned of it.

Sheri wanted to contact Jessica, but she was afraid to spook her. Cameron was busy on a case, so she walked into Owen's office. "Hey, okay, so I found a possible pilot that might have flown Gerard's plane, but it's weird. Jessica Gardener wished him a happy birthday, but there haven't been any postings of her with him. There's an uncanny resemblance between Jessica and Gerard. She's about twenty years younger than him. What if she's his—"

"Daughter, but not Betty's."

"Right. And Betty doesn't know about it."

"That's possibly what Fitz was blackmailing Gerard over then."

Sheri agreed. "It's bad enough that he might have had a girlfriend on the side, but a secret baby too? So I wondered how to approach this situation. I'm afraid to just contact Jessica to see if she knows anything about what's going on and then the cat is out of the bag. On the other hand, if she cares about her father and I tell her I'm trying to clear his name about the stolen merchandise and keep him safe, maybe she'll be honest with me."

"She might not buy it."

"That's what I'm afraid of."

"I think you need to meet her face-to-face and talk to her. Show her your credentials. Prove you're a PI and not one of Fitz's henchmen," Owen said.

"Okay. Maybe I can convince her that I'm only concerned about Gerard's safety."

"But you're working for Betty."

"Right. I'll think of something. Thanks," Sheri said. That was the interesting thing about this job. Every case was totally unique, involving different individuals, so they had to come up with different ways to solve them.

Sheri left Owen's office and tried calling Jessica. "Hi, Jessica Gardener?"

"Yes."

"I'm calling you about—" Sheri paused. She was so afraid she was going to screw up this case big time and possibly lose her only contact who might know where Gerard was. Sheri could pull a legitimate PI's ploy, or even a police detective's con, and say she had money Jessica had won or something to get her to meet with Sheri. But she just couldn't bring herself to do it with Jessica. Maybe because Sheri felt sorry for the young woman because her existence had to be kept a secret from Betty all these years. Of course, that was *if* Jessica was Gerard's daughter.

"Okay, listen, I'm trying to locate Gerard Connolly. I'm a PI, but I was involved in finding Gerard's plane wreckage and helping the police to recover some of the stolen merchandise that had been on that plane. My boyfriend and I saved Gerard's cousin after he had a heart attack in the Boundary Waters Canoe Area. Gerard's brother came to pick up Mr. Lincoln's dog, Jet, and his camping equipment, and we learned later that he was involved in the whole business of the stolen goods. One of his friends even shot at us."

"No," Jessica said, sounding shocked.

Sheri was glad Jessica was still listening to her and hadn't just hung up on her yet.

"Yeah, and at the police too. Anyway, I know Gerard's worried Fitz is wanting to take him down for this business and Gerard wasn't involved. His wife has hired me to make sure he's safe and he's found innocent of all charges."

"Why did you call me then? What do I have to do with any of this?" Jessica asked, sounding defensive.

"Fitz was blackmailing Gerard into delivering the goods, but the plane crashed." Sheri sighed. She might as well say what she had to say. "I believe you have a vested interest in Gerard staying alive."

Jessica didn't say anything.

"Okay, look, I believe Gerard doesn't want Betty to divorce him, but Fitz knew his brother had a love child."

Jessica gasped.

"I want both of you to be safe. I want Fitz and his friends

to be in jail for what they have been involved in. I don't want anyone to get hurt. You might have heard that one of Fitz's cohorts ended up getting shot by one of the police. He was the one who shot at them. He's in the hospital now."

"Um…"

"I'm not going to tell anyone who you are or what your relationship is to Gerard, but I need to talk with him. I need to prove he's not behind these thefts."

"I'll… I'll call him and see if he wants to talk to you."

"All right. Thanks, Jessica. And seriously, I'm not telling Betty about any of this. It's up to him to come clean about you if he wants."

"Thanks."

Then Sheri gave her phone number to Jessica and hoped she would get a message to Gerard, and he would call her.

"How did it go?" Owen asked, poking his head into Sheri's office.

"Well, time will tell. I talked to Jessica, and now it's in her court. I asked her to have Gerard call me. We'll see if it works or not."

"Okay, good. Let me know if you need me to help you with anything more concerning the case."

"I sure will. Thanks, Owen." Then Sheri got a call. She thought it might be Gerard, until she saw it was Slade. His call was most welcome. "It's Slade."

Owen smiled, then left her office.

Chapter 24

Eager to talk to her mate, Sheri answered Slade's call. "Hey, what are you up to?"

"I had a couple of tours of the pristine winter scenes over the BCWA after making more of a mess of my stuff in your apartment, but I'm done for now and it's lunchtime. Do you have some free time so you can have a bite to eat with me?"

"Oh, absolutely." The good thing about Sheri's job was that she could take calls while she was anywhere, if Gerard happened to get back with her.

"Good. How does the Boathouse Brewpub and Restaurant sound?" Slade asked.

"That's the place where you were going to take me before you had the flight to drop off the momma dog and puppies before the cabin stay."

"Yes."

"Oh, yes. I wanted to have one of their fresh burgers with mushrooms and Swiss cheese."

"You've got it! I'll be right over to pick you up."

"See you soon." Sheri waved to Cameron and Owen and said, "I'm having lunch out with Slade. See you later."

"Enjoy it for us," Cameron called out.

"Yeah, enjoy," Owen said.

"We will."

Then Sheri heard Slade's vehicle drive up. He must have been on the way to the office when he had called her. She pulled on her parka, gloves, and hat and went out to meet him. He got out of his vehicle and gave her a warm hug and kiss.

Then he got her door for her. "If you couldn't have gone out to eat, I was going to bring you something."

"You're so sweet and totally spoiling me," Sheri said, loving the attention.

"I'll be busier during the other seasons, so for now, I want to make this special for us. Besides, we missed our dinner date at the restaurant, so I wanted to make sure we still had time to do it, and I'm serious about the mess in the apartment. I didn't have time enough to do a lot of sorting and putting stuff away before I had the missions to fly."

"We'll get it done," she said. How hard could it be?

Then they arrived at the brewpub and went inside to see it all decorated for Christmas. "I know you're still working. I don't have any scheduled trips for this afternoon, so—"

"You're going to have a drink."

Slade smiled. "I've been wanting to try the blueberry blond."

She laughed as they took their seats and started looking at the menu. "It's a good thing we're mated. I might worry about you being interested in some blond otherwise. I'm getting the chocolate rye porter. And of course the mushroom burger and fries."

"I'm getting the bacon Gouda patty melt."

After they ordered their food and drinks, Slade asked Sheri, "So how is your investigation into Gerard coming along?"

Sheri got a call on her phone and saw it was from Jessica, not Gerard. She sighed. "Hold that question," she said to Slade, then answered the call. "Jessica?"

"Yeah. Gerard wants to know what you know about me."

"You're his daughter," Sheri guessed, "and he trained you to be a pilot. He has been taking care of you as much as he can, seeing you as much as he can. Caring for you."

"He has. I guess you could say he has been leading somewhat of a double life. He truly loves Betty. He always has and he doesn't want to lose her. I know people—his brother too—say that Gerard only stayed with her because of her money, but it isn't true."

"Because of the prenuptial agreement?"

"Yeah."

"So Fitz knew about the affair," Sheri said.

"Yeah. Fitz was with my dad when he met my mom at a restaurant. He knew all about their affair. The affair with my mother was a mistake. And he'd only been with her for a couple of nights when they were young, but they really didn't get along. When my mom learned she was pregnant with me, Gerard did everything he could to make sure I had everything I needed, including sending me away to college when it came time for that. He was sure Betty would divorce him over it, but he never had the courage to tell her the truth."

Sheri had a hard time believing Gerard hadn't told Betty because he loved her. "Okay, so why did your dad ask you to fly the plane? He must have known Fitz was up to no good. Why put you in that predicament?"

"Me? I didn't fly the plane."

"Who did then?"

"My dad wouldn't tell me."

"Will Gerard meet with me?"

"He's afraid to meet with anyone," Jessica said.

"I have to talk with him, even if it's just on the phone."

Their food was delivered to the table then. Sheri was glad that Slade didn't seem to mind that she was working on the case during their lunch date.

"All right. I'll tell him. You really are going to help him and not tell Betty about me or my mom?"

"Yes, I'm here to help him, and I'm not going to tell anyone about you and your dad, though I wonder how many people already know the truth besides Fitz."

"I–I don't know. Okay, I'll call him and get back to you one way or another."

"Thanks, Jessica." They ended the call and Sheri smiled at Slade. "Sorry about that."

"No problem. I'm glad I get to hear a little bit of what's going on."

Then they began eating their delicious burgers.

"So what do you think? Will Betty divorce Gerard when she learns the truth about his daughter?" Slade asked.

"I really don't know. The affair was long ago, so maybe not. When I was doing a search about Gerard and Betty, I learned they never had any kids. And Jessica can't help that she was born in that situation."

"Do you think he truly loves Betty and his not coming clean about his daughter doesn't have anything to do with the prenuptial?" Slade asked, lifting his hamburger to take another bite.

"I suspect the money has something to do with it, but maybe not. When it comes to fickle human relationships, I don't have a clue." Sheri sipped some more of her drink. "Now this is good."

"Mine is too." He asked then, "Will Gerard talk to you?"

"I sure hope so. What do you have planned for this afternoon?"

"I have to be up for any calls that come in. Tomorrow's my Santa gig. You're flying with me, right? Unless you have something that comes up concerning Gerard's case."

"Oh, absolutely." Sheri didn't get a call while they were eating, so she figured Gerard still didn't want to speak with her.

Slade paid for their meals and drove her back to the office. "I'll make dinner for us if I get off early."

"That sounds like a winner." Sheri loved how things were working out between them and their jobs so far. In the summer when Slade was so busy, things would change, but she was looking forward to all of it. She would be the one to make fun meals if he had long days.

"Good luck on your case," Slade said. "If Gerard wants to meet you and I don't have a flying commitment, let me know and I'll take you to meet him."

"All right, that sounds good."

Then they kissed and hugged. He left her at her office and drove off.

She filled Cameron and Owen in on the new developments in Gerard's case and began looking more into Jessica's background when she got a call from Betty. Ugh. Sheri wished Gerard would have just come clean with Betty and relieve her of having to keep the secrets.

"Hello, Betty."

"Yes, I wanted to call you and tell you Gerard called me. He said he couldn't talk, but he wanted me to know he loved me with all his heart. I'm so worried about him. Have you gotten any clues about where he is?"

This was the hard part. Not that Sheri knew where Gerard was. Still, she had a lot of new information about him that she couldn't share, even though Betty was her client.

"You're my only client and I'm working full time on this case. I'm sure I'll know something before long. I'm waiting to hear back on a couple of calls and have several leads right now. I'll let you know as soon as I have confirmed anything," Sheri said.

"Okay, thanks. I'm sorry if I sound impatient, but I really want Gerard to be all right."

"Yes, I totally understand. I would feel the same way as you, given the same circumstances." Betty really sounded sincere. Would she still feel that way if she knew the truth about Gerard's daughter? Then Sheri got another call on her cell phone and said to Betty, "I have an incoming call. It might be about Gerard. I need to go."

"Thanks. Let me know if you learn anything."

"I sure will." Then Sheri picked up the other call. It was from Jessica again.

"Gerard told me to tell you to meet me at a location and then I'll take you to where he is so you can talk to him."

Then Jessica gave her directions on how to reach her.

Sheri called Slade after that, but he didn't answer, so she called his mother, who scheduled all the plane trips.

"Hi, Sheri," Lolita said. "If you're trying to get ahold of Slade, he had a flight to take a pet to a new owner. He won't be longer than about two hours."

"Okay, thanks. I'll see him later then." Sheri hoped he didn't get upset with her for not waiting for him to go with her. Both Owen and Cameron were working on their own cases, but she let them know where she was going to and then headed out to the rendezvous site to meet up with Jessica. She called her just to let her know that she was coming alone.

When she finally reached the hotel where Jessica was waiting for her outside, Sheri recognized the pretty brunette right away from her Facebook photos. Sheri waved at her, and Jessica quickly joined her.

"Sheri Whitmore," she said, offering her gloved hand to Jessica.

"Hi, and thanks for wanting to help us," Jessica said. "After I spoke with you the first time, I checked the newspapers and read that you had done everything you had said—saving Mr. Lincoln, investigating Gerard's plane crash, even saving some other people during that awful storm. You and Slade White. We'll go in your car, all right?"

"Yeah, sure."

They got into Sheri's car and then Jessica made a call. "I'm with Sheri now. Her boyfriend couldn't make it. All right.

We'll go there." She ended the call and gave Sheri directions to a house.

"Who knows about this house?" Sheri asked, wanting to make sure Gerard would be safe there.

"No one. My grandparents on my mother's side owned it and when my mother passed, I inherited it. Normally, I rent it out, but the last renters moved out a few weeks ago, so my dad has been staying there."

"Fitz and his friends don't know about it though?" Sheri asked. If they knew about Jessica and her mother and the affair, then they might have learned Jessica inherited her grandparents' home.

"No one does," Jessica said.

Sheri hoped she was right.

When they arrived at the house, they went to the door and Jessica unlocked it. They walked inside and Gerard greeted them from the kitchen. "You're the PI my wife hired."

"Yes, Sheri Whitmore. You have to tell Betty about your past and about Jessica. It's the only way Fitz won't have a hold over you. He can't blackmail you if Betty knows about it, unless there's something else your brother has on you."

"No, nothing else. I just know Betty will want to divorce me over this, and I truly love her. I made that one mistake shortly after we were married, and I never wandered again."

"But since I was the result of it, he always had to worry about Betty learning about me," Jessica said.

"The thing of it is, Fitz is going to tell Betty or threaten you with it for the rest of your life. But I wonder why he didn't do this beforehand," Sheri said. "Why wait all these years until now?"

"He didn't know that I'd had a child. And he wanted to do this heist. Though someone else might be in charge of it. I'm not sure."

"Who did you hire to pilot the plane then?" Sheri asked.

"I didn't. I told Fitz I was going to fly it, but then I took off so he couldn't force me to pilot the plane. I really didn't believe he would hire anyone else to fly my plane. When I didn't show up for the appointed hour, Fitz must have gotten another pilot."

"Who would he be able to hire who could fly the plane?"

"I don't know. I mean, our cousin, Tex Lincoln, flies, but I know he wouldn't have done it. I don't know who else Fitz knows. Drug runners? But Fitz was mad enough to want to kill me because I didn't go along with the plan, the plane crashed, and he lost the stolen merchandise."

"But he didn't tell Betty about what he knew," Sheri said.

"True, he didn't. I figure if he doesn't kill me, he'll want me to fly another mission. Except now I don't have a plane."

"And you're unreliable." Sheri couldn't imagine Fitz trusting his brother to follow through on another case, if he tried to steal more merchandise and transport it the same way as before. "Has Fitz done any criminal activities before?"

"He was always stealing stuff when we were kids. Then he hooked up with Otis and Danbury and they decided on a bigger heist. But I don't know if they had done other ones before they wanted me to ferry the merchandise to New Mexico."

"Your brother didn't seem to like your cousin, Lincoln, all that much."

Gerard thought about that for a while. "Do you want a drink of something?"

"Water, if you don't mind."

"I'll get it," Jessica said.

"So about your cousin—" Sheri began again. "Tell me more about why you might think he could have been involved in this." Sheri always kept an open mind in the cases she worked because sometimes the most unlikely candidate could be the real culprit. Like Jessica even. She had a pilot's license too.

"Lincoln has talked about the ultimate theft where no one would be the wiser. Though I hadn't put two and two together before," Gerard said. "He has a pilot's license. It's like I said, he could have been the one flying my plane. He doesn't have his own plane any longer. I kind of dismissed the notion that he was a suspect when you found him in the BWCA having a heart attack a couple of weeks after the plane went down. If he'd been flying the plane and it had crashed, he most likely would have suffered a heart attack then and might not have survived."

Sheri was thinking the same thing.

Jessica brought in glasses of ice water. "We have to stop the charade, Dad. Sheri's right. You need to call Betty and tell her the truth. Maybe she'll hate you for it and she'll divorce you. Or maybe if Betty truly loves you like you love her, she'll be reasonable about it because it has been so many years since you had seen my mom. You can work things out. The truth is going to come out and it would be better if you told her."

They all sat down in the living room.

"All right, I'll do it," Gerard said, and got his phone out and made a call. "Hey, Betty. I need to tell you some things." Then he proceeded to tell her about the mistake he'd made that had resulted in having a daughter named Jessica. He didn't say anything for a while, then began to cry.

Sheri felt teary-eyed and saw that Jessica was too. What was Betty's response? She hoped Gerard's tears were of joy and not the sign of a breakup. But it had to be done.

"I'm so sorry. Yeah, okay. Uh—" Gerard looked at Sheri and smiled. "Yeah, Sheri is here, and she and Jessica convinced me to tell you. All right. Yeah. Okay. Sounds great." He gave her the address. "See you soon. Love you." He ended the call and as soon as he did, he looked like a huge weight had been lifted off his shoulders.

"Well, Dad, don't keep us in suspense," Jessica said. "Spill."

Gerard wiped away his tears with his hand. "Betty knew. All these years, she knew—about you, about your mother, all of it. She had hired a PI way back then and learned of it."

"And she never said anything to you about it?" Jessica asked, wiping away tears.

"No, she didn't. She was waiting for me to tell her. She didn't know that was what Fitz was blackmailing me over. She thought it was something else or she would have told me she already knew about the big secret."

"She's not divorcing you?"

"No. She wants to meet you. She wants you to come have Christmas with us. Or we might have it here if Fitz is still looking for my blood. She's coming here to see you right now. Well, the both of us."

Sheri smiled, glad that this part of the story, at least, was going to have a happy ending. "Okay, so then I need to talk to your cousin, Tex Lincoln, to learn if he knows anything about all this. I will use the ruse of checking on him to see if he's okay, after we found him having the heart attack in the BWCA."

"To learn if he flew the plane?" Jessica asked.

"Yes. And to learn if he was involved in stealing the merchandise."

"There's no need to learn if Tex piloted the plane. I flew it," Jessica said.

Shocked to hear the confession so freely given, Sheri didn't speak for a moment.

"No," her dad said, sounding just as astounded. Sheri was glad that her dad hadn't asked her to fly the illegal mission.

"Yeah. When you didn't fly, Fitz came to me and said he knew who I was, that I had access to the plane and a pilot's license and I had to fly it, or he was going to go to Betty and tell her all about the affair and about me. I did it because I knew you loved Betty and you were afraid she would divorce you." Jessica sniffled and wiped away tears.

Gerard gave her a hug. "I never wanted you involved in any of that."

"I had to do it for you."

"You crashed the plane. Thank God you weren't injured or killed."

"I had a dislocated shoulder, but I found a campsite about

a mile away. The guys who were camping there drove me home and I went to the hospital to have my shoulder fixed. I didn't tell the campers or you what had happened. I–I didn't really think the plane would be found until the spring. I have to admit I crashed it on purpose. I found the best place to land, based on stories you had told me about survivors of crashed airplanes. It was storming out, so I assumed it would cover the sound of the crash. I also had only enough fuel to make it there. I'd tested it out before they loaded the merchandise."

"What?" Gerard asked.

"I wanted to make sure they couldn't force you to fly for them again." Jessica wiped away more tears.

Sheri thought the world of Jessica for trying to save her father from his vengeful brother.

"Jessica."

"I did it for you."

"I'm sorry I didn't tell Betty a long time ago and got you mixed up in all this," Gerard said.

"It's going to work out," Jessica said.

"I agree. You just need to tell Betty the whole story." Sheri really thought it would work as long as Gerard was honest with her, and they talked things out. Not just now, but into the future. Fitz and the other men needed to be made to pay for their crimes though.

"I don't want to tell the police you were flying the plane," Gerard said to Jessica.

"They have to know, Dad. No more secrets. We need to tell the truth. I couldn't tell what was in the boxes, but I assumed the merchandise had been stolen. That's another reason I had to stop them. When I crashed the plane, I didn't recognize where I'd gone down exactly so I couldn't have given the police the coordinates."

"All right. We'll call them then."

"Call Conway King or Tanner Papadopoulos since they've been working the case. Tell them I'm here with you since I've also dealt with them while trying to help them find the stolen merchandise." Sheri didn't mention Dulcie because she was so new to their office, while the two detectives had been working this case all along.

"Okay." Gerard called Conway, and the officer said he and Tanner were on their way to their location, to stay put.

Chapter 25

WHEN CONWAY AND TANNER ARRIVED AT JESSICA'S house, they took both Gerard's and her statements. Now that they had more information, they could investigate further and pursue more charges against Fitz and his friends. They would look into Lincoln's involvement too, if he had any.

Then Betty arrived and talked to the police, corroborating Gerard's story. "But you need to put Fitz and the other men behind bars for what they have done."

"You'll be glad to know that after his hospital stay, Danbury was put in jail for attempting to kill police officers and Sheri's boyfriend, Slade. We'll deal with Fitz and Otis now that we have more of the story," Tanner said.

"We're having Christmas here," Betty said to Gerard, "and, Jessica, I've been waiting a long time to get to know you." She gave Jessica a heartwarming hug.

Sheri smiled as tears shimmered in her eyes and Jessica's.

Before Sheri left with the officers, Betty gave her a check. "Thanks again for your services. They were well worth it."

Sheri hadn't thought Betty would ever have used her services again, but she was glad it all had worked out well in the end. "We're always there for you anytime you might need our help."

"Hopefully, we won't, but if we do, we'll be sure to give you a call," Betty said.

Sheri left the house with the officers and Conway shook his head at her. "The White Wolf PIs have been helping us with cases ever since they arrived. But now they have a new investigator, and she's kicking butt too."

"Yeah, I totally agree," Tanner said.

Sheri laughed. She loved working with her PI partners, who made all the difference in the world because they really knew their stuff and taught it all to her and Elizabeth. Then she returned to the office and told everyone what was going on. Case solved. At least as far as she was concerned. The police would take it from there.

As soon as she arrived at the office to tell her partners what she had learned, she saw a Mrs. Claus suit sitting on her desk. It was a beautiful, long, red-velvet Victorian coat trimmed in white faux fur, elegant and perfect for cold weather. And suitable for Sheri to wear as a Mrs. Claus in front of a bunch of joyous kids eagerly waiting for presents from Santa!

All her partners joined her in her office—Elizabeth, David, Cameron, Owen, and Gavin smiled at her. Elizabeth said, "All of us got together and purchased it for you."

"Aww, this is gorgeous. I love it," Sheri said, running her hand over the plush material. "I can't wait to wear it tomorrow on the seaplane toy delivery."

Slade arrived at the office then. "Are you off for the rest

of the day?" Sheri asked, giving him a hug, then showed him the Mrs. Claus costume.

"Oh, now that's nice. You will make the perfect Mrs. Claus."

———————————

Slade hadn't had any other jobs to do and though he'd had a dog to deliver to his eager new family, Slade had wanted to be there for Sheri when she went to see Gerard. Though he knew when he got busy, he wouldn't be able to go with her on her cases. He just had been so involved in this one with her, he wanted to…well, protect her, if she had needed it, but also to learn what was going on with Gerard and everything else regarding this case.

"Yeah, I'm off and if you're done with your case…"

"I am." Sheri explained as much as she knew about the situation.

"So the daughter was the pilot," Slade said, surprised.

"Yeah, but the police will investigate claims further and if what she says is true about being forced to fly the plane, they didn't believe she would be up on any charges. They did tell her to get a lawyer, which I was glad for, just in case. The same for Gerard. That way, they would be better off if Fitz and his friends' lawyers tried to twist the story around."

"I'm glad it was resolved," Cameron said, and everyone agreed with him.

Then Slade and Sheri said goodbye to the other PIs and

drove home to their apartment. Slade had planned to make dinner for them, but he knew Sheri would be right there in the kitchen making dinner with him, as much as she liked to cook and assist. He enjoyed being mated to her and all that they did together.

He hoped she wouldn't be too upset with the mess he'd made while trying to dig out his clothes from the stacked boxes all over her place while he was trying to figure out where to stuff things. If they'd had a bigger house to move into, that would have been easy. But here, they were moving his things from a smaller apartment to hers that wasn't much bigger, and he would have to do some juggling.

Sheri looked at the disaster of the living room, just sighed, and walked past it, but then saw his Christmas stocking hanging next to hers on the mantel and her expression lit up. "You found your Christmas stocking."

"Yep. Santa hasn't filled it yet, but he filled yours."

She laughed. "I love it. I have my very own Santa Claus all to myself."

"Absolutely. But I don't expect Mrs. Claus to mend my socks."

"Good, because I don't sew things like that. Buttons, yes."

He cooked up spaghetti and meatballs, and then Sheri started preparing garlic toast while Slade got a bottle of wine and opened it. They finally finished making the meal and sat down to eat.

"You are a great PI."

"I got really lucky."

"If you had been someone else, or had approached Jessica

in the wrong way, you might not have solved the case. Or at least helped get some resolution on it as fast as you did."

"Well, thanks. I was glad to resolve it before Christmas. Hmm, so about tomorrow...Are you ready to play Santa?"

"I sure am."

———————

The next day Slade and Sheri dressed in their Santa and Mrs. Claus costumes at the airport, and she was so excited. She couldn't help but laugh when Slade ho-ho-hoed on the way to the snow-covered landing field to deliver the presents to the kids. All the wolf pack members were at the landing field to enjoy the fun.

Before they set down a few minutes later, they saw a couple hundred people there, all bundled up—families, kids, police, band members, eight carolers dressed in Victorian clothes singing Christmas songs, a television crew, and news reporters.

They landed on the snowy field and came to a stop. They had ended up with over a hundred presents for as many children. As soon as they landed, Slade and Sheri were having a ball. She gave him the gifts and then he handed them out to the kids while the band was playing Christmas songs.

Cameron and Faith served hot cocoa to warm the families that had shown up. Their triplets, dressed in elves' outfits, were handing out candy canes to all the kids, provided by a local grocery store, while they waited to receive their presents. The weather was perfect—cold, of course, but sunny and no wind, and that made it feel warmer.

The kids were thrilled to get their presents and the families were just as pleased that Henry and Lolita had set up the Santa Seaplane Toy Drop.

In truth, it was a pack affair since they had all been involved in gathering the toys for Christmas, the candy canes, hot chocolate, the band, and the Christmas carolers and getting the word out about the whole setup to the news media.

Dulcie waved at Slade and Sheri from where she was working to keep the peace. The only ones not there were Amelia, her mate, and the babies.

Once the gift giving was done and Slade and Sheri had some cocoa, they headed back to the plane and took off.

"That was so much fun," Sheri said, watching out the window as everyone waved at them.

"The kids and families were so happy. I thought that was a total success and I can't wait to do it again next year," Slade said.

"Me too. I'm all for it."

A few minutes later, he landed the seaplane at the airport and parked it. He removed his Santa outfit, while she slipped out of her Mrs. Claus suit and they dressed in their street clothes. Then they got in his SUV and headed back home.

"You know I would love to just go home and crash with you, but—"

"We have to make all my stuff magically disappear," Slade said. "Sorry, honey."

"We'll do it." At least Sheri sure hoped so. She hadn't realized how much of a neatnik she was until her apartment looked like a cyclone had hit it.

Chapter 26

THE MORNING BEFORE CHRISTMAS DAY SLADE GOT OFF the phone with his parents and said to Sheri, "My parents confirmed they are grilling steaks at their house for the Christmas Eve dinner. Your parents and Hans are all set to come. Amelia and Gavin will be there with the babies. And Elizabeth and David are coming."

"I'll make roasted garlic Parmesan baby potatoes," Sheri said.

"I'll help you with it. Amelia makes a creamy brussels-sprout bake that Mom always asks for."

"That sounds delicious."

"It is. Believe me."

"And tomorrow, my parents are hosting Christmas Day lunch. When we have a home of our own, we can take turns hosting one of the Christmas meals for the family."

"I agree. So for lunch tomorrow, my parents are bringing the turkey and stuffing, yours are having a glazed ham, and Hans said he was making the mashed potatoes and turkey gravy," Slade said.

"That leaves us with the cheesy green bean casserole and pfeffernusse cookies. I have all the ingredients."

"You mean those little white puff balls?" Slade asked.

"Yep. No extra decorating required," Sheri said.

Slade laughed. "You're afraid I'll make more green blobs with red eyes."

"Ha! I hadn't thought about it, but those could be your signature Christmas cookies."

If he ever wanted to create a signature dessert for the holidays, he would want it to look a whole lot more appealing to eat, though his cookie had tasted great.

"Oh, oh, what about Dulcie? She's here on her own and has no family. I'm sure one of the police officers' families will invite her over for a meal, but she's a member of our wolf pack now."

"And she and your brother are single. Have Hans invite her," Slade said.

"To both Christmas Eve dinner and Christmas Day lunch?"

"Sure, why not?"

"Okay. I'll give him a call then." She called her brother and put it on speakerphone, "Hey, Hans, we were just talking about the meals for Christmas Eve and Christmas Day."

"Yeah? What do I need to bring for the Christmas Eve dinner?"

"You always bring the best fresh bread and wine. But Slade and I were discussing that Dulcie doesn't have family here, and since she's one of the pack now—"

"You want me to invite her to Christmas Eve dinner and Christmas lunch?" Hans asked.

"Yeah, before one of the other families does," Sheri said.

"Okay, I'll ask her. I'll talk to you later."

"Good luck."

Then Slade got a call from his mom and put it on speakerphone. "Yeah, Mom?"

"I have another mission for you. Since you know the person involved, I thought you wouldn't mind going on this last-minute Pilots N Paws trip to fly to Minneapolis. You should arrive before lunchtime and return home well before Christmas Eve dinner," Lolita said.

"Yeah, sure." Slade knew it was important or they wouldn't need him to make the trip, but he was more than curious about who wanted the dog and why. "Who's it for?"

"Tex Lincoln."

"The man who had a heart attack in the Boundary Waters?" That really surprised Slade because he already had a dog.

"Yes. Benny is a German shepherd that's a fully certified cardiac-alert service dog. We just found one for him."

"Of course." Now Slade understood. He glanced at Sheri, and she nodded at him. "Is the dog ready now?" he asked his mom.

"He sure is. They're delivering him to the airport and should be here by the time you arrive. He was scheduled to go with another Pilots N Paws pilot, but the pilot became ill."

"Yeah, sure, Mom. I'm on my way." Then he said to Sheri, "Are you coming with me?"

"To see Mr. Lincoln and ask him a couple of questions? You bet." She smiled. "And of course to help deliver the dog."

"We could do a little last-minute Christmas shopping."

"Yes!" she said.

"And lunch."

"Yeah, that would be great. I love your job." Then she grabbed her purse and said, "Let's go."

Slade loved that about Sheri. She was always ready to go. He'd gotten her some things for Christmas, but he wanted to get something more for her since they were now mated. They didn't have a whole lot of shopping available in their small town, and ordering anything online now meant the presents wouldn't be delivered until after Christmas. So this was going to be fun. Besides, they could have a nice lunch there too and they would be helping a heart attack victim with a companion dog that might even save his life in the future. Even though Mr. Lincoln already had a dog, Jet, and the dog had alerted Slade and Sheri to come to his owner's aid in the Boundary Waters, Jet wasn't specifically trained on how to alert Mr. Lincoln that he was having a potential heart attack.

They reached the airport and made sure Benny was secure for the flight, then once Slade had done his flight checks and was given the go-ahead, they flew to Minneapolis.

"So what are you getting me for Christmas?" she asked.

Slade gave her one of his deep ho-ho-hos. "You don't sneak under the Christmas tree and peek at your presents in the middle of the night, do you?"

"I did once or twice when I was little. Did you?"

"Absolutely. And I should have warned you before we mated that when it's Christmas morning, there's no sleeping in."

"Oh, I wouldn't think of it. I'll be poking at you to get out of bed before you're trying to wake me," she assured him.

They were perfect for each other. "We could go to Mall of America to do our shopping after we drop off Benny. They have some great restaurants."

"Yeah, sure, that would be perfect."

The flight only took a little over an hour, and when they arrived, they rented a van so they could deliver the dog. Often the new dog owners would meet him at the airport, but in this case, because Mr. Lincoln was still at home resting up from his surgery and his wife was there caring for him, Slade didn't have any problem with taking the dog to his home.

When they arrived at the Lincolns' house and heard Jet barking, a woman opened the door and greeted them. "Hi, I'm Nancy Lincoln. Thanks so much for bringing the dog here for us. He could be a real lifesaver."

"That's so true. How is Mr. Lincoln doing?" Slade asked.

"Much better."

"That's good," Slade said, hoping Sheri would ask to see Mr. Lincoln before Nancy took Benny into the house and closed the door on them.

"I'm Sheri Whitmore, the one who called you when Slade"—Sheri motioned to Slade—"and I were in the BWCA and Mr. Lincoln had his heart attack."

Nancy's eyes widened.

"I'm a private investigator. I was looking into Mr. Lincoln's cousin Gerard's disappearance. I did locate him, but I still have some unanswered questions. You probably heard that we found Gerard's plane wreckage in the Boundary Waters."

To Slade's surprise, Mr. Lincoln came to the door and

motioned for them to enter the house. "Come in. I want to talk. You can call me Tex."

Glad he invited them in, Sheri and Slade walked inside with Nancy and Benny. Benny greeted Jet and thankfully the two dogs seemed to hit it off. Then Jet made Sheri and Slade feel as if they were old friends. They both petted him, glad to see him again.

They went into the living room to talk, and the two dogs sat down on the floor near Tex as he took a seat on a recliner, as if they wanted to be there for him if he needed their assistance should he have another heart attack.

Nancy asked, "Would you like sodas or water to drink? Coffee? Tea?"

"I'll take some hot tea, thanks," Sheri said.

"I'll have some too," Slade said.

Then Nancy went off to the kitchen to make the tea.

"So from what I heard you saying to Nancy, you're the PI Betty hired to locate Gerard," Tex said.

"Yes."

"You know about his brother blackmailing him?"

"Uh, yes, and the reason for it," Sheri said.

Tex let out his breath. "Gerard called me. I'm glad he's resolved that with Betty."

"Yes. So now Fitz doesn't have anything to blackmail Gerard with. Did Fitz approach you about piloting Gerard's plane when he didn't show up to fly it?" Sheri asked.

"Yes. And I said no. Fitz offered me money. I've been having some medical issues and I could have used the extra cash, but not from him."

"Why not?"

"Because…" Tex cleared his throat. Both dogs looked up at him. "Because Fitz was always a schemer. If he could get money from the government through some scam or conning people, even talking women into loaning him money and never paying them back, he would. I knew this couldn't be something legitimate that he was doing. I understand Gerard vanished and wouldn't do the job for him. I knew for sure it wasn't legit then."

"Did you worry about Gerard disappearing? That something might have happened to him?" Sheri asked.

"I did at first, but I knew Betty had contacted the police and then a PI to look for him. Later she told me that Gerard had shown up at home. Right before that, though, I got a call from him and a couple of text messages. He didn't want me to worry about him and told me not to fly the plane if Fitz tried to convince me to do it. He said he didn't know what the merchandise was but that if Fitz was involved, it was probably stolen."

"So do you know who ended up flying Gerard's plane?" Sheri asked.

Nancy brought in a tray of cups of tea and a bottled water for Tex.

"Thanks," Slade said.

"Thank you," Sheri said.

"You're welcome," Nancy said, and sat down to have her tea with them.

"No, I didn't know that he had gotten anyone else to fly the plane. I thought if I said no to flying it because I had health issues, they wouldn't risk my taking the mission. Truthfully, I had no idea I would end up having a heart attack in the BWCA or I wouldn't have risked that trip either," Tex said.

Nancy scoffed.

Everyone glanced at her.

"He was going ice fishing hell or high water," Nancy said. "I worried about him, of course, but I didn't realize the area would suffer such a damaging storm and it would lead to Tex having a heart attack." Under her breath, she said, "Cantankerous old fool."

Tex smiled. "I missed going last year. I didn't want to skip going this year again, not with my health being the way it is. But no, I don't know who flew the plane."

"Gerard's daughter, Jessica," Sheri said.

Nancy gasped. "No."

"Aww hell," Tex said.

"Fitz blackmailed her with the same reason he used on Gerard, that he would tell Betty about Gerard's affair and subsequently the child he had from their union."

"Bastard," Tex said. "Okay, I've got to tell you that one day my cousins and I were sitting around drinking beers a couple of years ago, and we were talking about this and that and the subject—Fitz started—was about making the perfect heist. So I proposed a way to do so because I used to work at a company that delivers packages. I never thought Fitz would buddy up with his friends Otis and Danbury and pull it off."

"Are you and Gerard on friendly terms?" Slade asked.

"Yes," Tex said.

"And it would be fair to say that you're not on good terms with Fitz," Slade said.

"Correct. He has always been the troublemaker in the family, but he has always managed to get away with everything he has done."

Slade heard a car pull up in the driveway and Jet began to bark. Because Benny was a service dog, he did not.

Nancy went to see who it was, and after she looked out the window, she turned, her face ashen, and whispered, "It's Fitz and that other guy. Otis, I think."

"Do you have a protective order against him?" Slade asked.

"No," Tex said, but already Benny was pawing at him, which was one of the indications that Tex's heart rate or blood pressure was elevating.

"Okay, I want you and Nancy and the dogs to go to a safe place in the home where there are no windows. With your permission, I'm going to call the police." Slade didn't want them to have to deal with this and for Tex to have another heart attack.

"We have a comfortable den in the basement and can lock the door," Nancy said.

"All right, then you go there, and we or the police will let you know when everything is all clear," Slade said.

Nancy looked at Sheri as if she thought she should stay with them.

"I'll be helping Slade. Do you have any security cameras inside your house?" Sheri asked.

"No," Nancy said, moving Tex protectively by the arm to the basement stairs.

"Outside security cameras?" Slade asked.

"Yes, front porch, corners of the property, back porch," Nancy said.

"You're going to have to tell the truth about what is going on with Fitz and this heist," Slade said to Tex. "It's the only way to get some protection from your cousin and his cohorts."

"Yes," Nancy said, speaking for her husband. "He is. And we'll get a lawyer."

"Good idea," Sheri said.

"I don't have a gun you can use to protect yourselves with," Tex warned. "But"—he glanced at Nancy—"she got me a good solid hiking stick that's under the Christmas tree. You can't miss it."

"You peeked," Nancy said, not sounding surprised.

"I love you for getting it for me. That means I'm going back to the BWCA hiking."

"Only with me. And both the dogs. It would be helpful if Sheri and Slade were in the vicinity at the same time, but we know that wouldn't be possible," Nancy said.

"Thanks—if we need it, we'll use it." Though Slade hoped if they needed it, he wouldn't break Tex's Christmas present.

Once the couple and the two dogs were securely locked in the basement, Sheri said to Slade, "I'm going to shift."

"Okay, I'll get the hiking stick." Then Slade hurried to the Christmas tree and found it way in the back of the presents, mostly hidden, but part of the Christmas wrapping paper on the hiking stick had been peeled away and Slade couldn't help but smile.

Sheri was hurrying to remove her clothes before she shifted while he pulled the wrapping paper from the hefty stick, the handle decorated in a hand-carved wolf's head.

"Oh, that's beautiful. Don't break it," Sheri said, then shifted.

"I'll try not to unless I'm stopping one of them from shooting us." Slade got on his phone and called the police. He noticed the men hadn't come to the front door. They had disappeared and he suspected they were going to a window or maybe even the back door. He raced back there to make sure the door was locked. Sometimes when an owner had a dog, they would let them out every so often and not always lock the back door.

Someone answered the phone and Slade said, "We have a break-in at Tex and Nancy Lincoln's house in progress. I'm Slade White, delivering a cardiac-alert service dog to Tex. He and his wife are secure for—"

He hadn't reached the back door when he heard it open. He whispered into the phone, "Two men involved in criminal charges in the Boundary Waters, Fitz Connolly and Otis Risotto, have unlawfully entered the Lincolns' home."

"Hello!" Fitz called out. "Tex? Where are you? You and I have some unfinished business to take care of." He was still standing at the back door.

His heart racing, Slade ducked into a hallway leading to the bedrooms. He didn't know where Sheri had gone to, but he didn't want her to be on her own.

"Are they armed?" the dispatcher asked.

"They were armed with illegal guns while they were in

the Boundary Waters," Slade said into the phone, his voice hushed.

"Hey, Tex, you don't want to have another heart attack, do you?" Fitz called out.

That would be an easy way to get rid of him for sure. Just upset him enough to give him a heart attack since he already had a heart condition. But Nancy would be a witness too.

"Come on, Tex. Let's not play games with each other." Fitz's voice was now near the kitchen, but Slade heard someone else moving through the house too.

At least Nancy and Tex were keeping Jet quiet, or he would have given their location away. He might not have been barking because he recognized Fitz's familiar voice.

"Maybe everyone's gone," Otis said, his voice low. "Maybe that's their son's van and he's off driving them around in Tex's car. You said he might come home for the holidays this year."

"Rarely. He rarely comes home. Come on, Tex, talk to me."

Slade thought it was telling that Fitz was staying put, as if he believed someone else might be in the house and he didn't want to get injured, so he was letting Otis do the exploring.

His footfalls muffled by the carpeting, Otis was nearly to the hallway where the bedrooms were. Slade moved into the first bedroom on his right. It looked like a master bedroom, and he mostly smelled Nancy's scent. If Otis was carrying a gun, Slade would whack him with the walking cane and hopefully knock it out of his hand.

Sheri suddenly moved out from behind a queen-size bed and bumped Slade's leg. He realized she'd gone into the bedroom to wait for one of the men to show up too. He patted her head and shoved his phone in his pocket, still open to the 911 operator.

Slade moved behind the door, but he couldn't see Otis if he peered into the room. Sheri was standing by the dresser nearby and she would be able to observe him. Slade didn't want her there, but he realized she intended to be the distraction. She looked as tense as he felt, her body held still. She was barely breathing, her gaze focused on the doorway, her tail held straight out. She was ready for the hunt.

Then Otis poked his head into the bedroom. Sheri's hackles raised, her body crouching, poising to pounce, she growled low and threatening. Slade came around from behind the door, swinging hard with the cane and connecting with Otis's gun hand. Slade heard a crack and knew the carved wolf head had broken the man's wrist, thankfully not the cane.

Otis cried out, dropped the gun, and fell to his knees in pain, clutching his injured arm close to his chest. "You," he said, when he saw it was Slade, murder in his blue eyes. He smelled of anger and agony.

Slade grabbed Otis's gun while Sheri guarded Otis. "Yeah, stay there or my dog will put you down. She's a trained police dog, retired, but she's good at her job." To Sheri, Slade said, "Watch him. If he moves, take him down." She would know Slade only meant for her to threaten him. They couldn't have her biting and turning him.

With the cane still in hand, Slade moved quietly down the hall. Fitz wasn't making a sound, and Slade wondered if he had taken off, abandoning his coconspirator.

Then from the kitchen, Fitz whispered, "Otis? Did you get him?" *Coward.*

Then Jet started to bark in the basement. *Aww damn it.*

Fitz said, "Someone's in the basement. Hurry up and join me." Then he headed for the basement door.

Slade was afraid Fitz would shoot his way through the door and kill both Nancy and Tex. Slade wouldn't have tried this risky move otherwise and rushed forward to stop Fitz from reaching the basement door.

For a second, Fitz's eyes widened as he saw his nemesis— the guy who had helped the police take him into custody the first time. Fitz raised his gun to shoot him. Slade jumped behind the wall and Fitz shot at him several times, the bullets hitting the wall, sending chips of plaster flying.

His breathing hard, Slade considered his options. He felt sure Fitz would continue to target him until he could take him out and then go after Tex and Nancy, leaving no witnesses behind. Slade waited for a heartbeat, not hearing any movement from Fitz, then came around the wall low, targeting him with Otis's gun. Fitz's eyes widened to see Slade was prepared to shoot him.

Fitz fired his weapon, the bullet whizzing by Slade, smacking the wall just to the right of him. He jumped a little, and then he pulled the trigger of Otis's gun to stop Fitz. Nothing happened. *Hell!*

Frustrated, Slade ducked behind the wall again, his heart beating hard. He tried to clear the gun, but he didn't have time. He heard Fitz quickly moving down the hall, getting closer, his knee cracking, his heart thumping, his breathing hard. At least Slade could pinpoint where Fitz was as he approached Slade's position. Slade moved to a bookshelf, glad Fitz couldn't hear *him* changing his location. Then Fitz ran the rest of the way to the corner of the wall. Trying to make sure Slade didn't have time to unjam the gun? That's what Slade would have done if the roles had been reversed.

Fitz came rushing around the corner, gun ready to shoot. Last chance to get this right. As soon as Slade saw Fitz, he threw the walking stick as hard as he could, aiming it at the center of him. Shocked to hell, Fitz didn't react until it was too late. The cane sailed through the air and struck Fitz hard in the chest. The round Fitz fired at the same time slammed into the ceiling above Slade's head, chips of paint and plaster falling from the ceiling. Slade instinctively ducked. Fitz fell back and landed on the floor from the impact, the breath knocked out of him.

Slade rushed to get his gun from him.

At the same time, a car pulled up in the driveway and Slade suspected it was the police. He realized at once the problem he had. Sheri was keeping Otis locked down in the bedroom, but she couldn't release him. Slade needed to get to the front door and open it for the officers. He told the 911 operator that the police were at the house. "Both men were armed, but I disarmed them. The back door's unlocked. Both men are down. I've got their guns."

Slade set them on a high table.

The police came through the backyard and then through the back door, slamming it against the wall, guns drawn. Slade held up his hands. "That's Fitz Connolly, cousin of the owner, Tex Lincoln, who is secure in the basement with his wife, Nancy. The other man, Otis Risotto, is in the bedroom. Guns are over there."

Slade knew this was going to be a problem because Sheri was still wearing her wolf coat, but he didn't know how to protect her. He was going to mention the dog in there but what if she had shifted and wasn't a wolf? How would he explain that? The dog had just…vanished?

A couple more police cars drove up to the house and one of the officers handcuffed Fitz and another went to take Otis into custody.

Slade made a move to go to Sheri since she hadn't left the bedroom, but the officers wouldn't let him for his own safety. This wasn't good.

Chapter 27

As soon as the police arrived, Sheri was in a bind. She didn't know what to do. Otis was terrified of her. For good reason. Every time he moved a muscle, she growled at him, and her hackles rose. She looked like a very growly wolf, ready to tear into him.

He tried to reason with her, telling her she was a good dog, but she had to keep him here out of Slade's way. She didn't want Slade to have to deal with two armed men at the same time in the event Otis retrieved his gun. When she heard the gunshots, Otis looked like he wanted to race out of the bedroom—and so did she, to save Slade—but she growled low at Otis, lowering her head, showing just how menacing her teeth could be.

Then she heard Slade talking to the police as they entered the back door. Someone headed down the hall toward the bedroom that she and Otis were in. She dashed into the closet, figuring the police officer would take Otis into custody. She didn't want them to find her wearing her Arctic wolf coat. The bedroom happened to be the master bedroom, the clothes in the closet all Nancy's. Sheri suspected Tex slept in another room.

She shifted, then hurried to pull off one of Nancy's

sweater dresses hanging in the closet. Sheri couldn't think of anything else to do at the time.

As soon as the police officer had Otis in hand, she came out of the closet and said, "Oh, I'm so glad you finally got here. I've been so scared." She wasn't wearing shoes, or anything else, just the sweater dress.

Otis was just staring at her, like he couldn't believe someone had been hiding in the closet all this time. She almost smiled.

"There's a vicious dog in there," Otis said, motioning to the closet with his good hand. The officer tried to cuff him, and he shouted, "Hey, hey, hey, my wrist is broken! Be careful."

Sheri needed to get her clothes. She was hoping she could grab them from the living room before Nancy saw her wearing her dress and wondered what that was all about. But it was already too late. She could hear the police escorting the couple into the living room and the officer was taking Otis there too.

They were all talking to the police, Tex saying, "Slade and Sheri have saved my life twice now." He explained about the BWCA incident and that they had brought him Benny because of his heart condition.

"Where's Sheri?" one of the officers asked.

"She stayed in the bedroom," the other officer said.

"I'll go check on her," Slade said.

She was so relieved when Slade walked into the bedroom, and he was carrying her clothes. He was the best mate ever. She hurried back into the closet with her clothes and rehung Nancy's dress and then slipped into her own things.

"Thank you." She hugged Slade. "I'm so glad you didn't get shot."

"That hiking walking stick came in handy. You should have seen Fitz's expression when he saw me."

"Oh, I bet! Everywhere he goes, we show up to thwart him."

Then they joined the others in the living room and Otis was claiming he wanted to charge Slade with breaking his wrist.

"You were going to shoot Slade," Sheri said. "He had no other way to stop you from shooting him."

One of the officers said to Sheri, "One of my former partners, Dulcie? She said both of you would make a couple of outstanding police officers."

Sheri was glad it had all worked out.

EMTs arrived to check out Tex to make sure his blood pressure and heart rate were okay, to wrap Otis's wrist, and to check out Fitz's chest after Slade hit him with the wolf walking stick. He would be wearing a hefty bruise, but that was all.

After getting everyone's statements, Otis and Fitz were hauled off in a couple of patrol cars. Slade and Sheri shared their witness statements and signed them.

Then the police left, and the Lincolns thanked Sheri and Slade for all their help, for bringing Benny to live with them, for saving them, and wished them a Merry Christmas.

Sheri smiled as she and Slade walked out of the house to the rental van to drive to the mall. "I think *this* time, Fitz and Otis will get a stay in jail."

"I agree. Which makes for a very merry Christmas for all the rest of us. When we get to the mall, do you want to shop together?" Slade asked.

"No way. Our presents are supposed to be a secret from each other."

"I don't want to lose you," he said.

"We both have our phones, no problem with reception here, so we should be good."

"It's going to be crowded. Oh, speaking of which, we need to make a reservation for lunch because of the crowds."

"I'm on it," she said. "How about a grill house? Another place has wings, shrimp, burgers."

"The grill house sounds good. After all we went through, we deserve something special."

She made reservations and then when they arrived at the mall, she looked at it in wonder. The whole place was filled with frosted Christmas trees, and it looked magical.

One section of the mall had a grouping of Christmas trees with a sign announcing MOA for Mall of America, giant Christmas presents, and enormous nutcrackers. Huge snowflakes and Christmas ornaments hung high above. Santa was sitting on a fancy white upholstered chair with a child on his lap while wearing a red vest, red pants, a green and red shirt, and a real long white beard. He totally looked like a real Santa.

The MOA also had a festival of more than fifty trees that Sheri and Slade enjoyed seeing, trees decorated in all different colors and with all different themes. The proceeds from the raffles for the trees were going to the Special Olympics Minnesota. Decorated by companies and sports teams, they featured purple, gold, blue, red and green, and silver trees, as well as a pink tree covered in flamingos, bows, and balls, some with winter themes, and others with features from a popular kids' TV show with search and rescue dogs. They were all beautiful.

Sheri and Slade hugged and kissed before they separated to do some shopping. She swore Slade looked uncomfortable to leave her and that he didn't like the crowds. She went to a department store first. She normally didn't regift things, but she was going to give Elizabeth the aqua waffle maker she got at the office Christmas party because Elizabeth had wanted it, and Sheri was going to get a waffle maker for two people and give it to Slade for Christmas. She had made sure when they were packing his stuff that he didn't have one in his own household goods. She also got him some stocking stuffers— special grilling spices, socks, his favorite chocolate mints.

She went to an electronics store that might have accessories for his drone and found a bundle of them that she thought would be perfect for her mate for Christmas. As soon as she took hold of the package to really look it over— and it was the only one the store had left—a redheaded, red-bearded man who was about six two, towering over her, grabbed hold of it.

He knew she already had hold of the package. He might be bigger than her, but she wasn't letting go of the package no matter what. She had it first! She wanted to turn into her wolf and growl at him. He actually had the nerve to tug at it, trying to pull it from her hands, but she tightened her grip on it, not about to let it go.

"Excuse me. I had ahold of this before you did." She knew it was the only one there, but she still wanted to look it over and see all the different goodies that came with the selection before she bought the set. She couldn't believe she had to even say that much to the guy.

Even then, he wouldn't let go of it. She wasn't letting go, though he actually pulled her toward him. It was good that Slade didn't see this, or she was sure there would be a real fight.

"Just let go of it, lady," the man growled.

Just then a customer arrived with a manager and the customer pointed toward the man who was still holding on to the drone accessory bundle and said, "He didn't grab the merchandise until she did." Sheri was glad that the other customer vouched for her.

The manager asked Sheri, "Is this the item that you want?"

"Yes." Sheri hoped after all the angst, Slade would really like it and get some use out of the items.

The other customer finally released the package.

"Do you need to shop for anything else?" the manager asked Sheri.

"No, thanks. That will do it."

"I'll ring this up for you then." The manager said to the other customer, "We can order it for you, sir."

"I'll shop somewhere else." he said, then he stalked out of the store.

"Sorry about that," the manager said.

"It's the holidays. For some, it totally stresses them out. But this was the only chance we had of coming to the big city to shop."

After finishing his shopping for Sheri, Slade pulled out his cell phone and called her, "Hey, are you ready to meet up for lunch?"

"Oh, yeah, it's about that time, isn't it. I'm on my way to the restaurant. I'm starving."

"Me too." When he finally reached the restaurant, she was just arriving. She always brightened his whole outlook on life. Despite the crowds at the store that made him want to return to the woods surrounding the lake where the wolf pack lived and get out of the crowded place, she made him feel like it was just the two of them there and everyone else just vanished. They hugged and kissed, then he took her hand and they went inside.

"Did you get everything you needed to?" Sheri asked as the hostess escorted them to their table, the restaurant beautifully decorated in garlands and Christmas ornaments, each of the tables having a candle surrounded by a wreath of greenery and red berries, adding to the holiday ambience.

"Yeah, how about you?"

"I sure did. I dropped off the packages at the van. You're not to peek now."

He laughed and they took their seats near one of the mall windows and began looking at the menus. "I dropped off the presents that I purchased in the van before I called you about our lunch date. I didn't see your packages in there." He'd worried when she said they were in there that someone had stolen them—which could happen at the height of the holiday season while thieves were on the prowl for easy snatching.

"I hid them in the back of the van."

Glad about it, he smiled. "I promise I'm *not* going to sneak a quick look."

"Not like Tex peeked at his hiking stick wrapped in Christmas paper under the tree?"

"I'm so glad he had and then offered it to me to use to protect ourselves from Fitz and Otis."

"Oh, me too. Hmm, after the wild time we had of it—not to mention fighting over a Christmas present for you when a man was bound and determined to have it instead—I need something really good. Like that shrimp pasta. I would have a rib eye steak, but we're having that for Christmas Eve dinner tonight."

"Yeah, I was thinking the same thing. I think I'll have the hamburger and chips." Once they had ordered, he said to her, "Okay, so what did you fight over?"

Sheri chuckled. "You are not learning what I picked up for you that easily. I might have let him have it, but I was still feeling rather growly about how Fitz and Otis arrived at the Lincolns' home to harm them, and it was the last one of the, um, items they had for sale that I really wanted to get for someone special in my life."

"Me."

She smiled. "Anyway, the guy was determined to have it. Period. And so was I. I saw it first, grabbed it first, end of discussion."

"Hell, you would think the other customer would have been nice enough—as it is the Christmas season, after all—to let you have it since you'd grabbed it first."

"Nope. So how was your shopping experience?" Sheri asked.

Bread and butter, their glasses of water, and salads were brought to the table, and they thanked the server.

"Well," Slade said, tearing off part of the loaf of bread for Sheri, "three older women were helping me shop for... I can't say what." He buttered his bread.

Sheri laughed. "Usually when I'm telling my family about Christmas shopping stories, I'll at some point let something slip about the actual present I bought."

"I know. It's hard not to do. So of course I didn't really need their help, but it was sweet of them to offer. I finally picked out what I thought you would love, even though some of their suggestions were for other items I was sure you wouldn't want. They were being nice and helpful, much more in the spirit of the holidays, unlike the guy you had to deal with."

"Well, that's cute."

Their meals were finally delivered to the table, and they were about to eat when Sheri glanced at the entryway to the restaurant and frowned. Slade glanced that way and saw a gruff-looking guy glowering at Sheri.

"Don't tell me he's the one you had a fight with over the Christmas present."

"He is."

Slade didn't plan to have any confrontation with the guy if he didn't cause her grief. He didn't want to ruin their lunch, but he was a wolf, and he wasn't going to back down if the guy got hostile.

Sheri took another bite of her shrimp pasta. "This is so good."

Slade watched another guy join the first and the hostess led them to a table deeper into the restaurant where they couldn't see them. He started eating his hamburger. "Hopefully, he'll eat and forget all about this until after we have a nice lunch and we leave."

"I sure hope so." But then Sheri's eyes widened as she saw someone else come into the restaurant. "Ohmigod, it's the man who was at our cabin."

Immediately, he thought she meant Fitz or one of his partners in crime, but then he saw it was the news reporter. "He won't recognize us." Slade hoped.

The reporter was with a woman, and he appeared not to notice them, thankfully. The hostess grabbed menus and headed straight in Sheri and Slade's direction. Sheri and Slade didn't look at them while they continued to eat and talk to each other, completely ignoring the reporter. But they should have figured he would notice them.

He continued past them as if he hadn't seen them, but Slade suspected that the reporter would have and would circle back once he and his companion had their table.

"He didn't stop here," Sheri said.

"Nope. But I wouldn't be surprised to see him return."

"Yeah. He saw us, but I thought maybe he didn't recognize us."

"Or he did," Slade said, seeing the news reporter head straight for their table. Slade took another bite of his hamburger. He really wanted to enjoy his meal with his mate in peace. But he wasn't going to hurry through the meal to avoid him.

"Hi, I'm Tom Briggs. You're Slade White and Sheri Whitmore, correct?" the reporter asked.

There wouldn't be any sense denying it. The reporter obviously had done his homework.

"We're enjoying a meal here on Christmas Eve," Sheri said, speaking up.

"I can relate. I just wanted to touch base and see if you would like to be interviewed about the—"

The customer who had the issue with Sheri over the gift at the store came over to the table. Immediately, Slade stood up. Now he was a wolf ready to get rid of a menace. The reporter was one thing. But someone who was there to give Sheri grief, that was another story.

Tom Briggs glanced at the approaching man, looking like he thought there could be a story here. Slade didn't want the reporter to get a story about some guy who had been fighting over a gift in a shop with Sheri.

"Yeah, sure, we'll give you an interview," Slade said, Sheri's jaw dropping. "We're heading home after lunch and it will have to be after Christmas and a trip we're taking, but we'll do it." He shook the reporter's hand, and he looked like he wanted to hang around to see what this was all about because the man approaching them looked angry. And reporters loved new news.

"Thanks, Mr. White. You and Ms. Whitmore have done some really wonderful things for folks this Christmas season and you epitomize what Christmas is all about," Tom Briggs said.

"Yeah, right," the disagreeable customer said as he

joined them at their table. "That woman forced me to let go of—"

Before the man could finish what he was saying, the reporter interrupted the guy. "They saved lives in the Boundary Waters Canoe Area a few days ago, helped catch some thieves, delivered a hundred toys to kids during the Santa Seaplane Toy Drop, and even today, they saved a couple from housebreakers who planned to murder them."

The disgruntled customer's eyes widened, and he said, "Hell." Without saying anything further, he turned around and walked back to his table.

Sheri shook the reporter's hand. "Thanks."

"I like to write about good news, though I have to admit I would love to know what that was all about," Tom said. "And knowing what I do about you and Mr. White, you deserve some praise."

Sheri smiled. "Thank you."

"I'll let you enjoy your lunch and look forward to hearing from you."

They shook hands again, and Tom left to join his companion at their table.

Slade sat down at the table again and they began eating their food.

"I was surprised you said we would do the interview, and then I realized you were trying to stop that other guy from giving us trouble. It worked." Sheri leaned over and kissed him.

He kissed her in return. "Yeah, I didn't want him ruining my gift by mentioning what it was, and I didn't want him giving the reporter a story he might want to share that would put us—"

"Me, you mean." Sheri forked up some more of her shrimp.

"Yeah. You in a bad light and I had no intention of him doing that."

"So now we have to do an interview," she said.

"Yeah, but Tom only likes to write feel-good stories and that won't hurt us a bit—for either of our jobs, you know."

"True, for promotional purposes. I hadn't thought of that."

Then they finished their meals and left the restaurant, but the customer Sheri had trouble with and his friend followed them out. Now what?

"Hey, sorry about the...gift," the guy said to Sheri. "Really. Merry Christmas."

Sheri smiled. "Thanks. Merry Christmas."

Slade inclined his head to the man, and then he held Sheri's hand as they left the mall.

"Well, that was a surprise," Sheri said.

"I'll say. But a welcome one."

"Maybe the guy just needed to get some food in him."

"I think the reporter's words made him feel like he had wronged some good Samaritans and he changed his tune. *And* that he needed to get some food in him. I can get grouchy when I'm hungry." They reached the rental van, and he unlocked the doors.

She laughed. "I'll have to remember that and send snacks with you when you don't have time to eat while you're flying missions."

Slade squeezed her hand. "I love you."

"I love you too."

Once they were in the rental van, they returned to the airport, then moved their packages into the plane. "I'll stay awake this time," Sheri said.

Slade smiled as he got ready to fly. "I love your company when I'm flying whether you're asleep or not."

She chuckled. "I knew you were the wolf for me when we mated. So I guess we'll tell everyone what went on at the Lincolns' home when we have Christmas Eve dinner with your parents tonight."

"Yeah. That will be an interesting topic and the family will be glad to hear that Otis and Fitz went to jail for Christmas."

"Yeah, glad just like we are."

When they landed at the airport in Ely, they carried all their presents to the SUV and then drove to the apartment. As soon as they walked into the place, still so cluttered with his boxes, Slade was thinking that he had to do something to put all this stuff away and fast.

They didn't have much time before they went to the Christmas Eve dinner at Slade's parents' home, and Sheri needed to make her potato dish. He was going to help her, but she said, "Go ahead and work on finding room for your things. I'll assist you after I get this started."

"Okay, sure." He wanted to help Sheri make her special dish for tonight like he'd planned to, but he knew she had things under control, and he figured she would be happiest if he got a lot of his stuff put away. They really needed to do that so that Christmas morning they could wake up to her beautifully decorated living room to open their Christmas stockings.

Then he had a thought. "Hey, you're not really using your second bedroom for much of anything. Can I store some of my stuff in there until the house is built? At least my stuff won't be cluttering up the whole apartment then."

"Yeah, sure. I just do some investigations on my computer in there at night sometimes after work. But you sure can. I suspect when we get home at night, we'll be busy with other stuff, and I won't be tempted to work on any cases."

He laughed. "I know what I'll want to be doing when we both are together after work. But I'll understand if you need to investigate your cases. Especially when I'm getting in late, or you have a clue you want to check out. I'll make sure that I don't block access to your computer in any way. And I'll continue to sort through things and put them away as much as possible."

"That'll be fine. I know we don't have that much room and I want you to feel like this is your place too, not that you just moved in on me. We rent it jointly—though of course your name isn't on the lease, but it can be. If you need to move some of my extra clothes or other items into the spare room, go right ahead. I don't need any of my summer clothes right now and that can make room for your winter things. When it warms up, we can move our winter things into the spare bedroom until our house is finished."

"Okay, but I'm leaving your bathing suits where they are because we'll be taking them with us on our honeymoon."

She smiled at him. "I can't wait."

Chapter 28

ONCE SHERI HAD THE GARLIC PARMESAN BABY POTATOES in the oven, she began helping Slade move the boxes he hadn't unpacked, consolidate others that were partially unpacked, and load the empty, flattened boxes in the SUV to recycle. She wanted Slade to know that he wasn't taking up some of her space, but they were sharing it together as mated wolves as if they had always been there together from the beginning.

They moved their summer clothes into the extra room and folded them into the chest of drawers in there and hung up the other garments in the closet. Everything was starting to look really organized again like she liked things. She could even see the Christmas tree, which reminded her she had to wrap some things when they got home tonight after dinner.

"Better?" he asked.

"Being with *you* makes *everything* better," she said, pulling him in for a hug and a kiss.

"I feel the same way about you."

They were just getting into the kiss when the oven timer went off. "Ooh, potatoes are ready. Which means we've got to go." She hurried into the kitchen and removed the casserole dish from the oven.

Then they got dressed in their Christmas sweaters—his

featuring the Grinch, which she had to smile at, and hers a snowman with a blue background, cardinals sitting on his branch arms.

"Who gave you the Grinch sweater?" she asked, pulling on her blue plaid skirt to match her sweater and then her boots.

"Amelia did. She teased me that she wanted me to buy her a laptop for Christmas one year, but of course I wouldn't, so she got me the Grinch sweater. I wear it proudly." He buckled his belt and pulled on his boots.

Sheri laughed. "That's an expensive gift."

"Yeah, I asked her for the same thing the next year."

Sheri raised a brow. "You didn't."

"I did."

"Don't tell me. She said no and you got her a Grinch sweater."

"I sure did. Well, a *Mrs.* Grinch sweater."

"Oh, how fun." She loved how Slade and his sister played with each other.

After they were dressed, he drove them over to his parents' home to have dinner. But when they got there, Hans said, "Dulcie sent her regrets. She had a call on a case, and she said she wouldn't be able to make it."

Sheri could tell Hans was disappointed but maybe Dulcie could make it for Christmas lunch. She was also disappointed because Dulcie should be able to enjoy the holidays too. But Dulcie was brand-new at the job and that meant since she was the rookie there, she would work some of the holidays when an important case came up.

Elizabeth and David had made Christmas cupcakes.

Sheri carried in the casserole dish of roasted garlic Parmesan baby potatoes. Hans arrived with bread and red wine to go with dinner.

Slade made Mrs. Claus cocktails of a blend of eggnog and peppermint schnapps, topped with whipped cream and crushed peppermint candy for everyone before they sat down to eat. Amelia and Elizabeth were drinking plain eggnog topped with whipped cream and crushed candy canes. "These are in honor of Sheri's participation as Mrs. Claus at the Christmas toy giveaway."

Sheri kissed Slade. "Thanks." She took a sip of her drink and had whipped cream and sprinkles of peppermint candy on her mouth which Slade quickly licked off. She smiled and he kissed her again.

Sheri and Slade finally shared what had happened at the Lincolns' house with everyone, and Lolita shook her head. "I can't believe I sent you on that mission to take Benny to Mr. Lincoln and you ended up having to fight Fitz and Otis to protect the Lincolns and could have been seriously injured or worse."

Henry and Fred started cooking the steaks.

"And that Sheri was with Slade at the time and put in harm's way," Henry said. "We're so fortunate the two of you protected the Lincolns and came out unscathed."

"And that the criminals are locked away now," Georgia said.

Gavin ended a call on his phone. "I checked with the DA's office, and they said that the judge didn't allow them to be bonded out this time."

Amelia nursed one of the babies. "They shouldn't have

been allowed out the first time. Not when they had both been found with illegal handguns in the BWCA."

"I agree," Fred said. "Hopefully they will stay in jail now and won't be any more trouble for anyone else."

"Here, here," Slade said, raising his Mrs. Claus cocktail to everyone.

They all lifted their drinks and cheered the outcome of the case as it stood today, though it probably wouldn't go to trial for months from now.

"I can't believe how dangerous this case has been for you," Gavin said.

"Yeah," David agreed. "Cameron would have never given it to you."

"But it all worked out in the end," Sheri said, "and I'm glad I was able to solve it."

"True. You and Slade have done an outstanding job," Elizabeth said, rubbing her tummy. David reached over and stroked her back.

Sheri loved how caring David was toward Elizabeth. He always was, but it was so endearing to see the way he took care of her while she was pregnant. "I love your Christmas sweater," Sheri said to Amelia. "Slade told me the reason for both of your Grinch sweaters."

Amelia laughed. "Yeah, you know, it's a twin thing."

"Okay, let's open a Christmas present before we eat dinner," Georgia said. Earlier, the parents had gotten together and decided Christmas pajamas were to be opened at the Christmas Eve dinner and let everyone know who was supposed to be purchasing what and for whom.

Hans and Sheri had gotten their mother and dad a matching howling wolf set of pajamas, hers with a pink, long-sleeved shirt and his with a gray, long-sleeved shirt, their pj pants plaid to match them. Their mom and dad had gotten Hans and Sheri wolf pj's with a wolf wearing a Santa hat. They had gotten David and Elizabeth the same thing. Slade and Amelia had picked out wolves on Christmas tree pajamas for their parents. Henry and Lolita had gotten Slade, Amelia, and Gavin pajamas that matched Hans and Sheri's, which Sheri thought was cute.

It seemed everyone had the same idea as far as buying *wolf-themed* Christmas pajamas. Tomorrow, for picture taking at the Christmas lunch, they would wear Christmas wolf sweaters and blue jeans.

Amelia nursed the other baby while Gavin changed the first one's diaper before they ate dinner. "When the kids are older, we'll have to bake Christmas cookies for Santa like we did when we were kids," Amelia said.

"For sure," Lolita said.

"What else do you usually do for Christmas Eve?" Slade asked. Since they had two different families combining the activities for Christmas, it was important to incorporate both their ideas, if they had special traditions they wanted to continue.

"Opening a Christmas Eve present, special drinks, and dinner are about it for us now," Georgia said.

"We open the gifts in our Christmas stockings, but we like the idea of pajama gifts for this year. That's fine for a new tradition for us," Lolita said.

"When the kids are older, we can make our own pizza dough and create our own pizzas. That's what we did when Hans and Sheri were younger," Georgia said.

"That was fun," Sheri agreed.

Amelia handed the baby she'd just finished nursing to Gavin, and he changed his diaper too. Then they rocked the twins to sleep, and everyone set the table and served up the food.

"Later, when the babies are older, we could do a karaoke Christmas song sing-along, but not while they need to sleep," Gavin said.

Slade laughed. "I would definitely wake the babies with my singing."

Everyone chuckled. Then they started passing around the food and eating their steak dinner.

"So when are you leaving on your mated honeymoon for Silver Town?" Henry asked Slade and Sheri.

"We're driving out on the day after Christmas," Slade said, "early that morning."

"Yeah, so we'll need to pack our stuff tomorrow night," Sheri said.

They had cupcakes after dinner, then it was time for everyone to start saying their good nights. Amelia and Gavin had been having a lot of sleepless nights with the new babies, and Elizabeth was feeling tired, so she and David were ready to go home. Hans teased everyone about getting old with being mated. Sheri knew their parents were probably tired too and they had a big day tomorrow with the Christmas celebration.

Slade and Sheri said their good nights to everyone, wished them a merry Christmas, and then left for home.

"That was so nice with all the families. Poor Hans. I think he felt a little left out. It would have been nice if Dulcie could have been his 'date' for the night," Sheri said.

"True, but she might have felt a little bit uncomfortable about being a date when she doesn't know Hans at all and everyone else was family," Slade said.

"You don't think she skipped out for that reason, do you?" Sheri would really feel bad about that.

"No way. She wouldn't have missed coming for that reason."

"Okay, good." They arrived at their apartment and started to pull off their parkas.

She was glad all of Slade's things were put away now so that he had easier access to what he needed, and they weren't tripping over boxes in the middle of the night. She still needed to figure out what to take to wear on their honeymoon. Winter clothes, some dressy skirts and sweaters for eating out, a swimsuit for the indoor pool, and her wolf pajamas. She thought of wearing them tonight, but she knew they would only have them on for a few minutes. They could wear them in the morning when they had breakfast and unwrapped the presents in their Christmas stockings before they dressed to leave to go to her parents' house for Christmas lunch.

"It's time to go to bed so we can get up early. After we open our presents in the morning, we'll have time to take a nap"— which meant make love—"shower and get ready for opening presents at your parents' place and having Christmas lunch," Slade said.

"That sounds like a plan." She grabbed his hand and tugged him to the bedroom, ready, eager to make love to her mate on Christmas Eve and every other night. It still seemed so unreal that the hot wolf she wanted to mate was now hers for real—before Christmas even.

They entered the bedroom, and he pulled her into a heartfelt embrace and kissed her cold nose, his mouth nice and warm against it. "When we return from our trip to Silver Town, we'll have to begin planning the wedding. I figure while things are kind of slow for me on scheduled trips, I would help you plan it as much as I can along with your mother and mine, of course, and all the ladies."

"You're so sweet." She hadn't figured he would want to plan anything, but she was glad he was eager to. But now, all she wanted was for them to make love to each other, snuggle, and sleep before they woke up bright and early on Christmas Day.

She slid her hands underneath his sweater and ran her palms over his pebbled nipples, and she loved that she could turn him on so easily. He pressed his hips against hers to show her just what else she had done to him as she felt the swell of his arousal. Just touching each other like this always made it happen, which made her feel sexy and loved that she could arouse him like that.

She kissed his stubbly chin and then pulled off his Christmas sweater, exposing his naked torso—glorious muscles that she wanted to touch all over. And she did, sweeping her hands all over his heated skin.

He smiled down at her as he cupped her face and began kissing her lips, taking a break to kiss each eye, her forehead, her cheeks, her jaw, and then her mouth again. He made her feel so special as she kissed him back, their heartbeats accelerating, their blood heating.

But then she pulled away from him to get this show on the road and slipped her boots off, and he yanked his off too. She laughed when she saw he was wearing Santa socks. "I didn't know you were wearing those. They're cute." She had gotten him some special socks for his Christmas stocking that she hoped he would get a kick out of.

"'Tis the season. And you're wearing Rudolph the Red-Nosed Reindeer socks." He leaned down and lifted her foot to kiss Rudolph's nose.

She laughed. "That tickles."

He ran his hands up her sweater and cupped her breasts. She sighed, loving how he molded his palms to them, massaging and lifting. But then he slid her sweater over her head.

She hurried to unbuckle his belt while he was kissing her bare shoulders. "I love your red lace bra and"—he unfastened her blue plaid skirt and peeked under the waistband—"your red lace panties."

"I wore them just for you for Christmas."

"I'm so glad you did." He removed his jeans and then unfastened her skirt and pulled it off.

She tugged off his boxer briefs, releasing his engorged erection. "You are so gorgeous," she said, running her hands over his abs, his arousal boldly showing he was as ready for her as she was for him. "Every bit of you."

He cupped her ass, his mouth sweeping over her jaw in a sensual caress. "You are too."

Oh, man, he was so hot, and her blood was on fire. Like it always did, a heady desire pooled between them. He pressed a kiss to each of her breasts, but then removed her bra and did the same thing, flesh to flesh, which felt even more sensual. Her panties were the last of the articles of clothing to go before he yanked their covers aside, scooped her up, and laid her gently on the bed.

No matter how many different ways they ended up in bed—falling into it while passionately kissing each other, him carrying her after a shower and dumping her on it and then ravishing her, him climbing onto the bed and her taking over like a wolf hunting its prey or tackling him like he did her, or like this, tenderly and lovingly—she loved him.

He covered her body with his, pressing his erection against her mons, kissing her like he couldn't get enough of her, like she felt about him all the time. His hands were gently combing through her hair, making her feel heavenly. He was a dream lover and made for loving. *Her* loving.

She rolled him over on his back and climbed on top, undulating against his body, rubbing herself against his erection, kissing his mouth with desire. Their pheromones were all over the place, ratcheting up the excitement, the anticipation of where this would lead.

But then, as if it was too much for him to take before he came, he rolled her on her back and began to pleasure her, using his finger to stroke her into an orgasm. Sheer pleasure streaked through her core as she moaned, and he kissed her mouth with a seal of self-satisfied approval.

"You're mine, my beautiful she-wolf," Slade said to Sheri, his voice hushed and saturated with lust. "Merry Christmas, honey."

She realized it was after midnight and truly Christmas Day. "You are likewise mine, my hunky wolf, a pilot after my own heart and piloting us toward adventures unknown. Merry Christmas."

"The holidays became even merrier once I met you." Slade was kissing Sheri again, so ready to come and he wasn't even inside her yet!

He spread her legs further, then pushed into her willing, heated body, thrusting. She was so tight, and she arched against him, making it even better, deeper, hotter. Every time he made love to her, he felt at home, that she had been the only one for him and she made him feel like he was the only one for her.

She moaned under his ministrations, digging her fingers into his shoulders possessively, seeking her own climax again as he was working toward his. He wanted her to come again, wanted them to have an orgasm at the same time, in union, together. So he slowed his thrusts, but she tightened her grip on him, both her fingers on his shoulders and her internal muscles stroking his erection. She was the stuff of dreams, magical, changing his world from so-so to extraordinary. He loved her with all his heart, and he managed to utter these thoughts aloud in a strained way. Then she was kissing him, nipping at his chin, his lips, his earlobe, and he sensed in her wildness that she was ready to come again, and he couldn't have been more satisfied than that. He started to thrust hard and deep and that sent them spiraling toward climax.

They both cried out and kissed and laughed.

Then they hugged each other close, listening to their rapid heartbeats, smelling their rampant pheromones that had cheered them on all the way to the climax. He was thinking about Christmas morning, about their ski trip, about the wedding, a million things before he drifted off to sleep, when she said, "The cookies!"

"Cookies?" That was one thing that hadn't been on his mind!

"I need to make the pfeffernusse cookies for tomorrow for Christmas lunch. I need to start them now, and the same thing with the green bean casserole. I don't know how I forgot about them. And I need to wrap your Christmas presents."

"Oh, I need to do that for you too. We had a lot going on."

She chuckled. "That's for sure."

"Okay, let's do this."

They got up and took a shower. No matter how much they tried to just shower—clean up, and nothing more—it always turned into something more. Then they finally dried off and went into the bedroom, and they pulled on their new Christmas wolf pj's.

In the kitchen, they started to make the dough. Once that

was done, she said, "I need to refrigerate them for two hours, then bake them."

He glanced at the clock.

"Yeah, I know. It will be really late, or really early, depending on your perspective. That's what takes the most time."

"Okay, set the timer, and I'll do it."

She smiled and kissed him. "You've never made them before. I've made them every year. I can practically do it in my sleep."

"You might be doing that."

She laughed, put them in the fridge while he set the timer on the oven, and then they made the casserole together, wrapped the presents they had bought for each other at Mall of America, and went to bed. Back to snuggling, kissing, and making love. Again.

Chapter 29

ON CHRISTMAS MORNING, SLADE WOKE FIRST, BUT SHERI was still sound asleep. He considered making her breakfast in bed. He had told her if he woke first, he was waking her to open their Christmas presents, but there was no way he was going to when he was enjoying being with her like this, cuddling, their first Christmas together. This was too special. He closed his eyes, enjoying the sweet scent that was all Sheri, and it wasn't until much later that he felt her stir.

She opened her eyes and smiled and kissed him. "You finally woke."

He chuckled. "*You* finally woke." He kissed her back.

"Me? I woke an hour ago."

He laughed and checked the clock. "I woke before that, but you were snuggling against me, sound asleep. It was too nice, and I didn't want to ruin the moment."

"Then you fell asleep."

"I did."

"What happened to us waking each other up first thing on Christmas morning?"

"I know, right? I'm sure it had all to do with having to get up and make the cookies, casserole, and wrap presents late last night. Oh, shoot, we have to hurry and unwrap the presents in our stockings or we'll be late for Christmas lunch," he said. "Or we'll have to open our stocking presents later."

"No way."

He laughed.

They hurried out of bed, threw on their Christmas pajamas, raced each other to the Christmas tree to turn on the lights and the mantel lights, and laughed. "Oh, let me start some coffee," Sheri said.

"I'll do it. You pick out the presents you want us to open first."

"We'll just do all the Christmas stocking presents, but we might have to tear through them as fast as we can so we can arrive on time at my parents' home."

"Yeah. We can do that." He started the coffee and then joined her in front of the lighted Christmas tree.

She handed him his Christmas stocking and dumped the presents out of hers onto the couch. "So what do we have here?" She started ripping open packages.

He opened a package of red and green boxer briefs featuring a Santa Claus that said *Delivering all night* and he laughed. "This is just too funny. For you, that's a promise."

"I'll hold you to it."

"I love a challenge." Then he unwrapped a pair of chili pepper socks that had *Hot Stuff* printed on the soles that were just as cute, and another pair that said *Superman*.

"You are both of those things, and I just wanted you to know it."

"I love them. I love you." He opened his last present, and it was an apron that said *An apron is a cape turned backward*.

"Because you truly are my superhero and because you need some place for the green icing to go when you decorate cookies in the future."

He chuckled. "I got a kick out of your dad saying he'd never decorated a cookie before, and his cookie still turned out great."

"I should warn you that he will be in a competition with you from now on."

Slade gave her one of his darling, dimpled smiles. "I'm up for it. I'll have to start practicing."

"Yes, you have all year to do it." She opened his first gift to her, and she found a blue body loofah-sponge back scrubber.

"But I get to use it on you," he said.

She smiled. "And I get to use it on you likewise."

"I look forward to. Tonight."

"You've got it." She opened her next present and pulled out a retro black-and-white-striped vintage apron with ruffles and a big black bow. It was absolutely adorable. She laughed. "That's to protect me while you're icing your cookies, right?"

"Absolutely."

She opened her next package, and it was a pair of cute wolf socks in aqua with little Arctic wolf heads. "Ooh, these look nice and cozy warm."

"They should be. They called them cabin socks and I figured you could wear them on our honeymoon at the ski lodge even."

"They're the cutest." Then she opened her last gift, a solar phone charger for two.

"I figured if we had electric issues, we could both use it."

"It's perfect."

They dressed in their wolf sweaters and blue jeans, boots, and parkas, grabbed the casserole, dessert, and presents for their families and some presents for each other and then drove to Georgia's and Fred's home. Except for Dulcie, everyone else had already arrived: Henry, Lolita, and Hans, Elizabeth and David, Amelia, Gavin, and the twins.

Everyone wished everyone a Merry Christmas, and hugs and kisses were shared all around. They took pictures of the whole family, then individual families, and the twins dressed in Santa elf sleepers. They were adorable.

Then everyone sat around the Christmas tree and began to open gifts. Slade laughed when he got a beginner's guide to cookie decorating from Fred. But he laughed even harder when Georgia got Fred one too.

"When Fred picked up that guidebook for you, I went back and got one for him," Georgia said.

Amelia and Gavin gave Sheri and Slade sky-blue silk pillowcases. They were so soft.

Hans got Sheri and Slade a blanket split in two but attached at the bottom. "So you don't have to worry about someone tugging the blanket away from you."

Everyone loved it. Then the couples found that Hans had given one to each of them. They loved them. Slade loved the aqua waffle maker for two that she had gotten them, and she gave her gift from the Christmas Eve party to Elizabeth, who was thrilled.

He was glad that Sheri loved her red cashmere sweater, just

as much as he loved the fleece sherpa sweater she'd given him. Her parents had given them both UGG slippers. And Slade gave Sheri a portable firepit they could use to make s'mores and roast marshmallows and hot dogs with guests or just the two of them inside their home anytime they wanted to.

"I'll be over to make s'mores on it," Hans said.

"You and everyone else is welcome to," Sheri said. "This will be fun to use."

Sheri had gotten Slade a portable, outdoor wood-fired pizza oven. "Now this is going to come in handy," Slade said.

"Hey, we're all going to love dropping by for pizza," David said, Gavin agreeing.

Then Slade opened his last present from Sheri and smiled. "Great. Lots of cool accessories to go with the drone."

"I'm going to get a drone license and take some shots of the wedding when you have it," Hans said.

"Oh, that would be perfect," Sheri said. "That was the gift that I had to fight over."

Then everyone had to hear the story.

"Well, at least he was man enough to apologize at the end," Georgia said.

Once they finished opening their gifts, everyone got ready to eat. The ham and turkey, mashed potatoes, dressing, gravy, cranberry, green bean casserole, and loaves of bread were set out on the table. Hans poured glasses of wine while Amelia and Elizabeth got glasses of milk.

A dessert table had been set up and Sheri put her pfeffernusse cookies on there. More desserts were already there, from a pecan pie to chocolate cupcakes.

Just then, the doorbell rang, and Sheri went to answer it. Slade saw it was Dulcie and everyone was thrilled she could make it for Christmas lunch. She was carrying a box of homemade fudge.

"Oh, yum, this looks great," Sheri said, and led Dulcie into the dining room. Everyone had already met her at the pizza party. They all greeted her and then they sat down to eat.

"So what did you get stuck working on last night?" Slade asked, knowing that she might not be able to say.

"Remember the delivery van that went missing in the case you were investigating, Sheri?" Dulcie asked.

"You found it?"

"Yes, it was found on a farm road. But we also located a video that showed the delivery van had been at Fitz's house. The video was from the house across the street. He'd even opened the van, looked inside, and locked it back up. It proves he knew it was full of packages."

Sheri sighed. "Good, so some more to charge him with."

"Exactly."

"And we have video and eyewitness testimony stating he wasn't a deliveryman but had been wearing a delivery uniform. Oh, but wait, the best news of all?"

Everyone was passing around dishes of ham, turkey, mashed potatoes, sweet potatoes, cranberry, and the rest of the side dishes, but Slade swore everyone stopped what they were doing to hear what Dulcie had to say.

"Otis flipped on the other two."

"Yes!" Sheri shouted with glee.

Dulcie laughed. "Yeah. Danbury was charged with

attempted murder, so he didn't have any leeway. Fitz was the head honcho, the man who planned the whole thing. So I talked to Otis, told him we had all this evidence and that though he was as involved in all of it too, he had a chance to testify against his cohorts and get a reduced sentence." She smiled and dished up some of Sheri's green bean casserole. "He took the deal."

"All right," Sheri said. "I'm so glad, as long as he doesn't change his mind at trial."

Then her father got a call and Slade wondered what that was all about. Fred built homes and all his family was right here, so Slade couldn't imagine he would be getting any calls from anyone on Christmas Day.

Fred smiled. "Thanks, Cameron. Yes, let them know where we live. Merry Christmas to you and your family too." Then he ended the call. "Well, apparently we're about to get some guests who are dropping off a package in about an hour."

"Oh?" Hans asked.

"Yeah." Fred didn't say anything more and began to enjoy his turkey leg.

"Dad," Sheri said. "You're not going to leave us hanging, are you?"

Fred laughed. "In the spirit of Christmas, yes. It's a surprise."

They were finishing up dinner when the doorbell rang, and Fred went to get it. "Come in," he said.

To Slade and everyone else's surprise, Gerard, his wife, Betty, his daughter, Jessica, Tex Lincoln, and his wife, Nancy, and his cardiac-alert service dog, Benny, and their dog, Jet, arrived with an extra-extra-large gift basket filled with cheeses, crackers, chocolates, teas, coffees, wine, just a little of everything.

"This is a small token of our appreciation for bringing us all together," Betty said, "and for saving Tex's life twice, once in the Boundary Waters and then at his home in Minneapolis, and Nancy's life too. Not to mention bringing Tex a cardiac-alert dog who is so loved by all of us, Jet also. And helping to put Gerard's brother away, but also making sure Gerard remained safe. This is the first Christmas we've spent together with Tex and Nancy in a decade, with the added special delight of having Jessica with us too, and Sheri and Slade made that all possible."

"Come in and have some drinks and dessert with us," Fred offered.

"Thank you. Is it all right that Benny and Jet come in too? We don't want to impose," Tex said.

"Yeah, Benny needs to be with you at all times. Jet was just as much of a lifesaver when he alerted us you were in trouble in the Boundary Waters, so he is welcome as well. And thank you for the lovely gift." Slade wrapped his arm around Sheri's shoulder and leaned down and kissed her. Sheri was the best gift he could have asked for, but through her diligence, and his own, they had aided the two families more than they realized and he was glad for that.

Sheri thanked them also and gave Slade a heartfelt hug, smiling up at him, just as glad things had worked out so well for the family.

Then they all sat down in the living room to have some Christmas cheer and talk about everything under the sun—except the thing they really couldn't discuss, the upcoming trial of Gerard's brother and the other men. But for Christmas Day, that was a good thing.

And when they finally had enjoyed their drinks and desserts, the two families left so that Slade and Sheri and their families could enjoy playing games until it was time to return home.

Since they were leaving the next day for Silver Town, Sheri and Slade left their gift basket with Elizabeth to take to the office and share with the rest of the pack. They were ready to enjoy all that Silver Town had to offer and a mated honeymoon without any issues.

They returned home to pack for their big trip to Silver Town tomorrow, but one thing led to another and they were back in bed enjoying each other like wolves who were very much in love, the perfect way to end their Christmas Day.

Epilogue

THE MATING HONEYMOON IN SILVER TOWN, COLORADO, after Christmas had been a great getaway for Sheri and Slade. They'd even met all the Wolff sisters and brothers and their extended family, two of whom were private investigators like Sheri and her partners. In June, Elizabeth had her babies, a girl and a boy, and she was still on maternity leave while David was taking off lots of time from the PI office to be with her and the babies to help out.

Sheri and Slade had moved into their new home—no more juggling seasonal clothes into the spare room. They'd had their wedding at the lake, and Hans had even gotten an operator's license so he could use Slade's drone and taken pictures of part of the wedding and reception.

They were delaying their honeymoon after the wedding because the trials for Fitz and his cohorts were coming up next.

They'd even had their interview with the news reporter, which had put them in a good light and given both the PI office and Slade's family's seaplane business a boost in clients.

Because they had barely settled into their new home with a few borrowed pieces of furniture, Sheri and Slade were so excited about just being there with each other.

Today, the dining room, living room, and bedroom

furniture were all coming. They couldn't wait to make love on their new mattress. The wolf pack had bought their dining room set and living room furniture.

"I wish we had a better idea when the deliveries were going to be made," Slade said.

"I know, right? The worst is that they delayed our bed's arrival." They'd been sleeping on a blow-up air mattress, but it wasn't the greatest for making love.

"I know. I was ready to have them ship a different kind just so we would get it sooner."

Then they heard a delivery truck pull up. It was like Christmas all over again, and Sheri hurried to see which delivery it was for. "The living room set!" She was so glad. They'd been sitting on lawn chairs to watch the TV on the wall.

"No bed."

"No. That's okay. It would be better if the bed is delivered last."

He smiled. "I'm going to grill the steaks, if you're ready for them."

She laughed and began making a spinach salad. "Watch everyone come over when they smell the steaks."

"They won't intrude. Not when we just got married and we would be on our honeymoon if it wasn't for the trial being suddenly scheduled."

"True." Of course, all the furniture was supposed to have been delivered and then Faith was going to supervise where they put it while Slade and Sheri were on their honeymoon. They'd given her the layout on where everything went, but they were glad they didn't have to ask her to do it now.

"But we'll run with them as wolves tonight, right?" she asked.

"Yeah, sure."

"I am so glad we're here now and can do that. We can just go out our wolf door and run together on our own or with the pack. I'm so happy."

"Me too. No more having to drive home afterward. We're already home."

Then they heard a knock on the door.

"I'll get that before I grill the steaks," he said.

"Too bad it wasn't the dining room set first."

He laughed. "The kitchen bar will work until then." He opened the door and the men started hauling in the two sofas, three recliners, a coffee table, and bookshelves.

"Wow, that's going to be so nice. It all looks so comfortable," Sheri said.

"It is."

Once the delivery men left, Sheri and Slade plunked down on one of the sofas, looked at the TV's blank screen, then turned to each and began kissing. Wow, this was so nice, not at all like sitting on lawn chairs.

"Man, I wish all the deliveries had already been made," Slade said.

"Even though the big bed isn't here."

"Yeah."

She laughed.

He sighed. "Okay, I'm going to get the steaks on."

Then someone else pulled up.

"Delivery truck number two." Sheri went to the window. "Dining room set. Go get the steaks ready."

"Coming right up." Slade saluted her and started to grill the steaks on the back patio.

Sheri had the men set the table, chairs, and hutch in the open dining room. Once the delivery men left, she made rice and cauliflower to go with their steaks and Slade brought in the grilled meat.

Sheri set the table and Slade opened a bottle of champagne. Then they sat down to have dinner and were enjoying it when they heard the final delivery truck.

"The bed!" Sheri said.

Slade smiled. "You know what that means."

"I sure do. We need to break out the sheets and get ready for what comes next."

"Christening the bed."

"Exactly."

"Yeah, from now until eternity. Well, maybe not the same bed," he said, smiling.

Slade went to the door and showed the delivery men where the bed, dresser, and bedside tables went.

Sheri was enjoying her dinner because she was always a slower eater than Slade. The men finished the job and left, and he rejoined her. "I figured we would finish our meals and then make the bed and you know the rest."

"Absolutely."

They finished dinner, cleaned up, and then when they found the fresh sheets in the linen closet, they made the bed together. They were stripping off their clothes when they heard the wolves of their pack howling. They were letting everyone know that they were headed out for a run.

Sheri and Slade looked at each other. They smiled.

"Okay, after we run with the pack," she said.

He laughed. "Yeah, after we join the pack."

Everyone in the wolf pack had done so much for them in helping them to set up their new home. They needed to show how much they appreciated them and finished removing their clothes and then raced out of their brand-new wolf door to join the white wolf pack to enjoy the woods, the leaves now yellow, red, orange, purple, and green. It was beautiful, even more so because she and Slade were running together as mated and married wolves with the rest of the pack.

They howled for joy, and a chorus of wolves—friends and family—howled back.

Read on for more of Terry Spear's wolfishly delicious Christmas romance in *Her Wolf for the Holidays*.

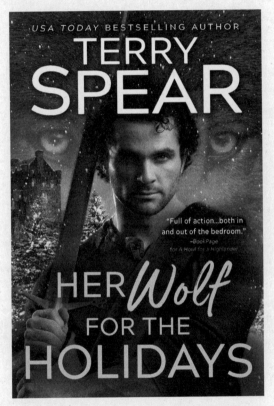

Now available from Sourcebooks Casablanca

Chapter 1

"WHAT DO YOU MEAN, THE PROPERTY ADJOINING OURS already sold, Lachlan?" Grant MacQuarrie practically roared at the youngest of his triplet brothers, his face reddening as he stood alongside his mate, Colleen, in the inner bailey of Farraige Castle in the Highlands of Scotland.

A smattering of snow fluttered around them. It was only two weeks until Christmas, and this wasn't the best of news for the holidays.

Lachlan MacQuarrie knew Grant, chief of the MacQuarrie clan and their gray wolf pack leader, would be furious about it. For centuries, Eairrdsidh James Campbell—known as EJ—and his kin had owned the nearby property, but EJ wouldn't consider selling to the MacQuarries before he died because of old wolf clan grudges. Grant was certain he would finally have the chance to buy it when the ornery old cuss passed on, since he had no offspring to leave it to. Any land that expanded their wolf territory was a good deal. What they didn't want was humans moving in next door to them, though thankfully, the MacQuarries still had a lot of acreage between them and EJ's property.

"The manor house and lands were sold to a private buyer," Lachlan said.

"They better not be planning on building some eyesore on the property. Hell, we live long lives, and we'll have to deal with this forever." Furious, Grant folded his arms across his chest.

Colleen said, "We know, dear. It's nearly Christmas. Think of pleasant and upbeat things. Like maybe we can befriend the new owners when EJ made it impossible to be friends with him. I can take over some Christmas shortbread cookies or plum pudding. I can even give them a Christmas poinsettia as a housewarming gift. Think positive thoughts."

Grant scowled.

Colleen sighed and ran her hand over his arm. "EJ would never hang Christmas lights on his manor house. Being located way out here and isolated from most everybody, he was more of a recluse and didn't have guests or friends or anyone that we know of. Maybe if the new owners want to decorate the outside of the manor house for Christmas at this late date, we could offer to help them put lights up or anything else they might want to do."

Grant grunted, rubbed his bearded chin, and frowned at Lachlan. "I told you the moment Campbell died you were to buy the land."

Lachlan had figured Colleen's gentle, kindhearted words wouldn't have any effect on Grant's irritated mood. "Aye. Everyone has been told to watch for any sign he was sick or an announcement of his death. If Campbell had any say in it, he would have sold it to someone who will hate us as much as he did. I'm sorry, Grant. The minute I heard the news, I was on it. I contacted our solicitor to learn if anyone had inherited the property. As far as we know, he didn't have any living relatives. I had hoped to find out when it was going on the market but discovered he'd already sold it to a private party a year ago with the provision that he would live there until he died."

Grant's brows shot up. "EJ sold the property a *year* ago?"

"Aye, and there was no way we could have learned of it. The whole thing was kept quiet."

"What about the deed to the property?" Grant asked.

"Whoever bought it recorded it in the name of Campbell, same initials even. EJ. So we hadn't thought it had changed hands."

"How do you know that someone else truly owns it?"

"The date on the deed showed it changed hands a year ago."

"Maybe we can convince the new owners to sell us the property since they haven't lived there yet," Grant said.

"I'll welcome whoever it is so that they know we're friendly." Colleen had been unable to make friends with EJ but sounded determined to do so with the new owner.

Grant cleared his throat. "We should just scare them away."

"Like you tried to scare me away?" Colleen smiled.

Lachlan chuckled. Grant cast her a small smile. When Colleen had inherited Farraige Castle, Grant had been afraid she'd change everything there when he and his kin had run things for centuries. Colleen had only been amused at Grant's tactics, and they'd ended up mating instead. Which had been the best thing that could ever have happened to the pack.

"Nay," she continued. "Unless Campbell told the buyers that the people at our castle are difficult to deal with, maybe we can have a fresh start. And, sure, if it might work, by all means make an offer for the property. I know you. If you could, you would buy up all of Scotland." Colleen kissed Grant's cheek. Lachlan loved how she adored Grant as much as he adored her.

"Then we could run as wolves anywhere we pleased," Grant said.

Which was something Lachlan wholeheartedly agreed with.

Suddenly, Frederick, their Irish wolfhound handler, came running to join them. "Daisy had her puppies. Hercules wants to see them also."

"The daddy can. Let's go see them." Grant took Colleen's hand, smiling, appearing to have dropped the subject about Campbell and the land. "You're feeling all right, aren't you, honey?"

"Aye, just a bit of upset stomach this morning," Colleen said.

"Good." Then they hurried off to the kennel. But as if he'd had an afterthought, Grant glanced back at Lachlan. "Learn who it is who actually purchased the property as soon as you can."

"Aye." Lachlan had hated to bring his brother the bad news ever since he had learned this morning that the property was in someone else's hands. He'd tried to learn who the new EJ Campbell was before he spoke to his brother, but to no avail.

Their middle triplet brother, Enrick, arrived at the castle, already wearing his Highland great kilt in the ancient tartan, sheathed sword hanging at his belt, and *sgian dubh* tucked in his boot just like Lachlan's was.

Enrick lived with his mate, Heather, at their home near her business, the Ye Olde Highland Pie Shoppe, but he still would drive here to help with pack and castle chores. From the expression on Enrick's face—his brows raised, waiting to hear if Lachlan had told Grant already—Lachlan suspected his brother already knew what had happened to the land next door.

"So a Campbell bought the place, but he can't be related to old Campbell. He had no living relatives," Enrick said.

"Aye." Or so they thought. "I have to discover who it is—"

"And then offer to purchase the bordering land?"

"Aye," Lachlan said.

"Or Grant can try to scare the new owners off," Enrick said.

Lachlan laughed. "Aye, and you know how well that turned out with Colleen."

"Exactly. Do we know if the new owners are even wolves?"

"Nay, and Grant's afraid they might try to develop the property into a block of flats filled with humans. He wouldn't put it past the old Campbell to sell it to someone like that to spite us."

"We have a forest and pastureland between us. Not to mention the dike running along the hill to the cliffs and across the pastureland that separates our properties. As long as they don't go hunting on our lands or causing other trouble, I don't see the difficulty."

"Unless they're not wolves and they're as cantankerous

as old Campbell was. Are you ready for some fighting?"
Lachlan was ready. They were both looking forward to their
sword training—something they did to keep in shape and to
hone their skills. They never knew when the training could
prove useful.

Enrick looked around the inner bailey where others were
gathering, all dressed in Highland plaids, ready to begin
sparring. "I am. Where's Grant?"

"With Colleen checking out the new pups. He'll join us
soon. You know how he likes to battle with his men."

"But especially with us."

Lachlan smiled. "Aye." The two of them loved to gang up
on him—because he was their pack leader and their oldest
brother and he had to prove his worth to them and to their
men in an endearing way.

———

As Edeen Campbell surveyed her land next to the
MacQuarries' property on that cold wintry day, she smiled,
thanking her lucky stars that EJ Campbell had come into
her life. He had warned Edeen she would have trouble with
Grant MacQuarrie and his kin in the castle on the hill, but he
told her to stand her ground.

She hadn't even known EJ. He'd looked her up—owing
to the fact she was listed as a Campbell on Facebook, living
in Edinburgh, single, and working out of her home. She did
well enough making Celtic clothes to sell at Renaissance fairs
and to shops all over the UK and overseas, so she could live

anywhere. But EJ made sure to check; he had to be assured she wouldn't lose the property over unpaid taxes or some such thing.

Some of Edeen's biggest markets were in the United States, and they were always expanding. Plus, she and her twin brother, Robert, an associate veterinary surgeon, had received an inheritance from an uncle and their parents, and she'd made a bundle off her home she'd sold in Edinburgh, so she could afford to pay the taxes and utilities on EJ's property in perpetuity. She was named Edeen Jane, same first and middle initials just like EJ, which he had been really glad for, though he wouldn't say why. But the clincher was that she was a wolf and so was he, which he'd only learned after talking to her in Edinburgh.

Robert was thrilled for her, but he worked in the city for now with a veterinary practice, so other than helping her move in, he'd had to get back to the city.

Of course Edeen had asked EJ if she hadn't been a wolf, then what would he have done? Tracked down all the Campbells in Scotland until he found one who was, he'd told her. Were she and her brother related to him? Maybe in the distant past his relations were her relations because they were both wolves, but she hadn't known him. He'd given her such a reduced price on the manor house and acreage that she couldn't say no to it. He'd said he would only do it for her because she was a wolf on her own, had an occupation that she could work at anywhere, and would carry on the Campbell name there.

She had no luck finding any wolf whom she'd been

remotely interested in while living in Edinburgh, and with neighbors here to be wary of, Edeen figured she had no chance of finding a mate here either. Being so remote out here, she didn't expect to find anyone else who was a wolf, at least. For now, she was fine with that.

Besides, she'd so screwed up things by dating humans in the last two years—both married, unbeknownst to her!—that she felt relief when she left the city. Not that she wanted anyone to believe she had left Edinburgh with her tail tucked between her legs. Though it did kind of seem like that.

She did wonder about the off chance of finding a wolf—slim chance of that, she thought—mating him, and maybe wanting to change her name to his. Then she would no longer be a Campbell who owned the property. EJ hadn't seemed to think of that, and she hadn't wanted to bring it up and nix the deal or promise him something she didn't want to promise.

When EJ died, Edeen and Robert had taken care of his wicker-coffin burial like he had wanted because he believed it was a more environmentally friendly alternative. They had felt saddened at the thought that he'd died alone like that with no family or friends to care, only them in attendance at his funeral. Though once she had met him and he had sold the property to her, she had made several trips out to see him during the year and bring him food. She'd even offered to help him decorate for Christmas, but he hadn't done so ever, and he wasn't starting now, he'd said. He did love the Christmas shortbread and other food she brought him. No one should be all alone in the world like that, though she guessed if he was happiest that way, then that was his life to choose.

After Robert helped her yesterday with moving in the bulk of her things—her sewing machine and cabinet and her own new bed—she'd finished moving into her new home this morning, glad to do so before the snowstorm that was due in a couple of days. She paused to step outside and admire the view. She would never tire of it.

The acreage was beautiful—a hundred acres in all, pastureland for Highland cattle, a pond, a loch even, streams meandering through the property. Some of the land was situated on a cliff overlooking the ocean. Just picturesque. Even Robert thought the same about the place. If he hadn't been so busy with his practice, he might have considered moving out there with her.

She'd fallen in love with the house and land as soon as she'd visited it. The home was a former inn built in the 1700s but had been refurbished several times. It was right on the shore of the loch and had views of the mountains off in the distance. With four bedrooms, a sitting room, a living room, utility room, two bathrooms, and a kitchen, the main part of the house was a nice size for a family. But the manor house also had a separate kitchen/dining/living room, two bedrooms, and two bathrooms that were perfect for renting out half the house to guests if she wanted to do that. But she would only want to house wolves. Plus, her brother could stay with her anytime he wanted to.

All the windows had been replaced to allow for ample natural light. The house had two wood-burning stoves, one of which could burn a variety of liquid fuels. Deep windowsills were perfect for plants or even seating. Rafters above were exposed, and the original board-and-latch doors inside the home gave it so much charm and made it perfectly unique. Deer, birds, and bunnies could be seen from the quarter acre of garden seating, and plenty of outdoor storage could be used for her ongoing garden projects in the spring, summer, and fall.

Right now, with winter upon them, she would be running as a wolf, just exploring her property and fantasizing about the wolf pack up at Farraige Castle. Though from everything EJ had told her, she needed to avoid them. In no way should she ever allow them to talk her into selling to them. She had no intention of it. This would be the perfect place to raise her own family if she ever found a wolf to mate.

She glanced up at the hill that was probably grassy in the spring but in the winter was rocky and bare of trees. An ancient six-foot rock wall wound its way across the hill. It extended down the hill and entered the forest below, separating her property from the MacQuarries' all the way to the main road.

EJ had warned her that last year a great battle had been waged below the hill on the other side—film style. He swore they did everything they could to irritate him. She'd seen the American-made film *A Twist in Time*, set at the MacQuarries' castle, but she'd never envisioned she'd be living next door to the castle where the movie had been filmed. She would have loved to see the battle going on when they were making the film. She wondered if she had sat upon the wall, would she have been able to see the film production from there? Though EJ also warned her the wall was the MacQuarries', so no touching it or they'd sic their hellhounds after her. She'd heard their dogs were wild giants. They better not mess with her little fox terriers, Jinx and Rogue, both of them in the house checking it out. They were fearless, but she still worried the MacQuarries' dogs could hurt hers.

Robert had said if she needed his help at any time, he'd be there for her. But her new home was a three-hour drive from Edinburgh, so she had reassured him she could handle the MacQuarries on her own.

That's when she saw a humongous dog jumping over the dike, the stone wall dike not slowing him down, and racing down the hill. Ohmigod, she swore he was about as big as a horse. She turned and shot toward the house, hating to feel as though she couldn't be outside enjoying her property without being chased inside by a ferocious monster of a beast. EJ had been right.

She just made it to her back door, her dogs wildly barking at the window, when she threw the door open and ran inside, slamming the door shut and locking it. She was glad she'd already locked the wolf door. She didn't want Jinx and Rogue to be outside unless she was watching them, afraid they might chase after rabbits or something and get lost until they knew their surroundings better.

The dog ran into her door with a big-footed thump. It better not have gotten big, dirty paw prints on the newly painted blue door.

She looked out the window and saw the dog staring through the window at her, his tongue hanging out, his ears perking up when he observed her. "Bad dog! Go home!"

The dog had a whole castle and lots of his *own* land to enjoy. Why was he bothering her?

She had to admit he was a pretty dog. A brindled Irish wolfhound, she thought.

Barking like crazy, her dogs were going nuts—standing on the window seat, jumping at the window, wanting to tear into the intruder. If she hadn't been afraid the giant dog would hurt them, she'd let them out so they could chase him off.

Thankfully, EJ had given her Grant MacQuarrie's cell phone number in case she had any issues with him. She hadn't believed the moment she'd practically moved into her new place, she would have to call him about some matter!

She grabbed her phone and called his number, but the call went to voicemail. *Naturally.* Which annoyed her even more. She needed this taken care of now!

Then she stiffened her back, threw on her coat, and grabbed a leash, hoping that she could put it on the dog and take him up to the castle without him biting her—though she was good with dogs, so she thought he would be fine. As soon as she unlocked the door and opened it, Rogue and Jinx raced passed her into the yard and took off after the dog.

"No! Get back here!" Oh, no. She hadn't expected them to bust out like that. Back home, they would never have. They had been model, well-mannered pets. Already her neighbors' dog was a bad influence on hers! Seeing the dog in their territory and then running off had been enough of an incentive for them to chase after him.

Jinx and Rogue were running as fast as they could after the dog as he bounded up the hill. With his long stride and head start, he was well ahead of them. At least if he jumped over the dike, the ancient drystone wall topped with a coping stone would prevent her dogs from following him.

She raced after them with only one leash, not having had time to grab another. Even though she was glad the Irish wolfhound was going home, she didn't want her dogs to bite him. He could very well turn and attack them in self-defense. She could see fur flying and being sued by the laird of the castle because her dogs ganged up on his dog even though it wasn't *her* fault that he let his dog loose and he trespassed on *her* property!

She was running up the hill as fast as she could, wishing she was wearing her wolf coat because she could run faster and maybe her dogs would listen to her better than as a human. Suddenly, she stepped in something squishy that didn't feel like the crunchy snow and looked down. Dog shit all over her boots. Oh, just great.

She could have chased all the dogs down in a heartbeat in her wolf form and maybe would have noticed the dog poop before she managed to get it all over the soles and sides of her wellies. As it was, she was lagging way behind the dogs. The Irish wolfhound leapt over the dike as expected, but to her shock, her dogs scrambled up and over the mossy rocks too! The wall was so ancient that it was covered in a cushion of green moss, a thin layer of white snow on top of it. Well-worn, rounded rocks jutted out from the dike from top to bottom, making them perfect stepping-stones for her dogs. For her too, she hoped!

She finally reached the wall where it was a little lower— the wall having settled over the years there, but not by much—and climbed over. If they'd owned the land on both sides of the wall, the stone builders might even have made an opening topped with a stone lintel, wide enough for sheep or pigs to go through to the other side of the wall to graze in the pasture there.

She landed on the other side in the white dusting of fresh snow, brown boot prints left behind, courtesy of the wild Irish wolfhound's leavings, and ran toward the castle. Off to the left was a stream filled with ducks and geese and a couple of swans. Her attention returned to the dogs and the castle surrounded by a massive, high stone wall, the portcullis open.

In the distance, men were yelling, and the clanking of swords could be heard inside the castle walls. She frowned. Was another film being made there?

"Jinx! Rogue! Come here!" she called out, trying to get their attention but attempting to not clue anyone else in that she was trespassing on the MacQuarries' property. *Great. Just great.* No one would believe the MacQuarries' dog was the culprit in the whole rotten scenario!

The Irish wolfhound ran straight through the open gates, as if finding safety there. Darned if her dogs didn't run right after him inside the castle walls and vanish! She hoped Grant and his people didn't hurt her dogs. She had to reach them in time to explain who was at fault.

She finally reached the big gate to the massive castle walls, which truly were spectacular, and saw men sword fighting in the inner bailey, working up a sweat in their kilts and boots, no shirts, despite that it was winter.

One of the men suddenly saw her dogs and said, "Whoa, where'd you come from?"

"They're mine, and *your* dog taunted them to chase him." As if that didn't sound ludicrous, she thought as soon as she said it.

The roguish-looking Highlander stared at her as if she had lost her mind. He glanced around at the inner bailey, where every man who had been fighting was now watching her. Their darn dog had vanished—probably hiding in the castle to pretend he didn't have anything to do with any of this, innocent as the day he was born.

"I'm Lachlan MacQuarrie, and who do I have the honor of addressing?" Lachlan asked.

His hazel eyes captured hers, and she swore she saw a hint of amusement in his gaze.

Appearing to have done their good deed for the day, Rogue and Jinx finally returned to her side after having lost their quarry. Thankfully, they hadn't found their way inside the castle and caused even more of a stir.

She hooked the leash on Rogue's collar and lifted Jinx in her arms. "Edeen Campbell. Your new next-door neighbor. Kindly keep your wild beast of a dog off my property."

Then she turned on her heel and took off for the gate. That first meeting with a MacQuarrie went well, she thought. *Not.*

Chapter 2

LACHLAN STARED AFTER THE FIERY REDHEADED, MOSSY-green-eyed spitfire as Edeen hurried off through the snow to get away from the castle. "Do you need to borrow another leash?" He immediately thought about inviting her to their Christmas party that was in six days. Before this, the person who bought the property could have been human, so inviting the owner would have been out. But Edeen certainly was *not* human. Though she might have a mate and family… What did he know? If she was single, he was completely intrigued.

In the back of his mind, he was thinking about Colleen's comments about befriending their next-door neighbor. He was all for being first in line for that before the other bachelor males in their pack showed how interested they undoubtedly would be.

She didn't answer him and continued to walk off. She looked like she was struggling to carry the one dog while the other walked beside her like a well-heeled pet. He wondered why she had concluded that their dogs had anything to do with luring her dogs here.

The MacQuarrie pack kind of knew now who they were dealing with as their new neighbor, so he could look into her further. Of course, she might have a whole family living there, not just herself; then they'd have more of her kin to deal with. Especially if she was mated and her mate didn't take kindly to Lachlan getting friendly with her. He wanted to chase after her and see what he could find out.

At least she was a wolf, and that was good news.

Grant shook his head at Lachlan, signaling he thought she was going to be trouble. But for Lachlan, she was going to be the kind of trouble he wouldn't mind handling.

Edeen disappeared from their sight as she moved beyond the castle gates.

"She's going to be just as difficult to deal with as EJ was," Grant said.

"Nay, worse," Enrick said. "She has a couple of beastly fox terriers. Did one of our dogs get loose? I was so busy fighting Lachlan, I didn't see any of ours out here, just suddenly the two fox terriers raced into the courtyard."

"Same here." Though Lachlan assumed she hadn't made up a tale.

"You'll apologize to the woman." Grant got ready to spar with Enrick this time, and his two brothers struck each other's swords.

"For what?" Lachlan was puzzled. If he'd seen one of their wolfhounds in the bailey, he would have apologized, though it wouldn't mean their dog was at fault. Her dogs could have just raced onto their property, heard all the ruckus of the men fighting in practice combat, and came to check it out. Which meant they had no reason to apologize for anything. Though in retrospect, he did like the idea of talking with her and getting to know her before any of the other guys had a chance.

He noticed several men were watching him speaking with Grant, looking as though they were ready to take on the task if he was in the least bit reluctant.

Grant and Enrick paused in their sword fight. "The lass obviously thinks we had something to do with her dogs coming here. Find out what it was and apologize to her," Grant reiterated.

"And ask if she wants to sell the property?" Lachlan asked.

"Nay, of course not. She's already riled up. We don't want to stir things up more by suggesting that. Once we get to know her better, aye. Make it your job. You were supposed to learn who bought the property. If she and her family did, then find out all you can about them. But go apologize to her first. Welcome her to the community also. Invite her and her family for dinner."

Enrick smiled. Lachlan knew his brother was glad Grant sent him on the mission instead.

"What about the Christmas party?" Lachlan believed that would be a great way to break the ice.

"Maybe wait on that," Grant said.

Lachlan sighed, grabbed his shirt, and pulled it on. He would have preferred wearing his regular clothes to talk with her, but when Grant wanted something done, he wanted it done now. "I'm off then." He sheathed his sword, another thing he wouldn't normally have carried with him to meet with the lassie who was already antagonistic toward him, but everyone would be fighting, and he didn't want to leave it just lying about. Plus, he intended to return to spar some more because he hadn't trained for all that long at today's session.

He took off after Edeen at a run, and then he smelled

Hercules's scent coming from the same direction she was headed. Why, that sneaky wolfhound! Hercules must have slipped back into the keep while they were getting in their sword practice without anyone being the wiser. Of course Lachlan had smelled Hercules's scent in the bailey, but he smelled all the dogs' scents in there because they'd all been outside at one time or another today.

Lachlan could see Hercules's paw prints in the light-snow-covered ground and of course the little terriers' paw prints and the woman's small boot prints. She was way up ahead, and he raced even faster to catch up to her. Hearing him coming, she glanced over her shoulder and raised her brows, her pretty mouth pursed, her cheeks red from the cold, reddish freckles sprinkled across the bridge of her nose, making her even prettier.

"What?" She was curt with him.

"Sorry. I should have brought a leash for you to borrow." But he wouldn't have had time to grab one from the kennel and reach her quickly enough. Not that he'd even thought about it again once he was trying to catch up to her. "Let me carry your dog for you at least." Even though he'd offered, she hadn't acknowledged his offer.

"Aren't you worried Jinx will bite you?" She looked cross with him, then glanced at his sword and the dirk sticking out of his boot.

Yeah, he did look a bit like a warrior on a deadly mission, not on a peaceful one. "If he's a biter, I'll let you continue to carry him, but I can hold the leash of the other dog." Dogs normally loved him, so he wasn't really too worried.

Smiling and looking amused that he might be afraid of her smaller dog, she handed the one dog over to him. He took hold of him and held him snug against his body. He was used to holding their Irish wolfhounds like this only when they were puppies. This one was so small and lightweight compared to his full-grown dogs. The dog seemed perfectly content to be carried home in Lachlan's arms. "Who might you be?" he asked the dog in his arms, as if he needed a proper introduction.

"That's Jinx. You can easily see the difference in that he has more of a white face, some tan, and the larger black saddle," she said. "This is Rogue, with a tanner face and more white and tan on his back, but just a little bit of black."

"Okay, got it. Rogue, Jinx," he said, greeting them. "I'm sorry Hercules went onto your property. That must have been the reason your dogs chased him back to the castle."

She raised a brow at Lachlan.

"I smell his scent and see his tracks. He was sneaky and got by us while we were fighting. None of us even saw him."

She released her breath. "Good. I didn't think you believed me."

"Nay, I do. He's normally well behaved."

"EJ said otherwise, and your dog Hercules proved it."

Lachlan stiffened a little. He didn't appreciate that even in death, EJ held sway over a Campbell's belief. Lachlan figured Hercules had realized there were dogs on the property next door, probably heard them barking at some point, and went to check them out. He was the most curious of their adult hounds and the greeter of the bunch. EJ had never owned dogs, and this was an interesting development for the MacQuarrie dogs to learn the new neighbor had some.

Lachlan figured it was time to change the subject. "We didn't think EJ had any relatives, so I was surprised to learn you had taken over the property."

"We were not related, unless it was very far back in our family roots and the families split up and lost track of each other. It's possible since we were both wolves."

"I think it's incredible that he sold his property to a Campbell wolf who isn't related to him. I mean, it sounds like a huge coincidence." Too much of a coincidence.

She didn't say anything, but when they came to the dike, he realized she had to have climbed over it and her dogs too. Definitely Hercules had leapt over the wall here. He felt bad for her then.

They both waited for her leashed dog to climb over the rock wall, but it was like Rogue didn't know how to or didn't want to now that he wasn't in hot pursuit of his prey.

Now Lachlan was in a quandary. He couldn't carry two dogs over the wall, and he didn't think Edeen could manage to carry one.

"Come on, Rogue, you did it before." She sounded exasperated with her dog.

"They need something to chase to make this work," Lachlan said.

She rolled her eyes at him.

He smiled. "Okay, let me see if I can carry both dogs over at the same time."

"You can't. You need at least one free hand to climb up the dike unless you can jump over the wall like your dog did."

"As a wolf, sure." He figured she was right. He needed at least one hand to climb up and over it. "Okay, give me the leash and you climb over the dike. I'll climb up and partway down to hand off Jinx and then go back for Rogue. I'll still be holding his leash so he can't run off." Luckily, the leash was long enough to accommodate the maneuver.

She looked skeptical, but unless they walked for a mile through the woods down to the road, the only other choice they had would be to walk back to the castle and he would give her and her dogs a ride home.

She climbed over the dike and then waited for him to ascend the stone wall with one of the dogs tucked under his arm while the other dog's long leash was tied securely to his belt.

"Do you always come armed for a fight when you see a new neighbor?" She eyed his *sgian dubh* and then his sword. She sounded like she thought they always did this when they had confrontations with EJ. Lachlan wondered if he'd told her that!

"Nay, never." Lachlan handed Jinx to her, then climbed back over and down the other side of the wall, but all of a sudden Rogue ran up the dike to the caprock all on his own. Lachlan figured he was afraid to be left behind. Then Lachlan climbed back up to where Rogue was still standing as if he'd changed his mind and descending the rocks or leaping to the snow down below was too much of a challenge. Lachlan lifted him off the wall and carried him the rest of the way down. He handed Rogue's leash to Edeen, then took Jinx from her so they could finish making their way down the hill.

He noticed then a smooshed bunch of Hercules's poop in the snow on the way to her house and her boot prints where she'd run through it. He sighed. He was sure she was annoyed about that too. He hadn't seen her footprints colored brown, so maybe it had come off just fine on her long trek to the castle in the snow.

"Your dogs seem to be very well trained," Lachlan said, which was a credit to their owner.

She scoffed. "When they're not chasing your beastie off my property." They finally reached the door to her house.

Because of the issues they'd had with EJ, Lachlan had never been here before. The manor house was beautifully maintained, freshly painted on the outside, and if this had been EJ's doing and not Edeen's, Lachlan respected EJ more for it.

Muddy paw prints covered the freshly painted blue door—definitely Hercules's. He'd been caught in the act. She took Rogue from Lachlan and let both dogs into the house, then shut the door. At least she was still standing on the porch to speak to Lachlan, her arms folded, not appearing happy.

He was glad she hadn't just slammed the door in his face. "To welcome you to the neighborhood and to apologize for Hercules's trespassing, we'd love to extend an invitation to you for dinner tonight. You can even see Hercules's brand-new pups."

She raised a brow. "Now there will be *more* of them?"

Okay, so he probably shouldn't have mentioned that part. "We usually find homes for them right away." He'd figured everyone would love to see the puppies and maybe that would brighten her mood. He guessed he was wrong.

"Thanks. But no thanks. I know what you're trying to do."

That caught him off guard. "And what is that?" Lachlan was afraid he was going about this all wrong. He suspected she could see just what he was up to with regard to wanting her to sell the property to his pack.

"You come down here all sexy in your ancient kilt and the rest of your"—she motioned to his garments—"clothes and armed to the teeth as if you were ready to do battle."

She thought he was sexy? He couldn't help but smile a little. "Uh, I didn't want to toss my sword and come after you—"

"And that's another thing. You're gallant, putting on the charm, friendly, apologizing—and, believe me, no Scotsman has ever apologized to me for anything—especially a wolfish one."

He wanted to laugh. "I—"

"Didn't do it on your own. I heard Grant speaking to you, telling you what to do—right? The laird told you to come after me, apologize, and invite me to dinner."

She hadn't been far enough away from the castle then when his brother had told him that. Which was the trouble with their enhanced wolf hearing.

"Aye. He's the pack leader. He asked me to apologize to you and learn what had happened because we hadn't seen

Hercules return to the keep. And he did ask me to invite you to dinner." Lachlan figured it was time to cut his losses and head back to the inner bailey to sword fight some more and give up on trying to make amends with their new neighbor for the moment. Not that he felt total defeat. "I'm sure you're just getting settled and now with our dog upsetting you—"

"How many more of them are there now?"

"Irish wolfhounds?"

"Aye."

He thought she didn't sound too eager to send him on his way or she wouldn't have talked to him further. That could be a good sign. "We have four adults—two males, two females—and the seven in the litter."

Appearing not to be happy that there were several more gentle giants at the castle, she shook her head. "If you truly want to apologize, you can wash Hercules's muddy paw prints off the front door." She checked the bottom of her small boots, and he looked too, hoping she didn't have any more of Hercules's poop on them. Then appearing satisfied they were fine, she went inside the house and closed the door.

He was just staring at the freshly painted blue door, thinking about how he could successfully clean it off. His kilt came to mind. Or his shirt. But before he could use either to wipe off the paw prints, she opened the door and handed him a wet rag. "Thank you and good day."

He took the rag, and she closed the door in his face. She was saucy. It was true love. He laughed at himself. He realized he should have asked if she had family staying here with her. Though he suspected she would have had someone helping chase after the dogs if she did.

After washing the door, he knocked on it to give her back her dirty rag and show her that he'd done a great job cleaning the door. When she opened it, she inspected the door, not surprising him. She nodded sagely, appearing to approve of his handiwork, but when he tried to hand her the rag, she shook her head. "You can take the dirty rag home and clean it and just leave it on the chair there when you have time." She pointed to a blue rocking chair. "Thanks." Then she flipped around and closed the door. The latch locked instantly.

He chuckled and headed back to the castle, climbing over the dike again. He was surprised she hadn't asked him to clean her boots too, but the long walk and the snow appeared to have cleaned them off sufficiently. He would have done it if she'd needed him to. Anything to rectify their rocky start.

She had spirit. He'd give her that.

Grant was going to have a real time trying to convince her that she should sell her property to him. Lachlan suspected that was *never* going to happen.

EJ had warned Edeen that Grant would begin trying to get on her good side as soon as she moved in. That he might even try to foist off his youngest triplet, bachelor brother, Lachlan, on her as a mate prospect. Though that would be foolish for Grant to even consider. *Lupus garous* lived long lives and they mated for life, so mating someone just to gain land for his pack wasn't going to happen, no matter how gallant Lachlan appeared to be. She had to admit if she was stuck with him for some catastrophic reason, she certainly wouldn't toss him from her bed. He definitely was more than easy on the eyes.

While he climbed up the hill, she watched him out the kitchen window, glad he hadn't seemed perturbed with her when she made him clean her door or take the rag home to wash. When she'd inspected her boots in case they needed to be cleaned off too, she'd wondered how he would have reacted if she'd removed her boots and handed them to him to wash up a bit.

But she reminded herself the MacQuarries would do anything to ingratiate themselves with her, just like EJ had said, so she wasn't letting them off the hook that easily.

Just as Lachlan was climbing the rock wall, the wind caught his kilt and it went flying up, exposing his naked arse. Her jaw dropped. He had gone commando? It figured.

She wouldn't get *that* image out of her mind for a while. If *ever*. Not that it was a bad thing; she was a wolf after all. He had one toned butt! She smiled but then frowned at herself. She had sworn off all men, and she was keeping up her guard when it came to the MacQuarries and their wolf pack. Then she sighed. She could still enjoy looking at one as hot as him, and according to EJ, Lachlan wasn't mated, so no issue there as far as getting involved with a man who already had a significant other. Not that she was going there with Lachlan or anyone else in his pack.

She went inside her home to sort out more of her boxes.

That was the downside to having the new place—unpacking and trying to figure out where everything would go. Then she'd spend weeks, months even, trying to figure out where she had put stuff!

She'd already piled up EJ's clothes from the closets in the spare bedroom to be packed in the boxes she was now emptying.

Other than unpacking her clothes and kitchen items so she could cook and setting up her sewing room so she could get back to work on her Celtic garment orders, she planned to leave the rest of the items in boxes until she needed stuff. Oh, she needed to put up her Christmas lights too. She'd been so excited about doing that at the new place. She'd always hung up lights at her previous home. She could just imagine the lights reflecting off the loch at night and how beautiful that would be.

Tonight, she was running as a wolf—her first time here. It was refreshing to be away from the city where she couldn't do that. Even the starry nights would be more brilliant out here in the darkness. After doing so much work, it would be fun to stretch her legs.

Both the front of the home and the back had wolf doors, so it was perfect for her coming and going as a wolf.

She thought about Hercules's puppies and wished that she could have seen them. *Truly.* She loved animals. If the MacQuarries only wanted her property, she didn't want to appear too eager to be friendly with them though. It *would* be nice to be on friendly terms, however. She'd always gotten along with her neighbors, and she hoped it would be like that here eventually—once they realized the land was hers and she wasn't selling it to them or anyone else.

She finally finished unpacking her dishware and utensils and then ordered a steak, bacon, and ale pie from Ye Olde Highland Pie Shoppe. Shopping for groceries was next on her list.

She tried to buy from local businesses whenever she could, and she loved Scottish pies. She'd never eaten at this restaurant as it had been too far from where she'd lived before, so this was the perfect opportunity to see if their food was just as delicious as customers' reviews had claimed.

She pulled her hair back into a chignon with a clip and then grabbed her coat. She'd been moving all her things into her new house all morning—except for when she'd chased after her dogs—and hadn't eaten breakfast, so she was starving. She figured she'd just pick up the food, grab some groceries from the market, and return home to do more unpacking. Tomorrow, she'd start working on the McIntyre wedding gown again. She needed to complete it, though the bride's wedding wasn't until March. But she liked to finish projects and get her final payment for them before a bride got cold feet—or the groom did—and Edeen got stuck with a half-finished gown that didn't have a buyer any longer.

She'd keep the down payment, which was half what was owed, in that case. That paid for the cost of the fabric at least, but not for all the work she'd put into the dress. Then she could have a hard time selling it unless she got lucky. Getting stuck with a dress didn't happen very often, but if it started to, she'd begin requiring full payment up front.

"Okay, pups, I'll be right back." She left the house, got into her car, and headed for the pie shop.

When she arrived, she loved the quaintness of the place, the big glass windows and white sparkly lights decorating them giving a bit of Christmas cheer, and for nicer weather, dining was available on the covered patio where little round tables and chairs provided seating. Inside, she soaked up the aroma of the baked goods, steak cooking, sweet confections. Red cinnamon candles were burning on each of the tables , scenting the air. The ladies managing the shop were dressed in ancient Scottish dress, and she smelled they were wolves! Her spirit was instantly lifted even more. Making she-wolf friends in the area would be great. Maybe they'd even need some new tartan outfits while they worked at the shop. She would love to make them some.

Ancient weapons and various shields hung on the wall, and a small Christmas tree decorated with little plaid Highland cows and colorful Christmas bows sat in the corner. Mistletoe dangled over the doorway, and boughs of holly and red bows adorned the walls. Christmas instrumental music played in the background, making for a special little Christmas retreat that was just delightful.

One of these days she might eat here, but she had so much to do at home that she just planned to get her order and leave.

When she walked up to the counter, a woman greeted her with a smile, but her smile broadened when she realized Edeen was also a wolf. They instantly had a connection.

"I'm Edeen, and I placed an order for a steak, bacon, and ale pie."

"Hi, I'm Heather, and I own the shop. I'm so glad to meet you. I'll be right back with your order."

Even though no one was at the counter picking up or placing orders, customers were seated at all ten tables inside, enjoying their lunches. The aroma of onions, steaks, and baking bread filled the air, and Edeen got a kick out of the old oven they were using for baking too.

All smiles, Heather set her steak pie order on the counter. "I hope you enjoy it."

"I'm sure I'll be back for more. Thanks so much. Oh, and if you ever need tartan clothing, I've got you covered. I do lots of historical, period, and fantasy Celtic pieces." Edeen handed Heather one of her business cards, figuring it wouldn't hurt to offer her services to a fellow business-woman, especially since Heather was dressed in the kinds of clothes Edeen created, and maybe she'd even get a sale or two. It wouldn't hurt if she made a few sales out here. This would be a totally new market for her.

"Oh, wow, thanks. Aye, we can always use new items to wear that are handcrafted by someone who knows what she's doing regarding the authentic, period styles. We wear them both at the shop and at other activities we're involved in."

"Great! Well, I'll be back for more pies soon, I'm sure. Thanks again, and it's so good to meet you." Then Edeen left with her pie, so glad to meet a she-wolf who she might be friends with who worked not too far from where Edeen lived. She hoped she really liked the pie after offering to get more! She loved that she might even get some more business. After she left, she realized she should have asked Heather what other functions she went to where she wore clothes like that. If they had a Celtic festival somewhere nearby where Edeen could set up a booth and take orders, that would be great.

Then she dropped by the market, picked up some groceries, and headed home. When she arrived at the manor house, she was shocked to see the kilted Highlander standing on her patio as if he'd become a permanent fixture there. Lachlan MacQuarrie gave her a sexy little smile and waved her rag at her—all clean. He was still wearing his kilt as if he wore it all the time, and he was still armed.

She had to admit he was a powerful sight to look at and totally appealing.

She got out of her vehicle, her purse in hand. "You're still in your battle tartan."

"We were still practicing sword fighting when I went to help you with your dogs."

"You didn't have to clean the rag and return it that quickly. Did Grant tell you to do it?" She opened her trunk to get her groceries.

"Nay. I didn't know if you might need it, so I wanted to get it back to you as soon as possible."

She was amused he was trying so hard to please her, though she suspected someone else actually washed and dried it. "I have others, thanks." She grabbed two bags of groceries, and he quickly tucked the rag into one of the bags and went to carry the others inside for her. "You don't have to help me."

He glanced at the meat pie sitting on the passenger's seat. "It's no trouble."

"Do you ever eat there?" The name of the shop and the

logo of a kilted warrior were featured prominently on the package, and since it was a wolf-run restaurant, she suspected he might dine there.

"Aye, the pies are really good." He brought her groceries into the house and said hi to the dogs. They greeted both of them as if they believed Lachlan was a long-lost friend and belonged there. Then he said, "If you need help with anything, just let us know."

"Not you? Us?"

"Uh, yeah, well, me, just anytime. I should have asked if you have family coming to stay here with you or—"

"I have a twin brother, Robert, but he's staying in Edinburgh. He's a veterinary surgeon."

"Ahh, okay. That's wonderful." Lachlan paused, looking as though he didn't know what to say exactly, but he wasn't ready to leave just yet. "Hey, if you plan to hang Christmas lights, I can help. I mean, I don't know if you even had plans to do that, but if you did…" He was looking at her boxes labeled *Christmas Lights* near the front door.

"You're just being neighborly, right?"

"Sure."

"At Grant's request."

Lachlan sighed. "His mate, Colleen, did mention it, but I'm offering on my own, not because she commanded me to."

"I'm fine, but thanks so much for the offer. And for carrying in the grocery bags." She walked outside to get her lunch out of the car, and then he said goodbye. He inclined his head a bit, not appearing to be disappointed that she had turned him down, and headed up the hill.

Seeing him return in that direction made her chuckle. She didn't know why she thought he would have come any other way when no other vehicle was sitting in her driveway. Since he was wearing his kilt, she just had to watch him, hoping he didn't turn and catch her in the act. Just as he crested the top of the dike, a breeze swept his kilt up, and she got a repeat performance. That was something she'd never get tired of seeing.

Smiling, she headed back inside the house to enjoy her meat pie.

Acknowledgments

Thanks so much to Darla Taylor and Donna Fournier for beta reading the book and giving me useful tips on changes. Also, thanks to Lor Melvin and Donna for brainstorming the book with me. Thanks to Deb Werksman for reminding me to add lots of Christmas cheer in the holiday books when I'm usually writing them under the hot Texas sun in the summer. And to the cover artists who always wow me.

About the Author

USA Today bestselling author Terry Spear has written over a hundred paranormal and medieval Highland romances. One of her bestselling titles, *Heart of the Wolf*, was named a *Publishers Weekly* Best Book of the Year. She is an award-winning author with two Paranormal Excellence Awards for Romantic Literature. A retired officer of the U.S. Army Reserves, Terry also creates award-winning teddy bears that have found homes all over the world, helps out with her grandchildren, and enjoys her two Havanese dogs. She lives in Spring, Texas.

Website: terrylspear.wordpress.com
Facebook: TerrySpearParanormalRomantics
Instagram: @heart_of_the_wolf

Also by Terry Spear

WHITE WOLF
Dreaming of a White Wolf Christmas
Flight of the White Wolf
While the Wolf's Away
Wolf to the Rescue (novella)

SILVER TOWN WOLF
Destiny of the Wolf
Wolf Fever
Dreaming of the Wolf
Silence of the Wolf
A Silver Wolf Christmas
Alpha Wolf Need Not Apply
Between a Wolf and a Hard Place
All's Fair in Love and Wolf
Silver Town Wolf: Home for the Holidays
Tangling with the Wolf (novella)

WOLFF BROTHERS
You Had Me at Wolf
Jingle Bell Wolf

RUN WITH THE WOLF
Wolf on the Wild Side
A Good Wolf Is Hard to Find

HIGHLAND WOLF
Heart of the Highland Wolf
A Howl for a Highlander
A Highland Werewolf Wedding
Hero of a Highland Wolf
A Highland Wolf Christmas
The Wolf Wore Plaid
Her Wolf for the Holidays

BILLIONAIRE WOLF
Billionaire in Wolf's Clothing
A Billionaire Wolf for Christmas
Night of the Billionaire Wolf
Wolf Takes the Lead

RED WOLF
Joy to the Wolves
The Best of Both Wolves
Christmas Wolf Surprise